Caroline E. Robinson, Daniel Berkeley Updike

**The Hazard Family of Rhode Island from 1635 to 1894**

Caroline E. Robinson, Daniel Berkeley Updike

**The Hazard Family of Rhode Island from 1635 to 1894**

ISBN/EAN: 9783337376055

Printed in Europe, USA, Canada, Australia, Japan

Cover: Foto ©Andreas Hilbeck / pixelio.de

More available books at **www.hansebooks.com**

# THE
# HAZARD FAMILY
### OF
# RHODE ISLAND
## 1635-1894

*Being a Genealogy and History of the Descendants of Thomas Hazard, with Sketches of the Worthies of this Family, and Anecdotes Illustrative of their Traits and also of the Times in which they Lived*

Embellish'd with Portraits and Fac=Similes, and with Map and Index

By
## CAROLINE E. ROBINSON

SINCERITAS

BOSTON
Printed for the Author
MDCCCXCV

The HAZARD FAMILY of
RHODE ISLAND

## AUTHOR'S NOTE.

HE compiler of this volume, who is a descendant of the Hazard family, has not endeavored to make a scientific, formal or final historical work, but simply a collection, more or less complete, of genealogical data in relation to the Hazard family. Such sketches of individuals have been inserted as the writer has been able herself to compile, or readily to obtain from sources of information open to everyone. The fac-similes and portraits have been, as is often the case in books of this class, secured where it was possible to secure them, without always bearing a strict relation to the importance of the individual represented. In many cases where it would have been desirable, owing to the eminence of the person in question, to have given them greater distinction by this means or by a very full biographical sketch, it has not always been possible to do so; while, in other cases, less known members of the family have obtained a fuller treatment, owing to sources of information more readily available. Of the defects of the volume the author herself is more fully aware than the reader can be; but she is also more cognizant of the many difficulties which have prevented the perfection which she wished to obtain.

¶ Valuable assistance has been given to the compiler of the records by Mr. Peleg F. Pierce of Wickford, Dr. Henry E. Turner of Newport, the late Mr. Stanton Hazard of Westerly, Mr. H. J. Cundall of Prince Edward Island, and Mr. James N. Arnold. Thanks are especially due to Mr. Thomas Crombe, Town Clerk of North Kingstown, and Mr. Howard Perry, who holds the same office in South Kingstown, for unvarying kindness and great assistance in searching the manuscript records of which they are the custodians. It should here be said, in passing, that the references to the Rhode Island Colonial Records allude to the printed volumes, not to the manuscripts themselves.

¶ She also desires to acknowledge her indebtedness to Mrs. William D. Moss of Westerly, for permission to copy the interesting portrait of Captain Stanton Hazard; to Mr. Rowland Hazard of Peacedale, for his kindness in furnishing the portraits of his father, Rowland G. Hazard, and of his uncle, Isaac Peace Hazard; to the President of Brown University for permission to reproduce the portraits of

*Oliver*

# The Author's Note.

*Oliver Hazard Perry and General Isaac Rodman, now in the dining-hall of the College; to Dr. William Elliot Griffis for permission to use the plate of Matthew Calbraith Perry; to Mrs. Richard K. Randolph of Kingston, for the use of the watercolor sketch of her great-grandmother, Abigail Hazard Watson; to General John G. Hazard, for the use of his portrait; to Mrs. Bond of Springfield, for the portrait of her father, Augustus Hazard; to Mrs. William Woodward, for the portrait of Samuel Rodman; and to the family of Mrs. Baldwin, for the portrait of their mother. The arms of the English Hassards, or Hazards, appear on the title page and are taken from those given in the " Reminiscences of Thomas R. Hazard." The portrait of Coddington, first Governor of Rhode Island, and of Abraham Redwood, as well as others of the older portraits, more or less in a direct line of ancestry, have been added at the suggestion of Mr. Berkeley Updike of Boston (himself a descendant of the family), who has carried the book through the press, and to whose care it owes its form of presentation.*

*¶ It only remains to express gratitude above all to one whose kindness has caused this work to be printed; but whose characteristic refusal to allow her name to be mentioned as so doing, will disclose her to the friends of the author.*

# A Table of CONTENTS, together with a LIST of the PORTRAITS, FAC-SIMILES, etc.

WILLIAM CODDINGTON.

# THE HAZARD FAMILY

## OF RHODE ISLAND

### First Generation

THOMAS HAZARD, the progenitor of the Hazard family in the United States of America, was born in 1610; he died in 1680; he married, 1st, Martha ———, who died in 1669. He married, 2d, Martha, widow of Thomas Sheriff; she died in 1691. His name is first found in Boston, Massachusetts, in 1635. In 1638, March 25, he was admitted freeman of Boston. Two years later he was admitted freeman of Portsmouth, Rhode Island. In 1639, April 28, he and eight others signed the following contract, preparatory to the settlement of Newport, Rhode Island: "It is agreed by us whose hands are underwritten to propagate a plantation in the midst of the island or elsewhere, and to engage ourselves to bear equal charge, answerable to our strength and estates, in common, and that our determination shall be by major voice of judge and elders, the judge to have a double voice." The founders and first officers of the town of Newport were William Coddington, Judge; Nicholas Easton, John Coggeshall, William Brenton, John Clarke, Jeremy Clarke, Thomas Hazard, and Henry Bull, Elders; William Dyre, Clerk. In 1639, June 5, he was named one of four proportioners of land in Newport, any three of whom might proportion it ; "the company laying it forth to have 4d. an acre for every acre laid." September 2, 1639, he was admitted freeman of Newport, and in 1640, March 12, he was appointed a member of the General Court of Elections. In 1665, he was for a short time in Newtown, Long Island. In his will, proved 1680, his wife Martha, whom he calls his "beloved yoke-fellow," is sole executrix, and he gives her "all movable and immovable estate, as housing,

housing, goods, cattle, and chattels, etc." To his son Robert he gives 1*s*. To his daughters, Hannah Wilcox and Martha Potter, wife of Ichabod Potter, 1*s*.

There is a long line of descendants from this daughter Martha, and Ichabod Potter, with frequent intermarriages in the Hazard family. In the early history of the family it was almost an exception to find a Hazard who did not marry a cousin, and it is a curious fact that the lines in which these marriages were the most frequent, were often marked by the strongest men and women, both mentally and physically.

These few meagre facts are about all that can be found at the present day of the founder of the Hazard family in America. But Thomas R. Hazard, in his *Recollections of Olden Times,* has given an account of the family that goes back, even beyond the name; its European founder being the Duke de Charante, living about 1060, on the borders of Switzerland. From the Duke de Charante he has given an interesting account of the changes in the name, until towards the close of the eighteenth century, when it was, and still continues to be, written Hazard. Willis R. Hazard, a descendant of Jonathan Hazard of Newtown, Long Island (according to whose opinion Jonathan was a son of Thomas Hazard, but by other authorities a nephew), has given us the chief characteristics of the family; and although his account was intended for the descendants of Jonathan of Newtown, it is equally applicable to the Rhode Island family. He says: "The Hazards are a strongly marked race, handing down and retaining certain peculiarities from generation to generation. One is, a peculiar decision of character, a certain amount of pride, and a pronounced independence, coupled with a slight reserve. Physically they are strongly marked. Generally speaking, they are of good stature and vigorous frames with rather a square head, high forehead, brown hair, blue eyes, straight or aquiline nose, and with will shown by a firmly set jaw. Their complexion is fair, a little inclined to florid."

Few families in Rhode Island have a brighter record than the Hazard family, where, if greatness is not always found, sobriety, honesty, and integrity make even the humblest lives worth studying; and when one finds, as is often the case, a retiring, unpretentious modesty combined with greatness, he must be pardoned for his enthusiastic admiration for the old family tree, that still sends out vigorous shoots after more than two hundred years of growth in America.

CHILDREN OF THOMAS HAZARD

2. ROBERT HAZARD, born 1635, in England or Ireland; died 1710; married *Mary Brownell.*
3. ELIZABETH HAZARD, married *George Lawton.*
4. HANNAH HAZARD, married *Stephen Wilcox,* son of *Edward Wilcox.*
5. MARTHA HAZARD, married 1st, *Ichabod Potter,* son of *Nathaniel* and *Dorothy Potter;* married 2d, *Benjamin Mowry,* son of *Roger* and *Mary Mowry.*

**End of the First Generation**

THE

# THE HAZARD FAMILY

## 𝕾𝖊𝖈𝖔𝖓𝖉 𝕲𝖊𝖓𝖊𝖗𝖆𝖙𝖎𝖔𝖓

ROBERT HAZARD 2 (Thomas, 1), was born 1635; he died 1710. In 1665 he was admitted freeman of Portsmouth, Rhode Island. From this time until 1698 his name often appears in the Colonial records as chosen to fill some important position. In 1658, he sold John Roome, of Portsmouth, all his interest in Conanicut and Dutch Island. In 1667, the Court at Plymouth ordered, in reference to a controversy between the English and Indians about bounds in Dartmouth, that in case Robert Hazard, of Rhode Island, could be procured, he should run the lines, etc. In 1670, he was juryman. In 1671, he bought five hundred acres of land in Kingstown, of the Pettaquamscutt purchasers. In 1676, he and three others of Portsmouth were a committee ordered by the Assembly to appoint their own men as keepers of Indians above twelve years of age. The Indians were to have "a sufficient place of security." Any master offending was to pay a fine of £5. In 1676, Robert Hazard was on a committee to procure boats for the colony's defence "for the present, and there were to be four boats with five or six men in each."[1] At the same date he and three others were empowered to take exact account of all the inhabitants on the island, "English, negroes and Indians, and make a list of the same, and also to take exact account how all persons are provided with corn, guns, powder, shot and lead." A barrel of powder was put in charge of himself and three others, and two great guns in the yard of the late William Brenton, were to be impressed into the country's service and carried to Portsmouth, and placed, one "in the Ferry Neck and one near the house of John Borden." Robert Hazard and three others were to see that the guns were set on carriages and fitted for service. In 1676, also, he was appointed as commissioner to take care of and order the several watches and wards on the island, and appoint the places. In 1687, he was taxed 11s. 7d. in Kingstown.[2]

Not long after this date, he built his house in Kingstown, which was still standing in the early part of the present century. It was on the site where now stands the house owned and occupied by the daughters of William Watson, Esqʳ., in the village of Mooresfield. The old house was very large, — possibly the largest in the town, not only at that time but for many years after. A well authenticated story is told of Dr. William Shaw, who, being called in to attend a

[1] R. I. Col. Rec., vol. ii, pp. 535-536.    [2] Col. Rec., vol. ii, p. 537.

3

sick

sick person in the house, drove into the back yard, and entered the house by the kitchen door. When he went out, he asked if the family always walked from the front door to the rear of the house, or did they have some conveyance? The ell was longer than the main body of the house, and in this ell was a capacious chimney. Inside the chimney were two stone seats, where, tradition says, the little slave children were wont to sit; the heat from the big oak-logs being no bad substitute for the hot sands of Africa.

In 1695, Robert Hazard gave to his son George the larger part of his Pettaquamscutt purchase. The deed runs: "I, Robert Hazard, late of Portsmouth, now of Kingstown, alias Rochester, for the natural affection that I have unto my son George, . . . . have given to him all my whole right and interest in or to the farm I live on now, by virtue of a deed from the whole Company of Purchasers, as may appear by a deed given under their hand. Said farm contains five hundred acres of land, more or less, bounded as in my original deed from aforesaid purchasers. Only I, said Robert Hazard, do reserve one hundred and twenty acres, and my now dwelling-house." The boundaries mention a big rock in the boundary line, about ten feet high. This rock is still to be seen in a substantial stone wall, and gave rise to the familiar name of his grandson Robert, who was called "Roc" Robert. This was also his signature, Robert Roc [his mark] Hazard. In 1710, a short time before his death, Robert sold the remaining part of this farm, with "my manor house where I now live," to his son Robert (for £300, current money), who, in 1718, gave it by will to his son Robert, after his mother's death; making three Roberts who had successively owned and occupied the old house. The last, upon the death of his mother in 1739, sold to his uncle George the remaining part of the farm. He in his turn gave the whole farm to his son, Col. Thomas Hazard, by will, in 1743. Col. Thomas, in 1748, sold it to John Rose. And thus, after sixty years, the old homestead passed out of the possession of the Hazard family.

Previous to the deed of gift to his son George, Robert had, in 1692, given to his son Stephen "all rights and interests in land belonging to Point Judith Neck, being yᵉ seventh part of yᵉ same, excepting one hundred acres and Little Neck, so called, next Boston Neck."

In 1695, he also gave his son Jeremiah two hundred acres of land in Tiverton; and that his eldest son Thomas had land given to him by his father, is proved by the fact that in his will he says, "land that came to me by inheritance from my father, Robert Hazard." By these deeds it would seem that Robert Hazard owned more than one thousand acres of land.

Robert married Mary Brownell, daughter of Thomas and Anne Brownell. She was born in 1639, and died in 1739, being exactly one hundred years of age. In an old copy of the *Boston Gazette*, dated Feb. 12, 1739, is found the following notice: "NEWPORT, Feb. 9. Mrs. MARY HAZARD, widow of Mr. ROBERT HAZARD, of SOUTH KINGSTON, and Grand Mother to the deceased GEORGE HAZARD, Esq., late Deputy Governor of RHODE ISLAND, departed this life the

28th

28th day of JANUARY last, in the HUNDREDTH Year of her age, who was decently interr'd the Wednesday following. She had 500 Children, Grand Children, and Great Grand Children, and left behind her now living two hundred and five of the aforesaid number. She was accounted a very useful Gentlewoman both to the Poor and Rich on many accounts, and particularly amongst Sick Persons for her Skill & Judgement, which she did Gratis."

CHILDREN

6. THOMAS HAZARD, born 1660; died 1746; married *Susannah Nichols.*
7. GEORGE HAZARD, died 1743; married *Penelope Arnold,* daughter of *Caleb* and *Abigail Arnold.*
8. STEPHEN HAZARD, died Sept. 20, 1727; married *Elizabeth Helme.*
9. MARTHA HAZARD, died 1753; married *Thomas Wilcox.*
10. MARY HAZARD, died before her father; married *Edward Wilcox.*
11. ROBERT HAZARD, died 1718, married *Amey* ——.
12. JEREMIAH HAZARD, born March 26, 1675; married *Mary Smith.*
13. HANNAH HAZARD, married *Jeffrey Champlin.*

§ 3. ELIZABETH HAZARD, 2 (Thomas, 1). She married George Lawton, of Portsmouth, Rhode Island. He was admitted an inhabitant of the island of Aquidneck in 1638. On April 30, 1639, he and twenty others signed the following compact : "We whose names are underwritten do acknowledge ourselves the legal subjects of his majesty King Charles, and in his name do hereby bind ourselves into a civil body politicke, unto his laws according to matters of justice."[1] In 1648, he was a member of the Court of Trials. In 1665, '72, '75, '76, '79, '80, he was Deputy. August 31, 1671, there was a meeting at his house of the Town Council, and Council of War of the two towns was ordered by the Assembly to be held on September 5th, at nine o'clock in the forenoon, "there and then to consider of some ways and means for securing the inhabitants and their estates in these times of imminent danger."[2] Twenty horsemen (ten from each town), completely armed, were to attend at same time and place for the defence of said council there sitting, treachery of the Indians being feared.
In 1676, April 4, it was voted by the Assembly: "That in these troublesome times and straits in this colony, the Assembly, desiring to have the advice and concurrence of the most judicious inhabitants, if it may be had for the good of the whole, do desire at their next sitting the company and counsel of sixteen persons,[3] among them George Lawton."
On May 2, 1676, he and John Easton were desired to go to Providence, with all convenient speed, to determine whether garrisons shall be kept there at charge of colony, a petition having been sent to the Assembly from that place concerning their distressed condition in these present times of wars with the Indians.[4]
In 1678 (October 30), there was ordered by the Assembly a meeting to be held at his house 13th of January next, to adjudge and audit all accounts between towns of Newport and Portsmouth, relating to late Indian wars.[5]

[1] R. I. Col. Rec., vol. i, p. 70.  [2] Col. Rec., vol. ii, pp. 409, 410.  [3] Col. Rec., vol. ii, p. 537.
[4] Col. Rec., vol. ii, p. 546.  [5] Col. Rec., vol. ii, p. 537.

On

On January 30, 1690, he and five other assistants, with the Deputy Governor, wrote a letter to their Majesties William and Mary, congratulating them on their accession to the crown, and informing them that since the deposition of Governor Andros, the former government under the Charter had been resumed, and mentioning also the seizure of Andros in Rhode Island, and his return to Massachusetts on demand of the latter colony.[1]

Lawton died October 5, 1693, and was buried in his orchard in Portsmouth.

CHILDREN

14. ISABEL LAWTON, died April 1, 1730; married *Samuel Albro.*
15. JOHN LAWTON, married *Mary Boomer.*
16. MARY LAWTON, married *John Babcock,* son of *James* and *Sarah Babcock.*
17. GEORGE LAWTON, died Sept. 11, 1697; married *Naomi Hunt,* daughter of *Bartholomew* and *Ann Hunt.*
18. ROBERT LAWTON, died Jan. 25, 1706; married Feb. 16, 1681, *Mary Wodell,* daughter of *Gershom* and *Mary Wodell.*
19. SUSANNA LAWTON, died Dec. 9, 1712; married *Thomas Cornell,* son of *Thomas* and *Elizabeth Cornell.*
20. RUTH LAWTON, died April 15, 1726; married *William Wodell,* son of *Gershom* and *Mary Wodell.*
21. MERCY LAWTON, died 1685; married Jan. 19, 1682, *James Tripp.*
22. JOB LAWTON, died Oct. 8, 1697.
23. ELIZABETH LAWTON, died 1724; married *Robert Carr,* son of *Robert Carr.*

§ 4. HANNAH HAZARD, 2 (Thomas, 1). There is no record found of birth or death. She married Stephen Wilcox (son of Edward). He was born 1633, or about that time, and died about 1690. They were married 1658. In 1658, Jan. 30, he had a deed of thirty-four acres from Thomas Hazard as dower with his wife. May 18, 1669, his name was in the list of inhabitants of Westerly. In 1670 he was complained of, with his partakers, by John Richards, Treasurer of Harvard College, for unjustly possessing five hundred acres in the Pequot country, on the east side of Pawcatuck River, within the bounds of Stonington.[2]

CHILDREN

24. EDWARD WILCOX, born 1662; married *Mary Hazard,* daughter of *Robert* (for children, see *No. 10*).
25. THOMAS WILCOX, died 1728; married *Martha,* daughter of *Robert* and *Mary Hazard.*
26. DANIEL WILCOX, married 1697, *Mary Wodell.*
27. WILLIAM WILCOX, married Jan. 25, 1698, *Dorothy Palmer.*
28. STEPHEN WILCOX, married 1704, *Elizabeth Crandall.*
29. HANNAH WILCOX, married *Samuel Clarke,* son of *Jeremiah* and *Ann (Audley) Clarke.*
30. JEREMIAH WILCOX, married *Mary Mallett,* daughter of *Thomas Mallett.*

§ 5. MARTHA HAZARD, 2 (Thomas, 1). There is no record of her birth. She married, first, Ichabod Potter, son of Nathaniel and Dorothy Potter. He died in 1676. She married, second, Benjamin Mowry.

---

[1] R. I. Col. Rec., vol. iii, p. 258.          [2] R. I. Col. Rec., vol. ii, p. 324.

CHILDREN

CHILDREN OF FIRST MARRIAGE

31. THOMAS POTTER, died 1728, married 1st, Jan. 20, 1687, *Susanna Tripp*; married 2d, *Lydia*, widow of *Thomas Sherman*, and daughter of *Daniel* and *Elizabeth (Cook) Wilcox*.
32. JOHN POTTER, born 1665; died 1715; married *Sarah*, daughter of *Samuel Wilson*.
33. ROBERT POTTER, died 1755; married *Elizabeth Wells*.
34. ICHABOD POTTER, died 1730; married *Margaret*, daughter of *Rouse* and *Mary Helme*.

CHILDREN OF SECOND MARRIAGE

35. ROGER MOWRY, died 1710; unmarried.
36. JOSEPH MOWRY, died 1718; married *Sarah* ——.
37. BENJAMIN MOWRY, died 1719.
38. JOHN MOWRY, died 1718; married *Mary* ——.

### End of the Second Generation

THE

# THE HAZARD FAMILY

## Third Generation

THOMAS HAZARD, 3 (Robert, 2; Thomas, 1), was born in 1669; he died in 1746. He seems to have taken little interest in town or Colonial affairs, for the records preserve a deep silence, when asked to give some items for a sketch of his life. The old books of land evidence, however, show his name more often than that of any other of the old planters, as a purchaser of large tracts of land, — not bought of the Indians for wampum or glass beads, but of the original purchasers, at good prices. Possibly the price £700, paid in 1698, for nine hundred acres, would have been considered a fair valuation one hundred and fifty years afterwards, before this neighborhood had become a fashionable resort in summer.

One can but speculate as to the nature of the business that enabled Thomas Hazard to invest so often, large sums in land. There could have been no sufficient home market for the products of his large plantations, where all men were planters; or for the increase of his stock of horses and cattle; but he may have been a large exporter. If Diedrich Knickerbocker, that veracious historian, can be trusted, the Narragansett pacers were even then in great demand. It may be that he built the ships in which he exported his farm produce and horses. The ships, if sold in England, with a deck-load of ship timber "for the King's navy," would have been a rich source of gain. There was certainly, previous to 1746, a ship-yard, "Great Pier" and ware-houses, on the farm that he gave by deed, in 1739, to his son Jonathan. This farm, situated on Boston Neck is now known as the Governor Brown farm and John J. Watson farm; and possibly the pier stood where the Watson pier now is. About 1746, or some time previous, Jonathan Hazard sold to his brother George one-half of the pier and one-half of the ware-houses and ship-yard.

In 1684, Thomas Hazard was admitted freeman from Portsmouth; after this date his name appears only twice in the Colonial Records, viz.: in 1696 as freeman from Kingstown, and in 1717, as appellant in a law-suit.[1] Previous to 1698, he made his first purchase of land in Narragansett, buying of Samuel Sewall nine hundred acres for £700, being the "land lately occupied by Robert Hannah." In 1710 he also bought of Samuel Sewall three hundred acres for £500, also five acres of salt marsh and eighty acres near the "great pond." In 1703, and in

---

[1] R.I. Col. Rec., vol. iv, p. 217.

1708,

1708, he bought two parcels of land from Benedict Arnold, one containing one hundred and sixty acres and the other twenty-six acres. This last purchase was what is called Little Neck Farm, and was afterwards given to his son George. In 1727 he bought of Samuel Vial six hundred and sixty acres in Boston Neck, and in 1738, eight hundred acres of Francis Brinley, adjoining the above purchase. Besides these lands, he at different times bought small pieces of land varying from ten rods to twenty-five acres, in different parts of the town. The whole amount of his land, including land that he mentions in a deed as "coming to me by inheritance," amounted to something less than four thousand acres.

The greater part of his land, he, according to the custom of the day, gave to his sons before his death; and as each son attained his majority he was given, "for natural affection," and, as sometimes was added, "valuable consideration," a farm of several hundred acres. On most of these farms thus given away were dwelling houses, out-buildings, and orchards. In his will he mentions no land, with the exception of three hundred and sixteen acres that he gave to his grandson and Fones Hazard, son of his deceased son, Stephen. The inventory of his personal estate shows no list of cattle and slaves, as is shown in the inventories of the estates of his brothers, all of whom, except Jeremiah, the youngest, he outlived. The inventory shows about £3,785. A few hundred pounds went to his daughters and granddaughters, and the rest to his son Robert, who was named residuary legatee. The manor-house and homestead farm also, not having been given away, became Robert's. In the early part of the present century the old house was still standing, not far from that now owned and occupied by Thomas G. Hazard, a lineal descendant of Thomas Hazard, [3].

Thomas Hazard divided his Boston Neck land by deeds to his sons thus, beginning north: —

Benjamin, three hundred and thirty acres [now called the Jencks farm]; Jonathan, three hundred acres [Governor Brown farm], and two hundred and nine acres [John J. Watson farm]; Robert, two hundred acres [the Updike farm]; George, two hundred acres [Thomas G. Hazard farm], and two hundred and nine acres [Thomas M. Potter farm].

He married, it is supposed, Susannah Nichols; she died before him.

CHILDREN

39. MARY HAZARD, born Oct. 3, 1683; married, 1st, *John Robinson*, son of *Rowland Robinson* and *Mary;* married, 2d, *Peter Easton*, son of *James Easton*.

40. HANNAH HAZARD, born April 11, 1685; married *Nicholas Easton*, son of *James Easton*.

41. SARAH HAZARD, born July 5, 1687; married *Stephen Easton*, son of *James Easton*.

42. ROBERT HAZARD, born May 23, 1689; married *Sarah Borden*, daughter of *Richard* and *Innocent Borden*.

43. THOMAS HAZARD, born May 11, 1691; died before his father. Tradition says that he married a member of the *Easton* family.

44. STEPHEN HAZARD, born June 13, 1693; married *Margaret Fones*.

45. JEREMIAH HAZARD, born June 5, 1697; He was admitted freeman from the town of Kingstown in 1722. In 1733, he sold to his brothers Robert and George, the land given to him by his father Thomas. The land sold is the farm now owned by W. B. Weeden in Matunuc. Jeremiah is mentioned in his father's will as having already had his share of his estate.

46.

46. GEORGE HAZARD, born Jan. 18, 1699; married *Mary*, daughter of *Enoch* and *Mary (Sweet) Place*.
47. BENJAMIN HAZARD, born Nov. 2, 1702; married *Mehitable Redwood*.
48. JONATHAN HAZARD, born Oct. 1, 1704; married *Abigail Macoon*.

§ 7. GEORGE HAZARD, 3 (Robert, 2, Thomas, 1), died in 1743. He was admitted freeman of the Colony in 1696. In 1701, '02, '06, '07, '09, '13, he was Deputy; in 1703 and 1704, Assistant. May 6, 1713, he was appointed by the Assembly one of a committee to make the public road leading through the Colony from "Pawtucket River to Pawcatuck River more straight and fair and passable."[1] In 1719 he was appointed Lieutenant-Colonel of Militia for the main land,[2] and was ever afterward called Colonel George Hazard. He became a large landholder like his brother Thomas. In 1695 his father gave him by deed three hundred and fifty acres, being a part of the original purchase; and after the death of his mother, in 1739, he bought of his nephew, Robert Hazard, the remaining part of the farm with the manor-house. Thomas R. Hazard, in his *Recollections of Olden Times*, has mistaken the graves of George Hazard and of his father and mother, upon this farm, for those of "Stout" Jeffrey Hazard and his family. But Jeffrey calls his farm in Exeter, that he gave to his son Jeremiah, "my homestead farm." Colonel George Hazard kept up a very large establishment until his death in 1743, when he must have been over eighty years of age. In the inventory of his personal estate, there are seventeen slaves. There were thirty or forty head of cattle, one hundred and fifty sheep, and other animals. On the homestead farm are still to be seen long lines of stone wall built by slaves; the work was so well done that the wall still stands firm and straight, after two hundred years of frosts and changing seasons.

In 1719 (April 29), Colonel George Hazard and Henry Gardiner gave to Thomas Culverwell, "late of Norrage, Connecticut, but now of Kingstown," for love and good will, "more especiailly for y⁰ promoting of y⁰ woolen manufacturing, which may be for my benefit and the public good," etc., a tract of land, "being a little part of my now dwelling place, and is bounded as follows : East and North on the Saucatucket river, South and West on said George Hazard." Henry Gardiner gave to Culverwell full powers to make a dam over said river upon his land, "said dam being for the promoting of a fulling mill and y⁰ fulling of cloth." That this dam was built, and also a mill, which, perhaps, was operated, is proved by the fact that two years later, September 29, 1721, Culverwell gave a quit-claim to George Hazard for this land, "with all houses, mills, and all improvements thereon made and done." The boundaries place this mill at what is now known as Lawton's saw-mill, about half a mile north of Rodman's mill at Mooresfield. This must have been almost the first mill in South Kingstown, as it antedates the old mill at Peacedale by nearly half a century.

In 1721, George Hazard gave to his son Caleb one hundred and fifty acres, "with all houses and outhouses, &c., . . . in a place called the Back Side of the

--------

[1] R. I. Col. Rec., vol. iv, p. 151.          [2] Col. Rec., vol. iv, p. 218.

Ponds.

Ponds." His will, proved in 1743, gives to his son Colonel Thomas Hazard "the homestead farm where I now live, with all housings, goods, chattels, and credit, and he to have profits till 1747 of northern part of Back Side farm, and profits of land given to grandsons Robert and Caleb, sons of my son Caleb, till said Caleb is twenty-one, my son Caleb having had his share of my estate before his death."

To his son Oliver was given three hundred acres of land in North Kingstown, this being in addition to other land given him by deed. Land in Point Judith, including the Foddering Place, with islands in the pond, had been given to his son Governor George Hazard, who died before his father. Colonel Thomas Hazard was made residuary legatee.

Mr. Hazard's slaves were named Jack, Jane, Cæsar, Ming, Prish, Betty, Jenny, Joe, Paro, Harry, Will, Jacob, John, Cuff, and infants Dinah and Moll. As the old slaves seem to be more or less identified with the old plantations and the old masters, it does not seem out of place to mention them here.

George Hazard married Penelope, daughter of Caleb and Abigail (Wilbur) Arnold, and granddaughter of Governor Benedict Arnold. She was born August 3, 1669, and died in 1742.

CHILDREN

49. ABIGAIL HAZARD, born March 19, 1690 ; married *Ebenezer Niles*, son of *Nathaniel* and *Sarah (Sands) Niles*.
50. ROBERT HAZARD, born Nov. 3, 1694 ; died young.
51. CALEB HAZARD, born Nov. 4, 1697 ; married *Abigail*, daughter of *William Gardiner*.
52. GEORGE HAZARD, born Oct. 9, 1700 ; married *Sarah Carder*.
53. THOMAS HAZARD, born March 30, 1704 ; married *Alice*, daughter of *Teddiman* and *Sarah (Sands) Hull*.
54. OLIVER HAZARD, born Sept. 13, 1710 ; married *Elizabeth Raymond*.

§ 8. STEPHEN HAZARD, 3 (Robert, 2 ; Thomas, 1). The date of his birth is not known ; he died September 29, 1727. He was an active and enterprising spirit in the affairs of the Colony. A large landholder, he early in the century saw the possibilities for water-power in North Kingstown, and bought large tracts of land so situated as to control the power, near Bissell's (now Hamilton) Mills. It is possible that he built the mill, that was after his death owned by his son Thomas. He was admitted freeman in the Colony in 1696, but previously to this date (in 1687), he was taxed 1s. in Kingstown. In 1702, '06, '08, '09, '15, he was Deputy ; in 1707, '08, '19, '20, '21, '22, he was Assistant. In 1707 he was appointed Justice of the Peace for Kingstown : [1] this office gave him the title of Judge, by which he is known by his descendants. In 1715 he was allowed 18s. by the Assembly for running the line between Eldred's purchase and Hall's purchase. [2]

On January 14, 1692, his father Robert gave him by deed "all my rights in Point Judith Neck, in Pettaquamscutt Purchase, being one seventh part of the land,

---

[1] R.I. Col. Rec., vol. iv, p. 19.     [2] Col. Rec., vol. iv, p. 189.

except

except one hundred acres, and the Little Neck, so called, next Boston Neck."
There was, as far as can be determined at this date, about three hundred acres of
this land.   In 1710 he bought of Samuel Clarke, one hundred acres for £150.
On July 9, 1713, Francis Brinley, "for the sum of £200 in silver, at eight shil-
lings the ounce, to me paid by Stephen Hazard," sells one moiety, or half-part
of a tract of land, containing one hundred acres.
In his will, written September 19, 1727, proved October 9, 1727, he gave his sons
Stephen and Robert three hundred acres of his Point Judith land to be equally
divided between them.  To his son Samuel, two hundred acres in North Kingstown, and a part of Mumford Island — now called Great Island.  To his son
Thomas, three hundred acres in North Kingstown, the remaining part of Mumford Island.  The inventory of his personal estate amounted to about £3000.
He had two hundred and twenty-five head of cattle and twenty-two horses.  This
will mentions silver buttons, silver shoe-buckles, a tankard and spoons.
Stephen Hazard married Elizabeth, daughter of Rouse and Mary Helme.  She
died in 1727, before her husband.

CHILDREN
55. MARY HAZARD, born July 20, 1695 ; died young.
56. HANNAH HAZARD, born April 20, 1697 ; married *Joseph Mumford.*
57. SUSANNAH HAZARD, born April 23, 1699; married, Sept. 13, 1718, *Samuel Perry,* son of *Samuel Perry.*
58. STEPHEN HAZARD, born Nov., 1700; married *Mary Robinson,* daughter of *John* and *Mary
     (Hazard) Robinson.*
59. ROBERT HAZARD, born Sept. 1702; married *Esther Stanton.*
60. SAMUEL HAZARD, born June 29, 1705; married *Abigail* ——.
61. THOMAS HAZARD, born July 28, 1707; married, 1st, *Hannah Slocum,* daughter of *Samuel Slocum ;*
     married 2d, May, 1738, *Hannah Updike.*
62. ELIZABETH HAZARD, born 170–; married July 16, 1729, *Benjamin Perry.*
63. SARAH HAZARD.

§ 9. MARTHA HAZARD 3 (Robert 2; Thomas 1).  She died in 1753 ; her husband was Thomas Wilcox, son of Stephen and Hannah (Hazard) Wilcox.  On
May 17, 1710, Wilcox and seventeen others bought two thousand acres of the
vacant lands ordered sold by the Assembly.   Their home was in Exeter.

CHILDREN
64. ROBERT WILCOX.
65. STEPHEN WILCOX.
66. JEFFREY WILCOX.
67. THOMAS WILCOX, born Oct. 24, 1693.
68. ABRAHAM WILCOX.
69. GEORGE WILCOX.
70. EDWARD WILCOX.
71. HANNAH WILCOX.

§ 10. MARY HAZARD 3 (Robert, 2; Thomas, 1), married Edward Wilcox,
son of Stephen and Hannah (Hazard) Wilcox.  After her death he married, second, May 1, 1698, Thomasin Stevens (daughter of Richard).

CHILDREN

Children of First Marriage
72. Mary Wilcox, married *Joseph Lewis*.
73. Hannah Wilcox, married *Ezekiel Garrette*.
74. Stephen Wilcox, married July 12, 1716, *Mary Randall*.
75. Edward Wilcox.

Children of Second Marriage
76. Sarah Wilcox, born May 30, 1700.
77. Thomas Wilcox, born Feb. 18, 1702.
78. Hezekiah Wilcox, born April 4, 1704.
79. Elisha Wilcox, born July 9, 1706.
80. Amey Wilcox, born Oct. 18, 1709.
81. Susannah Wilcox, born April 5, 1712.

§ 11. ROBERT HAZARD, 3 (Robert, 2; Thomas, 1.) The date of his birth is not known; he died in 1718. His will, proved November 10, 1718, gave to his son Jeffrey, called " Stout " Jeffrey, three hundred acres of land, which he called " the farm where I now live." It was probably in Exeter, then a part of Kingstown, as Jeffrey gave by deed to his son Jeremiah this farm, calling it " my homestead farm." To his son Thomas he gave two hundred acres in Kingstown, and one hundred and sixty-five acres in Westerly. To his son Robert, he gave the old manor-house, and one hundred and twenty acres, given to him by his father; but Robert was not to have possession of the house, and twenty acres, until after his grandmother's death. To each of his daughters he gave, when of age, £100. The inventory of his personal estate mentions three hundred and twenty-six head of cattle; his "cattle" including seventeen horses, six mares, five colts, four yearlings, riding beasts, &c.
He married Amey ——, who died a few months before her husband.

Children
82. Jeffrey Hazard, born Sept. 29, 1698; married Aug. 13, 1726, *Mary* ——.
83. Susannah Hazard, born Jan. 16, 1701.
84. Robert Hazard, born Jan. 19, 1703; married *Martha* ——
85. Thomas Hazard, born June 18, 1713.
86. Amey Hazard, born Sept. 20, 1715; married *Eber Sherman*.
87. Mary Hazard, born May 14, 1718; married June 6, 1739, *Ebenezer Druce*.

§ 12. JEREMIAH HAZARD, 3 (Robert, 2; Thomas, 1) was born March 25, 1675, he died February 2, 1768. His name is first found in the Kingstown records, in 1707, when he and his wife Sarah sold land to William Browning. In 1710, he and seventeen others bought seven thousand acres of the vacant lands ordered to be sold by the Assembly. In 1714, he bought a large tract of land of Samuel Sweet, near Ridge Hill, in North Kingstown. This land has been retained in the Hazard family until the present generation; the last of it (except ten acres, upon a part of which is the original burying ground of Jeremiah Hazard), having been sold in 1872. The ten acres were conveyed by deed for the first time, by the heirs of Wilbur Hazard to Hazard Burlingame, a few years ago.

ago. It is now owned by his heirs, he being a descendant in the female line of
Jeremiah Hazard.

Jeremiah Hazard married Sarah, daughter of Jeremiah and Mary (Geready)
Smith.

CHILDREN

88. MARY HAZARD, born March 16, 1699; died 1771.
89. ANN HAZARD, born Feb. 28, 1701; married *John Browning.*
90. ROBERT HAZARD, born April 1, 1703; married *Patience Northup.*
91. SARAH HAZARD, born Jan. 11, 1706; married, Oct. 24, 1728, *Robert Moore.*
92. MARTHA HAZARD, born Oct. 8, 1708.
93. HANNAH HAZARD, born April, 1714; married *Samuel Watson.*
94. SUSANNAH HAZARD, born May 21, 1716; married —— *Smith.*

§ 13. HANNAH HAZARD, 3 (Robert, 2 ; Thomas, 1) married Jeffrey
Champlin. She was his second wife, and died about 1713.

CHILDREN

95. THOMAS CHAMPLIN, born Sept. 3, 1708.
96. STEPHEN CHAMPLIN, born Feb. 16, 1710; married *Mary Hazard.*
97. WILLIAM CHAMPLIN, born March 3, 1713.

§ 14. ISABEL LAWTON, 3 (Elizabeth Hazard, 2 ; Thomas, 1). She married
Samuel Albro; died April 1, 1730.

CHILDREN

 98. JOHN ALBRO.
 99. DOROTHY ALBRO.
100. RUTH ALBRO.
101. SARAH ALBRO.

§ 15. JOHN LAWTON, 3 (Elizabeth Hazard, 2 ; Thomas, 1). He died in
1678 ; married Mary Boomer, daughter of Matthew and Eleanor Boomer. She
married, second, Gideon Freeborn.

CHILD

102. GEORGE LAWTON.

§ 16. MARY LAWTON, 3 (Elizabeth Hazard, 2 ; Thomas, 1). She died on
November 8, 1711 ; married John Babcock, son of James and Sarah Babcock.

CHILDREN

103. JAMES BABCOCK.
104. ANN BABCOCK.
105. MARY BABCOCK.
106. JOHN BABCOCK.
107. JOB BABCOCK.
108. GEORGE BABCOCK, born 1673; died May 1, 1756; married, Nov. 28, 1694, *Elizabeth Hall.*
109. ELIHU BABCOCK.
110. ROBERT BABCOCK.
111. JOSEPH BABCOCK.
112. OLIVER BABCOCK.

§ 17.

§ **17.** GEORGE LAWTON, 3 (Elizabeth Hazard, 2 ; Thomas, 1), died September 11, 1697; he married, January 17, 1677, Naomi Hunt, daughter of Bartholomew and Ann Hunt. She married, second, Isaac Lawton.

CHILDREN
113. ELIZABETH LAWTON, born Nov. 15, 1678; married —— *Curtis*.
114. GEORGE LAWTON, born April 30, 1685.
115. ROBERT LAWTON, born Oct 14, 1688.
116. JOB LAWTON, born Jan. 22, 1692.

§ **18.** ROBERT LAWTON, 3 (Elizabeth Hazard, 2 ; Thomas, 1), died January 25, 1706; married February 16, 1682, Mary Wodell, daughter of Gershom and Mary Wodell.

CHILDREN
117. GEORGE LAWTON, born Sept. 1, 1685.
118. ELIZABETH LAWTON, born Sept. 12, 1688.
119. MARY LAWTON, born Feb. 20, 1692; married —— *Sherman*.
120. ROBERT LAWTON.

§ **19.** SUSANNAH LAWTON, 3 (Elizabeth Hazard, 2 ; Thomas, 1), died Dec. 9, 1712; married Thomas Cornell, son of Thomas and Elizabeth (Fiscock) Cornell.

CHILDREN
121. THOMAS CORNELL, born Nov. 30, 1674.
122. GEORGE CORNELL, born 1676.
123. ELIZABETH CORNELL.

§ **23.** ELIZABETH LAWTON, 3 (Elizabeth Hazard, 2 ; Thomas, 1), died in 1724; married Robert Carr.

CHILDREN
124. ROBERT CARR.
125. ABIGAIL CARR, married —— *Honeyman*.

§ **26.** DANIEL WILCOX, 3 (Hannah Hazard, 2 ; Thomas, 1), married Mary Wodell.

CHILD
126. STEPHEN WILCOX.

§ **27.** WILLIAM WILCOX, 3 (Hannah Hazard, 2 ; Thomas, 1), married January 25, 1698, Dorothy Palmer.

CHILDREN
127. DOROTHY WILCOX, born Oct. 28. 1698.
128. ANN WILCOX, born June 14, 1701.
129. WILLIAM WILCOX, born June 3, 1703.
130. JEMIMA WILCOX, born July 21, 1705.
131. MARY WILCOX, born Dec. 1, 1709.
132. AMEY WILCOX, born July 7, 1711.
133. SARAH WILCOX, born Aug. 29, 1713.
134. NATHAN WILCOX, born Dec. 3, 1716.

§ 28.

§ **28.** STEPHEN WILCOX, 3 (Hannah Hazard, 2; Thomas, 1), married in 1704, Elizabeth Crandall, daughter of John and Elizabeth (Gorton) Crandall.

CHILDREN
135. STEPHEN WILCOX.
136. ROBERT WILCOX.
137. JOHN WILCOX.

§ **29.** HANNAH WILCOX, 3 (Hannah Hazard, 2; Thomas, 1), married Samuel Clarke, son of Jeremiah and Ann (Audley) Clarke.

CHILDREN
138. JOHN CLARKE.
139. AUDLEY CLARKE.
140. SAMUEL CLARKE.
141. DANIEL CLARKE.

§ **31.** THOMAS POTTER, 3 (Martha Hazard, 2; Thomas, 1), died 1728; he married, January 20, 1687, Susannah Tripp, born October 31, 1667, daughter of John and Susannah (Anthony) Tripp. He married after her death, Lydia Sherman, widow of Thomas, and daughter of Daniel Wilcox. She died in 1727.

CHILDREN OF FIRST MARRIAGE
142. SUSANNAH POTTER, born June 28, 1688; married —— *Sheldon*.
143. SARAH POTTER, born July 25, 1690; married —— *Earle*.
144. ICHABOD POTTER, born Sept. 23, 1692.
145. THOMAS POTTER, born Feb. 8, 1696.
146. JOHN POTTER, born Oct. 2, 1697.
147. NATHANIEL POTTER, born April 15, 1700; married *Elizabeth Bentley*.
148. BENJAMIN POTTER, born Jan. 19, 1703; married *Ruth Sherman*.
149. JOSEPH POTTER, born Jan. 30, 1706; married *Abigail Larkin*.
150. MARY POTTER, born Aug. 16, 1708; married —— *Sherman*.
151. MARTHA POTTER.

§ **32.** JOHN POTTER, 3 (Martha Hazard, 2; Thomas, 1), was born in 1665; died 1715; he married Sarah Wilson, daughter of Samuel Wilson. She was born in 1666, and died in 1739. In his will he gave to his son John Potter, all his land in Matunuck Neck, that joins Point Judith. He also mentions his daughter Martha Allen. In a deed somewhat earlier he gave to his daughter "Martha Allen" a small tract of land on Point Judith, not far from the Governor William Robinson place. The *Robinson Records* say that Governor William Robinson married, 1717, Martha Potter, daughter of John and Sarah (Wilson) Potter; if this is a fact, then she must have been the widow of Allen at the time of this marriage.

CHILDREN
152. MARTHA POTTER, born Dec. 20, 1692; married 1st, —— *Allen;* married 2d, *Gov. William Robinson*.
153. JOHN POTTER, born May 20, 1695; died April 11, 1739; married *Mercy Robinson*, daughter of *Rowland Robinson*.
154. SAMUEL POTTER, born Sept. 2, 1699; died young.

155. SARAH POTTER, born Sept. 15, 1702.
156. SUSANNAH POTTER, born Sept. 17, 1704.
157. MARY POTTER, born March 2, 1707.
158. SAMUEL POTTER, born July 28, 1715.

§ 33. ROBERT POTTER, 3, (Martha Hazard, 2; Thomas, 1), died in 1745; married Elizabeth Wells.

CHILDREN
159. BARBARA POTTER, born Feb. 2, 1688.
160. MARTHA POTTER, born Aug. 10, 1690.
161. ROBERT POTTER, born July 26, 1702.
162. ICHABOD POTTER, born Nov. 30, 1703.
163. SUSANNAH POTTER, born Feb. 14, 1705; married *Elisha Reynolds*.

§ 34. ICHABOD POTTER, 3 (Martha Hazard, 2; Thomas, 1), died in 1730; he married Margaret, daughter of Rouse and Mary Helme. She was born in 1679, and died in 1727.

CHILDREN
164. ICHABOD POTTER.
165. ROUSE POTTER, born Feb. 13, 1703.
166. THOMAS POTTER.
167. WILLIAM POTTER, born March 4, 1709.
168. MARGARET POTTER, born Oct. 11, 1714.

§ 36. JOSEPH MOWRY, 3 (Martha Hazard, 2; Thomas, 1), died in 1718; he married Sarah ——.

CHILDREN
169. MARY MOWRY, born Oct. 18, 1704.
170. ROBERT MOWRY, born Aug. 31, 1706.
171. JOSEPH MOWRY, born Aug. 14, 1708.
172. BENJAMIN MOWRY, born May 2, 1710.
173. ROGER MOWRY, born July 2, 1712.
174. MARTHA MOWRY, born Dec. 5, 1715.
175. SARAH MOWRY, born Aug. 31, 1717.

§ 38. JOHN MOWRY, 3, (Martha Hazard, 2; Thomas, 1), died in 1718; married Mary ——; she died in 1724.

CHILDREN
176. JOHN MOWRY.
177. JONATHAN MOWRY.
178. ABIGAIL MOWRY.
179. A DAUGHTER.
180. A DAUGHTER.
181. A DAUGHTER.

End of the Third Generation

THE

# THE HAZARD FAMILY

## Fourth Generation

MARY HAZARD, 4 (Thomas, 3; Robert, 2; Thomas, 1), was born October, 3, 1683; and died 1722; she married October 19, 1704, John Robinson, son of Rowland and Mary (Allen) Robinson; he died April 6, 1712. She married secondly, Peter Easton, son of James Easton.

CHILDREN OF FIRST MARRIAGE

182. MARY ROBINSON, born Sept. 30, 1705; married *Stephen Hazard,* son of *Stephen* and *Elizabeth Hazard.* [For children see *No. 58.*]

183. SARAH ROBINSON, born Jan. 22, 1707, married, 1st, Jan. 11, 1723-4, *Ichabod Potter ;* married, 2d, Feb. 10, 1742, *George Gardiner.*

184. RUTH ROBINSON, born March 12, 1709; married, April 27, 1732, *Joseph Underwood.*

185. SUSANNAH ROBINSON, born Feb. 9, 1712 ; married, March 30, 1731, *Peregrine Gardiner.*

CHILDREN OF SECOND MARRIAGE

186. MIRIAM EASTON, born Dec. 23, 1718 ; married, Oct. 11, 1739, *Fones Hazard,* son of *Stephen* and *Margaret (Fones) Hazard.*

187. HANNAH EASTON, born Oct. 1, 1720.

§ 40. HANNAH HAZARD, 4 (Thomas, 3; Robert, 2; Thomas, 1), was born April 11, 1685; she died October 1, 1765; she married Nicholas Easton, son of James Easton. He was born December 27, 1683, and died November 10, 1743.

CHILDREN

188. NICHOLAS EASTON, born Jan. 1, 1717 ; died March 14, 1772.

189. JONATHAN EASTON, born Nov. 24, 1719; married *Ruth Coggeshall,* daughter of *Benjamin* and *Sarah (Easton) Coggeshall ;* died Dec. 9, 1795.

§ 41. SARAH HAZARD, 4 (Thomas, 3 ; Robert, 2 ; Thomas 1), was born July 5, 1687 ; she married Stephen Easton, son of James Easton. He was born April 5, 1682, and died in 1732.

CHILDREN.

190. JAMES EASTON, born Aug. 8, 1710.

191. JOHN EASTON, born 1713; married April 17, 1735, *Patience Redwood,* daughter of *Abraham* and *Patience (Howland) Redwood.*

§ 42. ROBERT HAZARD, 4 (Thomas, 3; Robert, 2; Thomas, 1), was born May 3, 1689; he died May 20, 1762. Like nearly all the Hazard family of this

generation

generation he was a large landholder, although not large in proportion to the landholders of the preceding generation, whose estates numbered thousands, instead of hundreds of acres. A part of his land was given to him before his father's death, but the greater portion he obtained by purchase. In 1721, he was given by his father, one hundred and fifty acres on Tower Hill. This is the farm now owned and occupied by William Nichols. It was afterwards given by Robert to his son Thomas, called "College Tom." The old Mansion House (built perhaps by Robert), was still standing a few years ago. In 1739, he received from his father by deed, two hundred acres of his Boston Neck land. This Robert gave to his sons Richard and Jonathan, by will, having previously given them by deed when of age, as the custom then was, twenty acres. This land was not given as a means of support, but as a qualification for them to become freemen, or voters. His "mansion house," which was on the farm, now owned by Thomas G. Hazard, was given to his son Jonathan by will; also to Jonathan and Richard was given a farm of three hundred acres, near Worden's Pond, — land inherited from his father as residuary legatee. His father bought this land in 1710, of Samuel Sewall.

One hundred and thirty years have passed since the death of Robert Hazard. Perhaps his will shows us as much of his character, as can be traced at this late day. It shows us a man who left nothing to chance, and who attended to all minute details, and used an even-handed justice in the equal distribution of his worldly goods. The will bears date March 11, 1762. . . . " Being sick and weak in body but of a sound mind and in perfect memory, &c. *Item*, I give to my beloved wife *Sarah*, my Mulatto woman called *Lydia*, also four cows, such as she shall choose, to be kept yearly and every year, for and during the summer season, by my two sons *Jonathan* and *Richard*, and yᵉ winter season by my son *Thomas Hazard*, yearly and every year, also a black mare, called her mare, also sixty pounds of sheep wool to be delivered to her yearly and every year, twenty pounds by my son *Thomas Hazard*, and twenty pounds by my son *Jonathan Hazard*, and twenty pounds by my son *Richard Hazard*, also one equal share of my Puter, Brass, Iron, and wooden vessels; also two of my feather beds, with furniture belonging to them, such as she shall choose; also one room in my Mansion House, such as she shall choose, together with a privilege in the Kitchen, Cellar, Cheese House and well; also ten bushels of apples yearly and and every year, to be choosen by her in yᵉ Fall of yᵉ year out of yᵉ orchard adjoining my Mansion House; also three barrels of cider to be provided her yearly and every year by my son *Richard Hazard;* also one of my largest silver spoons, one salt spoon, also three silver spoons marked, *I. B.*, and *R. B., S. H., I. R. B.* and two other spoons, as she shall choose; also three hundred weight of good Pork to be provided for her yearly and every year, one hundred weight by my son *Thomas*, one by my son *Jonathan*, and one by my son *Richard*; also two hundred weight of good Beef to be provided in the same manner; also twenty bushels of Indian corn, . . . also two hundred weight of Flower; also the use of the improvement
of

of my garden annually; also the keeping of her mare; also sixty pounds in bills
of credit old Tenor to her paid yearly by my son Thomas.[1]

Also the use of my Mulatto man *Newport;* also one equal half of my tables, and
chairs, also my cupboard, desks, chests, one equal part of them all.   All above
bequests to be in Lieu of her Right of Dower, and power of thirds.

*Item;* I give to my daughter *Sarah,* one equal half part of my Puter, Brass,
Iron, and Wooden Vessels, also one silver spoon, one of yᵉ largest spoons, and
five other spoons, to be chosen by her after her mother's choice, also two feather
beds with furniture, to be chosen by her after her mother's choice, also one bay
mare coming four years old (to be kept by *Richard*); also one half part of my
tables, chairs, etc., also my negro woman *Bell* or *Isabel;* also privilege of living
in my Mansion House with her mother until her marriage day; also a thousand
pounds in Bills of Credit of yᵉ old Tenor, to be levied out of my movable estate;
also of my cupboards, desks and chests, yᵉ one-half part of them.

*Item;* I give to my daughter *Mary Champlin* five hundred pounds; one silver
salt spoon, and one of my largest spoons, and five other silver spoons.

*Item;* I give to my son *Thomas Hazard* a tract of land containing one hundred
fifty acres . . . also one other tract of land with dwelling house thereon, bounded
&c. ; . . . also all right in *Sege Island,* also one-third part of my right in *Susquehannah Purchase,* so called, he paying one-third part of the charges that may arise
in securing the same, also one-third right in *Pine* and *Cedar* swamp.

*Item;* I give to son *Jonathan* a tract of land with my Mansion House and the
buildings &c., . . . also tract of land lying west of *Wordens Pond,* . . . also one-third
right in *Susquehannah Purchase,* and in *Pine* and *Cedar* swamp.

*Item;* I give to son *Richard* a tract of land with dwelling-house, bounded
East on twenty acres given him by deed, &c., . . . also one-half part of land at
yᵉ westward of *Wordens Pond* &c., . . . also one-third part of *Susquehannah Purchase,*
and one-third part in *Pine* and *Cedar* swamp.

*Item;* son *Jonathan,* my mulatto man *Newport,* after his mother has done with
him, also mulatto boy called *Dick.*

*Item;* . . . to wife *Sarah,* negro child *Phyllis.*

*Item;* . . . to daughter *Sarah,* negro child *Phebe.*"

Robert Hazard married Sarah, daughter of Richard and Innocent Borden.
She was born July 31, 1694.

CHILDREN

192. MARY HAZARD, born 1716; Feb. 23, married *Stephen Champlin,* son of *Jeffrey* and *Hannah
(Hazard) Champlin.*
(For children see *No. 96.*)
193. THOMAS HAZARD, born May 9, 1718; died Dec. 2, 1719.
194. THOMAS HAZARD, born Sept. 15, 1720; married *Elizabeth* daughter of *Deputy-Gov. William
Robinson.*
195. JONATHAN HAZARD, born Aug. 1726; married April 15, 1747, *Mary Gardner.*

---

[1] At that time (1762), a pound of old tenor was equal to one-seventh of one Spanish dollar.  Seven pounds  was  the
value of a Spanish dollar.

196.

196. RICHARD HAZARD, born Dec. 31, 1730; married *Susannah Hazard*.
197. SARAH HAZARD, born June 27, 1734; married *Job Watson*.

§ 44. STEPHEN HAZARD, 4 (Thomas, 3; Robert, 2; Thomas, 1) was born June 13, 1693; he died December 24, 1718. He married Margaret, daughter of John and Lydia (Smith) Fones. In his will he leaves " all my estate both real and personal, to my beloved wife Margaret." She married in 1727, soon after the death of her young husband, Joseph Holmes. On a farm in North Kingstown, now the property of Warren Arnold, there is, a few rods south-east of the house, the family burial place of John Fones, containing twenty or thirty graves. On the east side of this ground there is a large rock, about fifteen feet broad, rising three or four feet above the ground with a perpendicular smooth side to the west, against which are the feet of the graves, each boxed to the height of about sixteen inches on the surface by common wall and flag-stones, not cemented. At the head of each there is a black slate stone about eighteen inches high, scrolled around the sides, and with the usual oval top with head and wings. The first grave at the right hand reads, " Here lies buried Stephen Hazard who died December y^e 24, 1718; aged 25 years."
The second reads, " Here lies buried Susannah daughter of Stephen and Margaret Hazard. Died, June 8, 1717; aged 2 years and 24 days."
For nearly two hundred years has the young husband and father rested beside his little daughter, under the shadow of the great rock, in the burial ground of his father-in-law, but no wife sleeps beside him.

CHILDREN
198. FONES HAZARD, born May 9, 1715; died in infancy.
199. SUSANNAH HAZARD, born May 9, 1715 ; died June 8, 1717.
200. FONES HAZARD, born Sept. 22, 1717 ; married *Miriam Easton*, his cousin.

§ 46. GEORGE HAZARD, 4 (Thomas, 3; Robert, 2; Thomas, 1), was born January 18, 1699 ; he died 1746. His will bears date October 11, 1746, about a month previous to the date of his father's will. On July 28, 1721, his father gave him by deed fifty acres, and in 1738 he gave him by deed four hundred and nine acres, being what is known as the Thomas G. Hazard and Thomas M. Potter farms. George, by his will, gave two hundred and nine acres on the Point to his son, Enoch Hazard, whose children sold in 1797 to Jeremiah Niles Potter, and which he in turn sold in 1798 to Elisha R. Potter.
There are many men of note that claim George Hazard as a direct ancestor, and judging from his descendants he must have been a man with a curious combination of pride and sensitiveness. Strong men do not spring from weakness. The qualities that made the Honorable Benjamin Hazard of Newport one of the best lawyers of his day, where were they not inherited ? The physique and strength of his great-grandson, Sylvester R. Hazard of Newport, could not have come from a dwarf in stature. An eye-witness says that he once saw Sylvester Hazard place himself under a medium-sized horse, and lifting it from the ground, he carried

ried it across the street. If one looks for gentle traits, they are found in the gracious courtesy of manner and the purity of life of his great-grandson, Dr. Rowland Hazard of Newport. These are speculations and history read backward, but it is history indeed, if one can judge him by the long line of honorable men and women who are his descendants.

He married, November 17, 1721, Mary, daughter of Enoch and Mary (Sweet) Place. She was born October 16, 1697.

CHILDREN

201. BENJAMIN HAZARD, born May 2, 1723; died 1748; married *Mary* ——.
202. SIMEON HAZARD, born Aug. 8, 1725; married, Feb. 6, 1745, *Abigail Mumford.*
203. MARY HAZARD, born Nov. 23, 1727; died 1777; unmarried.
204. GEORGE HAZARD, born Apr. 16, 1730; married, Nov. 7, 1752, *Sarah*, daughter of Colonel *Thomas* and *Alice* (*Hull*) *Hazard.*
205. SUSANNAH HAZARD, born Dec. 18, 1732; married *Richard*, son of *Robert* and *Sarah* (*Borden*) *Hazard.*
206. ENOCH HAZARD, born Dec. 6, 1735; married *Mary*, daughter of *John* and *Mary* (*Perry*) *Potter.*
207. THOMAS HAZARD, born Oct. 11, 1738; married *Mary*, daughter of *Jonathan* and *Ruth* (*Coggeshall*) *Easton.*

§ 47. BENJAMIN HAZARD, 4 (Thomas, 3; Robert, 2; Thomas, 1), was born November 2, 1702; he died in 1768. In 1738 he was given by his father three hundred and thirty acres in Boston Neck. He sold this land in 1750 to Daniel Jencks, and it is now known as the Jencks farm. Unlike his brothers, he did not increase his inheritance, and was not a large landholder. He died intestate, and probably insolvent, for after his death his daughter Hannah petitioned the town council to appoint George Hazard of Newport administrator of her father's estate, he being his largest creditor.

Though not a large farmer, he was an important man in the affairs of the Colony, and filled many positions with credit. In 1722 he was admitted freeman from South Kingstown; in 1744, '45, '46, '47, '48, he was Assistant. In 1745, " It was resolved and voted that Benjamin Hazard, Peter Bours, and Daniel Updike, Esq'., be, and they are hereby appointed a committee to take into consideration the last petition of the Massachusetts agent to the Right Honourable, the Lords of the Committee of His Majesty's Most Honourable Privy Council, respecting the controversy about the boundaries between the said Province of Massachusetts and this Colony, and make such remarks, and form such instructions thereon as they shall think necessary, and present the same to his Honour the Governor, in order to be sent to the agent by the first opportunity, and lay a copy thereof before this Assembly at their next session." [1] In 1749 he was on a committee appointed to burn the old tenor notes as fast as received, twenty thousand pounds of the new tenor being reckoned as eighty thousand of the old tenor. [2]

He married, September 13, 1739, Mehitable, daughter of Abraham and Patience

---

[1] Col. Rec., vol. v, pp. 116–117.          [2] Col. Rec., vol. v, p. 273.

47

ABRAHAM REDWOOD.

Redwood ; she was born in Salem, Massachusetts, September 16, 1722, and died June 18, 1761, aged 39.

CHILDREN

208. JONATHAN HAZARD, born Aug. 25, 1740.
209. THOMAS HAZARD, born Dec. 25, 1742 ; died young.
210. HANNAH HAZARD, born July 7, 1744 ; married, July 7, 1771, *James Tanner*.
211. MEHITABLE HAZARD.
212. BENJAMIN HAZARD ; died 1781, on board a prison ship.
213. REDWOOD HAZARD, born June 18, 1745 ; died June 24, 1836.
214. THOMAS HAZARD, born Jan. 23, 1756 ; married, Oct. 2, 1783, *Hannah*, daughter of *Joseph* and *Bathsheba Knowles*.

§ 48. JONATHAN HAZARD, 4 (Thomas, 3 ; Robert, 2 ; Thomas, 1), was born October 7, 1704 ; he died 1746. His will was recorded October 9. In 1739, his father gave to him by deed two hundred acres in Boston Neck. This land he ordered, in his will, to be sold to pay his debts. Thomas, his son, called " Virginia Tom," sold it to Stephen Champlin. In 1785 it was divided among Champlin's heirs, and was afterwards owned by Walter Watson, who gave it to his daughter Abigail. Walter Watson's wife was a granddaughter of Jonathan Hazard, and a daughter of "Virginia Tom" Hazard, so that this was family property. It is now known as the Updike farm, — the Updikes being descended from the Hazards and Bowdoins through the Watsons. Somewhat earlier than 1739, Thomas Hazard gave, by deed, three hundred and thirty acres to Jonathan. This land his son Thomas sold to Stephen Champlin, and it was afterwards owned by Deputy Governor George Brown ; now known as the Brown farm. A few years before his death, Jonathan conveyed to his brother George Hazard, a small part of the Watson farm, " with half the pier, half the warehouse, and half the boats and landing." This places a pier on the farm long before it was known as Watson's pier ; the deed also mentions "one-half the shipyard," which makes Jonathan one of the earliest shipbuilders in the town. In 1742, Jonathan Hazard was Deputy ; this is the only time that his name is found in the Colonial Records, with the exception that in 1728 he was admitted freeman from South Kingstown.

He married Abigail, daughter of Daniel and Sarah (Place) MacCoon. She was born December 14, 1707.

CHILDREN

215. THOMAS HAZARD, born Feb. 22, 1726 ; married, 1st, *Mary Preston*, daughter of *Peter Bowdoin*, of Virginia ; 2d, *Eunice*, daughter of *William* and *Mary Rhodes*, and great-granddaughter of Roger Williams.
216. SUSANNAH HAZARD, born March 24, 1729 ; died at her brother's house in Prince Edward Island, Dec. 27, 1815 ; unmarried.
217. MARY HAZARD, born March 22, 1737 ; married 1762, Colonel *Charles Dyre*.
218. GEORGE HAZARD, born May 22, 1742.
219. SARAH HAZARD.
220. ABIGAIL HAZARD.
221. JONATHAN HAZARD ; married *Patience*, daughter of *Jeffrey Hazard*.

§ 49.

§ 49. ABIGAIL HAZARD, 4 (George, 3 ; Robert, 2 ; Thomas, 1), was born March 9, 1690; she married Ebenezer Niles, son of Nathaniel and Sarah (Sands) Niles; he was born December 3, 1683. After her death he married Sarah Kenyon. He was brother to the Rev. Samuel Niles and Nathaniel Niles, and, with the last, owned several hundred acres in and about the village of Wakefield including a grist-mill and saw-mill. In a deed of land from his father, he was given permission to raise the dam to a certain stone, or to a certain mark on said stone. The picturesque old house in Wakefield now known as Dalecarlia was built by his brother, Nathaniel Niles, who died in 1766; so this makes the house certainly from a century and a quarter to a century and a half old.

CHILDREN
222. EBENEZER NILES, born March 4, 1710.
223. PENELOPE NILES.
224. SARAH NILES.

§ 51. CALEB HAZARD 4, (George, 3 ; Robert, 2 ; Thomas, 1), was born November 24, 1697; he died January 15, 1726. His father gave to him by deed one hundred and fifty acres, "land that I bought of George Whitman, bounded South on land of said Whitman, West on highway, North on land of William Congdon, East on Point Judith Ponds." This was the farm now owned by Elisha F. Watson. It was on this farm that Caleb was buried. If one can judge by the size of his grave, physically he could have been no exception to the Hazards of that day. He married, November 19, 1719, Abigail, daughter of William Gardiner. After his death his widow married, March 2, 1727, Deputy-Governor William Robinson, and was the mother of six of his children.

CHILDREN
225. WILLIAM HAZARD, born April 12, 1721; married *Phebe*, daughter of *John* and *Damaris Hull* of Jamestown.
226. ROBERT HAZARD, born May 1, 1723 ; married *Elizabeth*, daughter of Deputy-Gov. *Robert Hazard*.
227. CALEB HAZARD, born Jan., 1724; died young.
228. CALEB HAZARD, born Sept. 22, 1726; married *Mary* ——; he died March 4, 1784.

§ 52. GEORGE HAZARD, 4 (George, 3; Robert, 2; Thomas, 1), was born October 9, 1700; he died in 1738 ; his will was recorded May 22, 1738. He was admitted freeman of the Colony in 1721. In 1729 he was Deputy, and so continued six years. In 1733 he was Speaker of the House of Representatives, and in 1734 was elected Deputy Governor of the Colony, and was re-elected four years in succession, dying in office in 1738. In 1733 he bought of his father, for one thousand pounds, the farm then (and still) called " The Foddering Place." About this time he built the old house, taken down about twenty years ago by Joseph Peace Hazard. The old house, like all houses of the wealthy planters of that day, was very large, being fifty feet on the front, having a fan-light over the entrance door, above which was a large arched window which gave light to the hall. This hall was
square

square, with handsome oak staircase and balustrade. In the south end of the house was the parlor, a very large room, in one corner of which was the buffet, with the quaintly carved, scrolled back and top, that seems to have been a feature common to the houses of any pretension in Colonial days. The house was two stories high in front, but the roof ran down to the first story in the rear, a style still to be seen in some of the old houses that have been allowed to stand as monuments to the old builders. By his will, George gave this house, with all outbuildings and an "Island called Ram Island," to his son George Hazard, who was Mayor of Newport.

He married Sarah, daughter of James and Mary (Whipple) Carder. She was born May 14, 1705, and died 1738, after her husband.

CHILDREN

229. MARY HAZARD, born Sunday, July 16, 1722; married *Benjamin Peckham*.
230. GEORGE HAZARD, born Sunday, June 15, 1724; married, 1st, *Martha Wanton;* 2d, *Jane Tweedy*.
231. ABIGAIL HAZARD, born Sunday, March 12, 1726; married Sept. 5, 1753, 1st, Rev. *Peter Bours;* 2d, Rev. *Samuel Fayerweather*, Feb. 27, 1763.
232. SARAH HAZARD, born Sunday, Sept. 15, 1729; married *George Wanton*.
233. PENELOPE HAZARD, born Sunday, May 7, 1732.
234. CARDER HAZARD, born Sunday, Aug. 11, 1734; married, 1st, *Alice*, daughter of *Robert* and *Thankful (Ball) Hull;* 2d, *Alice*, daughter of Col. *Thomas* and *Alice (Hull) Hazard*.
235. ARNOLD HAZARD, born May 15, 1738; married *Alice*, daughter of *William Potter*. All of these children, excepting the last, were born on the first day of the week.

§ 53. THOMAS HAZARD, 4 (George, 3; Robert, 2; Thomas, 1), was born March 30, 1704, and died about 1787. He was Deputy in 1745, '48, '52, '53, '55, '56; in 1757 he was Assistant; in 1745 he was appointed Major, and in 1748, Colonel, by which title he is best known by his descendants. In 1725, he being then twenty-one years of age, his father, Colonel George Hazard, conveyed to him a "certain tract of land, being by estimation ten acres, be it more or less . . . with all Housings, Mills, Presses, Shears, and other things which may tend or belong to the Cloathing trade." This property was the fulling mill established by his father, Colonel George Hazard, in 1722–3, near what is now known as Moorsfield, at a place called Lawton's saw-mill. The land was a part of the homestead farm of Robert (2) Hazard. This whole farm of three hundred acres was given to Colonel Thomas by will, in 1743, and by him sold to John Rose in 1748. The residence of Colonel Thomas is not precisely known, although he was certainly living in Boston Neck in 1752, when his daughter Sarah was married to her second cousin, George Hazard, son of George, and grandson of Thomas (3) Hazard.

A certain unity of opinion, and tradition, all seem to point to the fact that he was a man of ability; and that he was well educated is proved by the formal, facile hand-writing seen in his family Bible, and in the few autograph documents which escaped the destroying touch of time, and have been handed down to his descendants.

descendants. He was both proud and gentle, and never violated a confidence. Surely one can be pardoned for giving credence to some of these old traditions, when the fact is recognized that many of these traits have been reproduced in some of his descendants.

Thomas Hazard married, December 11, 1729, Alice, daughter of Teddiman and Sarah (Sands) Hull; she died 1737.

CHILDREN

236. PENELOPE HAZARD, born Feb. 11, 1730-1; married Nov. 18, 1750, *William Potter*.
237. HANNAH HAZARD, born Aug. 5, 1732; married Nov. 21, 1752, Col. *John Wilson*.
238. SARAH HAZARD, born Jan. 27, 1734; married, Nov. 7, 1752, *George Hazard*. For children, see *George Hazard, No. 204*.
239. ALICE HAZARD, born Aug. 30, 1737 ; married, March 5, 1761, Judge *Carder Hazard*, her first cousin. For children, see *Carder Hazard, No. 234.*

§ 54. OLIVER HAZARD, 4 (George, 3 ; Robert, 2 ; Thomas, 1), was born September 13, 1710 ; died April 14, 1792. It is somewhat difficult to place the residence of Oliver Hazard, but probably he lived and died in South Kingstown. In 1734 he was admitted freeman of the Colony from that town, and in 1743 he had a valuable estate given to him by his father's will. A part of this land was trusteed, Colonel Thomas Hazard having the guardianship. He was also to have a part of the rents until 1747, but in 1744 he released the land to Oliver, doing so "in consideration of the love I have for my brother." In 1744 his nephews, William and Caleb, sons of Caleb, sold to him all the rights they had in their grandfather's estate. At the last date he was called Oliver Hazard of North Kingstown. His daughter Elizabeth was born in South Kingstown in 1737, and his daughter Mercy, grandmother of Commodore Oliver Hazard Perry, was born in North Kingstown in 1740.

He married, December 9, 1736, Elizabeth Raymond of North Parish, New London. This made him the grandfather of those remarkable men, Qliver Hazard and Matthew Calbraith Perry, and, through them, the ancestor of a long line of brave soldiers, both on land and sea. It would be interesting to know something of the family of Elizabeth Raymond, for, before the Civil War, the name Hazard was rarely found in army or navy lists, and it may be that the "fighting blood" was taken from the Raymonds. It was first developed in the Perry family in Christopher Raymond Perry, grandson of Oliver Hazard.

CHILDREN

240. ELIZABETH HAZARD, born Sept. 13, 1737.
241. OLIVER HAZARD, born March 30, 1739 ; married *Patience Greene*, widow of Captain *Samuel Greene*.
242. MERCY HAZARD, born Jan. 21, 1740-1 ; married Judge *Freeman Perry*.
243. SARAH HAZARD.
244. LUCRETIA HAZARD.

§ 56. HANNAH HAZARD, 4 (Stephen, 3 ; Robert, 2 ; Thomas 1), was born April 20, 1697; she married Joseph Mumford. He was born September 17, 1691,

1691, and was the son of Thomas and Abigail Mumford. His mother, Abigail, was murdered in May, 1707, by a slave, whom tradition says she had caused to be whipped for some misdemeanor. The slave's body was found on the shore of Little Compton. The Assembly ordered that his head and legs and arms should be cut from his body and hung up in some public place, and his body be burned to ashes, that it may be "something of a terror to others from perpetrating of the like barbarity in the future."

Joseph Mumford was admitted freeman of the Colony in 1722; in 1736, is found the following act: "Whereas, *Joseph Mumford*, of *South Kingstown*, in *Kings County*, yeoman, by petition, did set forth to this Assembly, that he, some time past, was at a great charge in building the pier at *Point Judith* in *South Kingstown*, aforesaid, which has been of great service to the country ; but by the late storm the said pier was very much damaged, and has cost the petitioner considerable to repair the same, and the petitioner having received three or four cords of timber, which was designed for *Block Island* pier, prayed that the same might be allowed him towards repairing his said pier."

"Upon consideration whereof, it is voted and ordered, that the said three or four cords of timber received by said *Joseph Mumford* be allowed to him for repairing his said pier, without any account to be rendered for the same."[1] This places the pier at Narragansett as being the first pier in the town, as there is no account of another until a few years later, at Boston Neck. Both were built by members of the Hazard family.

CHILD

245. STEPHEN MUMFORD, born March 2, 1718.

§ 57. SUSANNAH HAZARD, 4 (Stephen, 3; Robert, 2; Thomas, 1), was born April 23, 1697, and died 1756; she married Samuel Perry (son of Samuel, son of Edward Perry). In 1722 he was admitted freeman of the Colony from Charlestown. In 1735 he was on a committee appointed by the General Assembly to consider the feasibility of turning the Pawcatuck river into the largest salt pond in Westerly[2] in order to keep the breach open, thus providing a harbor. Point Judith was then the nearest place for water communication with Newport and Providence for the inhabitants of Charlestown.[3] The report was not favorable, and the project was dropped, to be taken up in 1892 by the United States Government, and a harbor provided for ships as well as for the people of Charlestown. The first project concerned the salt pond in Charlestown, and the second the salt pond in South Kingstown. In 1740, '41, '42, '46, Samuel Perry was Deputy for Charlestown, also in 1740 he was one of the trustees to George Ninegret, the Indian Sachem.[4] In 1744 " it was voted and resolved, that Joseph Whipple, Esq'., Deputy Governor Stephen Hopkins, Esq'., Mess^n. Stephen Brownell, Robert Hazard, Job Randall, and Samuel Perry be, and they are hereby, appointed a committee to determine what is rata-

---

[1] Col. Rec., vol. iv, p. 527.  [2] This was before Charlestown was set off from Westerly and became an independent town.  [3] Col. Rec., vol. iv, p. 511.  [4] Col. Rec., vol. v, p. 581.

ble

ble estate, and prepare a bill for the same, and present it to the next session of this Assembly." [1] He died previous to 1763.

CHILDREN

246. ELIZABETH PERRY, born Nov. 3, 1719; married, July 4, 1744, *Elisha Babcock*, son of *George and Susannah Babcock*.
247. MARY PERRY, born June 10, 1721; married —— *Dodge*.
248. SAMUEL PERRY, born April 19, 1723; married, Dec. 26, 1746, *Ann Clarke*.
249. SIMEON PERRY, born May 31, 1726; married, 1763, *Anne Browning*, widow of *Thomas Browning*; died Dec. 2, 1801.
250. HANNAH PERRY, born April 13, 1728; married, Dec. 26, 1746, *Joseph Clarke*.
251. EDWARD PERRY, born June 15, 1730; married *Deliverance Moore*.
252. JOHN PERRY, born May 15, 1732; married *Meribah Soule*.
253. STEPHEN PERRY, born Jan. 6, 1736; married, 1st, *Elizabeth Borden*; 2d, —— *Whitefield*.
254. SARAH PERRY, born March 30, 1738; married March 30, 1757, *David Babcock*.
255. RUTH PERRY, born 1740; married as second wife of *Edward Perry*.
256. SUSANNAH PERRY, born March 25, 1742; married, July 10, 1759, *Jonathan Babcock*.
257. MERIBAH PERRY, born 1744; married *Jeremiah Pierce*.

§ 58. STEPHEN HAZARD, 4 (Stephen, 3; Robert, 2; Thomas, 1), was born November 29, 1700; he died in 1746. His will was proved, July, 1746. His home was in Point Judith, on the farm now owned by the heirs of Carder H. Clark. His father gave him this farm by will, calling it "the farm where I now live, one hundred and fifty acres, also fifty acres of homestead farm, bounded South on Jeffrey Champlin, West on George Hazard, North on land in occupation of William Robinson, East on remaining part of said farm, he paying to the Colony what said farm is mortgaged for." In 1735 he was appointed Justice of the Inferior Court of Common Pleas.[2] This position gave him the title of Judge, by which he has always been distinguished from the other Stephen Hazard of his generation. He married, January 9, 1723, Mary, daughter of John and Mary (Hazard) Robinson. She was his second cousin; she was born September 30, 1705, and died 1780.

CHILDREN

258. STEPHEN HAZARD, born 1723; married *Sarah Nichols*, daughter of Governor *Jonathan Nichols*.
259. MARY HAZARD, born Sept. 18, 1725; married, Aug. 30, 1752, *John Potter*, son of *Ichabod Potter*.
260. ELIZABETH HAZARD, born July 26, 1729; married as second wife of *John Potter*, son of *John Potter*.
261. JOHN HAZARD, born June 26, 1731; died 1772.

§59. ROBERT HAZARD, 4 (Stephen, 3; Robert, 2; Thomas, 1), was born September 12, 1702; he died 1751. In 1722 he was admitted freeman of the Colony, in 1734 he was Deputy from South Kingstown; this position he held until 1749; in the following year he was chosen Deputy Governor, and died while holding this office, his last term being May, 1751. That he was a prominent man in the affairs of the Colony, active and able, and faithful in the discharge of his duties, is shown by the fact that from his thirty-second year until his

---

[1] Col. Rec., vol. v, p. 88.      [2] Col. Rec., vol. iv, p. 508.

death

death he is always found performing the duties attendant upon his position, making and sustaining the laws of the Colony.

His home was on Point Judith, on land given to him by his father's will, and was a part of the homestead farm. He married Esther, daughter of Joseph and Esther (Gallup) Stanton. Updike, in his *History of the Narragansett Church*, says: " Esther, the widow of Governor Hazard, was an extraordinary woman, portly and masculine.¹ She was styled Queen Esther, and when mounted on her high-spirited Narragansett pacer, proudly travelling through the Narragansett country, the people would almost pay her homage. To offend her required more than ordinary courage. In manner she was affable and courteous, but when irritated her sternness would compel obedience. In a lawsuit, the title to a considerable part of the patrimony of her children was jeopardized. That no omission should endanger a favorable result of the suit, she attended the trial in person, and, from courtesy, she was permitted to sit on the bench near the judges. On a motion to the Court by Mr. Honeyman, who was the attorney for the adverse party, she, by a quick and sarcastic reply to a severe remark of his, excited the laughter of the Court, bar and audience, to the complete discomfiture of the old barrister. The claim of the adversary was defeated, and Queen Esther became quite a heroine in the courts of law. The rights of an infant offspring were safe in the hands of such a mother.'' Unfortunately, the nature of this celebrated retort, being more witty and strong than delicate, forbids its repetition. That it was well deserved, and called forth by the attack, seems to have been understood by the court and bar, which evidently exulted in the discomfiture of the worthy Honeyman.

CHILDREN

262. JOSEPH HAZARD, born May 21, 1728 ; married, Sept. 28, 1760, *Hannah*, daughter of Deputy-Governor *Jonathan Nichols*.
263. ELIZABETH HAZARD, born May 31, 1730; married, April 19, 1752, Dr. *Robert Hazard*, her second cousin.  For children see *Dr. Robert Hazard, No. 226.*
264. ESTHER HAZARD, born Dec. 7, 1732; married *Jonathan Babcock.*
265. STEPHEN HAZARD, born Jan. 13, 1736.
266. ROBERT HAZARD, born Jan. 13, 1736.
267. SAMUEL HAZARD, born about 1739 ; married, May 3, 1763, *Hannah Perry.*
268. HANNAH HAZARD, born 1741; died 1798; unmarried.
269. JOSHUA HAZARD.
270. STANTON HAZARD, born Jan. 8, 1743; married *Elizabeth Wickham.*

§ 60. SAMUEL HAZARD, 4 (Stephen, 3 ; Robert, 2 ; Thomas, 1), was born July 28, 1705. He was admitted freeman of the Colony, from South Kingstown, in 1728 ; by his father's will he was given two hundred acres in North Kingstown, and also a part of Mumford Island, in Point Judith (now called Great Island). In the division of the slaves he was given "Short Joe" and the negro woman Megg. His home was for a time in North Kingstown, where he and his brother Thomas, in 1729, established a fulling-mill, on the present site of, or near Ham-

---

¹ Governor Hazard was an exceptionally small man.
² Updike's Hist. of the Narragansett Church, p. 250.

ilton

ilton Mills. In 1736 he sold his part to Samuel Bissell.¹ It is probable that about this time he removed to Newport, for in 1750 he and his wife Abigail, of Newport, sold to George Hazard, of Newport, their right in Mumford Island.

CHILDREN

271. SAMUEL HAZARD, married *Catharine* ——.
272. GEORGE HAZARD, married *Mary Mumford.*
273. SARAH HAZARD, born Nov. 26, 1736.

§ 61. THOMAS HAZARD, 4 (Stephen, 3; Robert, 2; Thomas, 1), was born July 28, 1707. He was admitted freeman in 1730. By his father's will he was given three hundred acres in North Kingstown, and a part of Mumford Island, in Point Judith Pond. The three hundred acres in North Kingstown were on the south side of the road that leads from Bissell's Mills (and is a part of that which is now known as the Hiscox home farm), and so on west to the country or Post Road. In 1729, Samuel Slocum, father-in-law to Thomas Hazard, sold to him, in company with his brother, Samuel Hazard, fourteen acres east of his home lot, with fulling mills and houses. In 1741 Thomas sold his interest to Daniel Fontain. At the sale there was conveyed fourteen acres of land with "mills, houses, fulling mill, tenter, brass and iron press plates, iron bars and a blacksmith shop." The whole farm was sold in 1772 to Gervase Elam, and was confiscated in 1775 by the State,² Elam being a royalist and accused of giving assistance to the enemy. About 1741 Thomas Hazard seems to have moved to South Kingstown, for his children by his second wife were born there, and their births recorded in that town. In 1748 he was paid £3 13s. from the estate of Benjamin Waite, who was a tenant on his three-hundred-acre farm in North Kingstown. He married, February 22, 1727, Hannah, daughter of Honᵇˡᵉ Samuel Slocum. He had a child by this marriage, "Short" Stephen Hazard, and perhaps other children. The North Kingstown records are so badly injured by fire that it is impossible to verify this. His wife Hannah died January 24, 1737. He married, second, in May, 1738, Hannah Updike.

CHILDREN

274. STEPHEN HAZARD, married *Elizabeth,* daughter of *Daniel* and *Renewed Carpenter.*
275. THOMAS HAZARD, born Nov. 30, 1741.
276. HANNAH HAZARD, born Dec. 22, 1745; died March 30, 1798.

§ 62. ELIZABETH HAZARD, 4 (Stephen, 3; Robert, 2; Thomas, 1), was born in 1709. She married, July 16, 1729, Benjamin Perry, son of Samuel Perry. He was styled "Junior" to distinguish him from his uncle Benjamin. He is called "youngest son" in his father's will, and was left by the will one hundred acres of land, "south of homestead already bequeathed, being land I purchased of Joseph Hull, Jr.; also the tract of land called Maple Swamp; and with son Edward, a tract of land lying partly on Wood River, of two hundred and seventy-nine acres to be divided equally between them." He lived in South

---

¹ The old name of Hamilton was Bissell's Mills.     ² Col. Rec., vol. viii, p. 325.

Kingstown,

Kingstown until March 1, 1731-2, when he was admitted freeman of Westerly, possibly that part of Westerly now Charlestown. He subsequently returned to South Kingstown, and took oath there May 6, 1735.

CHILDREN

277. DORCAS PERRY, married *Henry Potter.*
278. SUSANNAH PERRY.
279. ELIZABETH PERRY.
280. SARAH PERRY.
281. ALICE PERRY.
282. BENJAMIN PERRY, married *Ruth Potter.* He is probably the *Benjamin Perry* who was permitted by the General Assembly to take the test-oath, March 9, 1778; and allowed, Dec. 1778, £9 12s. for arresting a noted Tory. In 1778, *Benjamin Perry,* of South Kingstown, had a slave, *Garret Perry,* who enlisted in the army, and was valued at £120.

§ 82. JEFFREY HAZARD, 4 (Robert, 3 ; Robert, 2 ; Thomas, 1), was born September 29, 1696 ; he died in 1767. In 1718 his father gave him by will three hundred acres in Point Judith, with the Mansion House, "where I now live." Jeffrey was to bring up the younger children, all of them then being under age. In 1722 he bought of James Kenyon three hundred acres in Exeter, then in North Kingstown, as Exeter was not set off from that town until 1743. This land was bounded north on the estate of Benedict Arnold, west on dividing line of Pettaquamscut purchase, and south by land in possession of Jedediah Irish, east by undivided land, or on Cedar Swamp. By deed of gift dated 1751, he gave this land, calling it "my homestead farm," to his eldest son Jeremiah. One authority says that "Stout Jeffrey" lived in Boston Neck, on what is now known as the Governor Brown Farm. If this is a fact, then he must have been a tenant, and not owner of the farm, as this farm was, and had been since 1739, or earlier, in possession of Thomas Hazard (3), and his direct descendants. In 1746, Jonathan, son of Thomas, gave it to his son "Virginia Tom" Hazard ; in 1760 his first wife was buried there. However, the residence or non-residence of "Stout Jeffrey," on this farm, does not in any way affect the truthfulness of the tradition that he did show the slaves how to make a stone wall, by lifting a blue stone, weighing by the scales sixteen hundred and twenty pounds, to its place on the foundation. There is another legend equally marvellous and equally well vouched-for in proof of the great strength of the man. The second legend relates that he once had an encounter with a man of great strength, who had come from a long distance to meet the Narragansett giant. When the man dismounted from his horse and stated his errand, Jeffrey picked him up and tossed him over the wall (it should have been the same wall that he had helped to build), and then threw the horse over to keep his master company. Notwithstanding his splendid vitality he died comparatively young, from the effect of a slight cold, taken while attending to his duties as Councilman. He was Deputy from Kingstown almost uninterruptedly from 1735 until 1758. There are a few descendants of " Stout Jeffrey " in the town at the present day, and,

and, with scarcely an exception, the men are six feet or more in height, well developed and proportioned. Doctor Thomas A. Hazard of Kingston, and his brother Jeremiah of Jamestown, were men who did no discredit to their sturdy ancestor. There is living in New York State, a great-grandson over eighty years of age, who weighs over two hundred and fifty pounds, and is still hale and hearty. Jeffrey Hazard married Mary ———; unfortunately there is no record of this marriage, or of her maiden name. It would be interesting to know from which of the old Narragansett families his descendants draw their good blood.

CHILDREN

283. JEREMIAH HAZARD, born Aug. 13, 1726; married *Mary*, daughter of *Robert Hazard*.
284. SUSANNAH HAZARD, married, Feb. 5, 1753, *Wilkinson Browning*; died Feb., 1793; he died Oct. 28, 1805.
285. ROBERT HAZARD, married *Hannah Greene*.
286. JEFFREY HAZARD.
287. HANNAH HAZARD; married *Thomas Champlin*.
288. PATIENCE HAZARD, married *Jonathan Hazard* ("*Beau Jonathan*"); she died March 19, 1809. For children see *Jonathan Hazard, No. 221.*

§ 84. ROBERT HAZARD, 4 (Robert, 3; Robert, 2; Thomas, 1), was born January 9, 1703. He died 1775. He removed to East Greenwich early in life, and the births of all his children are recorded in that town. In 1739 he sold the old homestead, with a hundred acres, to his uncle George. By the terms of his father's will he was to have possession of the old home only after the death of his grandmother, which occurred in 1739, she being one hundred years old. He married in March, 1727, Martha ——— (the record of her last name is too indistinct to be read). The marriage was recorded in North Kingstown.

CHILDREN

289. ROBERT HAZARD, born Sept. 19, 1728; married *Alice Thomas*.
290. AMEY HAZARD, born Nov., 1733; married ——— *Wilcox*.
291. SARAH HAZARD, born May 6, 1734; married *John Richmond* Nov. 6, 1757.
292. JEREMIAH HAZARD, born July 25, 1736; married, March 6, 1760, *Phebe Tillinghast*.
293. MARY HAZARD, born Dec. 21, 1738; married, March 10, 1757, *Adam Richmond*.
294. HANNAH HAZARD, born March 19, 1741.
295. JEFFREY HAZARD, born Oct. 6, 1743.
295A. THOMAS HAZARD, died 1784; unmarried.

§ 86. AMEY HAZARD, 4 (Robert, 3; Robert, 2; Thomas, 1), was born September 17, 1715. She married, May 30, 1734, Eber Sherman, brother to Henry Sherman, who was grandfather to Judge Sylvester G. Sherman, of North Kingstown. Many of the descendants of Eber and Amey Sherman are now living in North Kingstown.

CHILD

296. EBER SHERMAN.

§ 89. ANN HAZARD, 4 (Jeremiah, 3; Robert, 2; Thomas, 1), was born February 28, 1701; she died in 1770; she married John Browning, son of William and Rebecca (Wilbur) Browning, April 21, 1721.

CHILDREN

CHILDREN
297. THOMAS BROWNING, married Feb. 2, 1767, *Anne Hoxsie.*
298. JEREMIAH BROWNING.
299. HANNAH BROWNING, married, Sept. 7, 1748, *Jedediah Frink.*
300. SARAH BROWNING, married —— *Stanton.*
301. JOHN BROWNING.
302. EPHRAIM BROWNING.
303. MARTHA BROWNING, married —— *Powers.*
304. ANN BROWNING, married, Jan. 31, 1754, *John Browning.*
305. MARY BROWNING, married *Robert Champlin.*
306. EUNICE BROWNING, married —— *Clarke.*

§ 90. ROBERT HAZARD, 4 (Jeremiah, 3; Robert, 2; Thomas, 1), was born April 1, 1703; he died October 8, 1789; he married Patience, daughter of Stephen and Mary (Thomas) Northup. She was born June 27, 1705, and died June 26, 1795.
CHILDREN
307. MARY HAZARD, married *Jeremiah Hazard.* For children see *Jeremiah Hazard, No. 283.*
308. JEREMIAH HAZARD, born 1735; admitted freeman from North Kingstown 1756. In 1779 he was impeached for disloyalty, and with his wife sent away from the town. On his petition to have the charges against him examined, and permission given him to return home, he was allowed to return on his parole.[1]
309. EPHRAIM HAZARD, born 1729; died May 28, 1825.
310. GIDEON HAZARD, born 1734; died June 15, 1814.

§ 93. HANNAH HAZARD, 4 (Jeremiah, 3; Robert, 2; Thomas, 1), was born April 17, 1714. She married, as second wife, Samuel Watson.
CHILDREN
311. SAMUEL WATSON.
312. FREEBORN WATSON.
313. HAZARD WATSON.

§ 96. STEPHEN CHAMPLIN, 4 (Hannah Hazard, 3; Robert, 2; Thomas 1), was born February 16, 1710; he died July 22, 1771; he married Mary, daughter of Robert and Sarah (Borden) Hazard; she died March 13, 1773.
CHILDREN
314. STEPHEN CHAMPLIN, born Sept. 29, 1734; married *Dinah,* daughter of *William* and *Mary (Wilkinson) Browning.*
315. HANNAH CHAMPLIN, born 1735; married *Nicholas Gardiner.*
316. SARAH CHAMPLIN, born Aug. 18, 1737; married *Samuel Congdon.*
317. MARY CHAMPLIN, born 1739; married, Feb. 12, 1761, *Joseph Browning.*
318. SUSANNAH CHAMPLIN, born March 26, 1742; married, Jan. 22, 1767, *Arnold Wilcox.*
319. JEFFREY CHAMPLIN, born March 21, 1744; married *Mary——.*
320. ROBERT CHAMPLIN, born April 12, 1747.
321. THOMAS CHAMPLIN.

[1] R. I. Col. Rec., vol. viii, p. 601.

§ 152.

§ 152. MARTHA POTTER, 4 (John Potter, 3; Martha Hazard, 2; Thomas, 1), was born December 20, 1692; she died November, 1725. She married first —— Allen; she married a second time, about 1718, Deputy-Governor William Robinson, son of Rowland and Mary (Allen) Robinson. William Robinson was born in the year 1693 and died in 1751. He was given by his father's will three hundred acres in Kingstown and three hundred acres in Westerly, and at his mother's death "all housings, mills and lands that were hers." To this estate he added largely by purchase, giving to his sons by will at his death one thousand three hundred and eighty-five acres. This was in addition to the farms given to them by deed at their majority. His South Kingstown farm extended from Point Judith to Narragansett Pier and thence to Sugar-Loaf Hill in Wakefield, a distance of several miles. When visiting the various points on his farm, superintending the work of his slaves, he always rode one of his Narragansett pacers. These horses he bred in large numbers. They were rather small in size, their peculiar merit consisting in an extremely easy gait. One could ride all day without feeling great fatigue. They were very fleet, and readily took the water when it was necessary to swim across a ford. These fords were apt to change after a great storm, especially in the Pettaquamscutt River, and a slave was usually sent on ahead, after one of these storms, to find the new ford for his mistress. But if a slave was not at hand and the mistress unwilling to wait, her trusty pacer would swim across the stream.

Governor William Robinson's public life covered a space of twenty-four years, and during this time he was always actively engaged in business of the Colony. He was Deputy in 1724, '25, '26, '27, '28, '34, '35, '36, '41, '48. In 1735, '36, '41, '42 he was Speaker of the House. In 1745, '46, '47, '48 he was Deputy Governor. The inventory of his estate is interesting, as showing not only the amount of his wealth, but the extent of his farming, and even the size of his house. The rooms were: great-room, great-room bedroom, dining-room, dining-room bedroom, store bedroom, northeast bedroom, kitchen, closet, store closet, cheese room, milk room, &c. All these were on the first floor, with corresponding sleeping rooms above. The large open attic, was the place for the looms, wheels, reels, &c., for converting the white fleece of his sheep and lambs into clothing for his family. His estate was inventoried at £21,573 5s. 5d. A pair of silver knee-buckles are now in the possession of his great-great-grandson, Benjamin F. Robinson of Wakefield. His silver "in the buffet in the great room" was inventoried at £374 8s. He possessed twenty slaves.

One of these slaves, called Abigail, was the daughter of that Abigail owned by Rowland Robinson, who grieved so bitterly for her son left behind in Africa, that her master sent her back to her native land to find the boy and bring him to her master's house, and to a state of bondage. The old man provided carefully for her comfortable sustenance on the voyage, giving the Captain a list of the things that he was to provide; these included cups and saucers, plates, knives and forks, with a certain amount of bread and meat and other necessaries, one bed with
                                                                furniture

furniture for the outward voyage, and two beds and furniture for the home voyage. Of course Rowland Robinson's friends and neighbors all laughed at his credulity in trusting his faithful slave, but as he had a crusty temper he was saved from an outward show of their amusement, for it was a bold man who offended him. A man that had such faith in human nature must have safely been trusted.

A short time before he left England for America, he quarrelled with one of his brothers; some ten or fifteen years afterwards a son of this brother came to seek his fortune in New England, and, of course, went to his uncle's house. The uncle refused to see him, but gave him the best room in the house, and detailed a servant to the young man's own service. He staid several months, and then his uncle bought for him an estate in Virginia, built a house, furnished it, and sent him, with the slave he had given to him, to take possession of the new home. It is to be hoped that the nephew had as fine a sense of honor as the slave, who returned with her boy, and served her master faithfully to the end.

Many years after Rhode Island had freed her slaves and provided for the old, weak, and feeble, a descendant of this Abigail, Bristol by name, worked for James Robinson, grandson of Governor William. One day, in mid-winter, the old man had been busy all day unloading a sloop. It was quite dark when the last load was brought home. Mr. Robinson met him and said, "Thee is late, Bristol, but never mind, the days will soon be longer." "'Fore God, massa," said Bristol, "I hope the days will *never* be any longer."

As Rowland Robinson is the ancestor of many of the Hazard family, he has been given a place in these records.

CHILDREN OF WILLIAM AND MARTHA ROBINSON

322. ROWLAND ROBINSON, born Oct. 8, 1719; married *Anstis Gardiner*, Dec. 3, 1741; she was a niece of his step-mother.
323. JOHN ROBINSON, born July 23, 1721; died 1739.
324. MARY ROBINSON, born Jan. 27, 1723; died April 16, 1723.
325. ELIZABETH ROBINSON, born June 16, 1724; married, March 27, 1742, *Thomas Hazard*, son of *Robert* and *Sarah*. For children, see *Thomas Hazard, No. 194.*
326. MARTHA ROBINSON, born Nov. 11, 1725; married, 1747, *Latham Clarke.*

§ 153. JOHN POTTER, 4 (John Potter, 3; Martha Hazard, 2; Thomas, 1), was born May 20, 1695; he died 1739; and married Mercy, daughter of Rowland and Mary Robinson, October 28, 1714. She died in 1762. He was called Colonel John Potter.

CHILDREN

327. JOHN POTTER, born Jan. 3, 1716; married, 1st, Oct. 20, 1736, *Mary Perry*, daughter of *James Perry*; 2d, *Elizabeth*, daughter of *Stephen Hazard.*
328. WILLIAM POTTER, born Jan. 21, 1722; married *Penelope*, daughter of Col. *Thomas Hazard.*
329. SAMUEL POTTER, born Jan. 20, 1724; married *Ann Seagar.*
330. MARY POTTER, born Aug. 15, 1727.
331. SARAH POTTER, born Aug. 11, 1730.

End of the Fourth Generation

# THE HAZARD FAMILY

## *Fifth Generation*

 SARAH ROBINSON, 5 (Mary Hazard, 4; Thomas, 3; Robert, 2; Thomas, 1), was born January 22, 1707; she married, January 16, 1722, Ichabod Potter, Jr.; after his death she married, February 19, 1742, George Gardiner.

### CHILDREN OF FIRST MARRIAGE

332. JOHN POTTER, born July 29, 1724.
333. SIMEON POTTER, born Sept. 25, 1726.
334. RUTH POTTER, born Jan. 19, 1728.
335. ROUSE POTTER, born Dec. 10, 1729.

### CHILDREN OF SECOND MARRIAGE

336. SUSANNAH GARDINER, born June 16, 1743.
337. GEORGE GARDINER, born March 18, 1745.
338. RUFUS GARDINER, born March 9, 1747.
339. WILLIAM GARDINER, born Sept. 8, 1749.
340. LEVI GARDINER, born Sept. 29, 1751.

§ 184. RUTH ROBINSON, 5 (Mary Hazard, 4; Thomas, 3; Robert, 2; Thomas, 1), was born March 12, 1709; married, April 27, 1731, Joseph Underwood.

### CHILDREN

341. JOHN UNDERWOOD, born Dec. 24, 1732.
342. JOSEPH UNDERWOOD, born April 12, 1734.

§ 186. MIRIAM EASTON, 5 (Mary Hazard, 4; Thomas, 3; Robert, 2; Thomas, 1), married Fones Hazard, son of Stephen and Margaret Hazard. They were first cousins. In the settlement of his estate, in 1749, he was called " Fones Hazard, Mariner." His grandfather, Thomas Hazard, gave him by will four hundred and sixty-six acres in " Matoonuck."

### CHILDREN

343. STEPHEN HAZARD, born May 18, 1740; died May, 1800; married *Hannah Sandford*.
344. NICHOLAS HAZARD, born Aug. 12, 1741; married, Jan., 1763, *Mary Dulucina*.
345. FONES HAZARD, born 1744; married, Jan. 17, 1768, *Rebecca Briant*; died 1803, at Mrs. Wells' house, Broad Street, Newport. His wife died Oct. 3, 1788.

§ 188. JONATHAN EASTON, 5 (Hannah Hazard, 4; Thomas, 3; Robert, 2; Thomas, 1), was born November 24, 1719; he married Ruth, daughter of Benjamin

36

Benjamin and Sarah (Easton) Coggeshall. He was called "Little Jonathan."
He died December 9, 1795.

CHILDREN

346. MARY EASTON, born May 20, 1743; married *Thomas G. Hazard*; died Nov. 26, 1794.
347. NICHOLAS EASTON, born June 29, 1744; married *Elizabeth Potter*, of South Kingstown; died
     June 21, 1789.
348. JONATHAN EASTON, born August 6, 1747; married *Sarah Thurston*, daughter of *Peleg* and
     *Sarah Thurston*, Dec. 3, 1778; died March 13, 1813.
349. SARAH EASTON, born Aug. 16, 1749; died Nov. 3, 1827.
350. HANNAH EASTON, born 1750; died Oct. 29, 1797.
351. BENJAMIN EASTON, born Aug. 28, 1752; died Sept. 16, 1807.
352. RUTH EASTON, born May 21, 1754; married, 1787, as second wife, *Godfrey Hazard*, and was
     the mother of Dr. Jonathan E. Hazard.
353. PATIENCE EASTON, born Sept. 24, 1756; died Aug. 30, 1811.
354. JOHN EASTON, born March 26, 1758; died Aug. 21, 1823; married, 1st, *Ruth*, daughter of
     *Robert Taylor*; she died March 11, 1806. He married, 2d, her sister, *Hannah Taylor*; she
     died Aug. 3, 1832, aged 79 years.
355. STEPHEN EASTON, born Oct. 18, 1759; died Oct. 19, 1759.
356. REBECCA EASTON, born Oct. 18, 1759; died Oct. 19, 1759. The mother died the follow-
     ing day, Oct. 20, 1759.

§ 191. JOHN EASTON, 5 (Sarah Hazard, 4; Thomas, 3; Robert, 2; Thomas,
1), was born 1713; he married, April 17, 1735, Patience, daughter of Abraham
and Patience (Howland) Redwood.

CHILDREN

357. NICHOLAS EASTON, born May 4, 1752; died Nov. 28, 1825.
358. MARY EASTON; married May 27, 1773, *Joseph Thurston*, son of *Thomas* and *Abigail Thurston*.
358 *a*. A CHILD; 358 *b*. A CHILD; 358 *c*. A CHILD; 358 *d*. A CHILD; 358 *e*. A CHILD.

§ 194. THOMAS HAZARD, 5, called "College Tom" (Robert, 4; Thomas,
3; Robert, 2; Thomas, 1), was born September 15, 1720; died in 1798. In 1742
he was admitted freeman of the Colony from South Kingstown. In 1748 was
Clerk of the Council. After 1742 his name appears several times in the Colonial
Records, not as a member of the General Assembly, but as a petitioner on various
matters that seemed to demand reform.

In 1769, "Thomas Steere, Ephraim Congdon, William Redwood, Joseph Congdon and Thomas Hazard, son of Robert, in behalf, and by appointment of the
Quarterly Meeting of Friends, held at Portsmouth, on Rhode Island, in October
last, preferred a petition to this Assembly, and, for the reason therein assigned,
prayed this Assembly to pass an act to prevent the selling of liquors, and the
playing at games, &c., on the days and near the place where the General Meeting
of Friends is annually held for religious worship; and the said petition being duly
considered, "It is voted and resolved, that the same be, and hereby is granted,
and the bill presented with said petition, pass into an act of this Assembly." [1]

In 1764, he, with about fifty others, among them being the most prominent

---
[1] R. I. Col. Rec., vol. vi, p. 578.

men

men in the Colony, petitioned the General Assembly to grant them full powers to " found, endow, order, and govern a College or University within this Colony. " [1]

The petition was granted, and Thomas Hazard, with ten others, were declared the "first and present Fellows and Fellowship, to whom the President, when here-after elected (who shall be of the denomination called Baptist, or *antipaedo* Baptists), shall be joined to complete their number."

This college, then founded under the name of Rhode Island College, afterwards was changed in name, and is now known as Brown University.

Thomas Hazard entered Yale University, and for this reason was called " College Tom," a name by which he is distinguished from the other Thomas Hazards of his generation ; he was not graduated from Yale, owing to the fact (as stated by Updike) " that he had become so thoroughly indoctrinated in the faith of the Quakers, that he became conscientious respecting collegiate honors, and left the institution before the regular period of conferring degrees." From the same authority is quoted, " Mr. Hazard was comely in person, large in stature, . . . and of great physical strength. He was a preacher of the Society of Friends for forty years before his death, and tradition speaks of him as a strong and forcible, argumentative speaker. He was deservedly popular in his denomination, and was the first in his society that advocated the abolition of negro slavery. He travelled much as a public Friend, preaching emancipation among his brethren."

In 1783, it was voted by the General Assembly " that the draft of an act authorizing the manumission of slaves, presented to this Assembly by the committee appointed to consider the petition of a committee of the people called Quakers, be referred to the third day of the next Session for further consideration," etc. Thomas Hazard was one of the signers of this petition, which was the opening wedge to the emancipation Act passed February, 1784.[2]

Pleasant landmarks in the history of these prominent men of the olden time, are the houses they occupied. To know that one is walking over the fields their feet have so often trod, or to stand on their own hearth-stone, gives one a feeling of reality and close connection with the dead, but not buried, past. Thomas Hazard's home was on Tower Hill, on the farm now owned and occupied by William Nichols ; his homestead, or manor-house, as it was called in old deeds and wills, was standing a few years ago. Some authorities say that Hazard was buried on this farm. Others say that he was buried in the yard of the Quaker Meeting-House ; but wherever buried, his spirit haunts the old home around which linger vestiges of his personality. It is not difficult for the imagination to see the beautiful wife (for the women of the Robinson family were noted for their beauty) standing at the gate to watch her husband mount his horse and ride away on one of his frequent journeys. On one of these occasions a relative, who was visiting the Hazards, accompanied Mrs. Hazard to the gate. After

[1] Col. Rec., vol. vi, p. 386.          [2] R. I. Col. Rec., vol. ix, pp. 735-738.

" Cousin

"Cousin Hazard" had mounted his horse and ridden over the brow of the hill well out of sight, she turned to enter the house. "Wait awhile," said Mrs. Hazard, "my husband will return, for he has forgotten something;" and presently was heard the clatter of the steel-shod hoofs of the returning horse. Without a word spoken, the rider, as he reached the gate, bent down and kissed the upturned face of the waiting wife. This incident occurred late in life, and is all the more touching for the reason, that it stands in proof of that steadfast love which naturally combines with "the steadfast convictions," that we are told controlled his life. He married, on March 27, 1742, Elizabeth, daughter of Governor William and Martha (Potter) Robinson; she was born on June 16, 1724; she died on February 5, 1804. She was a great-granddaughter of Thomas Hazard, the first in America, and consequently was third cousin to her husband.

The record of the children of Thomas Hazard was taken from a little book entitled *Extracts from the Journal of Sarah Howland*, published in 1890, by Howland Pell of New York.

CHILDREN

359. SARAH HAZARD, born the tenth of the 11th Mo., called January, 1747. She departed this life the 26th of the 3d Mo., called May, about 11 at night, in 1753, new style, being 5 yrs., 4 mos. & 5 days old.
360. ROBERT HAZARD, born Nov. 17, 1753, "it being the fourth day of the week, about fifty minutes after one in the morning."
361. THOMAS HAZARD, born the 13th of the 11th month, 5th day of the week, about 9 o'clock in the morning, 1755. He died the 15th of the 3d Mo., 2d day of the week, at 10 o'clock in the morning, 1756.
362. THOMAS HAZARD, "their second son of that name, born the 15th of the 11th Mo., 5th day of the week, about the 9th hour in the evening, 1758."
363. ROWLAND HAZARD, was born the 4th of the 4th Mo., 2d day of the week, about 10 o'clock in the forenoon, 1763.

§ 196. RICHARD HAZARD, 5 (Robert, 4; Thomas, 3; Robert, 2; Thomas, 1), was born December 31, 1730; he died September 30, 1762; his will, proved October 11, 1762 (written September 18, 1762), gave to his wife all the profits of his farm and Manor House, "lying in Boston Neck, given to me by my honoured father, Robert Hazard," towards her support and bringing up of "my family, also the use of all my estate, my negro man Tom and negro woman Esther, also my grey mare." He married Susannah, daughter of George and Mary (Place) Hazard, she was his first cousin. She died in 1767, when her youngest child was but six years old and the eldest, fourteen.

CHILDREN

364. HANNAH HAZARD, born April 14, 1753; died May 22, 1784.
365. ROBERT HAZARD, born April 11, 1755; died 1795; married, Dec. 29, 1782, *Hannah Gardiner*, daughter of *Nicholas Gardiner*.

366.

366. GEORGE HAZARD, born Sept. 22, 1756; married, March 7, 1782, 1st, *Sarah Scott;* 2d, Dec. 8, 1786, *Sarah Knowles,* daughter of *John* and *Susannah Knowles* (possibly no children by second wife). He was called "*Shoe-String*" *George.* He lived on a farm near the Great, or Worden's Pond. His will, proved Sept. 15, 1825, gave to his wife *Sarah* all his estate, both real and personal, to her, her heirs and assigns forever.

367. BENJAMIN HAZARD, born Dec. 26, 1757; married April 10, 1779, *Hannah,* daughter of *Simeon* and *Abigail (Mumford) Hazard ;* he died Oct. 15, 1784.

368. SUSANNAH HAZARD, born April 11, 1760.

369. RICHARD HAZARD, born Nov. 15, 1761; married, after the death of his brother Benjamin, his widow, *Hannah Hazard.*

§ 197. SARAH HAZARD, 5 (Robert, 4; Thomas, 3; Robert, 2; Thomas, 1), was born June 27, 1734. She married, February 11, 1760, Job Watson, son of John and Isabel Watson. She died in January, 1811.

CHILDREN

370. ISABEL WATSON, born Sept. 22, 1766.

371. JOB WATSON, born Oct. 25, 1767; married, Jan. 18, 1787, *Phebe Weeden.*

372. ROBERT WATSON, born Feb. 28, 1769; married *Catherine Weeden;* died Dec. 30, 1790.

373. WALTER WATSON, born June 10, 1770; married *Mary Carr.*

374. BORDEN WATSON, born Feb. 9, 1772; married *Isabella Babcock.*

375. JOHN WATSON, born Nov. 1, 1774; married, Jan. 24, 1799, *Sarah Brown,* daughter of Gov. *George* and *Hannah (Robinson) Brown;* married, 2d, Aug. 4, 1805, *Isabel Watson.*

§ 201. BENJAMIN HAZARD, 5 (George, 4; Thomas, 3; Robert, 2; Thomas, 1), was born May 2, 1723; he died in 1748. His father gave to him by will, in 1746, "all my right of land situate, lying and being in North Kingstown, containing four hundred acres, bounded Easterly, partly on country road, and partly on land of Jeremiah Hazard, Southerly on land of Samuel Watson, and partly on land of Ezekiel Gardner and others of yᵉ Gardners, and Northerly, partly on a lot of land that formerly belonged to my mother-in-law, Mary Wickham, deceased, and partly on land of Jeremiah Hazard, to him, his heirs and assigns forever." This is the farm now known as the Nathan G. Hazard farm. John, son of Benjamin, was called Wickham John, because a part of his inheritance came to him through his grandmother Wickham, or Wickom, as it is spelled in the deeds. Benjamin Hazard married Mary ——.

CHILD

376. JOHN HAZARD, born 1746; died June 20, 1813; married, 1st, *Sarah,* daughter of *Nathan Gardner ;* 2d, *Martha,* daughter of *Latham* and *Martha (Robinson) Clarke.*

§ 202. SIMEON HAZARD, 5 (George, 4; Thomas, 3; Robert, 2; Thomas, 1), was born August 8, 1725; he died in 1790. His father, by will, gave to him "a lot of land lying in Boston Neck, in South Kingstown, at the Pier, with half the Pier, half the warehouses and half the boats and landing, according as it is set forth and described in a deed of sale from my brother Jonathan Hazard, deceased, to myself, bearing date, &c., . . . and my negro man Olford. I also give and bequeath unto my son Simeon, the sum of three hundred pounds, current money of

New

New England, with all my silver, except what was given to Enoch Hazard and Thomas Hazard by their grandmother, Mary Wickom, deceased." The deed referred to above, "from my brother Jonathan," mentions "the great shipyard." The Pier is what is now known as Watson's Pier. This deed and will goes to prove that this line of the Hazard family were not only large farmers and exporters of the products of their plantations, but also shipbuilders. This would account for the great prosperity of Thomas Hazard, the third in descent, and the large amount of ready money, in "good silver Spanish dollars," that he invested in land at a time when money was extremely scarce. Mr. Weeden in his account of the early shipbuilding in New England, says that many of the staunch American ships were sent to England and sold with their cargoes, often consisting of ship-timber and tall masts for the King's navy. "They knew by experience that a present of huge masts was the surest approach to the favor and bounty of their sovereign." [1] Perhaps Thomas Hazard was one of those men who walked through their woodland, to mark the tall, straight trees, "For the King."

Simeon Hazard married, in February 6, 1745, Abigail Mumford.

CHILDREN

377. GODFREY HAZARD, married, 1st, Feb. 22, 1778, *Alice Hazard*, daughter of *George Hazard*; married, 2d, *Ruth Easton*.

378. SIMEON HAZARD.

379. MUMFORD HAZARD; married, Feb. 18, 1796, *Elizabeth*, daughter of *Christopher Robinson*. He died June 24, 1811; they had no issue. She was born 1761, and died 1824. An obituary notice from the *Rhode Island Republican*, dated June 26, 1811, says: "At South Kingstown, on the 24th, Mumford Hazard. A man universally beloved and esteemed for his inflexible integrity, industry, and humanity."

380. HANNAH HAZARD, married, 1st, *Benjamin Hazard*; married, 2d, his brother *Richard*. For children see *Nos. 367 and 369*.

381. ABIGAIL HAZARD, died June 17, 1839; married late in life Robert Rodman; she was his second wife.

382. GEORGE HAZARD, married *Content Wilbur*; died Nov. 29, 1836.

383. ELIZABETH HAZARD.

384. MARY HAZARD, married, Feb. 4, 1798, *Jonathan Carpenter*.

§ 204. GEORGE PLACE HAZARD, 5 (George, 4; Thomas, 3; Robert, 2; Thomas, 1), was born April 16, 1730. He was called "Little Neck George," because he owned and occupied the farm known as "Little Point Judith Neck Farm." This farm contained one hundred and thirty acres. He married November 7, 1752, Sarah, daughter of Colonel Thomas and Alice (Hull) Hazard; she was born January 23, 1734. They were second cousins.

CHILDREN

385. ALICE HAZARD, born Nov. 15, 1754; married *Godfrey Hazard*.

386. THOMAS HAZARD, born Oct. 3, 1756; died Nov. 14, 1761.

387. GEORGE HAZARD, born April 8, 1762; died Aug. 11, 1786.

388. THOMAS HAZARD, born March 30, 1765; married, Feb. 23, 1790, *Abigail*, daughter of *Sylvester* and *Alice (Perry) Robinson*.

---

[1] Weeden's Economic and Social Hist. of New England, vol. i., p. 156.

§ 205.

§ 205. SUSANNAH HAZARD, 5 (George, 4; Thomas, 3; Robert, 2; Thomas, 1), was born December 18, 1732; she married Richard, son of Robert and Sarah (Borden) Hazard. They were first cousins.
For children, see Richard Hazard, No. 195.

§ 206. ENOCH HAZARD, 5 (George, 4; Thomas, 3; Robert, 2; Thomas, 1), was born December 6, 1735; he died in 1785. In 1758 he was admitted freeman from South Kingstown, and in 1777-8 he was Deputy from the same place. In 1779, '80, '81, '82, '83, he was Assistant. He inherited from his father a farm, now known as the Thomas Potter farm, in Boston Neck. This farm contained two hundred and nine acres. The south part of it was sold in 1797, by his children, to Jeremiah Niles Potter, who in 1798 sold it to Elisha R. Potter. Enoch Hazard was a prominent man in the town. In 1777 he was one of a committee to procure blankets for the army; in the same year he was on a committee to receive the stock belonging to the farm " lately improved by Silas Niles." [1] In 1779, to " inspect the conduct of the tenants of the farms leased by the State." [2] In the same year he was to take possession of the " fat " cattle on the farm in Point Judith, in occupation of William Gorton, to be sold for rents due the State.[3] He married Mary, daughter of John and Mary (Perry) Potter. She died January 23, 1781.

CHILDREN
389. MARY HAZARD, born Sept. 6, 1763; married, May 6, 1782, *George Corliss.*
390. SARAH HAZARD, born Aug. 13, 1768; married, December 25, 1793, *Jeremiah Niles Potter;* were first cousins.
391. ENOCH HAZARD, born Dec. 28, 1775; died April, 1855.
392. ALICE HAZARD, born Jan. 1, 1778; died in 1868; married, as second wife, *Jeremiah Niles Potter.*

§ 207. THOMAS HAZARD, 5 (George, 4; Thomas, 3; Robert, 2; Thomas, 1), was born October 11, 1738; he died December 27, 1820. His father gave to him by will " the remaining part of my homestead farm in Boston Neck, in South Kingstown, containing two hundred acres, bounded Easterly on the sea, Southerly on the two hundred and nine acre lot given to Enoch Hazard, Westerly on Pettyquamscut river, and Northerly on land of Robert Hazard. I also give to my son Thomas all my deer, the clock in the great room, and a round table, and a great glass in the great room, to him, his heirs and assigns, when he shall arrive to the age of twenty-one years." He was but eight years old when his father died. This farm given to Thomas is now known as the Thomas G. Hazard farm, being owned and occupied by Thomas G. Hazard. After the death of Thomas Hazard, his son, George P. Hazard, bought out the rights of the other heirs, and gave it by will to his nephew, the present owner. Of all the several thousand acres bought in Boston Neck by Thomas Hazard, this farm is the only land that has never passed out of the direct line of inheritance. As it

---

[1] R. I. Col. Rec., vol. viii., p. 245.          [2] Ibid., p. 194.          [3] Ibid.

was

was given to George Hazard some time before his father's death, in 1746, it is possible, and probable, that he built the fine old house still standing, and occupied by the present owner. As far as one can judge from tradition and scanty documentary evidence, this line of the family has also retained, in a greater measure than other lines, the strongly marked characteristics peculiar to the earlier Hazard family. Through all this line one can trace a strong sense of justice, as shown in the equal distribution of property, and the care of the orphans of the family, and can perceive a pride of ancestry in many of the descendants at the present day, and an independence of spirit that unwillingly brooks opposition, and as unwillingly submits to an injustice.

Thomas Hazard's public life seems to have been confined to a few years' service in the General Assembly. He was called Thomas G. Hazard to distinguish him from others of the same name. It was equivalent to calling him Thomas, son of George. His name was entered on the town records without the G.; also his father in his will does not use the G.

There is a well supported tradition in the family, that Thomas Hazard's estate, being in some way jeopardized, his sister Mary, who was eleven years older than her brother, went into court herself to attend to his interests. It is also said that this same Molly made several journeys to Philadelphia on horseback.

He married Mary, daughter of Jonathan and Ruth (Coggeshall) Easton; she was his second cousin. She was born May 20, 1743, and died November 26, 1794.

CHILDREN
393. GEORGE PLACE HAZARD, born 1763; died April 16, 1839.
394. JONATHAN EASTON HAZARD, born 1764; died Jan. 31, 1849.
395. THOMAS G. HAZARD, married *Patience Borden.*
396. BENJAMIN HAZARD, born Sept. 9, 1774; married, Oct. 28, 1807, *Harriet Lyman.*
397. MARY HAZARD.
398. ENOCH HAZARD, married, Sept., 1804, *Mary,* daughter of *Nicholas Easton.*
399. JOHN ALFRED HAZARD, died July 21, 1799. He was purser on the U. S. Frigate "General Greene."
400. RUTH HAZARD, died Feb. 8, 1806.

§ 210. HANNAH HAZARD, 5 (Benjamin, 4; Thomas, 3; Robert, 2; Thomas, 1), was born about 1744. She died May 8, 1801; she married, July 7, 1771, James Tanner. He died September 6, 1778.

CHILD
401. JAMES TANNER.

§ 214. THOMAS HAZARD, 5, "Nailor Tom" (Benjamin, 4; Thomas, 3; Robert, 2; Thomas, 1), was born January 23, 1756; he died in Westerly, Rhode Island, September 28, 1845. He was the second son of his father of this name, for the Portsmouth records show that a Thomas, son of Benjamin Hazard, was born December 25, 1742. After his marriage, — before which he had led rather

rather an unsettled life, — he lived in the old house which was taken down about 1850 to give place to a more modern structure. This house was built by Robert Knowles, grandfather of Thomas Hazard's wife. He used to say that the mansion was one of the two oldest houses in the town. It was a quaint old structure, and evidently built for protection as well as shelter, as was shown by the strong wooden shutters and double doors inside. When Hazard was an old man he lost the possession of his home by the trickery of a trusted friend.

The " B." in Mr. Hazard's name was added, as so many other middle names were added, as a distinctive sign. He was also called " Nailor Tom," from one of his many occupations. He had a great fund of anecdote, and was an entertaining conversationalist. He was highly esteemed in his native town, and held numerous places of trust. For two years he was a Senator, and was elected by one hundred majority. He was a member of the Society of Friends, and appropriately to his belief was often a peacemaker and arbiter of differences. He impressed his personality strongly upon his associates. His features were sharply defined, so that people now living can describe him even to-day with singular fidelity to nature.

" Nailor Tom's " diary, or Blue Book, was highly esteemed by his townsmen, and was considered authority upon the matters noted. It is said that Mr. Wilkins Updike, the well-known lawyer and historian of Narragansett, used to say that he had rather see the Devil come into the court-room than " Nailor Tom " with his book. " Shepherd Tom " writes that the people of South Kingstown used to swear by " Nailor Tom's " book. Glancing through this famous book casually, its jottings would seem to be scanty and commonplace, but to one who reads carefully there are valuable data, and little incidents that give an insight into the manner of living and social condition of the people of the time.

Thomas Hazard was a most ingenious man, with a strong bias for invention. In the blacksmith shop that stood within a few rods of his house, he made many quaint and curious articles, — a self-acting rat-trap being amongst the number, so constructed that the captive rat set the trap for his successor.

Thomas Hazard was a great politician. Though not seeking office for himself, he was an indefatigable worker for his friends. He was not a demonstrative man. An anecdote told by an eye-witness is illustrative of his character and his manner of speech. He was once called as a witness in a lawsuit between James Robinson and Rowland Hazard, the question being as to the raising the mill-dam in Wakefield, which threw back-water on the wheel in Peacedale. When Thomas B. Hazard was called upon for his evidence, he commenced by quaintly remarking, " I had a goose once." This was met by a burst of laughter ; when quiet was restored, he repeated the remark, only to be met by repeated laughter on the part of Mr. Robinson. When this had subsided, he said with the same even, quiet voice with which he had made the first statement, " Friend Robinson, if thee will have a little patience I think that the goose will hatch something for thee." And it did hatch a defeat for " Friend Robinson." For this historical

goose

goose had for years made her nest and raised her brood on a point of land that made out into the pond, but after the raising of the dam, she had not been able to find a dry spot for her nest, nor in fact was the point above water. In connection with this the story continues: Thomas R. Hazard, son of Rowland, was at that time paying his addresses to the beautiful and accomplished daughter of Mr. Robinson; after the decision had been given and damages awarded and paid, Thomas R. Hazard sought to renew his visits at "Cousin Robinson's." His first remark, made possibly under some natural embarrassment, was most unfortunate; for he said, "Well, Cousin Robinson, thee has lost thy case;" "Yes," was the dry answer, "and thee has lost thy bride."
Thomas Hazard married, October 2, 1783, Hannah Knowles, the daughter of Joseph and Bathsheba (Seager) Knowles.

CHILDREN

402. BENJAMIN HAZARD, born Dec. 4, 1784; married *Joanna Carr*, May 12, 1814.
403. THOMAS HAZARD, born May 8, 1787; married *Ruth Carpenter*, March 13, 1714.
404. HANNAH HAZARD, born Dec. 14, 1791; died unmarried.
405. ISAAC SENTER HAZARD, born March 27, 1795; died March 29, 1795.
406. ISAAC SENTER HAZARD, born May 10, 1796; died May 11, 1796.

§ 215. THOMAS HAZARD, 5, "Virginia Tom" (Jonathan, 4; Thomas, 3; Robert, 2; Thomas, 1), was born February 22, 1727; he died April 27, 1804. His father gave to him three hundred acres in Boston Neck, now known as the Governor Brown farm, but it is probable that he did not live there for any length of time. He was too ambitious to be long content with the simple, uneventful life of a farmer; building ships to carry the products of his farms to distant markets, had little attraction for a man who could build fast-sailing privateers at his own shipyard, to chase the enemies of the King, and recover from them their ill-gotten gains. A cargo of rum to be exchanged for molasses had not as pleasant a savour, and was not as profitable as the sweet-smelling spices, fragant teas, or other luxuries that his ships brought back from their long voyages.
There are no records to prove that he ever became a large landholder in the Narragansett country. His Boston Neck farm he did retain, certainly until 1760, when his first wife was buried there. When a part of this farm was sold a few years ago, descendants of Thomas and this wife reverently moved the mouldering remains to the Boston Neck burying-ground of Wilkins Updike, whose wife (a daughter of Walter Watson) was a granddaughter of "Virginia Tom." Soon after Thomas Hazard's marriage he went to Newport, where he became a successful merchant, making a large fortune. His son, William Hazard, stated before the Loyalist Commissioners, in 1833, that his father had an estate of £20,000 confiscated in the United States. He was, like the greater number of the Hazard family of his generation, strongly conservative, and adhered to the cause of the King during the struggle for independence. It is not known that he took an
active

active part in actual warfare, but he was obliged to leave his family, and flee to New York, then in possession of the British. His property was confiscated ; he being the only member of the family who suffered in this way.[1] The others who were attainted, after a little discipline and a few months' absence from home, made their peace with the Colony, and were restored to their civil rights.

"Virginia Tom" was of too strong a build and too dominant a nature to yield his firm convictions to a matter of security to his person and estate. Even after the war was over, and he was offered free pardon and restoration of his property, he refused to accept either, at the price of submission. However, the Colony was most kind and gentle to her high-spirited children, and restored all his estate to his wife and children after the close of the war. His adopted mother proved herself but a step-mother, for of all the thousand acres of land granted to him in Ile S. Jean,[2] now Prince Edward Island, but a small part, if any, came into his possession. A great-grandson says: "As far as can be ascertained at present, he never profited by any grants of land in this Island, made to him as a loyalist." Very little is known of his life after he went to Prince Edward Island, in 1786 : shortly after his arrival there he is found filling some minor public offices ; also at an election in 1787, he was returned as a member of the House of Assembly on both opposing lists. He was peculiar in being the only person having that honor. A great-grandson who furnishes this information adds, " I think that election was set aside as void. I have not yet ascertained whether or not he ever sat in the House."

There is no record of office-holding while an inhabitant of the Colony of Rhode Island. His name first occurs in the Colonial Records in 1760, when he and Henry Wall of North Kingstown petitioned the General Assembly, "and represented that they, at their own costs and charges, equipped a private ship of war, against His Majesty's enemies, under the command of Captain Abel Michiner ; that the said ship, in her cruise, took a vessel belonging to the subjects of the French king, who are now prisoners of war, in Newport aforesaid, and supported at the sole expense of the petitioners ; whereupon they prayed that they be permitted to fit out and send a vessel with a flag of truce, to carry the aforesaid eleven Frenchmen to the West *Thomas Hazard* Indies, and there deliver them unto the commander in chief of such port or place, as they shall send to."[3] This petition was granted, " provided that they cause so many English prisoners to be brought back into Newport as the vessel will carry ; provided, also, that the vessel to be sent, be under the same regulations and restrictions with others going to the colonies, ports, or harbors of the enemy, with a flag of truce." [4]

Thomas Hazard married, about 1746, Mary Preeson, or Preston, Bowdoin, daughter of Peter Bowdoin of Virginia.

Pierre Baudouin, "who came to America in 1686, was one of the Baudouin

[1] R. I. Col. Rec., vol. ix., p. 530.
[2] The *Ile S. Jean*, in the Gulf of St. Lawrence, ceded by France to England in 1764. Its name was changed to Prince Edward Island in 1798.     [3] Col. Rec., vol. vi., p. 252.     [4] Col. Rec., vol. vi., p. 262.

family

*410*
ABIGAIL HAZARD.

family of La Rochelle, one of the most important and ancient " of that city. Its different branches were known by names taken from the numerous "seigneuries" which they possessed. They were descended from Pierre Baudouin, Ecuyer, Sieur de la Laigue, who married the daughter of Jean Bureau, mayor of La Rochelle, in 1448. The Baudouins were among the first disciples of the Reformed faith. Several of them distinguished themselves by services to the Protestant cause. In consequence of the severities practiced toward the Protestants, Pierre Baudouin left France and took refuge in the city of Dublin. Later he was induced to come to America, and settle in Maine, where he received a grant of land. He came to Boston in 1690, with his two sons, Jean and James. Jean, the elder, afterwards removed to Virginia, where his descendants may still be found. It was his granddaughter, Mary Preeson Bowdoin, who married Thomas Hazard. James Bowdoin, Governor of Massachusetts, was descended from Pierre, through James Bowdoin. It is from this branch of the Bowdoin family that Bowdoin College takes its name, as well as the square and street of that name in Boston. Mary Preeson (or Preston) Bowdoin Hazard died, in Rhode Island, April 17, 1760. The inscription on her gravestone reads, "She was a loving and kind wife." It is from this marriage that the Watsons, Updikes, and other Narragansett families are descended.

Thomas Hazard married, secondly, Eunice, daughter of William and Mary (Sheldon) Rhodes, and great-granddaughter of Roger Williams. She was born December 12, 1741, and died January 22, 1809. From this marriage the Haszards now living in Prince Edward Island are descended.

CHILDREN OF FIRST MARRIAGE

407. A CHILD, born Sept. 27, 1747; died March 26, 1748.
408. A CHILD, born Aug. 1748; died Aug. 10, 1749.
409. JONATHAN HAZARD, born July, 1750; married *Esther Watson*.
410. ABIGAIL HAZARD, born Dec. 25, 1751; married *Walter Watson*.
411. MARY HAZARD, born Aug. 14; 1753; died Aug. 31, 1754.
412. MARY HAZARD, born 1755; died Nov. 29, 1759.
413. A DAUGHTER, born 1757; died 1757.
414. A SON, born 1757; died 1757.
415. SUSANNAH HAZARD, born Aug. 24, 1758. Her name was changed to Mary; she died Sept. 18, 1841; married *William Cole*.

CHILDREN OF SECOND MARRIAGE

416. THOMAS RHODES HASZARD, born March 1, 1762 ; died 1839 ; married May 8, 1796, *Jane Bagnall;* she died Dec. 24, 1840.
417. EUNICE HASZARD, born Feb. 14, 1764; died March 9, 1832 ; married *John Gardiner*.
418. A DAUGHTER, born 1766; died 1766.
419. WILLIAM HASZARD, born May 3, 1767; died March 14, 1847 ; married *Ann Farrant Jones*, of London; she died Jan. 18, 1853.
420. SARAH HASZARD, born July 18, 1769; married Hon. *William Townshend*.
421. WAITSTILL C. HASZARD, born March 12, 1772; died May 23, 1804; married *James Douglas*, Jan. 30, 1789; he died Sept. 26, 1803.
422. BOWDOIN HASZARD, born 1774; died July 29, 1832; unmarried.
423. RHODES HASZARD, born Sept. 17, 1777; died 1806; unmarried.

§ 217.

§ **217.** MARY HAZARD, 5 (Jonathan, 4; Thomas, 3; Robert, 2; Thomas, 1), was born March 24, 1737; she married in 1762, Colonel Charles Dyre. In 1775 he was commissioned Major of militia for King's County, in the Colony of Rhode Island; in 1776 he was promoted to Colonel, which position he held until the close of the war, during all the time of which he was in active service.

CHILDREN
424. BOWDOIN DYRE.
425. CHARLES DYRE.
426. HAZARD DYRE.
427. CHRISTOPHER CORNWALLIS DYRE, married —— *Foster.*
428. ISABEL DYRE, married —— *Powel.*
429. MARY DYRE, married —— *Foster.*
430. ABIGAIL DYRE, born July 14, 1766; married, Sept. 14, 1783, *Arthur Aylesworth.*

§ **221.** JONATHAN HAZARD, 5, " Beau Jonathan " (Jonathan, 4; Thomas 3; Robert, 2; Thomas, 1), was born probably about 1744, as he was the last child mentioned in his father's will; he died some time after 1824, for he married a second wife after he was eighty years old. He was called " Beau Jonathan " because of his fondness for dress and his courtly manners. Updike, in his *History of the Narragansett Church*, has so well given a sketch of his life, that we quote it entire.

" Jonathan Hazard took an early and decided stand in favor of liberty in the Revolutionary struggle. In 1776 he appeared in the General Assembly as a representative from Charlestown, and was elected paymaster of the Continental Battalion in 1777, and joined the army in New Jersey. In 1778 he was re-elected a member of the General Assembly, and constituted one of the Council of War. He continued a member of the House most of the time during the Revolution. In 1787 he was elected by the people a delegate to the Confederated Congress. In 1788 he was re-elected, and attended the old Congress as a delegate from this State. Mr. Hazard was a politician of great tact and talent, and one of the most efficient leaders of the Paper Money party, in 1786, and their ablest debater in the General Assembly. He beat down the opposition raised by the Hard Money, or mercantile party. He feelingly depicted the lowering distress of the times produced by the avaricious course of the mercantile party. He represented that, prompted by exorbitant profits, they had shipped to England, our late enemy, all the remaining specie that could be obtained, to supply the country with fabrics which the war had exhausted; that the patriotism of the mercantile party was swallowed up by the lust of profit, and that the interest of money, by these selfish and avaricious speculations, had risen to twenty per cent per annum, and in some cases to four per cent per month; and that the paper money emission was the only measure of State policy to prevent civil commotion. He argued, likewise, in favor of the safety of the emission: that it was guaranteed by land security; that it was to be loaned on bond and mortgage of twice the value of the amount borrowed, to be estimated by a committee under oath; that it was an
emission

emission widely different from that of the States, being founded on real estate, and that as long as real estate remained, the money must retain its value, and that no bank could be more secure. That the public were alarmed without reason, and that the opposition were governed by avarice and prejudice.

"Mr. Hazard was the leader of the same party under the name of Anti-Federalists, and a fiery opponent of the adoption of the Federal Constitution. As a delegate to the Convention assembled at South Kingstown, in March, 1790, to take into consideration the adoption of that instrument, he successfully resisted the measure, and upon an informal vote, it was ascertained that there was a majority of seventeen against its adoption. Upon this event, the popular party chaired Mr. Hazard, their leader. The friends of the Constitution, however, obtained an adjournment to meet at Newport in the May following. In the meantime, all the influence and wealth of the State were brought to bear upon the members of the Convention, and whether Mr. Hazard was actually influenced by other means than conviction, cannot be ascertained; but his opposition became neutralized, and the Constitution was adopted by a bare majority of one (some say two, but the original paper upon which the yeas and nays were taken gives only the majority of one). The defection of Mr. Hazard, upon a question of this magnitude, and in relation to which his party confided in his integrity, shook the confidence of the public and his party, and he fell in the popular estimation, and never regained his former elevated position. He was subsequently a representative in the General Assembly, but his influence was so greatly impaired by his defection in the Convention, that he never could re-establish himself in the good opinion of his party or the people.

"Mr. Hazard was well formed, sturdy in body and mind, with a fine phrenological development of the head. He was a natural orator, with a ready command of language, subtle and ingenious in debate. He successfully contended against Marchant, Bradford, and Welcome Arnold, in the debates of the House at that period. He was for a long time the idol of the country interests, manager of the State, leader of the Legislature, in fact, the political dictator in Rhode Island; but his course in the Constitutional Convention was the cause of his political ruin. . . .

"The late Hon. Elisha R. Potter, and the late Benjamin Hazard, who knew Mr. Hazard in the zenith of his political influence, always spoke of him as a man of great natural power and sagacity." [1]

Mr. Hazard had a different opinion upon the causes of his fall, and must be allowed to speak for himself, as he does in a letter to his friend and kinsman, Thomas B. Hazard, which has been preserved by the descendants of the latter. The letter is given herewith : —

*Dear Kinsman:*                                        JAMESTOWN, June y⁰ 18.

I have thought of your disappointment in not being appointed Judge. You may be assured it is for your advantage that you are not chosen. It would have led you further into political

---

[1] Updike's Hist. of Narragansett Church, p. 328.

matters, than you are, and you have already, as well as myself, gone too far on that road. It is a pleasing thing while every thing moves with success and we are flying away before the wind and the tide of prosperity, and every one that meets you will greet you with submission and reverence; but let it only be in the power of these very men that you have served most, to sacrifice you to their own advantage, and you will find there is not one in a thousand but would embrace the opportunity. I speak from experience. The people that I have taken the most pains to serve have sacrificed me, as far as lay in their power. That is nothing new, it was ever so, and ever will be so. It is the greatest misfortune that is resident to man, that lack of resolution, stability, and integrity. Look back and read the history of the world, and you will find the greatest, and some of the best men in the world, have been brought to the block by traitorous companions. I hope you will profit by this little disappointment, and avoid thereby a greater mischief. All these disappointments are bitter, and of course disagreeable, but as they are suffered for our good, we ought to bear them with that manly fortitude that becomes great minds. I have been principal actor in three State revolutions, and if I was to show you the history you would not believe it until you paused, for I have been thrice sacrificed, once in the year 1790 and twice since, and although the authors have no thought that I am possessed of the means and instruments, I have them. I have not only the men's names, but the rooms in the houses where it was agreed upon. Two were in the dead scenes of the night. Notwithstanding I have ever been the slave of my friends, I find when they think there is a prospect of selling an old friend for a new one, they embrace the opportunity. Look back on time, and point out the man that has been deep in politics in this State, and you will find he died poor, if not in actual distress, and at the close of life I imagine miserable. Reflect on this and write me an answer.

*In haste, from your well wisher, friend and kinsman,*

JON'N J. HAZARD.

Mr. Hazard moved to Verona, New York, late in life, and purchased a valuable estate there. He became a prominent man in his adopted State and town, and was much respected. He retained his elegance of manner even to his last days, marrying for the third time after he was eighty years old. He married, first, Patience, daughter of "Stout" Jeffrey Hazard; she was his second cousin; she died in South Kingstown, March 19, 1809, at the home of Dr .George Hazard, aged sixty-six years. He married, secondly, Hannah Brown; his third wife was Marian, daughter of Moses Gage. She survived him many years, and married, as third wife, James Parker.

CHILDREN

431. JONATHAN J. HAZARD, married, Dec. 29, 1781, *Tacy Burdick;* died 1806.
432. GRIFFEN BARNEY HAZARD, born 1765; died 1822; married *Mary Parker.*
433. JOSEPH HOXSIE HAZARD, born June 16, 1777; died Oct. 22, 1838; married, Jan. 21, 1808, *Amey Williams.*
434. THOMAS JEFFERSON HAZARD, died aged twenty years.
435. SUSANNAH HAZARD (by one authority she is called MARY); married *Rowland Champlin.*
436. ABIGAIL HAZARD, married, as third wife, *Enoch Sherman.*


§ 225. WILLIAM HAZARD, 5 (Caleb, 4; George, 3; Robert, 2; Thomas, 1), was born April 12, 1721. He lived in Jamestown, where he kept a licensed tavern. He represented his town in the General Assembly in 1756,'57, '60, '62, as
Deputy

Deputy; in 1768–70 he was Assistant. He was called Captain William, having been for a few years a sea-captain. His name is found very often on the James-town records as Councilman, — generally Chairman of the Council. He married, September 12, 1744, Phebe, daughter of John and Damaris Hull.

CHILDREN

437. LYDIA HAZARD, married, June 8, 1763, *John Field*.
438. JOSIAH HAZARD, born Dec. 20, 1748; married, May 31, 1772, *Mary Carr*.
439. ABIGAIL HAZARD, married Oct. 5, 1796, *Sylvanus Wyatt*.
440. WILLIAM HAZARD, born March 21, 1753; married ——.
441. JOHN HAZARD, born Jan. 20, 1755.
442. BENEDICT HAZARD, born Jan. 26, 1758.
443. MARY HAZARD, born March 24, 1762.

§ 226. ROBERT HAZARD, 5 (Caleb, 4; George, 3; Robert, 2; Thomas, 1), was born May 1, 1723. He died February, 1771. He studied medicine in Boston, with his uncle Dr. Sylvester Gardiner, and was perhaps the best edu-cated physician in his own town at that time. His practice extended to the neigh-boring towns of Charlestown and Hopkinton. A halo of romance has always lingered about the name of Dr. Robert Hazard, and yet the reason for this would be difficult to define. That he attended the "unfortunate Hannah Robinson" in her last illness (two years after his own death, according to Thomas R. Hazard's account) may have added somewhat to this interest. His will gives one an insight into his character, and the inventory of his estate seems to place him almost with-in sight and touch of the present generation. The rooms of his dwelling-house are all mentioned, with the furniture belonging to each room, — in the parlor eight or ten chairs, tables, and the tea-table with its fine old china. In each of the sleep-ing rooms must be placed the "candle-stand," since called "light-stands," the chests, and the chest of drawers. In each room were andirons, shovel and tongs; and in the kitchen and apothecary shop was added a "slice." The "school-room chamber" shows that his children were educated at home. In the great open attic were the looms, wheels large and small, reels, combs, &c. On the farm was the apothecary shop, fulling-mill with presses, shears, plates, &c., to finish the cloth woven in the house; in the storehouse was a barrel of logwood, and a side of leather for the use of the itinerant shoemaker, who wandered about the country making the year's supply of shoes for the family. Robert Hazard's home farm was what is now known as the Elisha Watson farm; a few years ago the old house stood just as Dr. Robert Hazard left it.

His will was carefully worded, nothing being left to chance; even the interests of "my youngest son Francis," then but a baby of two years, were guarded with a jealous care. The little stream now known as "Brown's Brook" undoubtedly furnished the power for a fulling-mill, the foundations of which are still to be seen near the head-water or spring, on the Brown land. Dr. Robert was buried on his farm near the grave of his father, possibly with his wife beside him. But his children all lie in distant places.

He

He married Elizabeth, daughter of Deputy Governor Robert Hazard. The S. Paul's Church' record says: "On the third Sunday of April, 1752, being the 19th day of said month, Robert Hazard, commonly called Doctor Hazard, was married to Elizabeth Hazard, daughter of Robert Hazard, of Point Judith, deceased, at the house of her mother, Esther Hazard, and Colonel Joseph Hazard, her son, by the Reverend Doctor MacSparran." Also from the same record : "On the 12th of February, 1771, Doctor Robert Hazard was buried, having had a long and lingering illness. A considerable assembly present, and a funeral sermon preached, and on Sunday, the 24th, I preached at the house of mourning of the late Doctor Hazard, on mortality — a large congregation present. The Honourable James Honeyman was present, who came from Little Rest, where the Court had been sitting the whole week." [2]

CHILDREN

444. ABIGAIL HAZARD, born Aug. 29, 1753 ; married, Sept. 11, 1780, *Jared Starr*, of New London, Conn.
445. ESTHER HAZARD, born July 26, 1755 ; died March 25, 1831 ; married, 1st, Dec. 25, 1775, *Silas Niles ;* 2d, *Jared Starr*, of New London, Conn.
446. ELIZABETH HAZARD, born Nov. 28, 1757.
447. SYLVESTER GARDINER HAZARD, born July 27, 1760; died Feb. 14, 1812; married *Elizabeth*, daughter of *Richard* and *Sarah Greene ;* she died March 16, 1816, in her 53d year.
448. NANCY HAZARD, born April 20, 1764 ; died ——; unmarried.
449. CHARLES HAZARD, born July 14, 1766; married, Feb., 1795, *Ann Bours*, of Newport.
450. FRANCIS HAZARD, born 1769; died 1814; married *Rebecca Truman*.

§ 229. MARY HAZARD, 5 (Governor George, 4 ; George, 3 ; Robert, 2 ; Thomas, 1), was born July 16, 1722 ; she died in April, 1805, aged eighty-three years. She married, March 2, 1737, Benjamin Peckham, son of Benjamin and Mary (Carr) Peckham ; he was born March 22, 1715, and died in March, 1791. Their home was in Matunuck, on land given to him by his father, just south of the Potter Pond. In 1768, the Town Council of South Kingstown voted that "William Potter, Benjamin Peckham, Freeman Perry, Paul Mumford, Esquires, or a part of them, be a committee to consider of Proper measures to Recommend to the Inhabitants of this Town for Encouraging Industry, Frugality and American manufactories, and make a Report," &c.

CHILDREN

451. GEORGE HAZARD PECKHAM, born April 14, 1739–40; married, Jan. 17, 1763, *Sarah*, daughter of *Robert* and *Rebecca (Coggeshall) Taylor*.
452. JOSEPHUS PECKHAM, born Feb. 11, 1742; married, May 25, 1774, *Mary*, daughter of *Hezekiah Babcock;* he died March 27, 1814.
453. SARAH PECKHAM, married, April 9, 1761, *John Robinson*.
454. JOHN PAINE PECKHAM.
455. WILLIAM PECKHAM, born 1752; married *Mercy Perry*.
456. MARY PECKHAM, married Doctor *Joshua Perry*.
457. PELEG PECKHAM, born June 11, 1762 ; married, Aug. 25, 1785, *Desire Watson*.

[1] S. Paul's Church, North Kingstown, commonly known as the Narragansett Church.
[2] Updike's Hist. Narragansett Church, p. 343.

§ 230. GEORGE HAZARD, 5 (Governor George, 4; George, 3; Robert, 2; Thomas, 1), was born, according to the South Kingstown records, on June 15, 1724; but his tombstone in Newport is reported as inscribed June 13, 1721, which is undoubtedly an error. There is nothing more bewildering to an earnest searcher after truth than a gravestone record, for it is an exception if one finds it agreeing with town and church records. George Hazard was admitted freeman in 1745. Early in life he settled in Newport, and was a merchant there. In 1750 he was baptized in the church at Newport, and, as early as 1756, his name appears in the Colonial records as filling some important offices. He was almost constantly a member of the General Assembly. In 1764, he was one of a committee on paper money;[1] in 1766, he was Chief-Justice of the Court of Common Pleas; later he resigned this position, and was chosen Mayor of the City of Newport, under its first city charter. He was one of the incorporators of the Rhode Island College, now Brown University; also one of the trustees. In 1766 he was one of a committee appointed to prepare a humble address of thanks to His Majesty for giving his royal assent to the bill for repealing the Stamp Act.[2] He died in Newport, April 11, 1797, and was buried in the Common Ground. The inscription on his tombstone reads: —

"Sacred | to the memory of | the Hon. George Hazard, Esq., | who was born June 13, 1721, | and died August the 11th, 1797. | Almost Forty years of his Life | were spent | in the service of his Country, | Without Ambition | and without the hope of Reward | He accepted the various & important offices of | Legislator, Judge & Mayor of Newport | with diffidence, | and executed them with ability."

Mayor George Hazard, as he is called by his descendants and by others, married, November 24, 1745, Martha, daughter of George and Abigail (Church) Wanton. She and her mother Abigail are mentioned in her great-uncle Jahleel Brenton's will, and received valuable legacies of land in South Kingstown, Newport, and Boston. She died in March, 1763. He married, second, on July 28, 1769, Jane Tweedy.

CHILDREN OF FIRST MARRIAGE

458. EDWARD HAZARD, born (circa) 1746; married Sarah Cranston.
459. ABIGAIL HAZARD, born (circa) 1748; married, July 1, 1774, John Channing.
460. SARAH HAZARD, born 1751. She was baptized in that year. She married, 1st, Capt. Daniel Gardiner; 2d, Dr. George Hazard, her first cousin, Oct. 4, 1790.
461. GEORGE HAZARD, born March 30, 1758; married Martha Babcock.

CHILDREN OF SECOND MARRIAGE

462. ELIZABETH HAZARD, born 1771; died Jan. 12, 1788.
463. SOPHIA FREELOVE HAZARD, died 1790.
464. CARDER HAZARD, born 1774; married Sarah Coggeshall; died March 18, 1823.
465. NATHANIEL HAZARD, born 1776; married Sarah Fales; died Dec. 17, 1820.
466. WILLIAM TWEEDY HAZARD, born 1777; died Oct. 26, 1794.

---

[1] Col. Rec., vol. vi., p. 328.    [2] Col. Rec., vol. vi., p. 493.

§ 231.

§ 231. ABIGAIL HAZARD, 5 (Governor George, 4; George, 3; Robert, 2; Thomas, 1), was born March 12, 1726. She married, February 27, 1753, Reverend Peter Bours; he died February 24, 1762. She married, second, February 27, 1763, Reverend Samuel Fayerweather.

"The Reverend Peter Bours, A.M., was Rector of S. Michael's Church in Marblehead, from 1753 to 1762. He was the son of Peter Bours, Esq'., a member of the Council of the Government of Rhode Island. He graduated Bachelor of Arts at Harvard College in 1747, where he also afterwards received the Master's degree. For some time, before he proceeded to England for holy orders, he was employed in reading the service and sermons in several destitute churches with universal approbation, "both for his abilities and morals." His labors in the parish of S. Michael's were commenced in July, 1753, and appear to have been eminently successful. A contemporary describes him as a man of an excellent temper, good learning, and great piety, whose good character gained more to the Church of England than all who had preceded him. During the short period of his ministry in Marblehead (less than nine years), he baptized four hundred and fifty-six infants and adults. By the purity of his doctrine, his amiable manners, and his blameless life, he conciliated the enemies of the Church, and his congregation was much increased.[1]

A late rector of S. Michaels adds : " I have met with none who can speak of him from their own remembrance of his person. There is no parishioner of mine who received his edifying ministrations; but a traditionary veneration preserves his memory fresh among us ; and we are happy in having an excellent portrait of him from the hand of Blackburn. Mr. Bours is represented as sitting, and in his clerical robes. The figure is full, though not large ; and the face, which is fair, has an expression of quite uncommon serenity and sweetness . . . This excellent and amiable gentleman died, after a very short illness, February 24, 1762, at the early age of thirty-six. Above his mortal remains, which were buried in the graveyard contiguous to S. Michael's Church, a monument was erected which bears the following epitaph : —

"'Under This Stone | Lies the Body | of the Rev'd Peter Bours, | once | Minister of this Church : | which office | for the space of nine years | he discharged with faithfulness | Teaching the Doctrines of the Gospel | with plainness and fervency, | illustrating the Truth and Reality of what he taught | by his own Life | the goodness of which | joined | with great Candour | and unbounded Benevolence of Mind, | obtained for him | not only | the most sincere love of his own People, | but also | the esteem of virtuous Men | of every persuasion. He died Feb. y' 24th, 1762, | aged 36 years. | To his Memory | His people have erected this Monument, | in testimony | of his great worth, | and their sincere regards.

> Persuasion draws, Example leads the mind :
> Their double force compels, when meetly joined.' "[2]

---

Updike's Hist. Narragansett Church, p. 292.      [2] Ibid, pp. 270 and 359.

" After the death of Mr. Bours, his widow wedded, February 27, 1763, Reverend Samuel Fayerweather. They were married in Newport by the Reverend Marmaduke Browne, and the record adds : 'And on that day (an exceeding cold day), Mr. Fayerweather preached on the occasion from these words to a large auditory : " Do all to the glory of God." ' Mr. Samuel Fayerweather was the son of Thomas Fayerweather, of Boston. 'He was graduated from Harvard College in 1743; was ordained a Congregational minister, and settled over the second Congregational Church in Newport, in 1754. The Reverend Doctor Stiles was his successor. Mr. Fayerweather was ordained a Presbyter in the Episcopal Church, in 1756, in England. The degree of Master of Arts was conferred on him by the University of Oxford in the same year. Mr. Fayerweather died in 1781, aged about sixty-one." An extract from his will reads : "' I give all my library and books to King's (now Columbia) College, New York, and ten pounds sterling, and my large picture of myself. And my desire is, that the corporation may suffer said picture to be hung up in the library room of said College forever. Also my silver framed square picture of myself, to my sister Hannah Winthrope of Cambridge. My wife's picture of herself, to her niece, the wife of John Channing. My oval picture of myself, framed with silver, to my nephew, John Winthrope, of Boston, merchant.' " " The executor of his will, Mathew Robinson, Esquire, received Mr. Fayerweather's effects, and being aged and infirm, neglected the injunctions of the testator. He died ten years afterwards at an advanced age, and insolvent, and the pictures bequeathed by the Reverend Mr. Fayerweather were sold at auction as Mr. Robinson's property, there being no legatee, or friends in this quarter to claim them. The large picture, by Copley, in his academical honors at Oxford, is now (1847) in my house,' the others were in this town some years since. His library was also sold, and is now lost, except a few volumes in possession of the Church in Narragansett. The Reverend Mr. Fayerweather, while rector, baptized forty-five persons." '

§ 234. CARDER HAZARD, 5 (Governor George, 4; George, 3; Robert, 2; Thomas, 1), was born August 11, 1734; he died November 24, 1792. State and Colonial records give us something of the character of Carder Hazard, but it is from old papers, letters and family traditions, that we learn to know the grace of his private life. In the records we find his name in 1757, as admitted freeman of the Colony from South Kingstown ; from that time until 1787, when he was chosen Chief Justice, there is scarcely a year during which he is not found filling some position of trust in the Colony as assistant, deputy, or judge ; it is by his title of Judge that he is best known by his descendants. With justice, Carder Hazard could have written after his name, "Gentleman," a title often found in old deeds and wills ; but he, more in keeping with the modesty of his character, writes " Yeoman." In all the relations of his domestic life he was exceedingly gentle and lovable. In personal appearance he was tall and well formed, fair in

---

' The property of the estate of W. Updike.        ² Updike's Hist. Narragansett Church, p. 291.

complexion,

complexion, and (tradition says) an uncommonly handsome man. His sons inherited his beauty; one son, William, was wont to say jokingly, when reproached by his gentle mother for his dislike for manual labor, "My beauty must make my fortune, mother." Whether it was his beauty or merit is not known, but he did find a wife and a fair one in one of the Southern States, with an estate and fortune. Carder Hazard's life as a country gentleman gave him few opportunities for intercourse with his intellectual superiors, but in his frequent visits to "Town," as Newport was called in old times, in his official capacity and as a guest of his brother, Mayor George Hazard, he met many gifted men. In this intercourse, when subjects were broached with which he was not familiar, having the true spirit of the family, he rarely ever asked a question, but, following the advice of S. Paul to women, kept silent. Other members of the Hazard family left larger fortunes and more land to be divided amongst their children, but none of them left a name of sweeter savor.

His death was caused by a fall from a chair, upon which he had mounted in order to take a book from the top of the bookcase. He was at the house of his son, Doctor George Hazard, at the time, and died there.

An obituary notice, published in the *Providence Gazette*, December 1, 1792, expresses the public sentiment of one hundred years ago : —

" Last Sunday departed this life, at South Kingstown, in the 59th year of his age, Honorable Carder Hazard, Esq., one of the Judges of the Superior Court of this State. In political life he exhibited the honest citizen and upright judge; subject to laws, he reverenced them, and invested with power, he executed it without intrigue, and without a view of self interest.

In social Life the Goodness of his Heart and Simplicity of his Manners were peculiarly agreeable — but Death has closed his labours! and the Pity of that Death has evidenced the Innocence of his Life. With that of the Public, his particular Friends have united their own Sorrow."

Judge Carder Hazard married first, September 23, 1756, Alice, daughter of Robert and Thankful (Ball) Hull. She was born September 26, 1739, and died July 1, 1760, in the 21st year of her age. The inscription on her monument reads: "In Memory of | Alice, the wife of Carder Hazard | who died | July 1st, 1760, in the 21st year of her age. | She was a kind wife, a tender parent, and worthy friend."

He married, second, March 5, 1761, Alice Hazard, daughter of Colonel Thomas Hazard. They were married by the Reverend Samuel Fayerweather, who was afterwards Hazard's brother-in-law. History speaks of her as a fitting helpmeet to her husband. When she felt her stay on earth was short, she confided the care of her little twin daughters to her stepson, saying, "I only ask you to be just as kind to them as I have been to you." She died January 13, 1793.

CHILDREN OF FIRST MARRIAGE
467. ROBERT HULL HAZARD, born April 10, 1758.
468. PETER BOURS HAZARD, born Dec. 5, 1759; died May 15, 1807.

CHILDREN

CHILDREN OF SECOND MARRIAGE

469. THOMAS HAZARD, born Dec. 5, 1761; married, 1st, —— *Browning*; 2d, *Eliza*, daughter of *Thomas Arnold*.
470. GEORGE HAZARD, born April 13, 1763; married, 1st, *Sarah Gardner*; 2d, *Mary Hoxsie*; 3d, *Jane Hull*; he died Sept. 29, 1829.
471. WILLIAM HAZARD, born March 6, 1766.
472. EDWARD HAZARD, born July 7, 1768.
473. RICHARD WARD HAZARD, born Nov. 1, 1770.
474. CARDER HAZARD, born July 21, 1773.
475. ARNOLD HAZARD, born Jan. 9, 1776; unmarried.
476. SARAH HAZARD, born May 13, 1780; married *Peter Clarke*.
477. ALICE HAZARD, born May 13, 1780; married *George Congdon*.


§ 235. ARNOLD HAZARD, 5 (Governor George, 4; George, 3; Robert, 2; Thomas, 1), was born May 15, 1738; he married, November 30, 1777, Alice, daughter of Judge William, and Penelope (Hazard) Potter. They were second cousins.

CHILDREN

478. MARTHA HAZARD, born 1790; died March 28, 1861; married, Nov. 30, 1811, *Asabel Russell*.
479. BRENTON W. HAZARD, born 1793; died Oct. 4, 1864; married, Feb. 16, 1831, *Harriet Brown*.


§ 236. PENELOPE HAZARD, 5 (Colonel Thomas, 4; George, 3; Robert, 2; Thomas, 1), was born February 11, 1730–1. She married November 18, 1750, Judge William Potter, son of Colonel John and Mercy (Robinson) Potter. The records of the S. Paul's Church, Narragansett, read: " Nov. 18, 1750, Sunday, the banns being first duly asked, at St. Paul's, Dr. MacSparran married William Potter, youngest son of Colonel John Potter, to Penelope Hazard, eldest daughter of Colonel Thomas Hazard, both of South Kingstown, at Colonel Thomas Hazard's house." William Potter was great-grandson of Martha Hazard and Ichabod Potter; therefore there was a distant relationship between his wife and himself. Judge William Potter was born January 21, 1722. He was a member of the General Assembly from 1761 until 1776, when he was appointed Chief Justice of the Court of Common Pleas. When the General Assembly voted to raise an army of observation, he, together with the Governor, Joseph Wanton, and two others, made a protest against the measure. " We, the subscribers, professing true allegiance to His Majesty King George the Third, beg leave to dissent from the vote of the House of Magistrates, for enlisting, raising and embodying an army of observation, of fifteen hundred men, to repel any insult or violence that may be offered to the inhabitants, and also, if it be necessary for the safety and preservation of any of the Colonies, to march them out of this Colony, to join and co-operate with the forces of the neighboring Colonies.

" Because we are of the opinion that such a measure will be attended with the most fatal consequences to our charter privileges, involve the country in all the horrors of a civil war, and, as we conceive, is an open violation of the oath of allegiance

allegiance which we have severally taken, upon our admission into the respective offices we now hold in the Colony.

JOSEPH WANTON,    THOMAS WICKES,
DARIUS SESSIONS,    WILLIAM POTTER.

In the Upper House, Providence, April 25, 1775."[1]

This protest was the beginning of the end of Governor Wanton's public life. It cost him his position as Governor; but Judge Potter, finding the measure so obnoxious to his friends and the public in general, presented a second memorial to the Assembly at the June session, as follows: —

To the Honourable General Assembly, of the Colony of Rhode Island, at the session to be holden in East Greenwich, on the second Monday in June, A.D. 1775.

I, William Potter, of South Kingstown, in the county of Kings County, in the Colony aforesaid, humbly show: —

That at a session of the General Assembly, held at Providence, on the 22d day of April last, an act was passed for raising, with all expedition and dispatch, fifteen hundred men, as an army of observation to repel any insult or violence that might be offered to the inhabitants.

And also if necessary for the safety and preservation of the colonies, to march out of this Colony, and join and co-operate with the forces of the neighbouring Colonies, against which act, I, as one of the upper house of Assembly, together with Joseph Wanton, Esq'., then Governor, Darius Sessions, Esq'., the then Deputy Governor, and Thomas Wicks, Esq'., then also one of the Upper House, did enter my protest, which hath given much uneasiness to the good people of this Colony. To remove which, so far as respects myself, and as far as in me lieth, I beg leave to observe —

That a rough draught was drawn up, and delivered to a person to be corrected, which protest, as the same now stands, appears to me to be of a different import from my meaning at the time, and which, through the hurry attending the business before the House, was not so properly attended to as it might have been, and in that haste signed.

It is true, I was against the passing of the said act at the time, as I conceived the trade, and particularly the town of Newport, would be greatly distressed, which a little longer time might prevent, and because it was known that the very respectable Assembly of the Colony of Connecticut would soon sit, of whose wise deliberations we might avail ourselves. These were the true reasons of my conduct, however the contrary may appear from the protest signed.

No man hath ever been more deeply impressed with the calamities to which America is reduced, by a most corrupt administration, than myself. No man hath more exerted himself in private and public life to relieve ourselves from our oppression; and no man hath held himself more ready to sacrifice his life and fortune in the arduous struggle now making throughout America, for the preserva-

tion

tion of our rights and liberties, and in these sentiments I am determined to live and die.

Sorry I am, if any of the good people of this Colony should have conceived otherwise of me, and I greatly lament that the unguarded expression in the protest should give cause therefore. Should I from thence lose the confidence, just hopes and expectations of my countrymen, of my future conduct in the arduous American struggles, it might create an uneasiness of mind, for which nothing can ever compensate.

But should this public declaration ease the minds of my friends and the friends of liberty, and convince them of my readiness to embark, to conflict with them in every difficulty, and against every opposition, until our glorious cause shall be established upon most firm and permanent basis, it will be a consideration that will afford the highest satisfaction that human nature is capable of enjoying." [1]

This explanation proving satisfactory, the Assembly voted that it should be accepted, and William Potter be reinstated in the favor of the Assembly. At the same session he was re-elected Chief-Justice of the Court of Common Pleas in Washington county, and was successively elected until the year 1780, when he resigned.

"About this time (1780) Judge Potter became an enthusiastic and devoted follower of the celebrated Jemima Wilkinson. For the more comfortable accomodation of herself and her adherents, he built a large addition to his already spacious mansion, containing fourteen rooms and bedrooms with suitable fire-places. Her influence controlled his household, servants and the income of his estates. She made her headquarters here for above six years. Here was the scene of some of her pretended miracles. Susannah Potter, a daughter of the Judge, having deceased, she undertook to raise her to life. On the day of the funeral, a great concourse assembled to witness the miracle. The lid of the coffin was removed, and Jemima knelt in devout and fervent prayer for her restoration. The laws of nature were inflexible. The impious effort was unavailing. She imputed the failure to the old excuse—the want of faith in her followers. . . She induced most of her followers to sell their estates, and invest the proceeds in land in the Genesee country in the State of New York, for a common fund for the benefit of all. Judge Potter was the principal agent for that purpose. In 1784, with her train of deluded proselytes, she departed for her new residence in what in now called Yates County, called by Jemima herself 'New Jerusalem,' 'a land flowing with milk and honey.'"

Judge Potter's homestead was about a mile north of Kingston Hill, and was known for a great many years as the Old Abbey. He had a very large landed estate which he inherited, and was otherwise wealthy. He "returned in a few years after his emigration, and occupied his homestead, but his circumstances became so embarrassed in consequence of his devotion to this artful woman, that he was soon compelled to mortgage his estate; and finding it impossible to redeem it in its

[1] Col. Rec., vol. vii. p. 348.

deteriorated

deteriorated condition, he finally, in 1807, sold the remainder of his interest in it and settled in Genesee. The late Honorable Elisha R. Potter purchased the homestead, but the elegant garden with parterres, borders, shrubbery, summer-house, fruit-orchard, — his ancient mansion with the high and costly fences, out-houses, and cookery establishment, and the more recent erections for the accommo-dation and gratification of the priestess of his devotions, were in ruins, and within a few years the whole buildings have been removed, and a small and suitable house for a tenant has been built in its place. . . . The descendants of Judge Pot-ter are numerous in the State of New York. His son Arnold entered Harvard College, and remained there some time, but did not graduate. He was a man of great intelligence and enterprise. He owned a large estate in Middlesex, Yates County, now owned by William H. Potter of Providence. When the town of Middlesex was divided several years ago, the eastern part of it was named Potter, in honor of the memory of Judge Potter. Penelope, daughter of Arnold Potter, married Charles W. Henry, now living at Laporte, Indiana. Edward, son of Judge Potter, married a daughter of Captain Samuel Johnson, of Norwich, Con-necticut ; and a son, Doctor Francis M. Potter, is now (1847) living at Penn Yan, New York." [1]

CHILDREN

480. MERCY POTTER, born Nov. 26,1751 ; married 1769, *Joshua Perry;* died 1794.
481. THOMAS HAZARD POTTER, born Dec. 8, 1753 ; died Sept. 11, 1807 ; married *Patience,* daughter of *Jeremiah* and *Amey (Whipple) Wilkinson,* and sister to *Jemima Wilkinson.*
482. ALICE POTTER, born April 20, 1756 ; died 1818 ; married Capt. *Arnold Hazard* son of Gov. *George Hazard.* For children see *Arnold Hazard, No. 235.*
483. SUSANNAH POTTER, born April 25, 1758 ; unmarried.
484. WILLIAM ROBINSON POTTER, born July 13, 1760 ; died young.
485. BENEDICT ARNOLD POTTER, born Sept. 12, 1761 ; died 1810 ; married *Sarah,* daughter of *Benjamin Brown.* His daughter *Penelope* married *Charles W. Henry.*
486. PENELOPE POTTER, born March 7, 1764 ; died 1813 ; married, 1784, *Benjamin Brown,* Jr.
487. WILLIAM PITT POTTER, born April 10, 1766 ; died Nov. 6, 1800 ; married, 1793, *Mary Hazard.*
488. EDWARD POTTER, born Feb. 15, 1768 ; died Aug. 12, 1849 ; married *Eliza Johnson.*
489. SIMEON POTTER, born April 25, 1770 ; died Feb. 1, 1817 ; married *Catherine Klice.*
490. SARAH POTTER, born Dec. 13, 1771 ; died 1830 ; married, 1805, *George Brown.*
491. JOHN POTTER, born May 24, 1774 ; died 1815 ; married *Catherine Garrison.*
492. PELHAM POTTER, born Dec. 7, 1776.

§237. HANNAH HAZARD, 5 (Colonel Thomas, 4 ; George, 3 ; Robert, 2 ; Thomas, 1), was born August 5, 1732. She married, November 21, 1762, Colonel John Wilson, who was born May 11, 1726, and was son of Jeremiah and Mary Wilson, and had a twin brother Jeremiah. In 1761, John Wilson was appointed Major in the Colonial army. The next year he was promoted to the rank of Lieutenant Colonel, and by this title has he usually been known. In the struggle

[1] Updike's Hist. of Narragansett Church, p. 233.

for

for independence, he adhered to the cause of the Crown. Several of the Wilson family were attainted as Tories, and banished from their homes until the war was over, and, although Colonel John's name is not found with those thus banished, the absence of his name from all army records during the war is an indication that he did not participate in the struggle.

Colonel John Wilson lived on Tower Hill, in a house built by his grandfather Samuel Wilson. From this grandfather have descended seven generations, some of whom live on Tower Hill to-day, and own a part of the original land bought by Samuel as one of the purchasers of the tract of land known as the Pettaquamscut Purchase. "He built the first house on Tower Hill; this house was forty-two feet by fifty-six, two stories high with a roof of one-third altitude. The only architectural ornament was about the front door, which was constructed after the Ionic order with two large Ionic volutes, which formed the door-cap, and projected a foot and a half from the building. It had besides a modillion cornice. This house was silled three times, the last time in the year 1817. The manner of silling in those days was to frame the sill together, and then place large white-oak knees in the corners, after the manner of ship-carpentry. The house had a brick chimney fourteen feet square at the base, which contained three ovens (one of which was in the cellar) and eleven separate smoke-flues. There was also a boiling spring in the cellar, and a good well of water near each side of the house. The wells are still to be seen. The windows were of diamond-pane glass set in lead. The windows, and perhaps the frame of the house, was made in the mother country. The house was built soon after the Pettaquamscut Purchase, and was not taken down until the year 1823, when another was built very near the site of the old house. It is now the property of Charles Pollock, a great-grandson of Colonel John Wilson.

In the latter part of the eighteenth century Tower Hill was a prosperous place; the situation was incomparable, and nearly all of the wealthy families had representatives established there in younger sons or married daughters. It was the "court-end" of the town. There were fourteen houses, six of them with large gambrelled roofs, which were erected by wealthy and enterprising men who spared no pains to make them attractive. There were also several inns or taverns, as they were then called. A coach passed through the place twice a week from the South Ferry to New London, and returned, carrying passengers and the mails; as many as eight coaches have been known to arrive at the place in one morning. Balls and dances were of frequent occurrence, guests coming from Newport and the neighboring plantations of Boston Neck. Trees stood before each door, and in front of each house were little gardens filled with blooming shrubs.

During the war of 1812, the Atlantic coast was blockaded by a British fleet from Portland to Cape May, and it was difficult to carry any merchandise through Long Island Sound. Sometimes, however, an old molasses drogher would land a cargo at Stonington, which would be carried by land to Providence and Boston by means of oxen. Frequently there would be thirty ox-teams loaded with molasses on the
road

road at one time in close proximity to each other, straggling on to the extent of nearly half a mile. The drivers usually stopped over night at the old Brown house, where George and Rowland Brown kept a tavern."

The above account of the Wilson house and the old Tower Hill is taken, by permission, from the papers of Mr. James Wilson, a grandson of Colonel John Wilson. Mr. Wilson is now (1895) approaching his ninetieth year.

Hannah Hazard, and the other daughters of Colonel Thomas Hazard, were well educated and accomplished women for their day, when the women of the family were considered educated if they could read and write. Their accomplishments were spinning and weaving. But Hannah could work in wax, making figures and flowers that were very much admired. Some few of these pieces are treasured by her descendants to this day, while the fingers that wrought them so deftly have long been dust and ashes.

CHILDREN

493. JOHN WILSON, born July 24, 1763.
494. THOMAS HAZARD WILSON.
495. ROBERT ARNOLD WILSON.

§ 241. OLIVER HAZARD 5 (Oliver 4 ; George 3 ; Robert 2 ; Thomas 1) was born March 30, 1739. He lived in Jamestown, and kept a licensed tavern there. His name is often found in the town records, as Councilman and otherwise. In 1762, he exhibited an account (that was allowed) for £26 16s. for seventeen dinners and one punch-bowl, said dinner being for the comfort of certain public men on town-meeting day. He married Patience Greene, widow of Captain Samuel Greene and daughter of Ebenezer and Patience (Gorton) Cook. She died July 9, 1809, aged eighty years.

CHILDREN

496. MARY HAZARD, born March 15, 1762.
497. SAMUEL GREENE HAZARD, born Feb. 15, 1764 ; died April 4, 1765.
498-9. ELIZABETH HAZARD, born April 12, 1767.

§ 242. MERCY HAZARD 5 (Oliver 4 ; George 3 ; Robert 2 ; Thomas 1) was born January 21, 1740; she died in 1810; she married, in 1755, Freeman Perry, son of Benjamin and Susannah (Barber) Perry ; he was born January 23, 1733, and died October 15, 1813.

He was a physician and surgeon, also a man active in the public business of the town and Colony, holding from time to time several important positions. In 1780 he was appointed Chief-Justice of the Court of Common Pleas for the County of Washington, which position he held until 1791. Freeman Perry's home was what is now commonly but erroneously, called "Commodore Perry's birthplace," in Matunuck. In 1792, he gave a part of this, his homestead farm, to his son Dr. Joshua Perry, and the next year he gave ten acres of the same farm to his son Christopher Raymond Perry. By will, written in 1810, and proved in 1815, he gave the remaining part of the farm, "with my mansion house where I now live,"

live," to Christopher Raymond Perry. The will also gives to his grandson, George Hazard Perry, "my books on physics and surgery;" to his grandson, Freeman Perry, "my surveying instruments;" to his daughter, Elizabeth Champlin, wife of Stephen, "the beaufet in the great room where I now live, it having formerly belonged to her grandmother, Elizabeth Hazard;" to his grandson, Raymond Perry, "my watch (Richard Trapp, London, Maker, No. 11226 "); to his grandson, William Browning Champlin, "the silver spoons that I bought at the vendue of William Rodman, marked S.R.;" and to his granddaughter, Sarah Comstock, silver spoons marked M. H.

CHILDREN

500. JOSHUA PERRY, born 1756; died Nov. 1802; married, Oct. 17, 1780, *Mary*, daughter of *Benjamin and Mary (Hazard) Peckham*.
501. OLIVER HAZARD PERRY, lost at sea about 1783.
502. CHRISTOPHER RAYMOND PERRY, born Dec. 4, 1760; died June 4, 1818; married, Aug. 1784, *Sarah Alexander*.
503. ELIZABETH PERRY, born Aug. 20, 1762; died March 12, 1811; married, Dec. 20, 1782, *Stephen Champlin*.
504. MARY PERRY, died, aged 20, unmarried.
505. SUSAN PERRY, married, 1784, as second wife, *Elisha Watson*.
506. GEORGE HAZARD PERRY, married *Abigail Chesborough*.

§258. STEPHEN HAZARD, 5 (Stephen, 4; Stephen, 3; Robert, 2; Thomas, 1), was born September 12, 1723; he died August 6, 1800. He inherited a large landed estate in Point Judith. His father was a very rich man, and his grandfather was still more wealthy, for he gave away in legacies at his death over thirty-five thousand pounds, which, reckoned in old tenor (at that date seven pounds to a Spanish dollar), was still a little fortune. This did not include property left to his son Judge Stephen, who was made residuary legatee, and was given besides the " Mansion House and all buildings and farms." This mansion-house descended to " Long Stephen " through his father ; the house was on or near the site now occupied by the house of the late Carder Clark, and was provided with furniture imported from the " Old Country." " Long Stephen," as he was called, had also his town residence in Newport, where his family spent the winter. Unfortunately, during the absence of the family, the house, by the carelessness of the slaves left in charge, took fire and was completely destroyed with nearly all of its valuable contents, February 3, 1791 ; but the few remaining pieces of the ancient furniture that were saved, carefully treasured by descendants, bear witness to the elegance of the whole. Notwithstanding all his inherited wealth, Stephen Hazard died comparatively poor. His son Nichols, administrator on the estate, declared it insolvent, showing his father indebted to him for more than the whole amount of the property. These changes in his condition were caused, his descendants say, by the fact that his estate was confiscated during the war of 1776.

1776. There are no records in proof of this. But he did adhere to the cause of the Crown, and was for a time banished from his home for giving assistance and support to the enemy. He was, with his family, sent, not exactly to Coventry, but to the next town, Scituate, where several of the Point Judith families were dispatched to keep him company. The British paid good gold for fat cattle and provisions, and Point Judith was easy of access, — as easy as the conscience that made loyalty a fair-sounding word, whether it meant loyalty to England or America. However, the stringent measures adopted by the Colony soon brought its truant sons to a better understanding, for in 1779, " Stephen Hazard, Stephen Hazard, Jr., Samuel Hazard, Jeremiah Hazard, son of Robert, and the wife of said Jeremiah, and Christopher Robinson, have prayed this Assembly to be heard upon the charges brought against them," &c.[1] This petition was heard, granted, and permission given for them to return to their homes, they giving their paroles.[2] Samuel Hazard, Jeremiah Hazard, son of Jeffrey, and Thomas Hazard, son of Jeremiah, were also of this band of martyrs.

Stephen Hazard married, April 29, 1759, Sarah, daughter of Deputy-Governor Jonathan Nichols, and granddaughter of Deputy-Governor Jonathan Nichols, there being two Governors of the name, father and son. She was born in 1739.

CHILDREN

507. STEPHEN HAZARD, born Sept. 12, 1760 ; died March 17, 1788.
508. JONATHAN NICHOLS HAZARD, born Oct. 18, 1761; married, May 12, 1785, *Mary*, daughter of *Sylvester* and *Alice (Perry) Robinson.*
509. SARAH HAZARD, born July 14, 1763 ; died June 17, 1793.
510. MARY HAZARD, born Sept. 18, 1764 ; married *Robert Babcock* ; she died Aug. 26, 1851.
511. ELIZABETH HAZARD, born April 10, 1767 ; died 1820 ; married *Gideon Hazard*, son of *Samuel Hazard*. For children, see *Gideon Hazard, No. 546.*
512. NICHOLS HAZARD, born March 20, 1770; died May 13, 1848; married *Phebe Anthony.*
513. MARTHA HAZARD, born March 20, 1774; married, April 4, 1804, *Benjamin Hazard*, son of *Samuel Hazard.* For children, see *Benjamin Hazard, No. 545.*
514. JOSEPH HAZARD, born March 22, 1775; died April 1, 1776.
515. APLIN HAZARD, born July 20, 1777; died Jan. 20, 1778.
516. JOHN HAZARD, born Dec. 10, 1778; died Jan., 1805. He was a sea-captain.

§ 259. MARY HAZARD, 5 (Stephen, 4 ; Stephen, 3 ; Robert, 2 ; Thomas, 1), was born September 18, 1725 ; she married, August 30, 1752, John Potter, son of Ichabod and Sarah (Robinson) Potter. There is an uncertainty about the children of Mary and John Potter, for the *Potter Genealogy* gives the children mentioned below as a sister's, but the will of John Potter, who married her sister, does not mention them. Their grandmother, widow of Stephen Hazard, in her will, dated one year after the death of John Potter, calls these children her grandchildren. There were possibly sons, but there is no record of them.

CHILDREN.

517. ABIGAIL POTTER, born July 20, 1756; died March 1, 1784; married *Rufus Wheeler.*
518. SARAH POTTER, born April 12, 1762; died May 9, 1787.

[1] Col. Rec., vol. viii. p. 594.      [2] Ibid., p. 601.

519. HANNAH POTTER.
520. ELIZABETH POTTER.
521. RUTH POTTER, married *Benjamin Perry*, son of *Benjamin* and *Elizabeth* (*Hazard*) *Perry*. They were first cousins.

§ 260. ELIZABETH HAZARD, 5 (Stephen, 4; Stephen, 3; Robert, 2; Thomas, 1), was born July 17, 1729; she married, as second wife, John Potter. There is the usual relationship here between husband and wife, but a little remote, John being a great-grandson of Martha Hazard, daughter of Thomas Hazard, the first in America; Elizabeth his wife being related in the same degree to Thomas Hazard through Robert. John Potter lived in, and may have built, the old house in Matunuck known as the "Governor Potter" place. It is impossible to learn why it should have been called by this name, for there never was a Governor John Potter. Samuel J. Potter, his son, was the only Governor Potter of Rhode Island (and he was Deputy-Governor), and he lived in Point Judith, on what is now known as the George Pearse place. John Potter left a fortune to be divided between his children; he even gave to his daughters eight hundred pounds apiece, — a very unusual proceeding in those days, when fifty pounds and a home in the mansion-house until they were married seemed a plentiful provision. This was not as unjust as one would suppose such a proceeding to be at the present day, for where each man gave his property to his sons he simply provided for other men's daughters, and left it to other men to provide for his. John Potter could well leave a large fortune, for he made money easily by a process known to few, and approved of by fewer. There is a story well authenticated on this point. Nicholas Hazard of Newport, a nephew of John Potter's wife, when a lad, used to often visit his aunt, he being a great favorite with her. The Potters were hospitable people and kept open house for poor relations, as well as for the gentry of the town; during one of Nicholas Hazard's visits, there was a large dinner given to some prominent persons. It so happened that a poor pensioner, who was also a relative, was staying at the house at the time. She was occasionally a little out of her mind, and during a pause in the conversation at dinner she said, "Friend Potter, who made money in the Overing house?" Friend Potter made no reply but began a brisk conversation in order to turn the attention of the guests from the old lady. She however, watched for another pause, and at the first opportunity repeated her question with like success. At last, losing her patience, she gave Mr. Potter a smart slap on the knee, saying, "Friend Potter, I asked thee who made money in the Overing house?" At the end of *his* patience, he said incautiously, "I don't know, unless it was the devil." "I always said it was the devil," replied the old lady, "but my husband says it was Friend Potter." As the host and his guests were all Quakers, the turn of the conversation may have been somewhat startling to the company.

The old house at Matunuck was a very imposing structure, even in the early part of the present century, but it has been divided and sub-divided, until very little of the original is left. One room is almost all that can be seen, and this was

once

once a part of the great square hall, panelled from floor to ceiling. A painted panel that was over the mantel in the dining-room, is now carefully treasured by descendants of John Potter; it is said to represent members of Mr. Potter's family painted by some "famous" artist, much more probably by a house-painter, if one can judge by the character of the execution. John Potter died in 1787; his wife died in 1806.

CHILDREN OF FIRST MARRIAGE

522. JOHN POTTER, born 1751; married *Mary Niles.*
523. WILLIAM POTTER, born 1753.
524. MARY POTTER, born 1755.

CHILDREN OF SECOND MARRIAGE

525. SAMUEL J. POTTER, married *Ann Seager.*
526. STEPHEN POTTER, died 1793; married *Abigail,* daughter of *Christopher* and *Ruhamah Robinson.*
527. GEORGE POTTER, died 1787.
528. HENRY POTTER, married *Dorcas,* daughter of *Benjamin Perry.*
529. CHRISTOPHER POTTER.
530. MARTHA POTTER, died 1819; married *Hazard Browning.*
531. ELIZABETH POTTER, married *Nicholas Easton;* died June 17, 1800.

These children are all mentioned in John Potter's will, in the order given. The dates given in the *Potter Genealogy,* and the list of his children, are incorrect.

§ 261. JOHN HAZARD, 5 (Stephen, 4; Stephen, 3; Robert, 2; Thomas, 1), was born June 26, 1731; he died in 1772; he married Mary ——. There is no record of the birth of any children; but his father, in his will, dated 1762, mentions a "grandson John" Hazard, and as he had no other grandson by this name, the inference is plain that there must have been a son John, son of the above.

CHILD

532. JOHN HAZARD.

§ 262. JOSEPH HAZARD, 5 (Governor Robert, 4; Stephen, 3; Robert, 2; Thomas, 1), was born May 21, 1728; he died April 31, 1790. In 1756, when he was but twenty-eight years old, his name first appears in the Colonial records as Deputy from South Kingstown; in 1756 he was again Deputy, and in the same year he was appointed Lieutenant-Colonel of militia for Kings County.

From 1761 until 1777, he was Assistant, with scarcely an interval. In 1770, he, with Stephen Hopkins, formed a committee to examine the complaint of the Collector and Comptroller of the Port of Newport. In 1786 and 1787 he was Associate Judge of the Supreme Court. These few facts gleaned from the Colonial records, support the statements made by Updike, who says: "Colonel Joseph Hazard inherited all the lofty firmness, the unwavering perseverance, and sterling mind of his mother. He was elected to many important offices by the people, and sustained them with honor. Although a determined partisan, he never permitted his political attachments to sway him from the principles of right. His

motto

motto was ' to do right, and let consequences take care of themselves.'" He was on the bench of the Supreme Court of the State, when the General Assembly enacted the celebrated " Paper Money Laws " of 1786, and was one of the paper-money party. But when the question of the constitutionality of these laws came before the court for decision, in the case of Trevett *vs.* Weeden, in which cause General Varnum made his great and eloquent effort, this Court stood firm in defence of the cause of law in their country, and declared the Paper-Money Tender Laws unconstitutional and void. Their fiery partisans in the General Assembly ordered the Court to be arraigned before them for a contempt of legislative power, and they were required to give their respective reasons for overthrowing the laws of the Legislature that had created them. This novel procedure in judicial history, Judge Hazard met with firmness ; and when called on, unmoved, rose and said : " It gives me pain, that the conduct of the Court seems to have met with the displeasure of the Administration ; but their obligations were of too sacred a nature for them to aim at pleasing, but in the line of their duty. It is well known that my sentiments have fully accorded with the general system of the Legislature in emitting the paper-money currency. But I never did, and never will depart from the character of an honest man, to support any measures however agreeable in themselves. If there could have been any prepossession in my mind, it must have been in favor of the act of the General Assembly, but it is not possible to resist the force of conviction. The opinion I gave on the trial was dictated by energy of truth. I thought it right. I still think so. But be it as it may, we derived our understanding from God, and to him alone are we accountable for our judgment." " This," adds Updike, " was an instance where the heroic firmness of a few men saved the reputation of a State."[1]

Joseph Hazard married, September 28, 1760, Hannah, daughter of Deputy-Governor Jonathan Nichols.

CHILDREN.

533. ROBERT HAZARD, born Jan. 31, 1762 ; died Aug. 12, 1851 ; married *Alice,* daughter of *Peleg Anthony.* He was called " *Cold-Brook Robert.*"
534. MARY HAZARD, born May 29, 1764 ; died April 15, 1833.
535. LUCY HAZARD, born July 6, 1766 ; died Sept. 23, 1804 ; married, Dec. 25, 1801, *Teddiman Hull.*
536. RUTH HAZARD, born Feb. 4, 1769 ; died June 27, 1852.
537. JOSHUA HAZARD, born Oct 7, 1771 ; died Nov. 12, 1823 ; married, *Elizabeth Niles.*
538. STANTON HAZARD, born Feb. 3, 1774 ; lost at sea, 1798.
539. EVAN MALBONE HAZARD, born March 6, 1776 ; died at sea, 1805.
540. HANNAH HAZARD, born Aug. 10, 1778 ; died Aug. 26, 1827; married Dr. *Stephen Griffen.*

§ 264. ESTHER HAZARD, 5 (Governor Robert, 4; Stephen, 3; Robert, 2; Thomas, 1), was born December 7, 1732 ; she died March 25, 1831 ; she married, 1758, Captain Jonathan Babcock. He was son of James Babcock, of Westerly, Rhode Island, and was born October 11, 1736. He graduated from Yale Col-

---

[1] Updike, Hist. of Narragansett Church, p. 250.

lege

lege in 1755. Captain James Babcock distinguished himself in the English army during the French War, and he was also with General Wolfe at the taking of Louisburg. Soon after the close of the war, he, with his family, removed to Boston, where he engaged in business. In 1767, he was lost on his passage from Stonington to Boston.

CHILDREN

541. ESTHER BABCOCK, born June 23, 1759; married *Nathan Brand*, of Stonington, Conn.
542. JONATHAN BABCOCK, born May 30, 1762; married, Jan. 29, 1795, *Ruth*, daughter of *Benjamin* and *Hannah (Niles) Rodman*, of South Kingstown.
543. ROBERT BABCOCK, born Dec. 18, 1763; married, May 11, 1793, *Mary*, daughter of *Stephen Hazard*. He died Feb. 11, 1848.
544. HANNAH BABCOCK, born Feb. 11, 1768; unmarried.

§ 267. SAMUEL HAZARD, 5 (Robert, 4; Stephen, 3; Robert, 2; Thomas, 1), was born about 1739; he was admitted freeman from South Kingstown in 1760. He married, May 3, 1763, Hannah, daughter of Benjamin Perry, who died December 12, 1772. He married, second, Susannah Perry, sister to his first wife. They were married March 5, 1774. He married, third, December 11, 1785, Elizabeth, daughter of Deputy-Governor Jonathan Nichols. She died April 4, 1815, at the house of her nephew, Robert Hazard, in Charlestown, Rhode Island. Samuel Hazard died in 1787.

CHILDREN OF FIRST MARRIAGE

545. BENJAMIN HAZARD, born March 11, 1764; died July 12, 1849; married, April 4, 1804, *Martha*, daughter of "*Long Stephen*" *Hazard*.
546. GIDEON HAZARD, born Nov. 25, 1765; died April, 1806; married *Elizabeth*, daughter of "*Long Stephen*" *Hazard;* she died Nov. 21, 1818.
547. ESTHER HAZARD, born Oct. 5, 1767.
548. ELIZABETH HAZARD, born Dec. 2, 1769; married, Nov., 1798, *Atherton Wales;* died July 25, 1801.
549. JOSEPH STANTON HAZARD, born March 7, 1772; died in Havana while unloading his vessel.

CHILDREN OF SECOND MARRIAGE

550. SAMUEL HAZARD, born Oct. 10, 1776; died June 22, 1836, in Middleport Centre, New York.
551. JAMES HAZARD, born Aug. 27, 1778.
552. SUSANNAH HAZARD, born Aug. 21, 1780; died in South Kingstown, 1817.
553. PATRICK HAZARD, born May 10, 1782; died in 1805.
554. JOSHUA HAZARD, born Dec. 21, 1784; died in infancy.

CHILDREN OF THIRD MARRIAGE

555. HENRY HAZARD.
556. THOMAS HAZARD. These two last may have been twins. They were both mentioned in their father's will.

§ 270. STANTON HAZARD, 5 (Governor Robert, 4; Stephen, 3; Robert, 2; Thomas, 1), was born January 8, 1743; he died at Honduras in 1789. His death was caused by a wound from a sword, given by an adversary in a duel, in which he killed his opponent. He was a captain in the British Navy. His interesting portrait (here reproduced), in the dress of a post-captain, is now in the possession

270

CAPTAIN STANTON HAZARD.

session of a grand-nephew in Westerly, Rhode Island. It was painted in Rome, about 1776. At the beginning of the War for Independence, he offered his services to the Colony; but asking for the same rank as that which he held in the British Navy, and being refused, he remained in the service of the English.

Some time afterwards his vessel was captured by a Yankee privateer. The American vessel, having guns of longer range, and being much the faster of the two, was easily able to capture the British vessel. Upon the arrival of the prisoners in Newport, there was some embarrassment amongst the men in authority (all his old friends, and some of them relations), to know what to do with Captain Hazard, as they did not like to place him in confinement. He, however, solved the problem by asking to be sent to Narragansett, on his parole, to the house of his sister, the wife of Doctor Robert Hazard, promising not to leave the garden of the house until he was exchanged. This promise he faithfully kept.

In this connection is the following story: One morning, standing at the gate and seeing a travel-stained sailor going by, he hailed the man, asking if he was hungry, and being answered in the affirmative, Captain Hazard invited him into the house, and gave him a plentiful breakfast. He then asked the man if he had any money, and for answer the sailor turned his pocket inside out. Captain Hazard, putting his hand in his own pocket, took out two silver dollars, and said, "This is all the money I have; I will divide with you." This he did, and, giving the sailor one dollar, he then accompanied him to the gate, and said, "I can go no farther; my word of honour keeps me inside the gate."

Captain Hazard was rather a dandy in personal habits and dress, wearing fine lace ruffles on his shirt and at his wrists. Like the majority of the fine gentlemen of the day, he took snuff, and carried a gold and tortoise-shell box, and when in the performance of this duty, he always bent his head far forward, in order to prevent the least particle of snuff from soiling his fine ruffles. At one time, during an engagement between his vessel and the enemy, he took out his box, and taking a pinch of snuff, bent his head far forward. At that moment a shot from the enemy's guns passed over his head, and killed a man standing just behind him. This is, possibly, the only instance in history where a pinch of snuff has saved an officer's life or killed a man.

He married, July 3, 1785, Elizabeth Wickham. She died September 22, 1801. They had but one child, who died in infancy.

§ 271. SAMUEL HAZARD, 5 (Samuel, 4; Stephen, 3; Robert, 2; Thomas, 1), was born about 1730; he died previous to 1788. He was one of those who, in 1779, were sent out of the Narragansett country for giving aid to the enemy. His estate was not confiscated, and he was allowed to return to his home, on giving his promise to be loyal to the American interests.

He married Catharine ——.

CHILDREN
557. SAMUEL HAZARD.

558.

558. GEORGE HAZARD.
559. ELIZA HAZARD.
560. LODOWICK HAZARD, married a daughter of Dr. *William Robinson*, of Westerly, Rhode Island.
561. ROBERT HAZARD, married, and had one son, Rev. *Samuel Hazard.*
562. BETSY HAZARD, married —— *Worthington.*
563. NANCY HAZARD.
564. ABBY HAZARD, married *Ichabod Taylor ;* they had two children, *Robert* and *Dudley.*
565. HARRIET HAZARD, married —— *Bancroft.*

§ 272. GEORGE HAZARD, 5 (Samuel, 4 ; Stephen, 3 ; Robert, 2 ; Thomas, 1), was born in Newport, Rhode Island, about 1745. His father sold his manufacturing interest in North Kingstown in 1739, and soon after this date, sold his land in both North and South Kingstown, and removed to Newport, where his younger children were born, lived and died. George Hazard married Mary Mumford, daughter of John Mumford of New London. He died August 12, 1797.

CHILDREN
566. JAMES HAZARD, born 1770 ; died 1794.
567. MARY HAZARD, born 1773 ; died 1807 ; married, Nov., 1794, *Nathaniel Richmond.*
568. ESTHER HAZARD, married, Oct. 22, 1803, *Benjamin Pearce.*
569. CALEB HAZARD, born 1783 ; died 1804.
570. SALLY HAZARD, born 1785 ; died 1877.
571. CATHARINE HAZARD, born 1787 ; died June 11, 1819.
572. JOHN HAZARD, born 1790 ; died 1800.
573. A DAUGHTER, married —— *Dolbear.*
574. HANNAH HAZARD, married, 1st, May 12, 1822, *John Newman ;* 2d, *Erastus P. Allen.*
575. JAMES AUGUSTUS HAZARD, born 1798 ; died June 11, 1819.

§ 274. STEPHEN HAZARD, 5 (Thomas, 4 ; Stephen, 3 ; Robert, 2 ; Thomas, 1), was born about 1730. He died October 24, 1804, in North Kingstown. There is no certainty about the dates of his birth, of his marriage, or of the birth of his children, as no records of them can be found. He was called "Short Stephen," being one of the exceptional Hazards that could not boast of his six feet and great strength. His mother, Hannah Slocum, was a very small woman, not over five feet in height, and so slight that her husband could span her waist with his two hands. Stephen Hazard adhered to the cause of the Crown during the war of 1776, and was one of those sent out of the town for giving aid to the enemy. When allowed to return to the town, on his parole, he refused to serve when drafted. It is difficult to place his house, or the place where his children were born. At one time he was the keeper of the lighthouse at Point Judith, and at another he was living in Jamestown. He married, about 1760, Elizabeth, daughter of Daniel and Renewed (Smith) Carpenter.

CHILDREN
576. THOMAS HAZARD, married *Silence Knowles.*
577. MARY HAZARD, born 1765 ; married, Jan., 1781, *Joseph Oatley.*
578. MARTHA HAZARD.
579. SARAH HAZARD, married *Asa Carpenter.*

580.

580. ROUSE HAZARD, lost at sea when a young man ; unmarried.
581. ELIZABETH HAZARD, born (circa) 1783 ; married, 1799, Robert Rodman.

§ 283. JEREMIAH HAZARD, 5 (Jeffrey, 4 ; Robert, 3 ; Robert, 2 ; Thomas, 1), was born August 13, 1726. He died June 23, 1795. His father gave to him, by deed, three hundred acres in Exeter, and besides this fine farm, the *tradition* is, that " as his father died without a will, he, by the old English law *still in force* inherited all the estate, comprising three hundred acres given to Jeffrey by his father, and also a farm called the ' Great Neck ' farm, of several hundred acres, besides other land." But the law of 1719 for the settlement of intestate estates when not entailed, would have covered this case ; and this disproves the legend with regard to Jeremiah being his father's sole heir.
"Stout Jeffrey," while attending a meeting of the Selectmen of the town, took a sudden and violent cold, from sitting in his wet clothes. Feeling himself very ill he sent for a lawyer to make his will, but the lawyer delayed his visit until the next day, when "Stout Jeffrey," just in his prime, with his splendid physique and great vitality, was dead. This account is given by one of his descendants, who vouches for the truth of it.
Jeremiah Hazard married Mary, daughter of Robert and Patience (Northup) Hazard, his second cousin. She was born 1726, and died October 22, 1816.
CHILD.
582. THOMAS HAZARD, born 1753 ; died Feb. 15, 1815 ; married *Lucy Congdon*, born 1763, and died Dec. 30, 1807.

§ 284. SUSANNAH HAZARD, 5 (Jeffrey, 4 ; Robert, 3 ; Robert, 2 ; Thomas, 1), married, February 4, 1753, Wilkinson Browning, son of William and Mary (Wilkinson) Browning. He was admitted freeman from North Kingstown in 1756. When drafted, in 1777, he refused to serve, whether because of his religious or political belief is not stated. Susannah Hazard died February, 1795 ; he died October 28, 1805.
CHILDREN
583. HAZARD BROWNING, married *Martha Potter*.
584. AMEY BROWNING, married *Gideon Hoxsie*.
585. MARY BROWNING, married, Dec. 28, 1777, *Thomas Hoxsie*.

§ 285. ROBERT HAZARD, 5 (Jeffrey, 4 ; Robert, 3 ; Robert, 2 ; Thomas, 1). He married Hannah Greene, who was a sister of Captain Amos Greene.
CHILDREN
586. JEFFREY HAZARD, born March 24, 1771 ; died 1828.
587. ROBERT HAZARD, born Aug. 29, 1785 ; married *Abigail Seager*.

§ 289. ROBERT HAZARD, 5 (Robert, 4 ; Robert, 3 ; Robert, 2 ; Thomas, 1), was born September 19, 1728 ; married, December 13, 1753, Alice Thomas ; they were married by Philip Greene, Justice of the Peace.
CHILDREN
588. MARTHA HAZARD, born Feb. 27, 1755.

589.

589. RUTH HAZARD, born Feb. 26, 1759.
590. ABIGAIL HAZARD, born Jan. 4, 1762 ; married, Sept. 10, 1780, *Jared Bailey*.
591. JOHN HAZARD, born 1766 ; died 1851.

§ 292. JEREMIAH HAZARD, 5 (Robert, 4 ; Robert, 3 ; Robert, 2 ; Thomas, 1), was born July 25, 1736 ; he died in 1773. He married, November 6, 1760, Phebe Tillinghast. In his will, written June 21, 1773, he gave to his son Jeffrey "all my lands lying in Exeter and in West Greenwich ; to wife Phebe, all lands lying in Coventry (one hundred and fifteen acres) ; to daughter Abigail," &c. The will was admitted to Probate, December 14, 1773.

CHILDREN
592. JEFFREY HAZARD, born 1762 ; died June 3, 1840 ; married *Amey Tillinghast*.
593. ABIGAIL HAZARD.

§ 308. JEREMIAH HAZARD, 5 (Robert, 4 ; Jeremiah, 3 ; Robert, 2 ; Thomas, 1), was born (*circa*) 1727 ; he was admitted freeman from North Kingstown in 1756. In 1779 he was impeached for disloyalty, and with his wife, sent away from his home. On his petition to have the charges against him examined, and permission given to him to return home, he was allowed to return on parole. He married, first, Ruth Potter. She died about 1770. He married, soon after his first wife's death, Mary, daughter of John Cole, who was son of William, and grandson of John and Susannah (Hutchinson) Cole. Ann Hutchinson, after the death of her husband William, in 1643, removed to East Chester, New York, where she and seventeen persons of her household were murdered by the Indians. One only, Susannah, escaped, who, after being redeemed, married John Cole, of Boston, in 1651. They soon after settled in the Narragansett country, near what is now Hamilton Mills, formerly called Bissell's Mills.

CHILDREN OF FIRST MARRIAGE
594. JOHN HAZARD, born Aug. 24, 1749 ; married *Abby Boss*.
595. ROBERT HAZARD.
596. ROWLAND HAZARD, born in 1762 ; died April 3, 1834.

CHILD OF SECOND MARRIAGE
597. WILBOR HAZARD, born Dec. 15, 1774 ; died Feb. 14, 1827 ; married *Mary*, daughter of *Benjamin Stanton*.

§ 309. EPHRAIM HAZARD, 5 (Robert, 4 ; Jeremiah, 3 ; Robert, 2 ; Thomas 1), was born in 1729 ; died August 28, 1825 ; married Ann ———.

CHILD
598. EASTON HAZARD, born Sept. 13, 1783 ; died Sept. 2, 1826 ; married *Charlotte Bissell*.

§ 310. GIDEON HAZARD, 5 (Robert, 4 ; Jeremiah, 3 ; Robert, 2 ; Thomas, 1), married Sarah, daughter of Jonathan Chase, and widow of Benjamin Congdon. He married, second, Anna ———, who died November 3, 1822. He died June 13, 1814, at the homestead of his father and grandfather.

CHILDREN

CHILDREN OF FIRST MARRIAGE

599. EPHRAIM HAZARD, born Sept. 5, 1763 ; died April 23, 1836 ; married 1st, *Hannah*, daughter of Richard Updike; 2d, *Mary Smith*.

600. FREEBORN HAZARD, born in 1765 ; died Aug. 29, 1831 ; married *Susan Sherman*.

601. ROBERT HAZARD.

602. STEPHEN HAZARD.

CHILD OF SECOND MARRIAGE

603. ELIZABETH HAZARD, born Dec. 7, 1795 ; married *Joseph Hammond*.

§ 314. STEPHEN CHAMPLIN, 5 (Stephen Champlin, 4 ; Hannah Hazard, 3 ; Robert, 2 ; Thomas, 1), was born September 29, 1734 ; died in 1778 ; married Dinah, daughter of William and Mary (Wilkinson) Browning.

CHILDREN

604. MARY CHAMPLIN, born June 26, 1760.

605. STEPHEN CHAMPLIN, born Aug. 3, 1763 ; married, Dec. 20, 1782, *Elizabeth Perry*, daughter of *Freeman Perry*. For children, see *Elizabeth Perry, No. 503*.

606. HANNAH CHAMPLIN, born June 5, 1765.

607. SUSANNAH CHAMPLIN, born Dec. 9, 1772.

§ 315. HANNAH CHAMPLIN, 5 (Stephen Champlin, 4 ; Hannah Hazard, 3 ; Robert, 2 ; Thomas, 1), was born January 20, 1735. She married, about 1754, Nicholas Gardiner.

CHILDREN

608. STEPHEN CHAMPLIN GARDINER, born Dec. 3, 1755.

609. GEORGE GARDINER, born June 9, 1757.

610. ROWLAND GARDINER, born March 18, 1759.

611. HANNAH GARDINER, born Oct. 7, 1763.

612. JEFFREY GARDINER, born Nov. 12, 1765.

§ 316. SARAH CHAMPLIN, 5 (Stephen, 4 ; Hannah Hazard, 3 ; Robert, 2 ; Thomas, 1), was born August 18, 1737. She married Samuel Congdon.

CHILDREN

613. JOSEPH CONGDON, born March 1, 1758.

614. HANNAH CONGDON, born July 18, 1759.

615. GEORGE CONGDON, born Dec. 9, 1760.

616. SARAH CONGDON, married, March 15, 1795, Capt. *Robert Robinson*.

§ 317. MARY CHAMPLIN, 5 (Stephen, 4 ; Hannah Hazard, 3 ; Robert, 2 ; Thomas, 1), was born in 1739. She married, February 12, 1761, Joseph Browning.

CHILDREN

617. MARY BROWNING, born March 14, 1762.

618. SUSANNAH BROWNING, born Aug. 26, 1764.

619. WILLIAM BROWNING, born Sept. 5, 1767.

§ 319. JEFFREY CHAMPLIN, 5 (Stephen, 4 ; Hannah Hazard, 3 ; Robert, 2 ; Thomas, 1), was born March 21, 1744. He married Mary ———.

CHILDREN

CHILDREN
620. MARY CHAMPLIN, born April 7, 1769.
621. STEPHEN GARDINER CHAMPLIN, born Jan. 31, 1771.

§ 322.  ROWLAND ROBINSON, 5 (Martha Potter, 4 ; John, 3 ; Martha Hazard, 2 ; Thomas, 1), was born October 8, 1719 ; he died 1806. He married December 3, 1741, Anstis, daughter of John Gardiner. She was born March 23, 1721, and died in 1785. She was niece to Governor William Robinson's second wife.

CHILDREN
622. HANNAH ROBINSON, born May 10, 1750 ; died 1773 ; married *Peter Simmons.*
623. MARY ROBINSON, born Aug. 15, 1751; died 1777; unmarried.
624. WILLIAM ROBINSON, born Sept. 13, 1758; died 1804; married *Ann Scott.*

§ 326.  MARTHA ROBINSON, 5 (Martha Potter, 4 ; John, 3 ; Martha Hazard, 2 ; Thomas, 1), was born November 11, 1725 ; she died on September 7, 1760 ; she married April 18, 1745, Latham Clarke, the son of Samuel Clarke, of Jamestown. She died May 7, 1760.

CHILDREN
625. MARTHA CLARKE, married *John Hazard.*
626. SAMUEL CLARKE.
627. LOUIS LATHAM CLARKE.
628. HANNAH CLARKE, married *Peleg Gardner.*

**End of the Fifth Generation**

THE

# THE HAZARD FAMILY

## 𝔖𝔦𝔵𝔱𝔥 𝔊𝔢𝔫𝔢𝔯𝔞𝔱𝔦𝔬𝔫

 ROBERT HAZARD, 6 (Thomas, 5; Robert, 4; Thomas, 3; Robert, 2; Thomas, 1), was born November 17, 1753; died May 3, 1833; he married, in 1781, Sarah, the daughter of David and Lydia Fish; she died in 1847. February 26, 1794, he moved to Ferrisburg, Vermont, on Lake Champlain.

CHILDREN
629. THOMAS HAZARD, born Jan. 14, 1782; married *Lydia Rogers.*
630. ELIZABETH HAZARD, died young.
631. ROWLAND HAZARD, married *Fanny Carpenter.*
632. DAVID HAZARD, married *Sarah Rogers.*
633. ROBERT HAZARD.
634. SARAH HAZARD, married *Nicholas Holmes.*
635. LYDIA HAZARD, married *Schuyler Lewis.*
636. MARY HAZARD.
637. WILLIAM HAZARD, married, 1st, *Hannah Rogers;* 2d, *Lucy Burroughs.*
638. ROBINSON HAZARD.
639. STEPHEN HAZARD, married *Sarah Odell.*

§ 362. THOMAS HAZARD, 6 (Thomas, 5; Robert, 4; Thomas, 3; Robert, 2; Thomas, 1), was born November 15, 1758. He died at his home in New York, of apoplexy, July 24, 1828, aged seventy years, and was buried in the Friends' Cemetery. He married, September 6, 1780, Anna, daughter of Thomas and Mary (Borden) Rodman; born June 24, 1762; died June 14, 1845, aged eighty-four. After his marriage (at Leicester, Massachusetts), he went to live at Cranston, Rhode Island, near Providence, where several of his children were born. In 1789, he moved to New Bedford, Massachusetts, and in consequence was called "Bedford Tom." His house, a fine old colonial mansion on the corner of Elm and North Streets, is still standing. He made a large fortune in the whaling business, and took an active part in politics, being postmaster of New Bedford and a State Senator in 1812. He was the first president of the Bedford Bank, which commenced business in 1803.

He moved to New York shortly after the war of 1812, and lived at Nº. 80 Beekman Street, in a large brick house, near S. George's Church. He was actively engaged in business in New York, but owned interests in several vessels engaged

in

in the whaling trade. In 1824 he was one of the committee of thirty prominent men appointed at a mass-meeting held April 20, in City Hall, to secure the re-appointment of DeWitt Clinton, as Commissioner of the Erie Canal, — one of the most exciting incidents of the political history of that period.

Anna Rodman, the wife of Thomas Hazard, was born in the Rodman homestead, at Newport, Rhode Island, June 24, 1762. Her father was Thomas Rodman, son of Samuel Rodman and Mary, daughter of Colonel Thomas Willett, of Flush-ing, Long Island. Samuel Rodman was son of Thomas Rodman and Hannah Clarke, daughter of Governor Walter Clarke. He came to Newport, Rhode Is-land, in 1675, from the Barbadoes, where his father, John Rodman, owned a planta-tion. Thomas Rodman was born December 20, 1723–4, and was lost at sea, off Newport, November 16, 1766. He was returning home from England, where he had gone to collect a large amount of money due him, and being rendered help-less by an attack of gout, was the only person unable to save himself. He mar-ried, April 5, 1750, Mary, daughter of Abraham Borden and Elizabeth, daughter of Joseph Wanton. Mary Borden, mother of Anna Rodman, was born January 10, 1729, and died at New Bedford, February 19, 1798. Anna Rodman and her sisters were beautiful and accomplished women, in reference to whom the follow-ing tradition has been handed down to us: An Englishman of high rank, while drinking tea at Mrs. Rodman's, paid her the graceful compliment of saying, that " Newport was the garden of America, and her three daughters the choicest flowers therein." It must be remembered that before the Revolution, Newport was a large centre of wealth and refinement, and an important seaport. The discomfort occasioned by the Revolutionary war became so great that Mrs. Rodman and her family removed to Leicester, Massachusetts, in 1770, where they remained until peace was declared. Several letters which have been preserved, indicate that the young ladies did not enjoy the change of society, and tradition states that one reason Mrs. Rodman left Newport was, that she was afraid her daughters might marry English officers,— the profession of arms being contrary to the Friends' creed. It may be well to state here that the families were all Friends, and all wore their distinctive dress.

We insert an old love-letter of Thomas Hazard's, as a delightful specimen of old-time courtship: —

" *To Miss Anna Rodman*

Moſt divine and incomparable Charmer, Imagining a Lady of your Delicacy could not be agreeably Entertained with things of Earthly nature, I'm reſolved to take the Tour of the happy Regions above, preſent your Ladyſhip with a ſmall Collection of Gods and Godeſſes, for your particular Service, and as to Madam *Venus* you may depend upon't the Jade ſhall cry heartily through Envy before I have done with her, and confeſs in ſpite of her teeth, that there is one *Nancy Rodman* infinitely more charming than ſhe is ; I intend likewiſe to make *Sol* pop behind a Cloud, in acknowledgement of your Superior Lustre, and ſend the Stars pack-ing, as an unneceſſary Illumination, the *Moon* ſhall tramp off as aſhamed of her Dullneſs, and the weſtern Skies ſhall no more boaſt of their Colour ; in fine, Madam, I intend to perform
                                                                                                                    many

many more noble Exploits, as foon as ever I have projected a Scheme, to convey aloft without any danger of a broken neck.

Madam

your moft obedient

moft Devoted Humble fervant

and paffionate admirer,

THOMAS.

Young Thomas was certainly badly "hit" about the heart; but his head seemed
in no more danger of being broken than his neck. But then one must remember that "Miss Nancy" was really an exceptionally beautiful woman. Thomas
B. Hazard ("Nailor Tom"), was perhaps one of her
humble admirers. He often mentions in his diary the
fact that he went to Leicester to see "Cousin Rodman"; and one entry reads, "Tommy Hazard and
Nancy Rodman were married last week, AMEN." As
this is the only time in his diary where "Amen" is
used, it would seem to be a sigh of resignation, equivalent to, "The Lord's will be done."

CHILDREN

640. THOMAS R. HAZARD, married *Margaret Avery*, of Liverpool, England, in 1808, while United
     States Consul there; died near Cincinnati, Ohio, Oct. 18, 1822.
641. SAMUEL HAZARD, married *Rebecca Peace*, of Philadelphia, and lived in Franklin Street, New
     York, where they both died, leaving no children.
642. SARAH HAZARD, born Sept. 19, 1781; married *John H. Howland*.
643. ELIZABETH HAZARD, born Dec. 2, 1783; married *Jacob Barker*; died Dec. 29, 1866.
644. ANNA HAZARD, born at Cranston, Rhode Island, June 24, 1786; married, 1st, Oct. 2, 1809,
     *Philip J. Hone*, of New York; married, 2d, *Charles Stephens*, of Skidaway Island, Georgia, in
     1821, and died there, Oct. 7, 1823, leaving a daughter, *Joanna Hone*, who married *Charles
     Kneeland*, of New York.
645. EDWARD HAZARD, died young.
646. WILLIAM HAZARD, died young.
647. MARTHA HAZARD, died young.

§ 363. ROWLAND HAZARD, 6 (Thomas, 5; Robert, 4; Thomas, 3; Robert, 2; Thomas, 1), was born the fourth of the fourth month, second day of the
week, about ten o'clock in the forenoon, 1763; he died July 1, 1835. He married, in 1793, Mary Peace, daughter of Isaac Peace. She died June 28, 1852.
Peacedale was named in honor of this lady, and there Rowland Hazard early
established a manufacturing business. The first carding-machines set in South
Kingstown were in operation here, and as early as 1800 the industry was established which has since developed into the Peacedale Manufacturing Company.[1]
He also had shipping interests, first at Charleston, South Carolina, and afterward
in Narragansett. After the destruction of the Pier there in 1815, Mrs. Hazard
writes him she hopes he will not rebuild it, as it has always proved a trouble-

---

[1] Bagnall's The Textile Industries of the United States, p. 284.

some

some piece of property, quoting his grandfather, Governor Robinson, as having desired that none of his children would try to maintain it. Late in life he removed to Pleasant Valley, New York, where he died.[1]

CHILDREN

648. ISAAC PEACE HAZARD, born Oct. 3, 1794, in South Kingstown, Rhode Island, at the house of his grandfather, *Thomas Hazard.* He was educated at the Friends' School at West-town, near Philadelphia. On leaving school, about 1810, he returned to South Kingstown, and at once began to assist his father in business, passing the greater part of his life at Peacedale. He took a most kindly interest in the welfare of his neighbors there. He was constantly appealed to for advice and assistance, and no one whom he could aid ever applied to him in vain. He possessed the confidence and esteem of all who knew him. He never sought political power or office, but in response to the earnest solicitations of his townsmen, he on six occasions represented the town of South Kingstown in the General Assembly. From the organization of the Peacedale Manufacturing Company, in 1848, he was president of the company, until he retired in 1864. His brother, *Rowland G. Hazard,* was the treasurer, but the names of the offices do not indicate, with any exactness, the duties which each discharged. They divided the conduct of the business between them. After his retirement from active business, in 1864, he went to live with his sister at Newport. He was never married. He died on the second of March, 1879. He lies buried at Peacedale, in the Oak Dale Cemetery, among scenes with which he was so familiar, and among the people whose welfare he had so much at heart.[2]

649. THOMAS ROBINSON HAZARD, born January 3, 1797 ; married *Frances Minturn.*

650. ELIZA GIBSON HAZARD, born March 17, 1799 ; unmarried.

651. ROWLAND GIBSON HAZARD, born Oct. 9, 1801 ; married *Caroline,* daughter of *John Newbold,* of Bristol, Pennsylvania ; died June 24, 1888.

652. WILLIAM ROBINSON HAZARD, born Dec. 15, 1803 ; married, Oct. 2, 1828, *Mary,* daughter of *John* and *Lydia Wilbur,* of Hopkinton, Rhode Island.

652*a.* JOSEPH PEACE HAZARD, born Feb. 17, 1807, in Burlington, New Jersey, from whence his parents removed to Bristol, Pennsylvania, in his thirteenth year, when Peacedale became his home. In 1835, he erected a woolen mill at Peacedale, which was operated for several years, and subsequently leased, after which he abandoned business. Having a taste for travel, Mr. *Hazard* acquainted himself thoroughly with the land of his birth, and in 1856 made the tour of Europe, spending much time in London and Rome. For many years much of his time was spent abroad, until 1879, when he returned to his native land. Mr. *Hazard* was among the first to foresee the advantages presented by Narragansett Pier as a popular watering-place, and at an early day furnished means to aid in its development, and promote its growth. He was a considerable holder of land at that point, and in 1846 began the erection of what is known as the " Castle," — a picturesque structure surmounted by two towers. Mr. *Hazard* died at the residence of his brother, *Rowland G. Hazard,* in Peacedale, Rhode Island.[3]

653. ISABELLA WAKEFIELD HAZARD, born Aug. 3, 1809 ; died in 1838 ; unmarried.

654. MARY PEACE HAZARD, born Aug. 15, 1814 ; died in 1874 ; unmarried.

655. ANNA HAZARD, born Oct. 27, 1820.


§ 365. ROBERT HAZARD, 6 (Richard, 5 ; Robert, 4 ; Thomas, 3 ; Robert, 2 ; Thomas, 1), was born April 14, 1753 ; he died in 1795. He married, December 29, 1782, Hannah, daughter of Nicholas and Hannah Gardiner. She was born October 7, 1763.

1 Contributed by Caroline Hazard.        2 Condensed from Washington County History.        3 Ibid.

CHILDREN

648
Isaac Peace Hazard.

CHILDREN

656. SARAH HAZARD, born Jan. 11, 1784; married *Thomas A. Hazard.* For children, see *No. 767.*
657. A DAUGHTER, born Jan. 11, 1784.

Robert Hazard may also have had a son named Christopher, who had a son Ezekiel and a daughter Desire.

§ 366. GEORGE HAZARD, 6 (Richard, 5; Robert, 4; Thomas, 3; Robert, 3; Thomas, 1), was born September 22, 1756. He died Aug. 1, 1825. He married, first, March 7, 1782, Sarah Scott. She died April 12, 1783. He married, second, December 8, 1786, Sarah Knowles, daughter of John and Susannah Knowles, of Hopkinton, Rhode Island. Nailor Tom Hazard, in his diary, calls him "Blacksmith George"; he was also called "Shoe-String George." He lived and died on his farm near Worden's Pond, given to him by his father.

CHILD OF FIRST MARRIAGE

658. SARAH HAZARD, born March 28, 1783; died June 17, 1818. In a fit of melancholy she hung herself.

§ 367. BENJAMIN HAZARD, 6 (Richard, 5; Robert, 4; Thomas, 3; Robert, 2; Thomas, 1), was born December 26, 1757; he died of consumption, at the home of his brother-in-law, Godfrey Hazard, in Boston Neck, October 15, 1784; he married, April 11, 1779, Hannah, daughter of Simeon and Abigail (Mumford) Hazard.

CHILDREN

659. ABIGAIL HAZARD, born Dec. 7, 1781; married —— *Snow,* of Providence.
660. ALICE HAZARD, born 1782; died May 30, 1818; married *John Allen.*

§ 369. RICHARD HAZARD, 6 (Richard, 5; Robert, 4; Thomas, 3; Robert, 2; Thomas, 1), was born November 15, 1761; he moved to Newport, and died there at the age (tradition says) of one hundred and two years. Mr. Thomas R. Hazard, in his "Recollections of Olden Times," says that he died between 1845 and 1850. He married, 1787, his brother Benjamin's widow, Hannah Hazard.

CHILDREN

661. JOSEPH WANTON HAZARD, married, Jan. 18, 1818, *Mary Potter,* a niece of *Jeremiah Niles Potter.*
662. JOHN HAZARD.
663. MARY HAZARD, died young.
664. RICHARD HAZARD, born 1802; died July 18, 1823.
665. ROWLAND HAZARD.
666. MARY ANN HAZARD.

§ 371. JOB WATSON, 6 (Sarah Hazard, 5; Robert, 4; Thomas, 3; Robert, 2; Thomas, 1), was born October 25, 1767; he died July 25, 1832; he married, June 18, 1787, Phebe Weeden.

CHILDREN

667. DANIEL WEEDEN WATSON, born 1790; married *Mary Congdon*; he died March 5, 1873.
668.

668. SALLY WATSON, married *George Hull.*
669. PHEBE WATSON, married, Dec. 13, 1811, *Freeman Watson.*
670. HANNAH WATSON, married, Jan. 4, 1810, *Arnold Hazard*, son of *Thomas Hazard.*
671. ARNOLD WATSON.
672. HAZARD WATSON.

§ 372. ROBERT H. WATSON, 6 (Sarah Hazard, 5; Robert, 4; Thomas, 3; Robert, 2; Thomas, 1), was born February 29, 1769; he married, December 30, 1790, Catharine Weeden.

CHILDREN
673. ISABELLA WATSON, born July 31, 1791.
674. JOSEPH W. WATSON, born Aug. 25, 1793.
675. MERIBAH WATSON, born Nov. 20, 1795.
676. JOHN JAY WATSON, born Aug. 13, 1797.
677. SARAH WATSON, born Sept. 8, 1799.
678. DANIEL WATSON, born April 13, 1801.
679. HANNAH WATSON, born June 19, 1803.
680. ROBERT H. WATSON, born March 4, 1806.

§ 373. WALTER WATSON, 6 (Sarah Hazard, 5; Robert, 4; Thomas, 3; Robert, 2; Thomas, 1), was born June 10, 1770; he married Mary Carr.

CHILDREN
681. NICHOLAS CARR WATSON, born Oct. 10, 1794.
682. JOB WATSON, born Oct. 23, 1796.
683. ISABELLA WATSON, born April 17, 1798.
684. THOMAS HAZARD WATSON, born Jan. 22, 1800.
685. WILLIAM WATSON, born Sept. 15, 1803.
686. ELISHA WATSON.
687. WALTER WATSON.
688–9. JOHN WATSON.

§ 374. BORDEN WATSON, 6 (Sarah Hazard, 5; Robert, 4; Thomas, 3; Robert, 2; Thomas, 1), was born February 9, 1772; he married Isabella Babcock.

CHILDREN
690. JOHN WATSON.
691. BORDEN WATSON.
692. SARAH WATSON.
693. MARY WATSON.
694. ABIJAH WATSON.
695. ALBERT WATSON.

§ 375. JOHN WATSON, 6 (Sarah Hazard, 5; Robert, 4; Thomas, 3; Robert, 2; Thomas, 1), was born November 1, 1774. Married, first, January 24, 1799, Sarah, daughter of Deputy-Governor George Brown; she died February 19, 1804. They were married by Reverend Theodore Dehon. Married, second, August 4, 1805, Isabella, daughter of Walter Watson. They were married at Suffield, Connecticut,

necticut, by Reverend Daniel Waldo. She died January 9, 1858, aged seventy-three years; he died September 7, 1852, aged seventy-seven years.

CHILDREN OF FIRST MARRIAGE
696. WILLIAM R. WATSON.
697. HENRY WATSON.
698. GEORGE WATSON.
699. A DAUGHTER.

CHILDREN OF SECOND MARRIAGE
700. WALTER WATSON, unmarried.
701. JOB WATSON.
702. ISABELLA WATSON, born 1814; died April 6, 1856; unmarried.
703. EMILY WATSON, born July 29, 1816; died July 19, 1856; unmarried.
704. HARRIET WATSON, born Jan. 19, 1818; died May 22, 1858; unmarried.
705. THOMAS WATSON, born July 23, 1822; died Nov. 30, 1862.

§ 376. JOHN HAZARD, 6 (Benjamin, 5 ; George, 4 ; Thomas, 3 ; Robert, 2 ; Thomas, 1), was born in 1746; he died June 26, 1813. He was called, "Wickham John," because he inherited land which came into the family through his great-grandmother, Mary Wickham. Her first husband was Enoch Place. She married Samuel Wickham as his second wife; but the land that she gave to her son-in-law George (whom she called George Place Hazard), in North Kingstown, she inherited from her father, James Sweet. In this case there seems even less reason for the nick-name "Wickham" than usual. John Hazard married, first, Sarah, daughter of Nathan Gardiner, and second, Martha, daughter of Latham and Martha (Robinson) Clarke.

CHILDREN
706-7. JOHN HAZARD, born 1775; died 1806; married *Frances*, daughter of Capt. *Daniel* and *Sarah (Hazard) Gardiner*.
708. NATHAN GARDINER HAZARD, married, after his brother's death, *Frances Hazard*, his brother's widow. She was first cousin to her husband, through the *Gardiners*.

§ 377. GODFREY HAZARD, 6 (Simeon, 5 ; George, 4 ; Thomas, 3 ; Robert, 2 ; Thomas, 1). He married, February 22, 1778, his cousin Alice, daughter of George and Sarah (Hazard) Hazard. She died October 29, 1778, without children. He married, second, November 22, 1787, Ruth, daughter of Jonathan and Ruth (Coggeshall) Easton ; they were second cousins.

CHILD
709. JONATHAN EASTON HAZARD, married, Aug., 1812, *Sarah*, daughter of *George Lawton*, of North Kingstown.

§ 378. SIMEON HAZARD, 6 (Simeon, 5 ; George, 4 ; Thomas, 3 ; Robert, 2 ; Thomas, 1). He lived at the upper Narrow River Bridge, and for many years kept a tavern there. It is not known whom he married.

CHILDREN
710. GODFREY HAZARD, died Nov. 29, 1810, aged about 7 years.

711.

711. MUMFORD HAZARD, married —— *Jermain*. Moved to Albany, New York, and has descendants there.
712. ABBY HAZARD, unmarried ; died Nov. 9, 1819.
713. MARY HAZARD, unmarried.

§ 382. GEORGE HAZARD, 6 (Simeon, 5 ; George, 4 ; Thomas, 3 ; Robert, 2 ; Thomas, 1), was born May 15, 1773. He married, September, 1800, Content Wilbur ; she died, January 16, 1833, aged fifty years. He died November 29, 1836.

CHILDREN
714. MUMFORD HAZARD, born Feb. 1802; married *Sarah Tilley*.
715. ELIZABETH HAZARD, born Jan. 19, 1804; married, April 15, 1827, *William Wilbur*.
716. CHARLES HAZARD, born July 31, 1806; married *Sarah Cook*.
717. ARNOLD HAZARD, born Oct. 8, 1807; married, March 14, 1830, *Sarah Ann Stedman*.
718. ANN MATILDA HAZARD, born Sept. 30, 1808 ; married, Sept. 3, 1833, *Stephen M. Stedman*.
719. WILLIAM WILBUR HAZARD, born July 4, 1810 ; married, Oct. 27, 1834, *Sarah M. Armstrong*.
720. HARRIET HAZARD, born Jan. 23, 1813 ; married, Nov. 4, 1833, *Albert Armstrong*.
721. HENRY B. HAZARD, born Dec. 23, 1815 ; married, Aug. 11, 1840, *Eunice G. Wilbur*.
722. SIMEON HAZARD, born Jan. 7, 1817 ; married, Nov. 15, 1838, *Mary Ann Stedman*.
723. JAMES LAWRENCE HAZARD, born Feb. 21, 1818 ; married, 1842, *Frances B. Irish*.
724. GEORGE AUGUSTUS HAZARD, born March 26, 1819 ; married, Oct. 3, 1843, *Abby Card*.

§ 388. THOMAS HAZARD, 6 (George, 5 ; George, 4 ; Thomas, 3 ; Robert, 2 ; Thomas, 1), was born March 30, 1765. He was called Thomas Hull Hazard, although his name is entered on the records without the " H." Soon after his marriage, he sold his real estate in Boston Neck, and moved to Newport. His children, however, were all born in South Kingstown. He married, February 3, 1790, Abigail, daughter of Sylvester and Alice (Perry) Robinson. She died in March, 1818.

CHILDREN
725. SYLVESTER HAZARD, born March 3, 1791 ; married, 1st, July 3, 1817, *Hannah*, daughter of *Stephen Congdon ;* she died Jan. 8, 1820, aged 26 ; 2d, *Gulielma M.*, daughter of *Caleb* and *Waite Babcock ;* 3d, *Abby C.*, daughter of *Thomas* and *Abby Clarke*.
726. ROWLAND ROBINSON HAZARD, born Feb. 20, 1792 ; died Aug. 21, 1874 ; married *Anna*, daughter of *Charles Collins*.
727. SARAH ROBINSON HAZARD, married, as second wife, *George Congdon*.
728. GEORGE HAZARD, married *Ann Barnet*.
729. ALICE ROBINSON HAZARD, married, Feb., 1824, *Joseph Babcock*.

§ 390. SARAH HAZARD, 6 (Enoch, 5 ; George, 4 ; Thomas, 3 ; Robert, 2 ; Thomas, 1), was born August 13, 1768 ; she married, Dec. 25, 1793, Jeremiah Niles Potter. He was born January 23, 1769, and died February 27, 1849. She died September 11, 1817. He married, second, March 15, 1821, Alice Hazard, sister to his first wife.

CHILDREN OF FIRST MARRIAGE
730. MARY NILES POTTER, born Oct. 9, 1794 ; died Aug. 27, 1870 ; married, March 23, 1818, *George Champlin Robinson*.

731.

731. JEREMIAH NILES POTTER, born Oct. 10, 1796 ; died June 15, 1798.
732. ELIZABETH S. POTTER, born May 15, 1798 ; died May 14, 1799.
733. NILES POTTER, born Aug. 31, 1800 ; died Jan. 1864 ; married *Almira Fales.*
734. SARAH POTTER, born Aug. 19, 1802 ; married, in 1822, *Stephen Ayrault Robinson.*
735. ASA N. POTTER, born April 27, 1806.

CHILD OF SECOND MARRIAGE

736. ALICE POTTER, born Jan 16, 1822 ; died May 12, 1847 ; married *Benjamin Balch*, of Providence, Rhode Island.

§ 395. THOMAS G. HAZARD, 6 (Thomas Hazard, 5 ; George, 4 ; Thomas, 3 ; Robert, 2 ; Thomas, 1), died October 27, 1833 ; married Patience Borden, of Fall River.

CHILDREN

737. JOHN A. HAZARD, born April 11, 1804 ; died March 28, 1877 ; married, Sept. 4, 1839, *Phebe Sheffield.*
738. WILLIAM HAZARD, born Oct. 30, 1805 ; married *Harriet Brenton.*
739. THOMAS G. HAZARD, born Nov. 6, 1807 ; died Dec. 20, 1866 ; married, 1st, *Mary*, daughter of *Thomas Hull Hazard*, March 16, 1841 ; 2d, Oct. 15, 1861, *Sarah*, daughter of *Thomas H. Hazard*, and widow of *George Congdon.*
740. MARY E. HAZARD, born April 28, 1810 ; died Feb. 4, 1893.
741. GEORGE BORDEN HAZARD, born Dec. 25, 1813 ; married, 1st, *Martha Clarke ;* 2d, *Phebe Read.*
742. ENOCH HAZARD, born June 22, 1815 ; died March 3, 1854.
743. RUTH HAZARD, born June 30, 1817 ; died Feb. 13, 1888 ; married *Luther Bateman.*
744. BENJAMIN HAZARD, born Nov. 15, 1819 ; married *Hannah Davenport.*
745. ISAAC HAZARD, born Jan. 31, 1823.

§ 396. BENJAMIN HAZARD, 6 (Thomas G., 5 ; George, 4 ; Thomas, 3 ; Robert, 2 ; Thomas, 1), was born September 9, 1774 ; he died March 10, 1841. He graduated from Brown University in 1792, and was admitted to the bar in 1796. He began the practice of law in Newport, and followed his profession there with honor for the rest of his life. In 1809, he was elected a Representative to the General Assembly, and continued a member of the House until 1840. A contemporary says, " His ability was marked, and his integrity never questioned."

William Hunter, in a communication to Mr. Wilkins Updike, says : " There is one individual belonging to this numerous, wide-spread and highly respectable race (the Hazard family), who is deserving of particular notice and regard. We refer to the late Hon^ble Benjamin Hazard. . . . The ancient Constitution of Rhode Island, formed out of the provisions of its admirable Charter, was the most democratic, perhaps, that ever existed. It required a semi-annual election of Representatives to the General Assembly. Mr. Hazard was a Representative from the town of Newport in the General Assembly for thirty-one years, and, of course, was subjected to the ordeal of sixty-two popular elections ; a singular proof of the enlightened stability of his constituents, of his general high desert, and his peculiar fitness for this important office. This fact, independent of all
. others,

others, entitles him to claim rank as a distinguished man, and as it were, demon-
strates the possession of those impressive and useful qualities, whose combination renders character at once eminent and enduring. Mr. Hazard's course of
reading and study, operating upon a mind of genuine native strength, and con-
firming and justifying a native sturdiness of will (the germ and guaranty of
greatness), gave to all his literary efforts and political proceedings an air and
cast of originality. He read and dwelt upon such books as Rabelais, Burton's
*Anatomy of Melancholy*, Hobbes' *Leviathan*, Swift's *Gulliver*, Berkeley's *Querist*,
and, latterly, the dramas of Shakespeare and the romances of Sir Walter Scott.
In the middle and latter periods of his professional career, he was employed in
most of the important law-suits of the day, both in the courts of the State and
the United States. In politics, though his agency in the conflicts of parties, if
examined in the nicety of details, might betray some seeming inconsistencies, he
was in the main true to himself and the system of conservatism. His legislative
reports on banks, currency, &c., and on the extension of suffrage, are marked by
sterling thought and true and profound principles. In his style, as may have
been anticipated from what has been here said, there was nothing gaudy or
flashy; he aimed at and hit the mark of a plain, pure, Anglo-Saxon diction." [1]
In connection with this charming and honest tribute from Mr. Hazard's old
friend, it may be well to add that of an admirer, who, born too late to enjoy his
friendship, yet realized his brilliant qualities, said: —
"It was my misfortune to know little of the men who made the Newport Bar
celebrated in the early part of this century. Benjamin Hazard I never saw; he
died, I think, in 1840; but I have heard so much about him that I seem to have
known him well. He was one of those men who, vital in every part, live long in
memory and in tradition. There are those now among the living who could do
justice to his character; and the late Professor Goddard, in a few well-chosen
words, has left a portrait of him which Rhode Island people will not willingly
let die. I read every now and then his great report in defense of the suffrage
under the old Charter. Like the celebrated paper of Alexander Hamilton in
favor of the United States Bank, it is a monument to the patriotism, the ability and the integrity of its author; like that, also, it is a defense of a system
which the lapse of time and the change of circumstances rendered an obsolete
idea; but it was none the less a system which had the support of able, honest
men in a past generation; and it is too early, even now, to pass a final judgment
upon their wisdom and foresight." [2]
There are few men of Mr. Hazard's prominence and ability about whom so little has been written and given to the public. We conclude our sketch with the
"portrait" from Mr. Goddard's address: —
"Mr. Hazard felt himself at home in the General Assembly. There, and not in
our courts or primary assemblies, did he put forth, with the most effect, the un-

[1] Wm. Hunter, in Updike's Hist. of the Narragansett Church, pp. 478, 479.
[2] Payne's Reminiscences of the Rhode Island Bar, p. 48.

common

common powers with which he was gifted. His talents for debate would have won him no mean rank, even in the highest deliberative body in our country. The tricks of oratory, the artificial embellishments of rhetoric, he seemed to scorn ; but if his aim was either to support or defeat a measure, no man was a more skilful master of the language, and of the style of argument required for his purpose. No man more clearly comprehended, and at times more ably defended, the true merits of a public question. No man, too, it should be added, better knew how to perplex his adversaries by subtle objections, or to wither them by caustic sarcasm. Mr. Hazard was fond of reading. In my last interview with him, not many months before his death, he spoke, with great animation and emphasis, of his relish for Shakespeare, Sir Walter Scott, and Dean Swift. His predilection for the latter will not surprise those who recall to memory the celebrity of Swift as a politician, and the wonderful influence which, by the peculiar character and direction of his intellect, he obtained over the popular mind. Mr. Hazard could boast a true Rhode Island lineage, and he was in spirit a genuine Rhode Island man, attached to the old Charter, and to all the institutions which grew up under it. The Report on the Extension of Suffrage, made in the year 1829, is characterized by unusual ability. It is among the very few productions of his pen to which he attached his name, and in style and argument may perhaps be deemed one of the best specimens of his peculiar powers." [1]

It was thus that men and the world saw Mr. Hazard, but in his own home, he is best remembered by his tenderness to his wife and children, his courtly manner to the " some-time guest " ; his perfect unselfishness. A little-golden haired niece, whom he loved for her sweet voice in singing, remembers " Uncle Hazard's visits to her father's house ; when she was taken on his knee and asked to sing, over and over again, " Oft in the stilly night," and promised a guitar, when the little fingers should be strong enough to draw music from its strings. Though silver is now plentifully mingled with the gold of her hair, she still associates the sweet old song with the memory of " Uncle Hazard."

A plain block of granite, symbolical of the man, and beautiful for its strength and enduring qualities, marks his grave.

Benjamin Hazard married, October 28, 1807, Harriet Lyman, daughter of Major Daniel Lyman and his wife Mary Wanton, the beautiful daughter of John Wanton. He lived in the Wanton House on Broad Street, now Broadway, and died there, March 10, 1841, aged 67 years.

CHILDREN

746. EMILY LYMAN HAZARD, born Oct. 16, 1808; unmarried.
747. PEYTON RANDOLPH HAZARD, born April 9, 1810; died in St. Louis, July 2, 1849.
748. HARRIET HAZARD, born March 26, 1812; married, Oct. 18, 1837, Rev. *Charles T. Brooks.*
749. MARY HAZARD, born Dec. 14, 1813; died April 2, 1814.
750. MARY HAZARD, born March 5, 1815.
751. MARGARET LYMAN HAZARD, born April 8, 1817; married, Sept. 8, 1841, Gen. *Isaac Ingalls Stevens.*

[1] Writings of W. G. Goddard, vol. i, p. 135.

752.

752. NANCY HAZARD, born June 4, 1819; married, June 11, 1855, *John Alfred Hazard*, son of Dr. *Enoch Hazard*.
753. DANIEL LYMAN HAZARD, born July 19, 1821; married, May 20, 1869, *Delia Colton*.
754. THOMAS GEORGE HAZARD, born March 13, 1824; married, Dec. 8, 1858, *Mary King Brooks*.

§ 398. ENOCH HAZARD, 6 (Thomas, 5; George, 4; Thomas, 3; Robert, 2; Thomas, 1). He married, September, 1804, Mary, daughter of Nicholas Easton.

CHILD

755. JOHN ALFRED HAZARD, married *Nancy*, daughter of Hon. *Benjamin Hazard*. For children see *No. 752*.

§ 402. BENJAMIN HAZARD, 6 (Thomas, 5; Benjamin, 4; Thomas, 3; Robert, 2; Thomas, 1), was born December 11, 1784; he died June 4, 1845; he married, first, May 12, 1814, Joanna Carr. She died June 3, 1820. He married, second, June 3, 1823, Eliza Earl.

CHILDREN

756. SARAH HAZARD, born Sept. 11, 1815; died March 29, 1838; married June 4, 1838, Dr. *Amos Wilbur*.
757. HANNAH HAZARD, born June 9, 1817; died July 8, 1838.

Both these daughters died of consumption in early womanhood.

§ 403. THOMAS HAZARD, 6 (Thomas, 5; Benjamin, 4; Thomas, 3; Robert, 2; Thomas, 1), was born May 8, 1787; died April 16, 1846. He married March 13, 1814, Ruth, daughter of James and Ann (Rodman) Carpenter; she was born 1789; died August 7, 1860. He was a peculiar man. He was fond of hunting small game, and always ate the animals that he caught. He used to say that he never found anything that he could not eat, with the exception of crows, and these he did not care for. He was subject to a kind of cataleptic fit. If any one asked him about these fits, he would say, " Oh I can't describe them, but just wait a minute, I will have one for you." After a few minutes he would drop like a log, and go into convulsions, and this singular spasm was genuine and not pretended. It is said that these attacks were caused by a wound from a pistol-shot, on the right side of the head, when he was quite young; for this reason he was called "Pistol-head Tom." When younger, whatever he grasped in his right hand when attacked, he could not release without the aid of New England rum and music,— a curious combination. When a young man he enlisted in the United States service, and was sent to Newport. One day he had a quarrel with one of the soldiers, and springing upon him in a paroxysm of rage, seized him by the back of the neck. All known means were used to make him open his hand in vain, although his anger was gone; so he himself called for his usual remedies, and was thus enabled to release his prisoner. It is needless to add that, after this occurrence, he was, by the advice of the surgeon, sent home as unfit for service. Mr. James Wilson, who kindly gave this account, says that he saw him once on Tower Hill
with

with a handkerchief firmly grasped in his hand, which had not been opened in three days. He had walked to the place to beg Colonel George Brown to open his hand with the above-mentioned remedies. Colonel Brown had a good violin, and was a famous player, and after giving the patient his rum, proceeded to charm away the evil force with his music. When the hand opened, the inside was found to be of a dark purple, from the long continued pressure.

Mr. Hazard was exceedingly fond of flowers, especially the June pink, a large bed of which, near the door of his house, in its season, shone a bright spot in the surrounding green, sending its fragrance to the water's edge, and even across the stream. Scarlet beans and morning-glories were planted with the garden-beans, and a row of sweet-peas with the garden-peas; and he rarely left his house for a walk to the village, in the summer, without a large bunch of these fragrant flowers in his hand to be given to some "neighbor." Every man was either his " neighbor " or " cousin," for he, being a Quaker, was debarred the use of " Mr." or " Mrs." His home was near the centre of what is now the River Side Cemetery; and even to this day bunches of Napoleon's Dirge, and bits of moss-pink can be found in the early summer springing up near the site of the old house, a fitting memorial of this lover of flowers.

CHILDREN

758. PETER BOURS HAZARD, born Sept. 2, 1815; died June 22, 1871.
759. ABRAHAM HAZARD, born Dec. 9, 1817.
760. BENJAMIN HAZARD, died 1881.
761. THOMAS EDWARD HAZARD, born Aug. 19, 1823.
762. JONATHAN HAZARD.
763. RUTH HAZARD.
764. MARY ANN HAZARD, born Feb. 17, 1838; married —— Adams.

§ 409. JONATHAN HAZARD, 6 (Thomas, 5; Jonathan, 4; Thomas, 3; Robert, 2; Thomas, 1), was born July, 1750; he married Esther, daughter of Stephen and Abigail Watson. He was called Jonathan of Mumford's Mills, to distinguish him from the other Jonathans.

CHILDREN

765. GEORGE WATSON HAZARD, born Aug. 5, 1779; died Jan. 31, 1822; married Mary Lillibridge.
766. PATIENCE HAZARD, married Elam Holloway.
767. THOMAS ARNOLD HAZARD, born 1784; married Sarah, daughter of Robert Hazard (son of Richard).
768. BOWDOIN HAZARD, born Aug. 1785; married Theresa, daughter of Judge William Clarke.
769. ABBY HAZARD, married William H. Nye.
770. ESTHER HAZARD, married Robert Champlin.
771. SAMUEL HAZARD, born in 1794; died Jan. 14, 1866; married Lydia, daughter of Weeden and Mercy (Comstock) Eldred, of East Greenwich, Rhode Island.
772. NANCY HAZARD, born March 30, 1798; died May 20, 1850; married William T. Gardiner.

§ 410. ABIGAIL HAZARD, 6 (Thomas, 5; Jonathan, 4; Thomas, 3; Robert, 2; Thomas, 1), was born December 25, 1751; she married Walter Watson; he was born May 7, 1752, and died May 1, 1808; she died February 2, 1837.

CHILDREN

CHILDREN

773. WALTER WATSON, died young.
774. ISABELLA WATSON, born in 1785 ; died Jan. 9, 1858 ; married, as second wife, *John J. Watson.* For children, see *No. 375.*
775. ABBY WATSON, born June 22, 1792; died March 31, 1843 ; married *Wilkins Updike,* son of *Lodowick* and *Abigail (Gardiner) Updike,* of Cocumscussuc, Wickford.

§ 415. MARY HAZARD, 6 (Thomas, 5 ; Jonathan, 4 ; Thomas, 3 ; Robert, 2 ; Thomas, 1), was born August 24, 1758 or 1759. (The original record found in the old family Bible is indistinct.) The name was entered as Susanna, but was afterwards changed to that of Mary, after the death of Mary, her elder sister. She died September 18, 1841. Her tombstone reads, "in her 85th year," which is perhaps inaccurate. She married William Cole, son of John Cole, and great-grandson of John and Susannah (Hutchinson) Cole. The Coles were prominent in the country, and owned a large estate in North Kingstown. William inherited the homestead farm, with the manor-house, he to provide for his mother, and pay all legacies. Both he and his wife are buried on the farm. He died August 7, 1823.

CHILDREN

776. JOHN COLE.
777. ANN COLE, born in 1785 ; died Aug. 27, 1874 ; married, Jan. 5, 1806, *Elisha Watson.*
778. ABBY COLE ; married *Warren Gardiner.*
779. SARAH COLE.
780. WILLIAM COLE ; married *Lydia Gerry.*
781. MARY COLE ; married *William Watson.*

§ 416. THOMAS RHODES HASZARD, 6 (Thomas, 5 ; Jonathan, 4 ; Thomas, 3 ; Robert, 2 ; Thomas, 1), was born in Rhode Island, March 1, 1762, at nine o'clock at night ; he died November 30, 1839, at Prince Edward Island. He married, May 8, 1796, Jane Bagnall ; she died December 27, 1840. This line writes the name *Haszard.*

CHILDREN

782. JAMES DOUGLAS HASZARD, born June 27, 1797; died Aug. 17, 1875 ; married, 1st, *Sarah Sophia Gardiner* (his cousin), Jan. 27, 1825 ; 2d, *Susanna Jane Nelmes,* Oct. 29, 1835.
783. ELIZABETH HASZARD, born March 29, 1799 ; unmarried.
784. THOMAS RHODES HASZARD, born April 17, 1801 ; unmarried.
785. GEORGE HASZARD, born April 23, 1803 ; died June 17, 1824.
786. CHARLOTTE JOANNA HASZARD, born July 20, 1807 ; died July 1, 1890.

§ 417. EUNICE HASZARD, 6 (Thomas, 5 ; Jonathan, 4 ; Thomas, 3 ; Robert, 2 ; Thomas, 1), was born February 14, 1764, in Rhode Island ; she died March 9, 1832 ; she married, in Rhode Island, John Gardiner ; he died in Prince Edward Island, January 5, 1842.

CHILDREN

787. WILLIAM HASZARD GARDINER, born in Rhode Island, April 25, 1786 ; married, Feb. 7, 1811, *Ann Clark;* died in Charlottetown, Prince Edward Island.

788.

788. Sarah Gardiner, born at St. John's (Prince Edward) Island, Dec. 4, 1789.
789. Anna Matilda Gardiner, born May 29, 1791 ; married *James Bagnall.*
790. Thomas Gardiner, born May 8, 1796.
791. Bowdoin Gardiner, born May 8, 1796.
792. John Rhodes Gardiner, born April 24, 1798 ; married, 1st, about 1821, in Rhode Island, *Mary Gardiner ;* 2d, *Mary Hooper,* daughter of Major *Hooper,* a refugee from New Jersey.
793. George Scott Gardiner, born Sept. 9, 1800; died young.
794. Sarah Sophia Gardiner, born March 17, 1804 ; died Sept. 27, 1827.
795. Maria Waitstill Gardiner, born April 7, 1806 ; married *Thomas Hooper.*
796. Eunice Susannah Gardiner, born May 13, 1809 ; married *Joseph Pippy.*

§ 419. WILLIAM HASZARD, 6 (Thomas, 5 ; Jonathan, 4 ; Thomas, 3 ; Robert, 2 ; Thomas, 1), was born in Rhode Island, May 3, 1767 ; removed to St. John's (now Prince Edward) Island in 1785. He purchased two hundred and seventy acres of land, in the year 1792 (situate about three miles from Charlottetown). On part of the land, afterwards called " Bellevue," he settled in the following Spring (1793). He died March 14, 1847. He married, in London, Ann Farrant Jones, of London. The marriage settlement is dated March 11, 1797. She *[signature]* (1804) was born February 14, 1780, and died Jan. 18, 1858.

Children

797. Harriet Clarissa Haszard, born Sept. 28, 1798 ; died Feb. 4, 1841 ; married, Jan. or Feb., 1827, *William Compton;* he died Nov. 6, 1847.
798. Sarah Louisa Haszard, born May 20, 1800 ; died Jan. 18, 1871 ; married, Sept. 22, 1831, *William Cundall;* he died May 13, 1876.
799. Millicent Castle Haszard, born April 19, 1802 ; died in Oct., 1802.
800. Millicent Castle Haszard (2), born Aug. 10, 1803 ; married, Jan. 18, 1827, *William Hodges;* she died May 8, 1855 ; he died Jan. 26, 1857.
801. Waitstill Douglas Haszard, born Nov. 5, 1805 ; died April 23, 1844 ; unmarried.
802. William Jones Haszard, born July 12, 1808 ; he emigrated with all his family to New Zealand, by brig " Prince Edward," which sailed from Charlottetown, Nov. 30, 1858. He returned alone to Prince Edward Island, arriving Nov. 21, 1876, and died April 18, 1879, at Neil Stewart's, Harbor's Mouth.
803. Charles Haszard, born Feb. 29, 1812 ; married, Nov. 28, 1843, *Margaret Longworth.* He died June 4, 1862 ; she died Aug. 29, 1881.
804. Henry Bowdoin Haszard, born Dec. 8, 1813 ; died Nov. 24, 1872 ; married, Feb. 10, 1846, *Hannah Catherine Cameron;* she died June 20, 1889.
805. John Haszard, born March 4, 1816 ; died May 8, 1878 ; married, 1st, March 20, 1836, *Amelia McNutt;* she died April 6, 1860 ; 2d, Feb. 11, 1869, *Jane Davenport Davies.*
806. Ann Farrant Haszard, born Jan. 29, 1823 ; still living ; married, 1st, Jan. 22, 1857, Rev. *Andrew Lockhead;* he died Jan. 12, 1864 ; 2d, March 31, 1868, Rev. *William Ross Frame;* he died June 30, 1888.

§ 421. WAITSTILL CURTIS HASZARD, 6 (Thomas, 5 ; Jonathan, 4 ; Thomas, 3 ; Robert, 2 ; Thomas, 1), was born in Rhode Island, March 12, 1772 ; removed to St. John's (now Prince Edward) Island, in 1786 ; she died May 22, 1804 ; she married, January 31, 1789, James Douglas, Controller of Customs for Prince Edward Island. He died September 26, 1803.

Children

CHILDREN

807. SARAH DOUGLAS, born March 27, 1790 ; married Major *Edward Michael Dewend.*
808-9. MARY DOUGLAS, born June 4, 1791 ; married *Robert Brown.*
810. MARGARET DOUGLAS, born May 18, 1793.
811. SAMUEL JAMES DOUGLAS, born Nov. 7, 1794.
812. MARGARET DOUGLAS (2), born Oct. 20, 1796.
813. JOHN DOUGLAS, born Dec. 31, 1797 ; married —— *Gordon.*
814. SUSANNA WILSON DOUGLAS, born June 29, 1801.
815. WAITSTILL EUNICE DOUGLAS, June 15, 1803.

§ 431. JONATHAN J. HAZARD, 6 (Jonathan J., 5 ; Jonathan, 4 ; Thomas, 3 ; Robert, 2 ; Thomas, 1), was born in 1759 ; he married, December 29, 1781, Tacy Burdick, of Charlestown, Rhode Island, daughter of Edward and Thankful Burdick. She was born in 1755. Mr. Hazard, like his father, was an active man in the affairs of the town and Colony. He was often chosen representative of the town of Charlestown, and intrusted with commissions by the Colony. He did not, like the other children, follow his father to New York, but lived and died on his farm in Charlestown. He died in 1807.

CHILDREN

816. JONATHAN HAZARD, 3d, born about 1782 or 1783 ; died at sea. He was a sea-captain.
817. GEORGE V. HAZARD ; married *Miriam*, daughter of *John Potter*, of Rhode Island.
818. DANIEL SHERMAN HAZARD (commonly called *Sherman Hazard*) ; married *Susan Meek.*

§ 432. GRIFFEN BARNEY HAZARD, 6, (Jonathan J., 5 ; Jonathan, 4 ; Thomas, 3 ; Robert, 2 ; Thomas, 1), was born in 1765 ; died in 1822. He was the driver of an army-wagon in the Revolutionary War, though then but a mere lad. He was a man of energy and enterprise, and was much employed in public offices. He moved to Milo Center, Yates County, New York, in 1797 ; here he built a large dwelling-house, still standing ; a saw-mill in 1811, and a gristmill in 1812. From thence he moved to Starkey (near Dundee, Reading), about 1818. He left a large estate at his death, including seven hundred acres of land. He married, about 1792, Mary, daughter of James Parker, who died in 1845.

CHILDREN

819. JAMES PARKER HAZARD, born in 1794 ; died in 1866 ; married *Pamela Little.*
820. PATIENCE HAZARD, born in 1795 ; married, 1st, *John Walton ;* 2d, *Nicholas Yott ;* he died in 1862.
821. PENELOPE HAZARD ; died young.
822. JONATHAN J. HAZARD, born in 1799 ; married *Elizabeth Lake.*
823. GEORGE W. HAZARD, born in 1801 ; died in 1844 ; married, in 1822, *Sarah Card.*
824. ELIZABETH HAZARD ; married *George J. Wheeler.* She died young, leaving a daughter, who married Dr. *W. S. Crane.*
825. JOSEPH H. HAZARD.
826. THOMAS JEFFERSON HAZARD, born in 1807 ; married, in 1852, *Susannah Champlin*, daughter of *Jeffrey Champlin.*
827. CATHARINE HAZARD.

§ 433. JOSEPH HOXSIE HAZARD, 6 (Jonathan, 5 ; Jonathan, 4 ; Thomas, 3 ; Robert, 2 ; Thomas, 1), was born June 16, 1777 ; he died October 12, 1838.

1838. He moved, with his father, "Beau Jonathan," to Verona, New York, about 1806. He accumulated a large fortune there, and built a beautiful house near Penn Yan. His descendants speak of him as a man of noble appearance, and of great physical strength. His character seems to have been as strong and symmetrical as his person, unswervingly honest and courageous. He married, in Rhode Island, January 21, 1808, his second cousin, Amey Williams. She died September 25, 1871.

CHILDREN

828. JONATHAN HAZARD.
829. AMY SUSAN HAZARD, born Nov. 14, 1808 ; died March 6, 1838.
830. DANIEL WILLIAMS HAZARD, born in Rome, New York, Feb. 29, 1812; married, Nov. 13, 1837, *Ann E. Dyre*, his cousin ; he died June 27, 1888.
831. PATIENCE ANN HAZARD, born Jan. 29, 1814 ; died March 4, 1819.
832. ABBY M. HAZARD, born May 8, 1816 ; died in Kansas, Dec. 25, 1881 ; married —— *Williams*.
833. SARAH M. HAZARD, born March 3, 1818 ; married —— *Woodworth ;* died Sept. 16, 1887.
834. JOSEPH W. HAZARD, born July 5, 1820 ; died Nov. 8, 1860.
835. CAROLINE A. HAZARD, born Oct. 25, 1822 ; married —— *Lee*.
835*a*. ELIZA E. HAZARD, born April 6, 1825 ; died Aug. 6, 1825.

§ 436. ABIGAIL HAZARD, 6 (Jonathan J., 5 ; Jonathan, 4 ; Thomas, 3 ; Robert, 2 ; Thomas, 1) ; married, as his third wife, Enoch Sherman.

CHILDREN

836. PATIENCE SHERMAN ; married *George Vosbinder ;* died young.
837. ELISHA W. SHERMAN, married *Pamela*, daughter of *Lewis Sutherland*.

§ 438. JOSIAH HAZARD, 6 (William, 5 ; Caleb, 4 ; Colonel George, 3 ; Robert, 2 ; Thomas, 1), was born December 20, 1748 ; he married Mary ——.

CHILD

838. DAMARIS HAZARD, born Jan. 6, 1782.

§ 440. WILLIAM HAZARD, 6 (William, 5 ; Caleb, 4 ; Colonel George, 3 ; Robert, 2 ; Thomas, 1), was born March 21, 1753 ; married —— Perry.

CHILD

839. EDWARD HAZARD ; married, April 13, 1773, *Susannah Havens*, of North Kingstown, Rhode Island.

§ 444. ABIGAIL HAZARD, 6 (Doctor Robert, 5 ; Caleb, 4 ; George, 3 ; Robert, 2 ; Thomas, 1), was born August 29, 1753 ; she married, September 11, 1780, Jared Starr, of New London, Connecticut ; he was born in 1745, and died at Groton, Connecticut, in 1839.

CHILDREN

840. MARY STARR, born July 1, 1781 ; died Sept. 16, 1869 ; married *Samuel Greene*.
841. ROBERT STARR, born Aug. 11, 1783 ; died Jan. 20, 1808, in Demerara, West Indies.
842. CHARLES STARR, born Oct. 28, 1785 ; died July 17, 1817, in Demerara, West Indies.
843. GEORGE STARR, born June 14, 1787 ; died Aug. 4, 1869, in New York.

844.

844. HENRY STARR, born Dec. 22, 1788 ; died Sept., 1789, in New London, Connecticut.
845. NANCY STARR, born July 5, 1790 ; died when an infant.
846. ELIZABETH STARR, born June 23, 1791 ; died Oct. 20, 1861 ; married, about 1815, *Gilbert Saltonstall.*
847. FRANCIS HENRY STARR, born Aug., 1793 ; died April 3, 1836, in New London, Connecticut.
848. NANCY STARR, born Jan. 11, 1796 ; died Dec. 19, 1869 ; married Hon. *Hume R. Field.*

§ 445. ESTHER HAZARD, 6 (Doctor Robert, 5 ; Caleb, 4 ; George, 3 ; Robert, 2 ; Thomas, 1), was born July 26, 1755 ; she died March 25, 1831 ; she married, December 25, 1775, Silas Niles (probably son of Ebenezer and Abigail (Hazard) Niles. She married, second, March 5, 1805, Captain Jared Starr, her brother-in-law.

CHILDREN OF FIRST MARRIAGE

849. ROBERT HAZARD NILES, born Sept. 30, 1776 ; died in infancy.
850. MARY NILES, born Jan. 13, 1779 ; died in 1868 ; married *Ezekiel Watson Gardiner.*
851. WILLIAM NILES, born Aug. 3, 1780 ; lost at sea in 1819.
852. ELIZABETH NILES, born Dec. 7, 1784 ; died June 30, 1833.
853. CHARLES NILES, born June 30, 1786 ; died July 31, 1855, at Holly Springs, Mississippi.

§ 447. SYLVESTER GARDINER HAZARD, 6 (Doctor Robert, 5 ; Caleb, 4 ; George, 3 ; Robert, 2 ; Thomas, 1), was born July 27, 1760 ; he died February 14, 1812 ; he married, March 5, 1786, Elizabeth, daughter of Richard and Sarah Greene.

CHILDREN

854. RICHARD HAZARD, born March 7, 1787 ; died at sea, March 7, 1811.
855. HARRIET HAZARD, born 1788 ; died May 15, 1856.
856. ELIZA HAZARD, born May 5, 1790 ; died May 5, 1874 ; unmarried.
857. HENRY HAZARD, born April, 1792 ; died 1871 ; married, May 12, 1812, *Eliza Essex ;* she was born May 25, 1790, and died in 1857.
858. ESTHER HAZARD, born Oct. 1, 1793 ; died April 26, 1874 ; married, Aug. 15, 1815, *Edmund Bailey.*
859. HANNAH HAZARD, born May 26, 1796 ; died Feb. 9, 1878.
860. LUKE HAZARD, born Oct. 20, 1797 ; died June 9, 1878 ; married *Julia Miller,* who died June 15, 1835, at East Greenwich, Rhode Island.
861. JOB HAZARD.
862. ABBY HAZARD ; married *Jonathan Remington.*
863. LYDIA HAZARD, born Feb., 1802 ; died July 1, 1802.
864. MARY ANN HAZARD, born Feb., 1802.
865. ROBERT HAZARD, born 1807 ; died Sept. 11, 1811.

§ 449. CHARLES HAZARD, 6 (Doctor Robert, 5 ; Caleb, 4 ; George, 3 ; Robert, 2 ; Thomas, 1), was born July 24, 1766 ; he married, February, 1795, Ann Bours, of Newport ; she died at New London, Connecticut, October 17, 1810.

CHILDREN

866. JARED HAZARD, born 1798 ; died 1833, in Charleston, South Carolina. He was mate of the schooner " *Anjenora.*"

867.

867. CHARLES COURTLAND HAZARD, born 1800; died Nov., 1857, in Mobile. He was a merchant; he married *Cornelia Livingston*.
868. JOHN BOURS HAZARD, born in 1802; died Sept., 1833, in St. Stephen, Alabama; he married *Mary F. Ayott*.
869. ABBY HAZARD, born Nov. 3, 1804; married *Henry Snow*, of Alabama.
870. CAROLINE HAZARD, born Nov. 3, 1806; died Jan. 20, 1866, in Syracuse, New York.
871. ANN BOURS HAZARD, born 1809; married *William Hampton*, of Alabama.

§ 450. FRANCIS HAZARD, 6 (Doctor Robert, 5; Caleb, 4; George, 3; Robert, 2; Thomas, 1), was born in 1769; he died in 1814. He was born in South Kingstown, Rhode Island, and moved to New London, Connecticut. He married, in New London, Rebecca Truman. By this marriage, he became connected with a family who had for two or three generations been conspicuous in the commercial enterprise of the town.

CHILDREN
872. MARIA HAZARD, born in New London, 1799; died in 1864; unmarried.
873. HENRY TRUMAN HAZARD, born 1801; died of yellow fever, on the Ohio River, 1827.
874. ELIZABETH HAZARD, born 1803; died 1880; married Dr. *George Keifer*, of Ohio.
875. ROBERT HAZARD, born in 1805; died 1865; married *Sarah M. Greene*; he died at Lake Providence, Louisiana.
876. CHARLOTTE HAZARD, born 1807; died 1880, at Troy, Ohio.
877. GEORGE STARR HAZARD, born Dec. 5, 1809; married *Sarah Mercer*, daughter of Dr. *Archibald Mercer*, of New London, Connecticut.
878. WILLIAM SYLVESTER HAZARD, born 1812; died 1890; married *Marion*, daughter of Colonel *Snelling*, who built the fort of that name in Minnesota, in 1819; she died 1881.

§ 451. GEORGE HAZARD PECKHAM, 6 (Mary Hazard, 5; Governor George, 4; Colonel George, 3; Robert, 2; Thomas, 1), was born April 14, 1739; he married, January 7, 1763, Sarah, daughter of Robert and Rebecca (Coggeshall) Taylor, of Newport, Rhode Island. She died June 13, 1795; he died November 26, 1799.

CHILDREN
879. SARAH PECKHAM; married *Wheeler Watson*.
880. ABIGAIL PECKHAM; died unmarried.
881. REBECCA PECKHAM; married *Robert Potter*, son of *John Potter*.
882. BENJAMIN PECKHAM, born Oct. 22, 1773; married, Jan. 28, 1799, *Abigail*, daughter of *Benedict* and *Betsey (Ladd) Oatley*.
883. GEORGE PECKHAM; married —— *Lawton*.
884. CARDER PECKHAM; married *Achsa Brown*.
885. WILLIAM PECKHAM.

§ 452. JOSEPHUS PECKHAM, 6 (Mary Hazard, 5; Governor George, 4; Colonel George, 3; Robert, 2; Thomas, 1), was born February 11, 1742; he married, May 25, 1774, Mary, daughter of Hezekiah Babcock. He died March 27, 1814; she died March, 1807.

CHILDREN

CHILDREN

886. MARY PECKHAM, born May 27, 1793; married *Richard Ward Hazard.*
887. BENJAMIN PECKHAM.
888. HEZEKIAH PECKHAM.
889. JOSEPHUS PECKHAM; married *Mary Champlin.*
890. GEORGE PECKHAM; married, Nov. 14, 1805, *Betsey Cornell.*
891. WILLIAM PECKHAM.
892. HANNAH PECKHAM, born May 17, 1795; married *Freeman Perry,* grandson of Judge *Freeman Perry.*

§ 453. SARAH PECKHAM, 6 (Mary Hazard, 5; Governor George, 4; Colonel George, 3; Robert, 2; Thomas, 1), was born in 1744; she died in 1775; she married, January 13, 1761, John Robinson, son of Deputy-Governor William Robinson; he was born January 13, 1742-3; and died June 23, 1805; he married, second, Hannah, widow of —— Mumford, and daughter of Matthew and Abigail (Gardiner) Stewart, and great-granddaughter of Governor Winthrop. By this marriage he had one son, James Robinson.

CHILDREN

893. BENJAMIN ROBINSON, born Aug. 5, 1763; married *Elizabeth,* daughter of Deputy-Governor *George Brown.*
894. SARAH ROBINSON, born Dec. 10, 1764; married, Feb. 14, 1782, *Samuel Tabor,* of Waterford, Connecticut, who was born Oct. 29, 1750, and died Sept. 6, 1798.
895. WILLIAM ROBINSON, born April 25, 1766; married, March, 1802, *Phebe Dennison,* of Stonington, Connecticut.
896. JOHN ROBINSON, born Dec. 16, 1767; married *Abigail,* daughter of *James* and *Ann (Rodman) Robinson,* who was born 1768, and died 1805; he died 1831, in New Brunswick, New Jersey. They were first cousins.
897. SYLVESTER ROBINSON, born July 12, 1769; died 1807; married *Eliza,* daughter of *John* and *Marcia (Pell) Rodman,* of Pelham Manor, Westchester County, New York.
898. THOMAS ROBINSON, born May 5, 1771; died 1786.

CHILD OF SECOND MARRIAGE

899. JAMES ROBINSON.

§ 455. WILLIAM PECKHAM, 6 (Mary Hazard, 5; Governor George, 4; Colonel George, 3; Robert, 2; Thomas, 1), was born in 1752; he died May 19, 1820; he married Mercy, daughter of James and Mercy (Potter) Perry. She died July 24, 1810. He married, second, Dorcas Perry; she died July 15, 1831.

CHILDREN OF FIRST MARRIAGE

900. SARAH PECKHAM, born Nov. 28, 1777; married, Feb. 12, 1794, *Acors Rathbun.*
901. ALICE PECKHAM, born Jan. 19, 1780; married, Oct. 14, 1801, *Rowland Rathbun.*
902. WILLIAM PECKHAM, born Nov. 11, 1781; married, Feb. 13, 1803, *Susannah Stanton.*
903. MERCY PECKHAM, born July 11, 1783; married, Nov. 8, 1809, *John Bigland Dockray.*
904. DORCAS PECKHAM, born Feb. 7, 1787; married, Jan. 28, 1813, *Hezekiah Babcock,* of Dartmouth, Massachusetts. He was son of *Caleb* and *Waite Babcock,* of South Kingstown.
905. PERRY PECKHAM, born June 30, 1789.
906. ELIZABETH PECKHAM, born Dec. 9, 1792; died March 1, 1878; unmarried.
907. MARY PECKHAM, born March 27, 1795; died Jan. 27, 1827.

§ 456.

§ 456. MARY PECKHAM, 6 (Mary Hazard, 5; Governor George, 4; Colonel George, 3; Robert, 2; Thomas, 1). She married, October 17, 1780, Doctor Joshua Perry, son of Judge Freeman and Mercy (Hazard) Perry. He was born 1756, and died November, 1801. He was surgeon in Colonel Church's battalion of Newport, King's and Bristol Counties, in 1781. He and his wife were first cousins.

CHILDREN

908. SARAH PERRY, married Dr. *Joseph Comstock.*
909. ABBY PERRY, married *Thomas Rose.*
910. ELIZABETH PERRY, married *John Boss,* a lawyer of Newport.
911. MARTHA PERRY, married *James,* or *Joshua Barker.*

§ 457. PELEG PECKHAM, 6 (Mary Hazard, 5; Governor George, 4; Colonel George, 3; Robert, 2; Thomas, 1), was born June 11, 1762. He inherited from his father, Benjamin Peckham, land in Matunuck, on which he built, in 1784, a large house, and a store attached, as the custom then was. The house is standing to-day, a good specimen of the old-time mansion-house, so often mentioned in the wills of the last century. Here Peleg Peckham carried on a small business in connection with his farming, and dispensed to his neighbors the usual assortment of goods found in a country store, not forgetting the indispensable New England rum, without which a house or barn could not be raised, a man buried, or a child born. Near the close of the last or the beginning of the present century, he moved to Rensselaerville, New York, selling his house and farm to Doctor George Hazard, his cousin. Mr. Peckham was a member of the Society of Friends, among whom he held a prominent position. In 1784, "Nailor Tom Hazard" records in his diary that Peleg Peckham brought his mother "here," and adds, "I carried her to meeting behind me on horseback." She was then sixty-two years of age. He married, August 25, 1785, Desire, daughter of John Watson, Jr.

CHILDREN.

912. ELIZABETH PECKHAM, born in South Kingstown, July 25, 1786; married *Elijah Griggs,* a merchant in Rensselaerville, New York.
913. RUFUS WHEELER PECKHAM, born Sept. 27, 1789; died young; unmarried.
914. PELEG BENJAMIN PECKHAM, born July 17, 1792; married *Laura Griggs,* Oct. 4, 1814. He settled in Utica, New York.
915. GEORGE WILLIAMS PECKHAM, born in Rhode Island, Feb. 24, 1796; married *Mary,* daughter of *John Watson;* died 1873.
916. MIRANDA PECKHAM; married *Brockholst Livingston.*
917. WALTON HAZARD PECKHAM; married *Margaret A. Milderburger,* widow of *Robert Stuyvesant.* They had two children, viz.: *Margaret Augusta,* born in Aug. 1840, who married *Gabriel Mead Tooker,* and died in Rome, Feb., 1888, and *Walton Milderburger,* who married M. *Louise Chesebrough.*
918. RUFUS WHEELER PECKHAM, born Dec. 20, 1809; married, 1st, *Isabella,* daughter of the Rev. Dr. *Lacey;* 2d, *Mary Foote.*
919. HENRIETTA PECKHAM; married *Joseph S. Colt.*
920. ORIN PECKHAM; married —— *Thompson.*

§ 458.

§ 458. EDWARD HAZARD, 6 (Mayor George, 5 ; Governor George, 4 ; Colonel George, 3 ; Robert, 2 ; Thomas, 1), was born about the year 1746. He graduated from either Princeton or Rhode Island College (Brown University). After he left college, he was for a number of years a clerk in the store of Aaron Lopez, in Newport. His father left him the farm now known as the Foddering Place, in South Kingstown ; this estate was squandered away in his over-indulgence to an intemperate son. When his estate was gone, he moved from Newport to South Kingstown, and, with his wife and son, lived in the house now owned and occupied by the heirs of the late Nicholas Northup, on the old Kingston road. He brought, with his family, some of the elegant furniture that once adorned his Newport house ; also three portraits by Copley, of the Hon. Thomas Cranston, his wife and daughter. Mr. Hazard became so much reduced in circumstances that it was decided to remove him to the Town Asylum ; but death kindly gave him a narrow, but more honorable home. After his death, the fine old furniture was sold at public auction, and many pieces are still to be seen in the town, showing what the whole must have been. In some way the portraits escaped, and were left in the house. Many years afterwards, as Doctor Johnson, of Kingston, was returning from an early visit, in passing the house his horse shied, and came very near throwing him from his saddle. As this was a most unwonted proceeding of his staid beast, the Doctor dismounted and sought the cause, and, as he said, he was startled almost as much as his horse had been, to see a stately dame gazing at him from a canvas. The family had set the portrait outside their door, to be washed off by the rain, as there had been a slight summer shower. It was commonly used for a fire-board. Doctor Johnson, on his return home, went to see his old friend, Wilkins Updike, to recount the experience of the morning. Mr. Updike, who knew that such portraits were in existence, sent his daughter Mary to examine these, and prove their identity. The woman of the house was glad to be rid of the troublesome things, and was very willing to accept Miss Updike's offer to relieve her of the care of them. One was found in a chamber, pushed under the bed. As Thomas Cranston Hazard, son of Edward, was at that time living in Voluntown, Connecticut, in great poverty, Mr. Updike went to see him, and telling him what he had done about the portraits, asked him to sell them to him, which he gladly did.

Edward Hazard married, May, 1770, Sarah, daughter of Hon. Thomas Cranston, and great-granddaughter of Governor Samuel Cranston, of Newport, Rhode Island. She died June 6, 1821, aged seventy-two years. He died March 22, 1830.

CHILD

921. THOMAS CRANSTON HAZARD. He graduated from Rhode Island College in 1792.

This line closes here.

§ 460. SARAH HAZARD, 6 (Mayor George, 5 ; Governor George, 4 ; Colonel George, 3 ; Robert, 2 ; Thomas, 1), was born in 1750 ; she was baptized in 1751 ; she married, first, April 18, 1775, Captain Daniel Gardiner, son of Nathan Gardiner ;

Gardiner; he was a sea-captain, and on one of his visits to his home, his vessel being in port, he was drowned while fishing from the rocks on the shore; his body was recovered, and Doctor Jonathan Easton was called on the inquest; he took with him George Hazard, then a medical student in his office. The handsome young student succeeded so well in comforting the widow that she gave him her heart, her hand, and her three children. She was ten years older than her husband, but possibly more beautiful at forty than at eighteen. They were married in October, 1790. She had no children by her second husband.

CHILDREN OF FIRST MARRIAGE

922. FRANCES GARDINER; married, April, 1800, *John Hazard*, son of *John* and *Sarah (Gardiner) Hazard*; married, 2d, his brother, *Nathan G. Hazard*.
923. MALBONE GARDINER.
924. NILES GARDINER.

§ 461. GEORGE W. HAZARD, 6 (Mayor George, 5; Governor George, 4; Colonel George, 3; Robert, 2; Thomas, 1), was born March 30, 1758; he died November 6, 1834. He was unlike the old type of the family in characteristics and in physical development. He was scarcely five feet four inches in height, yet extremely agile in movement. He was called "Crazy George," because of his many eccentricities. He used to say: "My father was a money-getting man, he raked the money in, and I can pitchfork it out faster than he raked it in," — rather an ignoble ambition. He entered college quite young and was to be educated like his brothers, but hostilities commencing between the Colonies and the Mother Country soon after he had entered, he ran away and joined the army, saying that he much preferred "following the God of War to courting the Muses." It can not be ascertained now which college had the privilege of erasing his name from its books; by one authority it was Princeton, by another Rhode Island College, but one fact that he used often to relate, ought to give the name of the College. A daughter of the President entered on a full college course the same year, and was graduated with honors, possibly not publicly. A man of unquestioned veracity, now living (1893), who was in his early days a shoemaker, relates that one morning Mr. Hazard came into his shop and ordered a pair of boots, "Fine boots," he said, "nothing on the common order, for I wish them to be buried in." He said that they must be finished and delivered on a certain day, as he was to be buried on that day. The man laughingly promised that they should be ready, and entered the order on his books with the stipulated time of delivery. On the day and date, as agreed, the boots were delivered, and "Crazy George" was buried. Perhaps the boots were buried with him, but on this point history is silent. This is one of those curious coincidences that suggests nothing and proves nothing, but is for a moment startling.

He married Martha, daughter of Christopher and Martha (Perry) Babcock. She was a cousin to her husband, but in this case not quite as nearly related as usual, although the connection was double.

CHILDREN

CHILDREN

925. SALLY HAZARD, born June 14, 1780; married *David Larkin.*
926. MARTHA HAZARD, born Jan. 25, 1782; married *Marlbury* [*Marlborough ?*] *Stanton ;* he died Dec. 2, 1835.
927. BRENTON HAZARD, born Jan. 15, 1784; married *Ann G. Childs,* of Bristol.
928. GEORGE CHAMPLIN HAZARD, born July 4, 1787; married *Eliza Butter.*

§ 464. CARDER HAZARD, 6 (Mayor George, 5; Governor George, 4; Colonel George, 3 ; Robert, 2 ; Thomas, 1), was born in 1774 ; he died March 18, 1823. He settled in Norwich, Connecticut, and made a large fortune in business. He died young. His descendants speak of him as a man of fine physique, charming in manner as in person. Some old letters, carefully treasured by his descendants, illustrate somewhat the beauty of his domestic relations. The following was written soon after the death of his wife, to his friends in South Kingstown: —
" Some time has elapsed since I lost the only comfort of my life, the very best of wives, far dearer to me than my own life. She was beloved by every one, as was evidenced during her most distressing sickness of several months, which she bore with perfect composure and resignation, and retained her senses to the last moment ; for forty-five nights I never removed my clothes, and for months, night and day was out of her room scarcely for a moment ; yet with all that I could do, all that physicians could do, all that her numerous friends could do, could not keep her here to me a day longer. She died a week ago to-day, and left me a little son, by name, George Carder.
" As I have not seen the death of my beloved Sally noticed in the papers, I wish to have it done for my numerous friends in Rhode Island. My wife was in her thirty-fourth year, she died November 27, leaving five children. I have enjoyed fourteen years of true love ; never, no never was there her equal. My eldest child is twelve years old, and takes charge of my family, a remarkable child."
Mr. Hazard being a handsome man, was much courted, after his wife's death, by marriageable dames. His daughters were afraid that he would give them a stepmother ; he however assured them that he would never marry again as long as one of them remained at home as his housekeeper ; but he added, " If you all leave me, I will marry again if I am so old and feeble that I am obliged to be carried into church on a cot-bed."
These few facts are gleaned from correspondence with his great-granddaughter. He graduated from Rhode Island College, and commenced his married life in Middletown, Rhode Island, where several of his children were born. It was about 1809 that he moved to Norwich, Connecticut, and passed the remainder of his life in that city. He married, April 4, 1804, Sarah Coggeshall, of Boston ; she was called the most beautiful girl of her day. She had wonderful rich-brown hair, which at twenty-eight was as white and shining as silver.

CHILDREN

929. JULIA SOPHIA HAZARD, born in Middletown, Rhode Island, Feb. 6, 1806; married *Abiel Sherman.*
930. WILLIAM COGGESHALL HAZARD, born in Middletown, Rhode Island, Aug. 15, 1807; died Nov. 6, 1807; buried in Middletown.

931.

931. ANGELINE MARGARET HAZARD, born in Norwich, Connecticut, Jan. 3, 1810.
932. ALMIRA JANE HAZARD, born in Norwich, Connecticut, Aug. 11, 1811; died at Norwich, Connecticut, Feb. 16, 1884.
933. SARAH ELIZA HAZARD, born in Norwich, Connecticut, March 5, 1813; died at New York, July 3, 1858; unmarried.
934. CARDER HAZARD, born in Norwich, Connecticut, Sept. 3, 1815.
935. GEORGE CARDER HAZARD, born in Norwich, Connecticut, Oct. 18, 1817; he died March 5, 1840. When about eighteen years of age, he was thrown from his horse, receiving injuries that eventually caused his death. He was a young man as beautiful in person as in mind, with gentle, graceful manners. He was the idol of his sisters. A quaint and old-fashioned obituary notice, evidently from the hand of his old pastor, is here given as a tribute to his goodness: "Died, in this town, on the 5th inst., at the residence of Mrs. *A. B. Sherman* (his sister), Mr. *George Carder Hazard*, aged 22, only son of the late Mr. *Carder Hazard*, of this town. If there is profit or usefulness in comment, or a consolation in sympathy, in no instance can that tribute be more justly due than at present. The long-protracted illness under which the deceased suffered for about four years, is well known; but the extraordinary fortitude and patience, which he has exercised under his sufferings and confinement, is not only worthy of remark, but, for one of his years, of the highest admiration; during the whole of the time, and under all circumstances, he was never known to complain, but gave up his own will with entire faith and confidence and resignation to the will of his Heavenly Father, in full hope and trust in His unbounded wisdom, love, and mercy. The ardent sympathy of his human friends is sufficient evidence of one among many of a peculiar trait of his character, that of treating and speaking well of all, whether present or absent. His kind and generous heart, and gentle, manly deportment, have left a deep impression on the affections of a great number of friends and relations both at home and abroad; and the grief especially of those of the family, from which he has been taken, can be described only by those who have a heart to feel. . . . Much might be said of the manly bearing and excellent qualities of young *Hazard*, but suffice it to say, in the language of another, 'The grave never closed on a nobler youth than *George Carder Hazard*.'

> " ' *I stay not to gather the lone ones of earth,*
> *I spare not the young in their gay dreams of mirth,*
> *But I sweep them all on to their home in the grave,*
> *I stop not to pity, I stay not to save.*' "

§ 465. NATHANIEL HAZARD, 6 (Mayor George, 5; Governor George, 4; Colonel George, 3; Robert, 2; Thomas, 1), was born in 1776; he died December 17, 1820. He graduated from Brown University about 1792. In 1818, he was a member of the General Assembly and Speaker of the House. In 1820, he was a Representative in Congress; he died in office, and was buried in the Congressional burying-ground. He was an eloquent speaker, and much admired for this gift by his contemporaries. There is now in existence a programme, printed by the order of the House of Representatives, of the funeral services, which seem to have been observed with great solemnity.

He, like all the sons of Mayor George Hazard by his second wife, was a man of fine physical development and great personal beauty; he had the misfortune in early life to lose one of his hands by the accidental discharge of his gun. The loss was supplied by one very artistically made of cork. This hand he used so skillfully that his wife never knew that the hand he offered her was removable until after her marriage. He married, November 2, 1801, Sarah, daughter of

Judge

Judge Fales, of Taunton, Massachusetts. She was, like all her sisters, beautiful. She was engaged to be married to George DeWolfe, of Bristol, Rhode Island; but, just before the wedding-day, she eloped with Nathaniel Hazard. Singularly enough, two of her children married two of the children of DeWolfe's family.

CHILDREN

936. SAMUEL HAZARD ; married *Martha,* daughter of *Charles DeWolfe,* of Newport, Rhode Island ; he died 1865.

937. GEORGE HAZARD ; died young ; unmarried.

938. WILLIAM HAZARD ; died about 1879 ; married —— *Nailor,* of Missouri.

939. SARAH HAZARD ; married *Charles,* son of *Charles DeWolfe,* of Newport.

940. JANE HAZARD ; married *David Bugbee,* of Bangor, Maine.

§ 469. THOMAS HAZARD, 6 (Judge Carder, 5 ; Governor George, 4 ; George, 3 ; Robert, 2 ; Thomas, 1), was born December 5, 1761 ; died November 1, 1834. He was called Thomas C. Hazard, which was equivalent to Thomas, son of Carder ; he was also called " Fiddle-head Tom," because of the peculiar shape of his head. He married, first, January 3, 1790, —— Browning ; he married, second, January 8, 1812, Eliza, daughter of Thomas Arnold, of Newport. His second wife was a beautiful and accomplished woman, and a great favorite in the society of her native town. Even in middle age she was much admired, especially by the young, who loved to listen to her tales of the gay life led in Newport, and read the notes and love-letters addressed to her by men whose names are historic. Two playing-cards are even now in existence, — one, the two-spot of clubs, bears, written on the back : " Lord Percy asks the favour of Miss Eliza Arnold's company to a Ball at the Crown Coffee House, on Saturday, the 18th of January, being His Majestie's birthday." On the

back of a six-spot of clubs is written : " Lord Howe's compliments to you, and requests the honour of your company to a Ball at the Assembly Rooms on Monday, the 19th Instant."

CHILDREN OF FIRST MARRIAGE

941. JOSEPH HAZARD ; married *Rubama Champlin.*

942. SUSAN HAZARD ; married Judge *Nathan Kenyon.*

§ 470. GEORGE HAZARD, 6 (Judge Carder, 5 ; Governor George, 4 ; George, 3 ; Robert, 2 ; Thomas, 1), was born April 13, 1763 ; he died September 29, 1829. After a few years at school in Plainfield, Connecticut, he commenced the study of medicine under Judge Freeman Perry, who was a skilful physician and surgeon, as well as a judge. He afterwards studied with Doctor Jonathan Easton, of Newport, and after a regular course, was graduated at the Medical School in Philadelphia. (These facts have been extracted from his son, Edward Hazard, with some difficulty, being thrown in as slight episodes, during interesting discourses on his favorite theme, Lions, or rather Heroes, and therefore the order of

Doctor

Doctor Hazard's studies may not be exact; an attempt to bring Mr. Hazard back to the desired subject being answered by, "Will you be quiet and let me talk; I am a hero-worshipper.") Of course this is not intended as a history of Doctor Hazard, but is only given as a memorandum for future reference.

Doctor Hazard married, first, his cousin Sarah, widow of Captain Daniel Gardiner, and daughter of Mayor George Hazard, of Newport. She was several years older than Doctor George, but he remedied this as far as possible, by carefully cutting from his father's family Bible the record of his birth, a heroic and chivalrous act, which should place him among his son's "Heroes." Mrs. Hazard died a few years after her marriage, leaving no children. He married, second, December 25, 1804, Mary Hoxsie. She died March 30, 1806, leaving one daughter. He married, third, May 16, 1807, Jane, daughter of Robert Hull, a remote cousin. Mrs.

Jane Hazard was a remarkable woman in many ways, energetic and capable. She was left with a large family of children, the youngest being but eight years old; her resources were not large, but yet she brought up her family well, and gave them all a good education. Her features were more strong than beautiful, yet her husband when asked, "Whom do you consider the handsomest woman in the town?" always answered, "Jane Hazard." She was an interesting woman in conversation, even in extreme age: one always felt a little wiser on leaving her than one had been before the meeting. She was a shrewd observer and possessed great tact. She made no enemies, and one was apt to feel better satisfied with himself after a conversation with "Friend Hazard." She was a little proud of her heavy brown hair, that showed but few threads of silver, even at eighty years of age.

After her husband's death, she joined the Society of Friends (having always had a strong leaning in that direction), and was a worthy member of the Society.

Her son-in-law, Mr. Attmore Robinson, used to tell with delight a story of taxing his mother's patience to its utmost capacity. He drove with her one fine, cool morning to Wickford, a distance of twelve miles, to see an old friend. The drive gave Mrs. Hazard a good appetite, and when dinner was served the "*pièce de résistance*" proved to be a delicious boiled ham; Mr. Robinson was asked to carve the ham, and, willing to show how well he could carve, he cut the slices so thin that one could easily see through them; Mrs. Hazard was helped as often as she dared to be helped, and as she afterward assured him, left the table hungry. When they were well on their way home, she took him to task, saying, "Attmore, when thee cuts ham for a hungry person, thee must never cut it thin."

She was very fond of flowers. Her little garden, of which she was proud, and of which she took the entire charge, was a mass of color from the early tulip to the late chrysanthemum. She allowed no one to work in her garden but herself,

for

for fear that some carefully nursed weakling might receive too rough handling. In the early morning, and in the late afternoon, a dark brown patch in the garden, if looked at steadily, would resolve itself into a long cloak and Quaker bonnet, within which was Mrs. Hazard, busily engaged in pulling the weeds from her loved flowers; nothing that she ever planted, died.

For several years before her death she lived with her daughter, Mrs. Attmore Robinson, and as her grandchildren love to tell, she kept a little twig behind the tall old clock, with which she "tingled" their fingers when disobedient. She was a strict disciplinarian, and often said, "Children must be made to obey or they will end on the gallows"; the word gallows, as she spoke it, was a mystical word of fearful portent to the younger children, and they wondered what sort of a thing this was upon which they were to end their days. Another axiom of hers was, that children must be taught to work: "A man who is ashamed to work with his hands, will never amount to anything" was an often repeated assertion. She died January 18, 1862.

CHILD OF SECOND MARRIAGE
943. MARY HOXSIE HAZARD, born March 20, 1806; died March 6, 1808.

CHILDREN OF THIRD MARRIAGE.
944. WILLIAM HENRY HAZARD, born Feb. 12, 1808; married, March 15, 1840, *Louisa*, daughter of *Lemuel* and *Sally* (*Lyman*) *Arnold*. She was born April 25, 1820.
945. CARDER HAZARD, born Aug. 20, 1809; married *Eliza*, daughter of *Elisha* and *Ann* (*Cole*) *Watson*.
946. JANE HAZARD, born Dec. 5, 1810; married Dr. *Daniel Howland Greene*.
947. EDWARD HULL HAZARD, born Sept. 29, 1812; unmarried.
948. GEORGE HAZARD, born Aug. 25, 1813; died Feb. 12, 1864.
949. MARY HOXSIE HAZARD, born March 10, 1815; married Rev. *James Carpenter*.
950. LAURA HAZARD, born Nov. 4, 1819; married *Attmore Robinson*.
951–61. ALICE JOANNA FITZGERALD HAZARD, born Sept. 7, 1821; died April 11, 1881; unmarried.

§ 473. RICHARD WARD HAZARD, 6 (Judge Carder, 5; Governor George, 4; George, 3; Robert, 2; Thomas, 1), was born November 1, 1770; he died December 2, 1844; he married Mary, daughter of Josephus Peckham. She died September 27, 1869. He was a very worthy man, a farmer, and lived and died on his farm in Matunuck. He was for years an honored member of the Baptist communion, and was always in his seat on Sunday morning, with a pew full of children. Late in life, when the children were stalwart men and healthy pleasant-faced women, the seat was always full, with Mr. Hazard at the head. His usual dress was a blue coat with brass buttons, but in the winter he wore a long brown surtout, with a high collar. This dress gave him a distinctive personality, making him seem like a man left over from another generation, and also (be it added) making him seem the best-dressed man in church. He had a fine face, fair, with blue eyes, — a face to be trusted. He was respected by his townspeople, possibly for negative, rather than positive qualities; but he was a good type of the honest, upright country gentleman.

CHILDREN

CHILDREN
962. BENJAMIN HAZARD, died in infancy.
963. ELIZABETH HAZARD, died in infancy.
964. MARY HAZARD, married *John Nichols*.
965. JOSEPH HAZARD, born Sept. 14, 1814; married Jan. 7, 1847, *Susan Congdon*.
966. DANIEL HAZARD, unmarried.
967. JOSHUA HAZARD, born Nov., 1820; died Jan. 19, 1877; unmarried.
968. ALICE HAZARD, married *Jonathan Allen*.
969. HANNAH HAZARD, born Oct., 1827; married, 1st, *Hezekiah Babcock*; 2d, *Jonathan Allen*.
970. CHARLOTTE HAZARD, died aged fifteen years.
971. JANE MARIA HAZARD, died aged five years.

§ 476. SARAH HAZARD, 6 (Judge Carder, 5; Governor George, 4; George, 3; Robert, 2; Thomas, 1), was born May 13, 1780; she died January 10, 1852; she married, January 2, 1807, Peter Clarke; he was born in 1788.

CHILDREN
972. JAMES E. CLARKE, born March 3, 1809.
973. CARDER HAZARD CLARKE, born July 21, 1811; married *Hannah Allen*.
974. PETER CLARKE, born March 12, 1815.
975. NICHOLAS CLARKE, born 1818; died Sept. 2, 1844, unmarried.

§ 477. ALICE HAZARD, 6 (Judge Carder, 5; Governor George, 4; George, 3; Robert, 2; Thomas, 1), was born May 13, 1780; she died December 25, 1831; married, September 18, 1800, George Congdon. After her death he married Sarah Robinson Hazard, daughter of Thomas H. Hazard and his wife Abigail (Robinson) Hazard. He had no children by his last wife.

CHILDREN OF FIRST MARRIAGE
976. CARDER HAZARD CONGDON; unmarried.
977. MARY CONGDON; married *Lee Perkins*.

§ 500. JOSHUA PERRY, 6 (Mercy Hazard, 5; Oliver, 4; George, 3; Robert, 2; Thomas, 1), was born in 1756; he died November, 1802; in 1871 he was appointed surgeon in Colonel Church's battalion. Mr. Perry married, October 17, 1780, Mary, daughter of Benjamin and Mary (Hazard, daughter of Governor George) Peckham. For children, see *Nº. 456*.

§ 502. CHRISTOPHER RAYMOND PERRY, 6 (Mercy Hazard, 5; Oliver, 4; George, 3; Robert, 2; Thomas, 1), was born December 4, 1761; he died June 4, 1818. He served with distinction during the Revolutionary War, upon armed vessels fitted out in the Colonies.
There is a tradition, well authenticated, that during the war he was sent out on a foraging expedition in his native town, South Kingstown. A very respectable man, by the name of Tucker, resisted the authority of the boy-captain (for he could not have been over seventeen or eighteen years of age at the time), and Perry discharged his gun, killing the man. He was obliged to flee for his life from the enraged relatives of Tucker, and ran his horse to the South Ferry. He was for a great many years after this rather timid about visiting his native town,

town,—so reads the story; but he married, in 1784, and his first child was born in the town. In June, 1798, he was appointed a Captain in the United States Navy, to command the frigate *General Greene*, and was commissioned a captain March 1, 1799, to rank from the first date. He was discharged under the Peace Establishment Act of April 3, 1801, and was subsequently Collector of Internal Revenue for Newport, Bristol, etc., in Rhode Island.

In the *Rhode Island American*, July 31, 1812, is this notice: "Captain Christopher R. Perry is appointed to succeed Captain Bainbridge as Superintendent of the United States Navy Yard, at Charlestown, Massachusetts, the latter being required to take command of the frigate *Constellation*, now refitting at Washington." He married, August, 1784, Sarah Alexander. She came from Scotland in Captain Christopher Perry's vessel, and the acquaintance thus formed ripened into love and marriage. Soon after the marriage they lived in the house of William Rodman, then but recently built,—a large, commodious house, still standing in the village of Rocky Brook. William Rodman was a bachelor, and lived with them. He was a well-read, well-informed man, and excellent company, exceedingly quick at repartee; but occasionally he was a little merry after dinner, from the effects of good wine. On these somewhat rare occasions, Mrs. Perry would place her hand on Mr. Rodman's arm and say, very gently, "William, I think thee had better go to thy room for a little rest." "William" always went away as meekly as a lamb, with a parting bow to the ladies, and a merry twinkle in his eyes. Christopher Perry's first child, Oliver Hazard Perry, was born in this house.

In 1798, Robert Rodman was married to Elizabth Hazard, and they also lived in their uncle's house where their first child, Samuel, was born, in 1800. When the child was a few days old, Captain Christopher Perry being at the house to see "Cousin Elizabeth," and glancing round the room (the large west chamber), said, "My son Oliver was born in this room."

In 1793, his father gave Christopher Raymond Perry ten acres of his homestead farm in Matunuck, and at his death the remaining part of the farm, "where I now live." It is possible that the family of Christopher Perry lived with his father several years before he came into possession of the farm in 1813, as Commodore Oliver Hazard Perry always spoke of the place as his early home, and of Judge William Peckham, who lived on the next farm, as his early playmate and companion.

CHILDREN

978. OLIVER HAZARD PERRY, born Aug. 20, 1785; married, May 5, 1811, *Elizabeth Champlin Mason*.

979. RAYMOND PERRY, born Feb. 11, 1789; died March 2, 1826; married, May 16, 1814, *Mary Ann*, daughter of *James DeWolfe*, of Bristol, Rhode Island; she married, Oct. 4, 1826, Gen. *W. H. Summer*, of Massachusetts. Perry was a lieutenant in the United States Navy, and had two sons and one daughter.

980. SARAH WALLACE PERRY, born April 28, 1791; died Jan., 1851; unmarried.

981. MATHEW CALBRAITH PERRY, born in Newport, April 10, 1794; died March 4, 1858; married, Dec. 24, 1814, *Jane*, daughter of *John Slidell*, of New York.

982.

982. ANN MARIA PERRY, born Nov. 10, 1797; died Dec. 7, 1856; married, July, 1815, Commodore *George W. Rogers*, United States Navy.

983. JANE TWEEDY PERRY, born Dec. 15, 1799; died July, 1875; married, Dec. 15, 1819, Dr. *William Butler*, surgeon United States Navy.

984. JAMES ALEXANDER PERRY, born June 26, 1801; he was drowned in the harbor of Valparaiso, March 9, 1822, while attempting to save the life of a friend. He was a lieutenant in the United States Navy. He was the "midshipman mite," who was on his brother Oliver's ship during the battle on Lake Erie, and who was slightly wounded in the beginning of the battle. When the terrible affray was over the Commodore anxiously sought the little brother, and found him curled up in his berth, fast asleep.

985. NATHANIEL HAZARD PERRY, born Nov. 27, 1802; married *Lucretia Mumford Thatcher*, of New London, Connecticut. He was purser in the United States Navy.

§ 503. ELIZABETH PERRY, 6 (Mercy Hazard, 5; Oliver, 4; George, 3; Robert, 2; Thomas, 1), was born August 20, 1762; she died March 12, 1811. She married, December 20, 1782, Stephen Champlin. He was the grandson of Stephen and Mary (Hazard, daughter of Robert, 4) Champlin, and the great-grandson of Jeffrey and Hannah (Hazard, daughter of Robert, 2) Champlin. This gives three strains of Hazard blood to her descendants, one of whom is now "the first lady of the land," Mrs. Grover Cleveland. Stephen Champlin removed to Lebanon, Connecticut, in 1795, where he remained until his death, and was buried there. He died July, 1848.

CHILDREN.

986. MERCY CHAMPLIN, born Sept. 19, 1783; died Aug. 14, 1857; married Rev. *James Rogers*, of Wheatland, New York.

987. WILLIAM B. CHAMPLIN, born Feb. 13, 1785; married *Olive Manning*.

988. ELIZABETH CHAMPLIN, born Dec. 2, 1786; married *Sherman Loomis*.

989. HANNAH CHAMPLIN, born June 19, 1788; died 1878; unmarried.

990. STEPHEN CHAMPLIN, born Nov. 17, 1789; married *Minerva Pomeroy*.

991. MARY PERRY CHAMPLIN, born April 17, 1791, in South Kingstown; died in infancy.

992. MAY PERRY CHAMPLIN, born Feb. 7, 1793; married, in Lebanon, Connecticut, *Gordon Bailey*.

§ 505. SUSAN PERRY, 6 (Mercy Hazard, 5; Oliver, 4; George, 3; Robert, 2; Thomas, 1). She married, as second wife, Elisha Watson, in 1784.

CHILDREN

993. FREEMAN PERRY WATSON, born May 16, 1787; married, Dec. 13, 1811, *Phebe*, daughter of *Job* and *Phebe* (*Weeden*) *Watson*.

994. SUSANNAH WATSON, born March 13, 1789; married *George Watson*, called "Bold Cæsar."

995. ELIZABETH WATSON, born June 24, 1790; married *Benjamin Brown*.

996. MIRIAM WATSON, born Oct. 30, 1793; married *Stephen Browning*.

§ 506. GEORGE HAZARD PERRY, 6 (Mercy Hazard, 5; Oliver, 4; George, 3; Robert, 2; Thomas, 1); married Abigail Cheesborough.

CHILDREN

997. GEORGE HAZARD PERRY.

998. FREEMAN PERRY; married *Hannah Peckham*. To him was given his grandfather *Freeman Perry's* books on surveying.

There

There is no record of the birth of these children other than the mention of their names in their grandfather's will.

999. GIDEON PERRY, born in South Kingstown, Oct. 11, 1800; died in Hopkinsville, Kentucky, Sept. 30, 1879; married *Abby*, youngest daughter of *Nathan Stewart*, of Brookfield, New York; she died July 14, 1887, aged eighty-two years. He graduated from Hamilton College, New York. In addition to his first degree, those of D.D. and LL.D. were conferred upon him, and, after a course of study and lectures in medicine and surgery, he received the degree of M.D. from Jefferson College, Philadelphia, Pennsylvania. They had four children : *Oliver Hazard Perry*, M.D., deceased ; Rev. *Henry G. Perry*, M.A., of Chicago ; *Willis G. Perry*, and *Emily B. Perry*.

§ 508. JONATHAN NICHOLS HAZARD, 6 (Stephen, 5; Stephen, 4; Stephen, 3; Robert, 2; Thomas, 1), was born October 18, 1761; he died in 1802; he married, May 12, 1785, Mary, daughter of Sylvester and Alice (Perry) Robinson. She was born in 1763, and died in 1837, and was buried in the old family burying-ground at Point Judith, which was laid out by Governor William Robinson as a final resting-place for himself, his sons, grandsons, and descendants for all time. It was on that part of his farm that he gave to his son William Robinson, who sold it to Sylvester, his brother, in 1770–1. Governor William was possibly the first man buried here, in 1751. Unfortunately, a great-grandson, moved by a spirit of progress, translated the mouldering bones of his ancestor to a village cemetery, and one by one the bodies of the sons of Governor William have been moved, until only his son John is left, with his young wife beside him. The property has long since passed from the possession of the Robinson family, but the old graveyard, with its substantial stone wall, remains a monument to the provident care of Governor William for his posterity.

CHILDREN

1000. JAMES ROBINSON HAZARD, born Feb. 10, 1789; married *Sarah Barney*.
1001. ALICE ROBINSON HAZARD, born Dec. 12, 1790; died Jan. 1, 1837; unmarried. She was buried in the Robinson family burying-ground, Point Judith.
1002. STEPHEN HAZARD, born Sept. 10, 1792.
1003. JONATHAN NICHOLS HAZARD, born Jan. 16, 1795; married *Mary Congdon*.
1004. SYLVESTER ROBINSON HAZARD; married *Alice*, daughter of *Robert Hull*.
1005. MARY A. HAZARD, born July 3, 1799; died April 6, 1855, unmarried; buried at Point Judith, in the family burying-ground.

§ 512. NICHOLS HAZARD, 6 (Stephen, 5; Stephen, 4; Stephen, 3; Robert, 2; Thomas, 1), was born March 11, 1770; he died May 13, 1848; he married Phebe Anthony. Mr. Hazard was well known by a large number of people who made his "Inn" their home when in Newport. He was a most popular landlord, and his house was known far and wide for its good cheer, as well as for the kindly reception by its master. His kindness to old friends who had not means to pay for their entertainment is well known. He had a few pensioners of this kind, who had orders from him to come every day, and were as well placed and served as his most distinguished guests. Of his large family, not one married, so that this line closes with the death of his last child.

CHILDREN

CHILDREN
1006. ALICE HAZARD, born 1801 ; died March 11, 1868 ; unmarried.
1007. MARY HAZARD, born July 16, 1805 ; died Nov. 5, 1883 ; unmarried.
1008. PHEBE HAZARD, born July 12, 1807 ; unmarried.
1009. RUTH HAZARD, born Feb. 11, 1809 ; died Sept. 9, 1882 ; unmarried.
1010. SARAH HAZARD, born March 4, 1811 ; died Feb. 21, 1843 ; unmarried.
1011. HANNAH HAZARD, born April, 1813 ; unmarried.
1012. NICHOLAS HAZARD, born Nov. 21, 1815 ; died Nov. 21, 1836 ; unmarried.
1013. EDWARD HAZARD, born Feb. 9, 1820 ; died April 10, 1878 ; unmarried.

§ 525. SAMUEL J. POTTER, 6 (Elizabeth Hazard, 5; Stephen, 4; Stephen, 3; Robert, 2; Thomas, 1), was born about 1752. One year after his mother's marriage to John Potter, in her will, she calls "son Samuel J. Potter" "eldest son." Samuel J. Potter died in 1804. He was Deputy-Governor of the State from 1790 to 1799, when George Brown was elected Deputy-Governor over him, after a severe and close canvass. "This vote," says Mr. Updike, "drew the lines in this State between the two great political parties of the country; the Federalists, under Mr. Adams, and the Democrats, under Mr. Jefferson." Governor Potter, the Republican, now styled Democratic, candidate, succeeded Mr. Brown in 1800; and in 1801 the State became Republican, and remained so until the war of 1812. Governor Potter continued in office until 1803; he died the following year.

His father gave him a farm in Matunuck; this is what is now known as the John Babcock estate. It was sold to William Peckham, grandfather of Mr. Babcock. In the attic of the house, after it came into Mr. Peckham's possession, were found two portraits, supposed to be those of Governor Potter and his wife; they are now in the possession of Mrs. John Potter Sherman. His father gave him also a farm in Point Judith, where he lived and died. This is the farm now owned and occupied by George Pearse. He married Ann Seager. In his will he called John Seager "brother-in-law." He also mentions seven children by name. He died September 26, 1804.

CHILDREN
1014. SAMUEL J. POTTER.
1015. ANN POTTER.
1016. FENNER POTTER.
1017. MARY POTTER.
1018. JOSEPH POTTER.
1019. SARAH POTTER.
1020. ELIZABETH POTTER.

§ 526. STEPHEN POTTER, 6 (Elizabeth Hazard, 5; Stephen, 4; Stephen, 3; Robert, 2; Thomas, 1), was born about 1754; he died in 1793. He married, about 1772, Abigail, daughter of Christopher and Ruhamah Robinson. She was born in 1754, and died in 1803.

CHILDREN
1021. ROBINSON POTTER.

1022.

1022. ABIGAIL POTTER ; unmarried.
1023. A DAUGHTER, who married Capt. *Gardiner*, of Newport.
1024. A DAUGHTER, who married —— *Chadwick*.

§ 535. LUCY HAZARD, 6 (Joseph, 5 ; Governor Robert, 4 ; Stephen, 3 ; Robert, 2 ; Thomas, 1), was born July 6, 1766 ; she died September 23, 1804 ; married, December 25, 1801, Teddiman Hull.

CHILD
1025. LUCY HULL, born Sept. 7, 1804 ; married, July 28, 1834, *Harry Clarke*.

This line closes here.

§ 537. JOSHUA HAZARD, 6 (Joseph, 5 ; Governor Robert, 4 ; Stephen, 3 ; Robert, 2 ; Thomas, 1), was born October 7, 1771 ; he died November 12, 1823 ; he married, October 7, 1807, Elizabeth, daughter of Silas and Esther (Hazard) Niles. They were first cousins.

CHILDREN
1026. STANTON HAZARD, born April 21, 1809 ; died Aug. 16, 1892 ; married *Bethany Brattle Aborn*.
1027. EVAN MALBONE HAZARD, born Oct. 1, 1811 ; married, Jan. 25, 1836, *Jane Hume*.
1028. MARY NILES HAZARD, born Oct. 13, 1813 ; married, Nov. 5, 1831, *Ebenezer Dennison*.
1029. ROBERT HAZARD, born March 11, 1815 ; died June 8, 1815.
1030. ESTHER HAZARD, born May 30, 1817 ; died Aug. 31, 1851 ; married Capt. *Waterman Cliff*, of Mystic, Connecticut.
1031. CHARLES PHILLIPS HAZARD, born Nov. 25, 1820 ; died Oct. 17, 1847, at Memphis, Tennessee, *en route* for Mexico as First Lieutenant of Capt. *Little's* company of mounted volunteers, in the Mexican War.

§ 540. HANNAH HAZARD, 6 (Judge Joseph, 5 ; Governor Robert, 4 ; Stephen, 3 ; Robert, 2 ; Thomas, 1), was born August 10, 1778 ; she died August 26, 1827 ; she married, November 16, 1807, Doctor Stephen Griffen.

CHILDREN
1032. EVAN MALBONE GRIFFEN, born Jan. 4, 1809 ; died in infancy.
1033. JOSEPH HAZARD GRIFFEN, born July 25, 1810 ; died June 27, 1879.
1034. CHARLOTTE R. GRIFFEN, born Oct. 23, 1812 ; died Sept. 16, 1884 ; married, July 19, 1839, Capt. *William Montgomery*.
1035. HANNAH HAZARD GRIFFEN, born July 14, 1814.
1036. MARY C. GRIFFEN, born May 14, 1816 ; died April 5, 1886.
1037. STEPHEN AUGUSTUS GRIFFEN, born Aug. 21, 1818 ; married, July 27, 1856, *Eliza Card*.

§ 542. JONATHAN BABCOCK, 6 (Esther Hazard, 5 ; Governor Robert, 4 ; Stephen, 3 ; Robert, 2 ; Thomas, 1), was born May 30, 1762 ; he married, January 29, 1795, Ruth, daughter of Benjamin and Hannah (Niles) Rodman ; she died December 16, 1795. She was one of the six beautiful daughters of Mr. Rodman. Tradition says that a gentleman who had been a great traveller was once asked, "What is the most beautiful sight you have ever seen in your travels?" and he answered, "The six lovely daughters of Benjamin Rodman."
They

They were not only beautiful in person, but were gifted with good voices, and sang delightfully. Ruth was brought up in the village afterwards called Peacedale, in the old house which stood on the site of Mr. John Hazard's mansion-house. Her grandfather, Nathaniel Niles, built the old house, still standing near the village of Wakefield, called " Dalecarlia."

CHILD

1038. RUTH HANNAH BABCOCK, born Nov. 26, 1795 ; married, Oct. 20, 1831, *Solomon Harley.*

§ 543. ROBERT BABCOCK, 6 (Esther Hazard, 5 ; Governor Robert, 4 ; Stephen, 3 ; Robert, 2 ; Thomas, 1), was born December 18, 1763 ; he died February 11, 1848 ; he married, May 11, 1793, Mary Hazard, who was the daughter of " Long Stephen " Hazard.

CHILDREN

1039. JARED BABCOCK ; died Oct. 16, 1838 ; married, Dec. 7, 1817, *Diadema Douglass;* she died May 18, 1877.
1040. SARAH BABCOCK ; died May 21, 1870 ; married, June, 1833, *John Wiltrey,* of Hoboken, New Jersey.
1041. ESTHER BABCOCK ; married, May, 1825, *Robert Tripp.*
1042. NICHOLAS BABCOCK ; married *Maria Hamblin.*

§ 545. BENJAMIN HAZARD, 6 (Samuel, 5 ; Governor Robert, 4 ; Stephen, 3 ; Robert, 2 ; Thomas, 1), was born March 11, 1764 ; he died July 12, 1849 ; he married, April 4, 1804, Martha, daughter of " Long Stephen " Hazard.
Benjamin Hazard owned a farm in Westerly, Rhode Island, where he lived and died. According to the old custom, he set apart a piece of ground on his land for a family burying-ground, which he walled with heavy masonry, leaving a space for a gate. When he died, he left orders that when the last member of his family died, the gate should be removed and the opening be closed with solid masonry. When his daughter died, these instructions were carried out, and this line ends with the four graves within the four walls.

CHILDREN

1043. MARTHA HAZARD, born May 31, 1805; died July 15, 1889; unmarried.
1044. BENJAMIN HAZARD, born July 3, 1808; died May 10, 1876; unmarried.

§ 546. GIDEON HAZARD, 6 (Samuel, 5 ; Governor Robert, 4 ; Stephen, 3 ; Robert, 2 ; Thomas, 1), was born November 25, 1765 ; he died April 18, 1806. He married Elizabeth, daughter of " Long Stephen " Hazard ; they were first cousins. She died November 21, 1818.

CHILDREN

1045. JOHN G. HAZARD.
1046. JOSEPH STANTON HAZARD.

§ 548. ELIZABETH HAZARD, 6 (Samuel, 5 ; Governor Robert, 4 ; Stephen, 3 ; Robert, 2 ; Thomas, 1), was born December 2, 1769 ; she married July

25,

25, 1798, Atherton Wales ; he was born May 26, 1773. He was the son of Peter F. and Lydia (Potter) Wales.

CHILDREN
1047. ROUSE POTTER WALES, born July 21, 1802.
1048. LYDIA POTTER WALES, born May 17, 1804.

§ 560. LODOWICK HAZARD, 6 (Samuel, 5; Samuel, 4; Stephen, 3; Robert, 2; Thomas, 1); he married Susan, daughter of Doctor William Robinson, of Westerly, Rhode Island.

CHILDREN
1049. LODOWICK HAZARD.
1050. JAMES HAZARD.
1051. WILLIAM HAZARD.
1052. ABBY HAZARD.
1053. GEORGE HAZARD.
1054. NANCY HAZARD.

The sons of Lodowick Hazard [7] are settled in one of the islands of the Pacific Ocean.

§ 561. ROBERT HAZARD, 6 (Samuel, 5; Samuel, 4; Stephen, 3; Robert, 2; Thomas, 1). There is a record of but one child.

CHILD
1055. SAMUEL HAZARD. He was a clergyman.

§ 564. ABBY HAZARD, 6 (Samuel, 5; Samuel, 4; Stephen, 3; Robert, 2; Thomas, 1); she married Ichabod Taylor.

CHILDREN
1056. ROBERT TAYLOR.
1057. DUDLEY TAYLOR.

§ 568. ESTHER HAZARD, 6 (George, 5; Samuel, 4; Stephen, 3; Robert, 2; Thomas, 1), was born in Newport, Rhode Island, about 1775; she married, October 22, 1803, Benjamin Pearce.

CHILDREN
1058. GEORGE PEARCE; lived at Bristol, Rhode Island.
1059. WALTER PEARCE.
1060. JOHN PEARCE ; lived at Newport, Rhode Island.
1061. JAMES PEARCE.
1062. CATHARINE PEARCE, married —— *Liscomb.*

§ 574. HANNAH HAZARD, 6 (George, 5: Samuel, 4; Stephen, 3; Robert, 2; Thomas, 1), she married, first, May 12, 1822, John Newman ; she married, second, Erastus P. Allan, son of William S. N. Allan.

CHILDREN
1063. ABBY ALLAN.

1064.

1064. WILLIAM S. N. ALLAN, married ——— *Lyon.*
1065. ERASTUS P. ALLAN, married *Sarah Barker.*

§ **576.** THOMAS HAZARD, 6 (Stephen, 5; Thomas, 4; Stephen, 3; Robert, 2; Thomas, 1), was born probably about 1760. There is no record of his birth, but as he was the eldest child the above date is not far from correct; he married about 1782, Silence, daughter of Hazard and Margaret (Congdon) Knowles. In early life he was a sea-captain, but towards the latter part of the last century he lived in Peacedale, and improved what is known as the "Broad Rock Farm," now owned by Rowland Hazard, and even then owned by ancestors of Mr. Hazard. This land has for nearly two hundred years been in possession of this branch of the family, having been handed down from father to son by will or deed. In about 1814, Thomas Hazard removed with his family to Columbia, Connecticut, but his children were all born in Rhode Island. His wife Silence died November 25, 1827, aged sixty-eight years.

CHILDREN
1066. WILLIAM HAZARD, born 1785; died at Columbia, Connecticut, July 28, 1849.
1067. MARGARET HAZARD, died October 20, 1812.
1068. MARY HAZARD, married, June 22, 1807, *John Knowles.*
1069. STEPHEN HAZARD, married *Abby Knowles,* sister of *John.*
1070. ROUSE HAZARD, married, and left several children.
1071. ELIZA HAZARD, unmarried.
1072. STANTON HAZARD, married ——— *Gridley.*
1073. AUGUSTUS GEORGE HAZARD, born April 28, 1802; died May 7, 1868; married, July 24, 1822, *Salome Goodwin Merrill.*

§ **577.** MARY HAZARD, 6 (Stephen, 5; Thomas, 4; Stephen, 3; Robert, 2; Thomas, 1), was born in 1765; she died May 20, 1857, aged ninety-two years. She married, January, 1781, Joseph Oatley, son of Benedict and Betsey (Ladd) Oatley. He died November 29, 1815.

CHILDREN
1074. MARY OATLEY, died young.
1075. HANNAH OATLEY, born Nov. 6, 1783; married *Rodman Carpenter.* She was a member of the Society of Friends, sat on the "High Seat," and often preached eloquent sermons, peculiar for their good, practical common-sense. Even to this day there are people living who remember these sermons, and the advice given under the head, "Be thou not a stumbling block in the way of thy neighbours."
1076. BETSEY OATLEY, born Feb. 16, 1786; married *Jonathan Carpenter.*
1077. NANCY OATLEY, born March 28, 1788; married, after the death of her sister *Betsey, Jonathan Carpenter.*
1078. JONATHAN OATLEY, born July 7, 1790; married, May 29, 1813, *Mary,* daughter of *Joseph Champlin.* He was ordained a preacher in the Baptist Church in Wakefield, Rhode Island, and preached more or less during his life. He lived to be nearly ninety years old. When he was over seventy-five years of age, he walked from Connecticut to South Kingstown, stopping to visit relatives and friends on the way.
1079. JOSEPH OATLEY, born Sept. 13, 1793; married, 1823, *Eliza Wells,* of West Hartford, Connecticut.
1080. STEPHEN OATLEY, born June 10, 1796; married *Mary,* daughter of *Jonathan Carpenter.*

1081.

1081. MARY OATLEY, born Aug. 28, 1798; married, April 28, 1816, *Stephen Congdon.*
1082. SUSAN OATLEY, born May 2, 1803; married, 1st, *Davis Mumford;* 2d, *Isaac Hopkins.* She is still living (Feb. 25, 1894).
1083. ROUSE OATLEY, born July 30, 1806; died Feb. 8, 1812.

§ 581. ELIZABETH HAZARD, 6 (Stephen, 5; Thomas, 4; Stephen, 3; Robert, 2; Thomas, 1), was born about 1783; she married, July, 1799, Robert Rodman, son of Robert and Margaret (Carpenter) Rodman. He was born May 18, 1774, and died April 1, 1838; she died May 6, 1870.

CHILDREN
1084. SAMUEL RODMAN, born May 3, 1800; died May 9, 1882; married, 1st, *Mary Peckham;* 2d, *Mary Anstis Updike.*
1085. ELIZABETH RODMAN, born July, 1801; married *Henry Money.*
1086. ABBY RODMAN, born May 21, 1804, died May 31, 1829; married *Thomas Hiscox.*
1087. SARAH RODMAN, born Sept. 19, 1805; died Aug. 10, 1845; married *William Knowles.*
1088. AMOS PEASLEY RODMAN, born 1806; married *Clarissa Allen.*
1089. PENELOPE RODMAN, born March 24, 1807; died May 1, 1856; married *Daniel Gould.*
1090. BENJAMIN RODMAN, born Sept. 13, 1808; died April 15, 1860; married *Hannah Brown.*
1091. HANNAH RODMAN, born 1815; married *Erasmus D. Campbell.*
1092. ANN RODMAN, married *Lorenzo Hall.*
1093. ROBERT RODMAN, born 1820; married *Mary Gardiner.*

§ 582. THOMAS HAZARD, 6 (Jeremiah, 5; Jeffrey, 4; Robert, 3; Robert, 2; Thomas, 1), was born in 1753; he died February 15, 1815; he married Lucy Congdon; she was born in 1763, and died December 30, 1807. In 1804, he and his wife Lucy gave a deed of Dutch Island to Hazard Knowles.

CHILDREN
1094. ABBY HAZARD, born in 1789, married, 1st, Jan. 30, 1806, *Hazard Knowles;* married, 2d, *Elder Chapin.* She died June 8, 1865, aged seventy-six years, nine months.
1095. ARNOLD HAZARD, born 1792; died March 19, 1856; married Hannah, daughter of *Job* and *Phebe (Weeden) Watson.*
1096. LUCY HAZARD.
1097. JEREMIAH HAZARD.

§ 525. MARY BROWNING, 6 (Susannah Hazard, 5; Jeffrey, 4; Robert, 3; Robert, 2; Thomas, 1). She married, October 20, 1777, Thomas Hoxsie.

CHILDREN
1098. HAZARD HOXSIE, born June 17, 1782; married, Dec. 25, 1806, *Chloe Bailey*, of Lebanon, Connecticut.
1099. MARY HOXSIE, born April 28, 1786.

§ 586. JEFFREY HAZARD, 6 (Robert, 5; Jeffrey, 4; Robert, 3; Robert, 2; Thomas, 1), was born March 24, 1771; he died in 1828.

CHILD
1100. JOHN P. HAZARD, born 1804. He is alive (1893), and has two sons living in New York State.

§ 587.

§ 587. ROBERT HAZARD, 6 (Robert, 5; Jeffrey, 4; Robert, 3; Robert, 2; Thomas, 1), was born August 29, 1785; he married Abigail Seager. In her will, dated 1825, she mentions four children, in the order given below, to whom she gives " all my estate given to me by my father, John Seager; " her brother, Francis Seager, was executor.

CHILDREN

1101. JEREMIAH B. HAZARD, died July 23, 1883.
1102. JOHN S. HAZARD, born Feb. 14, 1816.
1103. JOSEPH P. HAZARD.
1104. HANNAH HAZARD, born 1820; married *Jesse Reynolds*.

§ 591. JOHN HAZARD, 6 (Robert, 5; Robert, 4; Robert, 3; Robert, 2; Thomas, 1), was born in 1766; he died in 1851.

CHILDREN

1105. ALICE HAZARD, born Aug. 2, 1788; died March 19, 1879; married *J. P. Stone.*
1106. ROBERT HAZARD, born June 26, 1790; died March 21, 1871; married, Dec. 28, 1815, *Amey*, daughter of Gov. *Jeffrey Hazard.*
1107. THOMAS T. HAZARD, born March 2, 1792; died Aug. 2, 1874.
1108. MARY HAZARD, born May 11, 1794; died May 3, 1815; unmarried.
1109. PHEBE THEODOSIA HAZARD, born Nov. 21, 1796; married *Easton Lewis.*

§ 592 JEFFREY HAZARD, 6 (Jeremiah, 5; Robert, 4; Robert, 3; Robert, 2; Thomas, 1), was born in 1762 and died in 1840; he married Amey, daughter of Thomas Tillinghast; she was born in 1773, and died June 3, 1870. His father, in his will, dated June 1, 1773, probated December 14, 1773, gives "my son Jeffrey all my lands lying in Exeter and in West Greenwich."
He was Lieutenant-Governor of the State from 1833 to 1835, and again from 1836 to 1837; he was also for many years Representative in the General Assembly, and Chief Justice of the Court of Common Pleas, and Judge of the Supreme Court from 1810 to 1818.

CHILDREN

1110. AMEY HAZARD, born 1791; died 1864; married *Robert*, son of *John Hazard.*
1111-2. THOMAS JEFFERSON HAZARD, born June 17, 1795; died Aug. 2, 1874.
1113. WILLARD HAZARD; married, April 4, 1826, *Mary Ann,* daughter of *George W. Hazard.*
1114. JOHN HAZARD; married *Margaret Crandall.*
1115. PHEBE HAZARD; married *Reuben Brown,* of Hopkintown, Rhode Island.

§ 594. JOHN HAZARD, 6 (Jeremiah, 5; Robert, 4; Jeremiah, 3; Robert, 2; Thomas, 1), was born August 24, 1749; he died November 26, 1832. He lived and died on a farm near Hammond's Mills, on land given to his grand-mother, wife of Robert Hazard [4], by her uncle, Benjamin Northup, by free deed of gift, dated November 17, 1747. He married, first, Abby Boss; she died about 1800. He married, second, Sarah Cranston.

CHILDREN OF FIRST MARRIAGE

1116. GEORGE HAZARD; married *Henrietta Freeborn.*

1117.

1117. JOHN BOSS HAZARD, born Feb. 17, 1778; died May 28, 1848; married *Mary Potter* ; she was born Aug. 31, 1774; died Oct. 21, 1838.
1118. RUTH HAZARD; married, 1st, *Daniel Bates;* 2d, *John Buckover;* 3d, ——— *Mitchell.*
1119. SARAH HAZARD, married *Elisha Gardiner.*
1120. PATIENCE HAZARD, born Jan. 30, 1784; died March 3, 1869; married, Nov. 5, 1802, *William Battey,* Jr.
1121. MARY HAZARD; married, 1st, *Henry Chapell;* 2d, *Edward Alb;* 3d, *Shadrach Card.*
1122. ABBY HAZARD, born June 24, 1789; died Feb. 21, 1864; married *Elisha B. Johnson.*
1123. HANNAH HAZARD, born 1790; died Nov., 1840; married *Benjamin Hammond.*
1124. JEREMIAH HAZARD, born Oct. 10, 1792; died Oct. 19, 1878; married *Harriet Moore.*
1125. CATHARINE HAZARD, born 1796; died Oct. 16, 1876; married *Edward Carr.*

CHILDREN OF SECOND MARRIAGE
1126. CALEB HAZARD, born June 24, 1804; married, 2d, *Susan Hazard.*
1127. BETSY HAZARD, born May 24, 1809; married *James Hight.*

## § 596. ROWLAND HAZARD, 6 (Jeremiah, 5; Robert, 4; Jeremiah ,3 ; Robert, 2 ; Thomas, 1), married Elizabeth, daughter of William and Chloe Hammond.

CHILDREN
1128. MARY HAZARD.
1129. ELIZABETH HAZARD; married *Nicholas Gardiner,* of Exeter.
1130. RUTH HAZARD; married *Elisha R. Potter,* of South Kingstown. In 1884 she was living at Norwich, Connecticut, with her son, *William Potter,* and was then ninety-four years old.
1131. ESTHER HAZARD.
1132. RODMAN HAZARD, born 1797; died Aug. 10, 1842; married, 1st, *Deborah Congdon;* 2d, *Martha Congdon.*

## § 597. WILBOR HAZARD, 6 (Jeremiah, 5; Robert, 4; Jeremiah, 3; Robert, 2 ; Thomas, 1), was born December 15, 1774; he married, in 1804, Mary, daughter of Benjamin Stanton, of South Kingstown. He died February 14, 1827. His wife was born December 14, 1786, and died October 15, 1876.

CHILDREN
1133. ANN HAZARD, born Feb. 12, 1805; married, Dec. 26, 1831, *Samuel C. Cottrell.*
1134. JEREMIAH HAZARD, born Oct. 12, 1807; married, Feb., 1857, ——— *Zubero,* of Mississippi.
1135. RENEWED HAZARD, born Feb. 22, 1808; married, Dec. 8, 1833, *Edward Slocum;* she died May 10, 1857.
1136. MARY HAZARD, born Sept. 25, 1810; married, 1837, *Benjamin Cottrell.*
1137. BENJAMIN HAZARD, born Aug. 25, 1812; married, March 19, 1840, *Charlotte Cole Atwood,* daughter of *Jeremiah* and *Izett Atwood,* of Warwick, Rhode Island.
1138. WILBUR HAZARD, born Feb. 27, 1814; married, Dec. 25, 1843, *Lydia,* daughter of *William* and *Abby (Sandford) Pierce.*
1139. RUTH HAZARD, born April 29, 1817; married, Oct., 1839, *John C. Gardiner.*
1140. SUSAN HAZARD, born June 10, 1819; died April 28, 1883.
1141. SAMUEL HAZARD, born Oct. 22, 1821; married, May 10, 1847, *Sarah,* daughter of *William D.* and *Mercy Pierce Cole,* of Warwick; he died April 29, 1878.
1142. DANIEL S. HAZARD, born Jan. 26, 1824; married, June 20, 1847, *Hannah S. Congdon,* daughter of *Benjamin S.* and *Mary Congdon,* of North Kingstown. They live in Providence, Rhode Island.

1143.

1143. WILLIAM HAZARD, born Jan. 22, 1827; he lives in Oregon, where he settled in 1852, after prospecting in the gold-mines of California.

§ 598. EASTON HAZARD, 6 (Ephraim, 5; Robert, 4; Jeremiah, 3; Robert, 2; Thomas, 1), was born September 13, 1783; he married Charlotte Bissell; and died September 2, 1826.

CHILDREN

1144. CHARLOTTE HAZARD, born Nov. 23, 1803.
1145. VARNUM HAZARD, born Oct. 5, 1805; died 1836.

§ 599. EPHRAIM HAZARD, 6 (Gideon, 5; Robert, 4; Jeremiah, 3; Robert, 2; Thomas, 1), was born Sept. 5, 1763; he died April 23, 1836; he married, first, Hannah, daughter of Richard Updike; she died June 22, 1808. He married, second, Mary Smith; she died in 1835.

CHILDREN OF FIRST MARRIAGE

1146. NANCY UPDIKE HAZARD, born Nov. 19, 1787; married *Henry Burlingame.*
1147. JAMES HAZARD, born May 15, 1794; died aged nineteen years.
1148. HANNAH HAZARD, born April 20, 1801; married *Ezekiel Reynolds.*

CHILDREN OF SECOND MARRIAGE

1149. MARY HAZARD, born Aug. 21, 1810; married, Feb. 21, 1830, *Samuel Pierce.*
1150. LOUISA HAZARD, born Nov. 24, 1814; died June 22, 1868; married *Ezekiel Pierce.*

§ 600. FREEBORN HAZARD, 6 (Gideon, 5; Robert, 4; Jeremiah, 3; Robert, 2; Thomas, 1), was born in 1765; he died August 29, 1831. He married Susan Sherman; she died March 11, 1829.

CHILDREN

1151. ROBERTSON HAZARD, born Aug. 27, 1785; married *Elizabeth Marshall.*
1152. STANTON HAZARD, born Aug., 1786; married *Phebe Bush.*
1153. SUSAN HAZARD, born Nov. 11, 1788; married *Stephen Hazard.*

§ 601. ROBERT HAZARD, 6 (Gideon, 5; Robert, 4; Jeremiah, 3; Robert, 2; Thomas, 1).

CHILDREN

1154. PELEG HAZARD, married *Mary Northup.*
1155. STEPHEN HAZARD, married his cousin, *Susan Hazard.*
1156. EDWARD HAZARD, married *Hannah Smith.*

§ 603. ELIZABETH HAZARD, 6 (Gideon, 5; Robert, 4; Jeremiah, 3; Robert, 2; Thomas, 1), was born December 7, 1795; she died October 20, 1868; she married Joseph Hammond, son of Benjamin.

CHILDREN

1157. ELIZA ANN HAMMOND, born 1816; married *Stephen G. Slocum.*
1158. JOSEPH WILLETT HAMMOND, born 1817.

1159

1159. Waity Frances Hammond, born 1820.
1160. Ruth Hammond, born 1824.
1161. Benjamin Franklin Hammond, born 1826.
1162. George Newton Hammond, born 1828.

## End of the Sixth Generation

# THE HAZARD FAMILY

## Seventh Generation

THOMAS HAZARD, 7 (Robert, 6; Thomas, 5; Robert, 4; Thomas, 3; Robert, 2; Thomas, 1), was born January 14, 1782; he married Lydia Rogers. The Christian name of the eldest son of this, the eldest branch of the family, alternated from Thomas to Robert for eight generations. When Robert [6] Hazard married, he carried his wife home to the house of his father, "College Tom" Hazard, on Tower Hill. "Nailor Tom" Hazard, in his oft-quoted diary, says, on the 13th of December, 1782: "Robert's wife very sick; I went for Granny Stedman." On the 14th he says, "Robert had a son born." A few days later he says, "Robert got a name for his son, last night, from his father." This addition to the family made it necessary for the house to be enlarged, and soon "Robert and I" are at work digging a trench for the addition to "Cousin Hazard's" house. "College Tom's" house was originally a "half house," with one side of the chimney exposed. The addition was put on this side of the house, making the chimney answer for the new part.

CHILDREN
1163. ROBERT HAZARD, married *Elizabeth Alexander.*
1164. RUFUS HAZARD, married, 1st, *Sarah Allen;* 2d, *Ruth Holmes.*
1165. SENECA HAZARD, married, 1st, *Elizabeth Allen;* 2d, *Persis Hoag.*
1166. ACHSAH HAZARD, married —— *Taber.*

§ 632. DAVID HAZARD, 7 (Robert, 6; Thomas, 5; Robert, 4; Thomas, 3; Robert, 2; Thomas, 1), married Sarah Rogers.

CHILDREN
1167. SARAH HAZARD.
1168. JOHN HAZARD.
1169. ANN HAZARD.

§ 634. SARAH HAZARD, 7 (Robert, 6; Thomas, 5; Robert, 4; Thomas, 3; Robert, 2; Thomas, 1), married Nicholas Holmes.

CHILDREN
1170. ROBERT HOLMES.
1171. TITUS HOLMES.
1172. JOHN HOLMES.
1173. MARY HOLMES.
1174. JULIA HOLMES.

§ 637.

§ 637. WILLIAM HAZARD, 7 (Robert, 6; Thomas, 5; Robert, 4; Thomas, 3; Robert, 2; Thomas, 1), married, first, Hannah Rogers; married second, Lucia Burrough.

CHILDREN

1175. WILLIAM B. HAZARD, born March 20, 1843; died May 17, 1888; married, April 21, 1868, *Gertrude M. Holmes.*
1176. ROBERT HAZARD.

§ 639. STEPHEN HAZARD, 7 (Robert, 6; Thomas, 5; Robert, 4; Thomas, 3; Robert, 2; Thomas, 1), married Sarah Odell.

CHILDREN

1177. GEORGE G. HAZARD.
1178. HENRY HAZARD.
1179. LYDIA HAZARD.
1180. ROBERT HAZARD.
1181. ELIZABETH HAZARD.

§ 640. THOMAS RODMAN HAZARD, 7 (Thomas, 6; Thomas, 5; Robert, 4; Thomas, 3; Robert, 2; Thomas, 1), married, in 1808, Margaret Avery, of Liverpool, England. He died near Cincinnati, Ohio, October 18, 1822.

CHILDREN

1182. ELIZA HAZARD, born 1810; married, 1826, *Allan Callom.*
1183. THOMAS R. HAZARD, born 1812; lost at sea in 1842.
1184. SAMUEL L. HAZARD, born 1813; married, 1840, *Olivia Woodman.*
1185. EDWARD HAZARD, born 1816; married, 1839, *Mary Anderson.*
1186. WILLIAM HAZARD, born 1818; died 1849.
1187. ROBERT HAZARD, born 1821; died 1865; married, 1842, *Eliza Mixer.*

§ 642. SARAH HAZARD, 7 (Thomas, 6; Thomas, 5; Robert, 4; Thomas, 3; Robert, 2; Thomas, 1), was born September 18, 1781, at Cranston, Rhode Island. At the close of the Revolutionary War she went to live with her grandmother, Mary Rodman, at Newport, where she remained until she was eight or nine years of age. She was her grandmother's favorite grandchild. It is without doubt due to this early association that she preserved the letters, papers and relics of that period. Though born in the midst of the Revolutionary struggle, scarcely any references are made to the stirring events of that period, either in the letters she has preserved or in the traditions which have been handed down to her descendants; for war was abhorrent to the creed of her family. Her grandmother Rodman, being an invalid in her old age, was unable to attend the receptions given to persons of distinction visiting Newport, and many of them called upon her. Her granddaughter remembers, among them, Washington's visit. Living with her grandmother, she saw a great deal of her mother's sisters, and from the many affectionate references to her in their letters, must have been a favorite with them.

After

After finishing her education at Newport, she joined her parents at New Bedford, where she remained until her marriage, visiting her grandmother Rodman at Newport, her grandfather Hazard at South Kingstown, her sister Mrs. Jacob Barker in New York, and her aunt, Mrs. Samuel R. Fisher, in Philadelphia. She married John H. Howland, November 3, 1803, at the Friends' Meeting House in New Bedford, before a large gathering of friends and relatives. Mrs. Howland had a great love for poetry and objects of art, but being a Friend did not enter much into the social amusements of New York, although, as her Journal would indicate, she was fond of travelling.

In person Mrs. Howland is described as being slightly over the medium height, with dark hair and eyes, resembling her grandmother Rodman, who was considered very beautiful. Mrs. Howland died suddenly, April 29, 1847, and was buried beside her husband.

John H. Howland, was born at the Round Hills farm, at Dartmouth, near New Bedford, Massachusetts, February 8, 1774. He was the sixth son of Gideon Howland and his wife Sarah, daughter of Captain Thomas and Judith Hicks. He spent his early days on his father's farm, but disliking the life of a farmer, ran away to sea at the age of fourteen, and before many years was in command of a vessel. He made many voyages to the West Indies in his brother Joseph's vessels, and by good management, about the year 1798, was able to begin business on his own account. In 1803 his name appears as a director in the Bedford Bank, of which his father-in-law, Thomas Hazard, Jr., was the first president. He was also one of the first directors of the Marine Insurance Company. He was named John Howland, but as there were so many of that name, about this time he signed himself " John H. Howland," the H. being for Hicks, the name of his mother. He married first, in 1800, Sylvia, daughter of Captain Isaac Howland; she died in 1802, leaving a son who died young ; he married Sarah Hazard in 1803, and about 1810 moved to New York, where he soon became prominent as a shipping merchant. His office was at 159 Front street, and his residence on the south-west corner of Broadway and Leonard street. Joseph Grinnell, a nephew of Mr. Howland, was his partner in 1810, the firm name being " Howland and Grinnell." Mr. Grinnell withdrew in 1815, forming a partnership with his cousin, Captain Preserved Fish. Mr. Howland continuing the business as " John Howland and Co." He subsequently admitted his son William to partnership, the firm being known as " John H. Howland & Son." [1]

Mr. Howland's summer house, at Bloomingdale, was on a high bluff overlooking the Hudson River (at what is now Eighty-sixth Street and Riverside Drive), with over ninety acres of lawn and gardens. Mr. Howland owned many vessels, among them being the ships " Martha Howland," " Mary Howland," and " William Howland," named after his children. The " Mary Howland " brought over the first English passenger locomotive engine used in this country, on the Mohawk and Hudson River Railroad. [1]

---

[1] Abridged from Howland Pell's Journal of Sarah Howland.

During

During the war of 1812, Mr. Howland subscribed for fifty thousand dollars of the war-loan, authorized by the United States Government, to raise funds for defence of the nation. Mr. Howland died highly esteemed by all who knew him, at his home in Eighty-sixth Street, New York, March 13, 1849.

CHILDREN

1188. MARTHA HAZARD HOWLAND, born at New Bedford, Mass., Dec. 12, 1804, died in New York, March 7, 1875; married *Thomas Hooker*.

1189. WILLIAM HAZARD HOWLAND, born at New Bedford, Feb. 3, 1807; died in New York, March 3, 1865; married, Nov. 3, 1841, *Annie M. West*, of South Carolina.

1190. ALGERNON SIDNEY HOWLAND, born at New Bedford, Feb. 10, 1809 ; died at New York, Aug. 23, 1813.

1191. MARY RODMAN HOWLAND, born in New York City, Nov. 26, 1810 ; married, March 12, 1830, *Morris*, son of *William Ferris Pell*, of New York, and *Mary Shipley*, of London.

1192. JOHN HOWLAND, born in New York, Nov. 2, 1812, and died there in 1870 ; married *Adele Flandon*.

1193. SARAH RODMAN HOWLAND, born in New York, Jan. 12, 1817 ; married, 1st, *David G. Gillies ;* 2d, *Samuel S. Osgood.* She has no children. Mrs. Osgood is interested in the condition of the colored people and the Indians, and has done much to help them.

§ 643. ELIZABETH HAZARD, 7 (Thomas, 6 ; Thomas, 5 ; Robert, 4 ; Thomas, 3 ; Robert, 2 ; Thomas, 1), was born December 2, 1783 ; she died December 29, 1866 ; she married, August 27, 1801, Jacob Barker, son of Robert and Sarah Barker. He was born December 17, 1779, and died December 26, 1871. She was buried in the Friends' Ground, in Brooklyn, Long Island.

CHILDREN

1194. ROBERT BARKER, born June 11, 1802 ; died Sept. 28, 1803.

1195. ROBERT BARKER, born July 20, 1804 ; died at sea, Dec. 24, 1830.

1196. THOMAS BARKER, born June 21, 1807 ; died 1876 ; unmarried.

1197. WILLIAM BARKER, born Aug. 21, 1809 ; died Sept. 17, 1879 ; married *Jeanette B. James*.

1198. ANDREW BARKER, born Nov. 11, 1811 ; died 1846 ; unmarried.

1199. ANNA HAZARD BARKER, born Oct. 25, 1813 ; married *Samuel Gray Ward*.

1200-1. JACOB BARKER, born May 23, 1816 ; died April 27, 1842.

1202. ELIZABETH HAZARD BARKER, born July 14, 1817 ; married, 1st, *Baldwin Brower ;* 2d, *William T. Van Zandt ;* 3d, *John McCaulis*.

1203. SARAH BARKER, born July 27, 1819 ; married, 1st, *John C. Harrison ;* 2d, *William H. Hunt*.

1204. ABRAHAM BARKER, born June 3, 1821 ; married, 1st, *Sarah Wharton ;* 2d, *Katharine Crane*.

1205. MARY BARKER, born June 27, 1823 ; died Jan. 9, 1826.

1206. JOHN WELLS BARKER, born and died Dec. 18, 1825.

§ 644. ANNA HAZARD, 7 (Thomas, 6 ; Thomas, 5 ; Robert, 4 ; Thomas, 3 ; Robert, 2 ; Thomas, 1), was born at Cranston, Rhode Island, June 24, 1786 ; she married, first, October 2, 1809, Philip J. Hone, of New York; she married, second, Charles Stephens, of Skidaway Island, Georgia, in 1821, and died there October 7, 1823.

CHILD

1207. JOANNA HONE, born June 26, 1811 ; died Feb. 20, 1837 ; married *Charles Kneeland*.

§ 649.

§ 649. THOMAS ROBINSON HAZARD, 7 (Rowland, 6; Thomas, 5; Robert, 4; Thomas, 3; Robert, 2; Thomas, 1), was born in South Kingstown, Rhode Island, January 3, 1797, and died in New York City. When quite a youth, he assisted his father in his mill, but as early as March 29, 1821, he bought of Abigail Rodman, widow of Robert Rodman, ten acres of land in the village of Rocky Brook; and at about the same date, March 25, 1821, he leased from Freeman P. Watson a water-right, with right to erect a dam and flow ten acres of land. The same year he made his reservoir, and built a small wooden mill that contained one set of machinery. The year following, he bought of his father, Rowland Hazard, seventy acres adjoining. He combined farming with his manufacturing business, raising large quantities of sheep; for this reason he was called "Shepherd Tom," a name with which he was much pleased. In 1838 he sold this property, having accumulated what at that time was considered a small fortune, and retired from active business, buying an estate in Newport, where the remaining part of his life was spent.

When over eighty years of age he wrote a book called *Recollections of Olden Times*. Possibly no book has been more thoroughly read in the South County than this one. The few of his contemporaries that Time had spared read it in order to live over again the golden days of youth, while the rising generation read it as veritable history. This book was followed by the *Jonny-Cake Papers*, which was equally well read by South County folk, as it contains many characteristic anecdotes mingled with the romance. Mr. Hazard had a fine imagination, and was a good *raconteur*, — qualities that he inherited, perhaps, from his Robinson ancestors.

The nature of Mr. Hazard's books is such that he rarely speaks of himself in a serious way; therefore it is to be very greatly regretted that lack of material necessarily renders this sketch incomplete. In *Recollections of Olden Times* he says: "Thomas R. Hazard, the compiler of these tables, has been an earnest worker in the cause of what is called 'Modern Spiritualism' since the year 1856, and whatever may be his merits or demerits otherwise, he has no higher ambition than that his name should be handed down to the coming generations associated with this fact alone."

In his last illness, a few hours before his death, he said to his brother, Joseph Peace Hazard: "I am afraid that I am better, and am sorry, for I am anxious to commence the new life in the 'spiritual world.'"

After Mr. Hazard's removal to Newport, "he became very much impressed with the necessity of improved and more humane methods in the care of the insane and poor of Newport. His personal investigation, and the reports he made, brought about a revolution in the State, and a very general reform. He, with his brother, Isaac Peace Hazard, working together, were largely instrumental in securing the establishment of the Butler Hospital for the Insane, which Cyrus Butler liberally endowed. Rowland G. Hazard aided in obtaining necessary

necessary funds, so that the three brothers are connected with the founding of that institution."[1]

He married, October 12, 1838, Frances, daughter of Jonas Minturn, of New York.

CHILDREN

1208. MARY ROBINSON HAZARD, born 1839; died 1842.
1209. FRANCES MINTURN HAZARD, born 1841 ; died 1877.
1210. GERTRUDE MINTURN HAZARD, born 1843 ; died 1877.
1211. ANNA PEACE HAZARD, born 1845 ; died 1868.
1212. ESTHER ROBINSON HAZARD, born 1848 ; married *Edwin J. Dunning.*
1213. BARCLAY HAZARD, born Dec. 4, 1852 ; married *Ada Blake.*

§ 651. ROWLAND GIBSON HAZARD, 7 (Rowland, 6; Thomas, 5; Robert, 4; Thomas, 3 ; Robert, 2 ; Thomas, 1) was born in his grandfather's house on Tower Hill, South Kingstown, October 9, 1801. In early childhood, he was taken to Bristol, Pennsylvania, to the home of his maternal grandfather, Isaac Peace. He attended school in Burlington, New Jersey (across the Delaware), and in Bristol, and in 1813 was sent to West Town school. Here he remained five years, and developed a strong taste for mathematics, discovering some new modes of demonstration in conic sections. This school gave him a thorough training in the branches it taught, and though he lamented his want of a classical education, yet by reading he early acquired a knowledge of classical history.

In 1819 Mr. Hazard returned to Rhode Island, and, with his brother, Isaac Peace Hazard, took charge of the manufacturing business at Peacedale, in which their father was engaged. Under the management of the brothers the business largely increased. From 1833 to 1843 Mr. Hazard made yearly visits to the South, and had an opportunity to see the workings of slavery, an institution he abhorred. In New Orleans, through his efforts, many free negroes unjustly detained in the chain-gang were released. His speech on the Fugitive Slave Law, in the Rhode Island Legislature, in 1850, while generous and appreciative of the slave-owners' position, is a powerful denunciation of the institution.

For several years he represented his town in the General Assembly, always taking a prominent position. During the adjourned session of the General Assembly, in the autumn of 1854, he delivered an address condemning the discriminative rates for freight and passengers charged by the Stonington Railroad Company, — an address that the officials of that corporation regarded as highly offensive. Some time afterwards, in order to test the rights of the Company in granting stop-over privileges on through tickets, he was ejected from one of the Company's trains. This measure excited much indignation, and a set of resolutions was adopted by the Town Council of his native town, in which is to be found the germ of the Interstate Commerce Law of 1886.[2] But it is as a writer that Mr. Hazard is best known. In his books he will live long after the houses he builded and the fortune he accumulated have become matters of tradition.

---

[1] Washington County History (Preston & Co.), New York, 1889.          [2] Ibid.

In

*651*
ROWLAND GIBSON HAZARD.

In 1836 his essay on "Language" appeared, and gained for him the friendship of William Ellery Channing, who said of the book, "I have known a man of vigorous intellect, who had enjoyed few advantages of early education, and whose mind was almost engrossed by the details of an extensive business, but who composed a book of much original thought, in steamboats and on horseback, and while visiting distant customers." This essay was possibly the dearest to Mr. Hazard of all his works. It is written in a less studied, more graceful style than his purely metaphysical works, and contains many charming bits of imagery. As an illustration of the remarkable concentration and dual quality of his mind is given this anecdote: In 1840, or about that time, a gentleman occupied a seat with Mr. Hazard on the train from New York. Not long before the train reached Kingston he took a letter from his pocket, also a pencil, and, while still keeping up the conversation of a purely business nature, occasionally wrote a few words. Just as he was leaving the train, he with a smile tore off the back of the letter and gave it to his friend, who, to his surprise, found a charming little poem addressed to a young girl whom he had seen, the evening before, enter a room with a rosebud between her lips.

A biographical sketch of Mr. Hazard has been written by his granddaughter, Caroline Hazard, and is prefixed to his collected works.

Rowland Gibson Hazard, married Caroline Newbold, daughter of John Newbold, of Bucks County, Pennsylvania, September 25, 1828.

CHILDREN

1214. ROWLAND HAZARD, born Aug. 16, 1829, in Newport; married, March 29, 1854, *Margaret,* daughter of Rev. *Anson Rood;* she died Aug. 7, 1895.
1215. JOHN NEWBOLD HAZARD, born Sept. 11, 1836, in Peacedale.

§ 652. WILLIAM ROBINSON HAZARD, 7 (Rowland, 6; Thomas, 5; Robert, 4; Thomas, 3; Robert, 2; Thomas, 1), was born December 15, 1803. He married, October 2, 1828, Mary, daughter of John and Lydia Wilbur.

CHILDREN

1216. JOHN WILBUR HAZARD, born 1830; married *Adelia Hoag.*
1217. MARY G. HAZARD, born 1833; died Aug. 19, 1884; married *Samuel G. Cook.*
1218. LYDIA C. HAZARD, born 1835; married *Franklin E. Hoag.*
1219. ELIZABETH HAZARD, born 1837.
1220. ROWLAND HAZARD, born 1839; married *Phebe Ann Moore.*
1221. ANNA HAZARD, born 1841; married *Thomas Tierney.*
1222. WILLIAM WILBUR HAZARD, born 1843.
1223. ISAAC PEACE HAZARD, born 1847; married 1871, *Elizabeth Howland.*

§ 706. JOHN HAZARD, 7 (John, 6; Benjamin, 5; George, 4; Thomas, 3; Robert, 2; Thomas, 1), was born 1775; he died 1806; he married, April, 1800, Frances, daughter of Captain Daniel and Sarah (Hazard) Gardiner.

CHILDREN.

1224. MARTHA HAZARD, born about 1801; married *Osmus Stillman.*

---

1 See Writings of R. G. Hazard (Houghton, Mifflin & Co.), 4 vols.

1225.

1225. FRANCES HAZARD, born about 1803; married, 1st, May 11, 1827, *Elnathan Brown*, who died Jan., 1830; 2d, *Osmus Stillman*.

## § 708. NATHAN GARDINER HAZARD, 7 (John, 6; Benjamin, 5; George, 4; Thomas, 3; Robert, 2; Thomas, 1). He married, after his brother's death, his widow, Frances Hazard; they were second cousins.

CHILDREN

1226. WILLIAM ROBINSON HAZARD, born Jan. 11, 1810; died Sept. 26, 1873; married *Sarah*, daughter of *Joseph* and *Mary (Norris) Potter*.
1227. SARAH GARDINER HAZARD, born July 2, 1811; unmarried.
1228. CATHARINE HAZARD, born June 2, 1818; married *Peleg Noyes*.
1229. JOHN HAZARD, born April 30, 1821; unmarried.

## § 714. MUMFORD HAZARD, 7; (George, 6; Simeon, 5; George, 4; Thomas, 3; Robert, 2; Thomas, 1), was born February, 1802; he died November 13, 1876; he married Sarah Tilley.

CHILDREN

1230. GEORGE HAZARD, born March 13, 1822; married *Almira Sweet*.
1231. CHARLES H. HAZARD, married *Sarah Smith*.
1232. JAMES T. HAZARD, born May 2, 1828; married, March 10, 1851, *Phebe*, daughter of *Thomas Gould*.
1233. BENJAMIN HAZARD, born March, 1831; married *Sarah*, daughter of *Thomas Ingalls*, of Taunton, Mass.
1234. WILLIAM HAZARD, born 1833; married *Mary Ryan*.
1235. SARAH HAZARD, born 1836.
1236. THOMAS T. HAZARD, born 1839; married *Margaret Kellogg*.
1237. MARY S. HAZARD, born 1842.

## § 715. ELIZABETH HAZARD, 7 (George, 6; Simeon, 5; George, 4; Thomas, 3; Robert, 2; Thomas, 1), was born January 19, 1804; she married, April 15, 1827, William Wilbur.

CHILDREN

1238. JOSEPH WILBUR.
1239. WILLIAM WILBUR.
1240. HARRIET WILBUR.
1241. CAROLINE WILBUR.

## § 716. CHARLES TILLINGHAST HAZARD, 7 (George, 6; Simeon, 5; George, 4; Thomas, 3; Robert, 2; Thomas, 1), was born July 31, 1805; he married Sarah Cook; she was born October 6, 1805, and died, January 16, 1874.

CHILDREN

1242. GEORGE SULLIVAN HAZARD, born May 18, 1827; married *Mary Wilson*.
1243. CHARLES GODFREY HAZARD, born Nov. 9, 1830; married *Mary Warner*.
1244. JOHN C. HAZARD, born May 16, 1833; died July 29, 1833.
1245. LUCRETIA S. HAZARD, born Aug. 5, 1835; died Sept. 1, 1845.
1246. WILLIAM C. HAZARD, born Aug. 16, 1837; married *Mary Peckham*.
1247. SILAS H. HAZARD, born Jan. 27, 1840; married *Sallie Burdick*.
1248. EDWARD HAZARD, born April 13, 1843.
1249–50. CHARLES T. HAZARD, born Dec. 30, 1845.

§ 717.

§ 717. ARNOLD HAZARD, 7 (George, 6 ; Simeon, 5 ; George, 4 ; Thomas, 3 ; Robert, 2 ; Thomas, 1), was born October 8, 1807 ; he married, March 14, 1830, Sarah Ann Stedman.

CHILDREN
1251. GEORGE A. HAZARD, born Aug. 5, 1831; married *Mary Barber*.
1252. STEPHEN STEDMAN HAZARD, born Feb. 3, 1833; died Sept. 3, 1834.
1253. SARAH CONTENT HAZARD, born Oct. 14, 1834; married *Jethro C. Carr*.
1254. MARY ELIZABETH HAZARD, born Nov. 19, 1836; died Oct. 23, 1842.
1255. HARRIET A. HAZARD, born June 5, 1838; married *Charles F. Palmer*.
1256. JAMES STEDMAN HAZARD, born Jan. 4, 1841; married, 1st, *Sarah E. Harvey*; 2d, *Sarah A. Titus*.
1257. ELIZABETH S. HAZARD, born Oct. 7, 1845; died Sept. 28, 1846.
1258. SIMEON HAZARD, born Dec. 3, 1847; died Jan. 8, 1848.

§ 719. WILLIAM WILBUR HAZARD, 7 (George, 6 ; Simeon, 5 ; George, 4; Thomas, 3 ; Robert, 2 ; Thomas, 1), was born July 4, 1810 ; he died January 11, 1874 ; married October 27, 1834, Sarah Armstrong.

CHILDREN
1259. ISABELLA DONALDSON HAZARD, married *Joseph M. Bokee*.
1260. THEOPHILUS DUNN HAZARD.
1261. GEORGE ARMSTRONG HAZARD, married *Josephine Augusta*, daughter of *Thomas Carr*.
1262. MARY ESTELLE HAZARD.
1263. HELEN BANNISTER HAZARD.
1264. ALITHEA LENNOX HAZARD.

§ 720. HARRIET HAZARD, 7 (George, 6 ; Simeon, 5 ; George, 4 ; Thomas, 3 ; Robert, 2 ; Thomas, 1), was born January 23, 1813 ; she married, November 4, 1833, George Albert Armstrong.

CHILDREN
1265-6. WILLIAM ALBERT ARMSTRONG, born Oct. 11, 1834; married *Caroline Lewis*.
1267. HARRIET AUGUSTA ARMSTRONG.

§ 721. HENRY B. HAZARD, 7 (George, 6; Simeon, 5; George, 4; Thomas, 3; Robert, 2 ; Thomas, 1), was born December 23, 1815 ; he married, August 11, 1840, Eunice G. Wilbur.

CHILDREN
1268. LEBBÆUS ENSWORTH HAZARD, born July 3, 1841; married, Aug. 3, 1865, *Amelia J. Ludlum*.
1269. ABBY CONGDON HAZARD, born Oct. 8, 1843.
1270. HENRY BOND HAZARD, born Dec. 26, 1845.
1271. FRANK HAZARD, born July 6, 1848.
1272. ARTHUR HAZARD, born Nov. 30, 1850.
1273. EMMA HAZARD, born Jan. 18, 1853.
1274. RENÉ HAZARD, born July 18, 1858.

§ 722. SIMEON HAZARD, 7 (George, 6 ; Simeon, 5 ; George, 4 ; Thomas, 3 ; Robert, 2 ; Thomas, 1), was born January 7, 1817 ; he died August 20, 1855 ; he married, November 15, 1838, Mary Ann Stevens.

CHILDREN

CHILDREN
1275. SARAH W. HAZARD, born Oct. 2, 1839; married *Edwin G. Spooner.*
1276. ELIZABETH S. HAZARD, born Oct. 28, 1841; died Sept. 26, 1842.
1277. ELIZABETH S. HAZARD, born Nov. 13, 1843; died May 29, 1846.
1278. GEORGE S. HAZARD, born June 4, 1846; married *Sarah Amanda Stoddard.*
1279. ANNIE W. HAZARD, born June 26, 1849.
1280. WILLIAM S. HAZARD, born Nov. 5, 1853.

§ 723. JAMES LAWRENCE HAZARD, 7 (George, 6; Simeon, 5; George, 4; Thomas, 3; Robert, 2; Thomas, 1), was born February 21, 1818; he married, in 1842, Frances Irish.

CHILD
1281. MARTHA SIMPSON HAZARD, born Sept. 30, 1843; married *Eben H. Godbald.*

§ 724. GEORGE AUGUSTUS HAZARD, 7 (George, 6; Simeon, 5; George, 4; Thomas, 3; Robert, 2; Thomas, 1), was born March 26, 1819; he married, October 3, 1843, Abby C. Card.

CHILDREN
1282. CHARLOTTE THAYER HAZARD, married, March 27, 1878, Professor *John M. Cross,* of Johns Hopkins University, Baltimore.
1283. CAROLINE CLARKE HAZARD.

§ 725. SYLVESTER ROBINSON HAZARD, 7 (Thomas, 6; George, 5, George, 4; Thomas, 3; Robert, 2; Thomas, 1), was born March 3, 1791, on Little Neck Farm on Point Judith. When he was nine years old, his parents, leaving the old home that had been in the possession of the Hazard family for over one hundred years, made a new home in Newport, Rhode Island, almost in sight of the paternal Hazard and Robinson mansion-houses. Here he received his education. In the war of 1812, being then twenty-one years of age, he promptly responded to the call for soldiers, and served through the war as Captain in the Newport Artillery, and took an active part in the engagement off Sachuest Beach with the British man-of-war, *Nimrod.* It was he who carried many of the field-pieces from the town to assist in this brief battle. He was one of the few pensioners of the war of 1812. Later he turned his attention to farming, which occupation he followed for thirty years. When about fifty years old, he accepted the office of Overseer of the Poor of the town of Newport, and faithfully performed its duties until about six months previous to his death.

> " *Who sweeps a room as to Thy laws,*
> *Makes that and the action fine."*

He also held several other offices under the municipal government.
Mr. Hazard was a "tall, strong, good man," so says Mr. Thomas R. Hazard, in his *Recollections of Olden Times,* and so say many of his contemporaries. He never had a week of illness during his life until within two weeks of his death. He was an industrious, unselfish man, of a kindly, genial nature. He is said to have been a great and rapid talker, and was wont to preface his conversation,
with

with, "I am a man of few words." There was no limit to his hospitality. He died September 16, 1875, respected and beloved in the community where he lived so long.

He married, in 1817, Hannah, daughter of Stephen Congdon; she died January 8, 1820, aged twenty-five. He married second, Gulielma M., daughter of Caleb and Waite Babcock. He married as third wife, Abby C., daughter of Thomas and Abby Clarke.

CHILDREN OF FIRST MARRIAGE
1284. CHRISTOPHER C. G. HAZARD, born March 3, 1818; died in infancy.
1285. CHRISTOPHER GRANT CHAMPLIN HAZARD; married, Dec. 15, 1846, *Eliza Gardiner Coggeshall*.

CHILD OF SECOND MARRIAGE
1286. ABBY ROBINSON HAZARD, born Jan. 3, 1833; married, Nov. 19, 1849, *William Attmore Whaley*.

§ 726. ROWLAND ROBINSON HAZARD, 7 (Thomas Hull Hazard, 6; George, 5; George, 4; Thomas, 3; Robert, 2; Thomas, 1), was born 1792; he died August 21, 1874; married Anna, daughter of Charles Collins. From an obituary notice published in a Newport newspaper the following account is taken: "Dr. Hazard died at his residence in this city, on Friday evening, August 21st, in the eighty-third year of his age. It is sad for us to chronicle the decease of one of our oldest and best citizens, perhaps as thoroughly an old Newporter as any now living, springing as he did from an ancient Rhode Island family, remarkable for its strong, distinctive characteristics for many generations.

"Dr. Hazard was born at Narragansett, within sight of the beautiful Bay; when about eight years old his parents removed to Newport, bringing him with them. He was an accurate and painstaking boy, known at school for his mathematical skill and elegant penmanship, which he retained almost to the close of his life; he was a pupil of Mr. Frazier, and subsequently of that strict but excellent teacher, Mr. Levi Tower. He delighted to narrate the incidents and scenes of his school-boy life, painting them with all the freshness of early youth. He was, for the times, a good Latin scholar, and had more than usual mechanical ingenuity. He early turned his attention to the study of medicine, and after leaving school entered the office of Dr. William Turner, well remembered by our older citizens as an eminent medical practitioner. He remained with him about four years, when, having completed his studies, he continued to practice with Dr. Turner, and won the confidence of the entire community, and was a favorite of Dr. Turner, and all the physicians of Newport. His most intimate associate and friend was Daniel Turner, distinguished in our naval history as a brave and talented commodore.

"About 1827, Dr. Hazard purchased the apothecary establishment of the late Charles Feke, on the Parade, and the mantle of that charitable and excellent man could have fallen on no more worthy shoulders. About this time he married Anna Collins, daughter of Governor Charles Collins, and removed to the fine old-fashioned old-fashioned house fronting on the Mall, which his kindly presence brightened to the day of his death. The light of his pleasant wood-fire in winter has smiled through the flower-graced windows upon all the passers-by. Dr. Hazard continued the practice of surgery and medicine in connection with the drug business, and we may safely say has prescribed for more men, women, and children, than any other living physician in the city. His manner was indescribably kind and gracious, his tenderness toward children was unvarying, and his charity and devotion to the suffering poor was without limit. He literally prescribed and gave medicine and attention gratuitously, to thousands who were unable to pay ; our older people will recall him in his little office, which was the perfection of neatness and order, devoting himself at almost all hours to his patients, humming an old tune as he prepared his medicines, or beaming with kindly eyes upon some little child.

" He had great love for agriculture, and purchased two fine farms near the town, which he delighted to cultivate and beautify, in what he called his leisure hours. He was athletic, erect and agile, and at seventy years of age could outwalk almost anybody, delighting to allude to the ' Narragansett white-oak ' of his bones and sinews.

" His house was overflowing with hospitality, and we doubt if there was a residence in Newport where more friends were welcomed and entertained.

" He was a man of great modesty and reticence, but of strong convictions of right, and great fixedness of purpose, and healthy conservatism ; he abhorred shams, and detested ill-advised radicalism.

" About twenty years ago he retired from active business and surrendered his drug establishment to his nephew, Rowland Hazard, and Mr. Philip Caswell, and shortly after removed to his country seat, which he called " Bird's Nest," because there the feathered songsters most did congregate, attracted by his kind attentions, and protected and fed by his hand ; he used to say that he could recognize them as they came back to their nests year after year. As he grew older and more infirm he returned to his city home, and resided there until he died, surrounded by his many relatives and friends, and comforted and cared for by his faithful and devoted wife, sustained and soothed by a trusting faith which seemed like that of a little child towards a kind father. The morning of the day of his death as he lay upon his bed, calm and patient, the only words he could utter were ; ' God is Master of the World ' ; and unto the hands of that God we commit his spirit."

§ 728. GEORGE HAZARD, 7 (Thomas, 6; George, 5; George, 4; Thomas, 3; Robert, 2 ; Thomas, 1), married Ann Barnet, of England.

CHILDREN

1287. VICTORIA HAZARD.
1288. OLIVER HAZARD.
1289. ROWLAND ROBINSON HAZARD, married *Margaret Rhodes.*

1290.

1290. Louis L. Hazard, married *Sarah Congdon*, daughter of *Jonathan N. Hazard*.
1291. Alice Hazard.
1292. Abby Hazard.
1293. Mary Hazard, married *Thomas G. Hazard*.

§ 730. MARY NILES POTTER, 7 (Sarah Hazard, 6 ; Enoch, 5; George, 4; Thomas, 3 ; Robert, 2 ; Thomas, 1), was born August 9, 1794. She died August 27, 1870; she married, March 23, 1818, George Champlin Robinson, son of Christopher and Ruhamah Robinson.

Children

1294. Jeremiah Potter Robinson, born Aug. 18, 1819; married *Elizabeth DeWitt*.
1295. Sarah Robinson, born 1821; died May 22, 1860; married *William Rhodes Hazard*.
1296. Elizabeth Robinson, born 1823; died Feb. 18, 1879; married *James Stewart*.
1297. George Champlin Robinson, born 1823; married *Mary Lyman*, daughter of Gov. *Lemuel Hastings* and *Sally (Lyman) Arnold*.
1298. Mary Niles Robinson, born 1827; married *George G. Pearse*.

§ 732. JEREMIAH NILES POTTER, 7 (Sarah Hazard, 6; Enoch, 5; George, 4; Thomas, 3 ; Robert, 2 ; Thomas, 1), was born in 1800; he died January 1, 1864 ; he married, in Tiverton, Rhode Island, October 7, 1831, Almira, daughter of Judge Samuel Fales, of Taunton, Massachusetts. She was born in 1800, and died in 1869.

Children

1299. Sarah Fales Potter, born July 26, 1833; married, Feb. 20, 1868, *Walter Watson*.
1300. Mary Niles Potter, born Dec. 25, 1834.
1301. Alice Hazard Potter, born Jan. 14, 1836.
1302. Frances Ann Potter, born Feb. 4, 1839.
1303. Jeremiah Niles Potter, born March 12, 1842.

§ 736. ALICE POTTER, 7 (Alice Hazard, 6; Enoch, 5; George, 4; Thomas, 3; Robert, 2 ; Thomas, 1), was born January 16, 1822 ; she died May 12, 1847 ; she married Benjamin Balch, of Providence, Rhode Island.

Child

1304. A Child, born and died 1847.

§ 737. JOHN A. HAZARD, 7 (Thomas G., 6 ; Thomas, 5 ; George, 4 ; Thomas, 3 ; Robert, 2 ; Thomas, 1), was born April 11, 1804 ; he died March 28, 1877 ; he married, September 4, 1839, Phebe Sheffield.

Children

1305. John A. Hazard, born 1843.
1306. Ida Hazard, married *J. F. Flynn*.
1307. Harriet Hazard.

§ 738. WILLIAM HAZARD, 7 (Thomas G., 6 ; Thomas, 5 ; George, 4 ; Thomas, 3 ; Robert, 2 ; Thomas, 1), was born October 30, 1805 ; he died February 17, 1883 ; married, May 19, 1836, Harriet Brenton ; she was born July 24, 1810, and died November 25, 1885.

Children

CHILDREN

1308. ELIZABETH HAZARD, born April 15, 1837.
1309. WILLIAM HAZARD, born Feb. 16, 1839; died April 17, 1841.
1310. HARRIET MARIA HAZARD, born Jan. 16, 1842; married *John G. Clarke.*

§ 739. THOMAS G. HAZARD, 7 (Thomas G., 6; Thomas, 5; George, 4; Thomas, 3; Robert, 2; Thomas, 1), was born November 6, 1807; he died December 20, 1866; he married, first, March 16, 1841, Mary, daughter of Thomas Hull Hazard. He married, second, October 15, 1861, Sarah, daughter of Thomas Hull Hazard. She was widow of George Congdon.

CHILDREN OF FIRST MARRIAGE

1311. MARY ANNA HAZARD, born April 16, 1842; died Oct., 1843.
1312. THOMAS H. HAZARD, born 1843; died 1887; married, Feb. 20, 1871, *Sarah* ——.
1313. JAMES ROBINSON HAZARD, born 1846; died 1848.
1314. MARY ANNA HAZARD.

§ 741. GEORGE BORDEN HAZARD, 7 (Thomas, G., 6; Thomas, 5; George, 4; Thomas, 3; Robert, 2; Thomas, 1), was born December 25, 1813; he married, first, Martha Clarke; second, Phebe Read.

CHILDREN

1315. RUSSELL CLARKE HAZARD.
1316. J. ALFRED HAZARD.
1317. LIZZIE HAZARD, married *William Cotton.*

§ 743. RUTH HAZARD, 7 (Thomas G., 6; Thomas, 5; George, 4; Thomas, 3; Robert, 2; Thomas, 1), was born June 30, 1817; she died February 13, 1888; she married Luther Bateman.

CHILDREN

1318. WILLIAM H. BATEMAN.
1319. HENRY BATEMAN.

§ 744. BENJAMIN HAZARD, 7 (Thomas G., 6; Thomas, 5; George, 4; Thomas, 3; Robert, 2; Thomas, 1), was born November 15, 1819; he married Hannah Davenport.

CHILD

1320. THOMAS B. HAZARD; died 1867.

§ 745. ISAAC HAZARD, 7 (Thomas G., 6; Thomas, 5; George, 4; Thomas, 3; Robert, 2; Thomas, 1), was born January 31, 1823; he married, first, Elizabeth Bosworth; second, Penelope Mann.

CHILDREN

1321. E. ESTELLE HAZARD.
1322. MARIA HAZARD.
1323. WILLIAM HAZARD.
1324. FRANK B. HAZARD.

§ 748.

§ 748. HARRIET HAZARD, 7 (Benjamin, 6; Thomas, 5; George, 4; Thomas, 3; Robert, 2; Thomas, 1); she was born March 26, 1812; she married October 18, 1837, Rev. Charles T. Brooks. He was born in Salem, Massachusetts, June 20, 1813, being the second child of Timothy and Mary King (Mason) Brooks. For the first fifteen years of his life he remained in his father's house, attending meanwhile different elementary schools. In 1824, he attended the Latin Grammar-school in Salem, where he completed his preparation for college. In 1828, the youth of fifteen entered Harvard University. Among his classmates were Henry W. Bellows, George Ticknor Curtis, John S. Dwight, John Holmes, Estes Howe, Samuel Osgood, John Parkman, William Silsbee, Henry Wheatland, and Augustus Story. Other college-mates were Charles Sumner, J. Lothrop Motley, and Oliver Wendell Holmes. Young Brooks seems to have engaged in the work of securing a higher education with great seriousness and ardor. The list of his studies and literary appointments is truly formidable for one of his slender strength. In 1832, he entered the Cambridge Divinity School, and graduated with honors in 1835. His first, last, and only pastoral charge was the Unitarian Church in Newport, he being called to this church in 1836; this call he accepted January 1, 1837, and entered upon that ministerial relation which, during the thirty-seven years of its continuance, so abounded in labors for truth, virtue, and piety, and proved such a blessing for the parish and the larger community.

Mr. Brooks wrote voluminously for the reviews and the periodical press of his day. He always entertained an ambition to write an English life of Martin Luther; and the thirty-six lectures on that great spiritual hero and his times, which he read to his people at Newport, were perhaps intended as material for this end. But it was as a poet, gifted by nature with a facile and graceful muse, that Mr. Brooks was best known to the world of American letters. Shining with a mild and genial ray, he became, from choice as well as disposition, the poet of the home-life of his friends, contributing the wealth of his sympathetic imagination and the lyric sweetness of his verse, to voice their joy, or lift their sorrow. His versatility and productiveness were amazing. Literary and theological essays, reviews, historical monographs, odes and hymns for religious, patriotic, and festive occasions, drolleries, children's books, translations from masterpieces of foreign literature, both in prose and verse, occasional verses and jeux d'esprit, flowed in a steady stream from his busy pen.

Mr. Brooks died in June, 1883, a few days before the seventieth anniversary of his birth; and his pure and amiable spirit ascended to those mansions of light to which he had so often pointed the hopes of his sorrowing friends.[1]

CHILDREN

1325. CHARLES MASON BROOKS, born July 24, 1840; married, April 19, 1866, *Eleanor Williamson MacIntire.*

1326. HARRIET LYMAN BROOKS, born July 18, 1841; married, Oct. 1, 1863, *George Stevens.*

---

[1] Condensed from Memoir by Charles W. Wendt, in Poems by Charles T. Brooks.

1327.

1327. JONATHAN MASON BROOKS, born Sept. 12, 1844; died March, 1863.
1328. MARY ELIZABETH BROOKS, born April 6, 1847; married Lieut. *Washburn Maynard.*
1329. PEYTON HAZARD BROOKS, born Sept. 26, 1850.

§ 751. MARGARET LYMAN HAZARD, 7 (Benjamin, 6; Thomas, 5; George, 4; Thomas, 3; Robert, 2; Thomas, 1), was born April 8, 1817; she married, September 8, 1841, General Isaac Ingalls Stevens, United States Army. Major-General Isaac Ingalls Stevens was born in North Andover, Massachusetts, on the 15th of March, 1818. In 1835, at the age of seventeen, he entered the Military Academy at West Point. Here he distinguished himself, and in 1839 he graduated at the head of his class. He was appointed a second lieutenant in the Corps of Engineers in the United States Army, and promoted to the rank of first lieutenant, July 1st, 1840.

From August, 1839, to September, 1841, Lieutenant Stevens was employed as an assistant at Fort Adams, Newport, Rhode Island. From September, 1841, to March, 1843, he had charge of the Government works at New Bedford. In March, 1843, he was placed in charge of those at Portland, Maine, and Portsmouth, New Hampshire, and also of Fort Knox, at the narrows of Penobscot river. Of these works he was in charge until December, 1846, when ordered to join General Scott's army at Brazos. He served on the staff of General Scott, from the investment of Vera Cruz to the capture of the City of Mexico. He was at the siege of Vera Cruz and at the battles of Contreras, Cherubusco, Molino del Rey, Chepultepec, and the capture of the City of Mexico. At the San Cosmo gate he was severely wounded. For his gallant conduct in the battles of Contreras and Cherubusco, he was breveted captain, and for his bravery at the battle of Chepultepec, which resulted in the taking of the city, he was breveted major. Having been disabled by his wound, he returned to the United States in January, 1848, and resumed charge of the works in Maine and New Hampshire.

In September, 1849, Major Stevens accepted the position of assistant in charge of the office of the United States Coast Survey, in Washington, and there continued on duty until March, 1853. He was a warm friend of President Pierce, and was by him, soon after his inauguration, appointed governor of the new territory of Washington. As governor of that territory, he was *ex-officio* superintendent of Indian affairs; and at the same time, having volunteered for the service, he was placed in charge of the exploration and survey of the northern route for a railroad to the Pacific. He determined the entire feasibility of the route for a railroad, and by his surveys established the practicability of navigating the Upper Missouri and Columbia River by steamers. As Indian Superintendent his labors were very successful. From December, 1854, to July, 1855, he negotiated treaties of cession of lands with some twenty-two out of the twenty-five thousand Indians of the territory, and extinguished the Indian title to more than one hundred thousand square miles of territory. His Indian policy was one of great beneficence to the Indians. He guarded their rights most carefully, provided for their civilization, and guaranteed to them homesteads on their assuming the
habits

habits and adopting the usages of civilized life. His treaties were confirmed, and his policy adopted by the Government, with the most benign results. At the end of his term of office, he was sent delegate to Congress from the Territory. When Congress adjourned, Governor Stevens proceeded to Washington Territory. On the fall of Fort Sumter he offered *carte-blanche* to the Government, came in person as soon as possible, accepted the colonelcy of the Seventy-ninth High-landers, New York Volunteers, and steadily devoted himself to the duties of the field. In September, 1861, in command of a force of eighteen hundred men, he made the reconnoissance of Lewinsville. September 29th, he was made a brig-adier-general. In October, he was ordered on the expedition against the coasts of Carolina, Georgia and Florida. On the first day of January, 1862, he attacked, and, with the aid of gun-boats, carried the enemy's batteries in the Coosaw, and, in command at Beaufort, he held possession of the site until ordered to the Stono in June. Placed then in command of a division, he landed on James Is-land, forming the right wing of the army under General Benham, and, whilst his force was landing, drove in the advance of the enemy, capturing a battery of five guns, and establishing his permanent picket-line. In July, General Stevens with his division was ordered to Virginia, and reported to General Burnside. The fol-lowing month he was ordered to Fredericksburg, and thence marched up the Rap-pahannock, and joined Pope's army at Culpepper Court House. At the second battle of Bull Run, he was almost incessantly engaged for two days ; his troops suffered terribly, and his own horse was shot dead beneath him. Among the last to leave the field, he was placed in charge of the rear the day after the battle, with a force of two divisions of infantry, a brigade of cavalry, and several batteries of artillery. On the following day, September 1st, 1862, General Stevens, in con-junction with the Second Division (Ninth Corps), was sent to arrest the advance of a force of the enemy, threatening the road to Washington, by which the army was retiring. This force, consisting of Stonewall Jackson's troops, was advancing with great resolution and rapidity, and was already within sight of the road when met by General Stevens. Forming his division into a column of brigades with the greatest rapidity, he charged the enemy with bayonet, knowing full well that the safety of the army depended in their repulse. The enemy, meantime, had taken position behind a fence on the edge of a wood, and opened a deadly volley upon our advancing troops. General Stevens, seeing the head of the column waver and hold back, rushed forward, seized the colors of the seventy-ninth High-landers from the hands of the wounded color-bearer, and calling on his troops to follow him, led them to a resistless charge which swept back the enemy like chaff and gained the position — a position dearly bought, for, in the very moment of success, he fell pierced through the brain by a rebel bullet. In recognition of his services during the civil war, General Stevens was made a major-general, to date from July, 1862.[1]

---

[1] Condensed from Memoirs of Rhode Island Officers.

CHILDREN

CHILDREN

1330. HAZARD STEVENS, born June 9, 1842.
1331. JULIA VIRGINIA STEVENS, born June 2, 1844.
1332. SUSAN STEVENS, born Nov. 20, 1846; married, Oct. 27, 1870, Captain *Eskridge*, United States Army.
1333. GERTRUDE MAUD STEVENS, born April 29, 1850.
1334. KATE STEVENS, born Nov. 28, 1852.

§ 752. NANCY HAZARD, 7 (Benjamin, 6; Thomas G., 5; George, 4; Thomas, 3; Robert, 2; Thomas, 1), was born June 4, 1819; she married, June 11, 1855, John Alfred Hazard.

CHILD

1335. NICHOLAS EASTON HAZARD, born Oct. 14, 1856; died May 18, 1874.

§ 753. DANIEL LYMAN HAZARD, 7 (Benjamin, 6; Thomas G., 5; George, 4; Thomas, 3; Robert, 2; Thomas, 1), was born July 19, 1821; he married, May 20, 1869, Delia Louise Colton.

CHILDREN

1336. EMILY B. HAZARD, born Oct. 20, 1870.
1337. PEYTON RANDOLPH HAZARD, born April 13, 1873.

§ 754. THOMAS GEORGE HAZARD, 7 (Benjamin, 6; Thomas G., 5; George, 4; Thomas, 3; Robert, 2; Thomas, 1), was born March 13, 1824. Mr. Hazard resides in Boston Neck, in the old house built by his great-grandfather, George Hazard. This house was probably built in the early part of the eighteenth century; the farm being given to George [4] by his father, Thomas Hazard, who died in 1746. When the house was being built, Thomas advised his son to lower the second story, which was intended to be as high as the first story. He thought that in this way the house would be better able to withstand the strong winds that came blowing in without a break from the broad Atlantic. George being a "wise son," took the advice of his father, and cut down the post of the second story, and the house is still standing to-day. This house with the farm, was given by George to his youngest son Thomas G. Hazard; several pieces of the old furniture, given with the house, are still there, — the old family clock, marking the time as accurately as it did almost two hundred years ago. This farm came to the present owner from his uncle, George Place Hazard, who was called " Barley George," as his father Thomas G. Hazard was called " Gentleman Tom." The present owner of the farm has also his sobriquet, as there are still several Thomas Hazards living. " Gentleman Tom " was, tradition says, a very handsome man, tall and large, with fair, rather ruddy complexion, and blue eyes, — the true Hazard type. His descendants get their dark complexion (and sobriquet) from his wife, who was an Easton, — the Eastons being a dark race. Mr. Hazard is a farmer, improving his family acres, and, like his ancestors, taking a keen interest in the affairs of the town; he has represented the town in the General Assembly on several occasions. In 1875, he was elected Senator. He

He has been greatly interested in all questions tending to the advancement of the town, especially in schools, both public and private. Mr. Hazard is, in one sense, an ideal farmer, being extremely fond of books, and reading only the best, and he has thus been able to bring his society to him, and in the quiet of his old manor-house hold communion with the best minds of all times. He married, December 8, 1858, Mary King Brooks, a sister of the Reverend Charles Brooks the gentle poet and preacher.

CHILDREN

1338. MARY KING HAZARD, born Feb. 20, 1860 ; died Jan. 2, 1874.
1339. THOMAS G. HAZARD, born July 20, 1862. He is a civil engineer.
1340. DANIEL LYMAN HAZARD, born Aug. 26, 1865. He is a graduate of Harvard University, and a civil engineer.

§ 765. GEORGE WATSON HAZARD, 7 (Jonathan, 6 ; Thomas, 5 ; Jonathan, 4 ; Thomas, 3 ; Robert, 2 ; Thomas, 1), was born August 5, 1779. He died January 31, 1862 ; he married Mary Lillibridge ; she was born in 1789, and died March 23, 1828.

CHILDREN

1341. GEORGE LILLIBRIDGE HAZARD, born Nov. 21, 1808 ; died May 23, 1886.
1342. MARY ANN HAZARD, born March 19, 1810 ; died March 25, 1883 ; married Col. *Willara Hazard*. For children, see *No. 1113*.
1343. HANNAH REYNOLDS HAZARD, born July 21, 1819 ; died August 21, 1871 ; married, Nov. 23, 1840, Hon. *Elisha Watson*. For children, see *No. 1389*.

§ 767. THOMAS A. HAZARD, 7 (Jonathan, 6 ; Thomas, 5 ; Jonathan, 4 ; Thomas, 3 ; Robert, 2 ; Thomas, 1), was born January, 1784 ; he died July 16, 1852 ; he married, February 22, 1805, Sarah, daughter of Robert Hazard, son of Richard Hazard. She was born December 25, 1787, and died April 1, 1873.

CHILDREN

1344. THOMAS G. HAZARD, married *Sarah Kenyon*.
1345. HANNAH HAZARD, married *Stephen Barrow*.
1346. SUSAN HAZARD, born Dec. 15, 1811.
1347. SARAH HAZARD, born 1814 ; married *Benjamin Carpenter ;* she died 1836.
1348. WANTON R. HAZARD, married ―― *Munroe.*
1349. GEORGE WALTER HAZARD, born 1819 ; married *Susan Arnold.*
1350. ALBERT ARNOLD HAZARD, born April 10, 1821 ; died Nov. 5, 1868. He was born in Richmond, Rhode Island, and died at Perryville, Rhode Island. He graduated from Harvard College in 1844.
1351. REBECCA HAZARD, born 1825 ; died July, 1862 ; married *Stanley Webb.*
1352. LAURA E. HAZARD, died 1863.
1353. SUSAN ABBY HAZARD, born Sept. 1828 ; died Nov. 18, 1846.

§768. BOWDOIN HAZARD, 7 (Jonathan, 6 ; Thomas, 5 ; Jonathan, 4 ; Thomas, 3 ; Robert, 2 ; Thomas, 1), was born February 14, 1785 ; he died in 1873 ; he married, December 6, 1810, Teresa, daughter of Judge William Clarke.

CHILDREN

CHILDREN

1354. ELIZA CLARKE HAZARD, born Sept. 1, 1813; married, Dec. 13, 1840, *William Robinson*, son of *Christopher Robinson*.
1355. ARNOLD W. HAZARD, born Oct. 4, 1815; married *Sarah Hoxsie*.
1356. ALFRED HAZARD, born Jan. 15, 1820; married *Ruth White*.
1357. HARRIET THERESA HAZARD, born Jan. 15, 1820; married, March 12, 1843, *John G. Perry*.
1358. WILLIAM RHODES HAZARD, born April 1, 1821; married, 1st, *Mary Lyons*; 2d, *Sarah Robinson*; 3d, ——.
1359. MARY ETTA HAZARD, born Feb. 18, 1823; married *Joseph Nichols*.
1360. JOHN L. HAZARD, born Feb. 4, 1825; married *Julia Humphry*.
1361. NATHANIEL HAZARD, born Feb. 4, 1827; married *Emma Davis*.
1362. ISAAC PEACE HAZARD, born Feb. 4, 1829.
1363. EDWARD CLARKE HAZARD, born April 4, 1831; married, 1st, *Mary Kimball*; 2d, *Emily Howe*; 3d, *Frances Frothingham*.

§ 771. SAMUEL HAZARD, 7 (Jonathan, 6; Thomas, 5; Jonathan, 4; Thomas, 3; Robert, 2; Thomas, 1), was born in 1794; he died January 14, 1866. He married Lydia, daughter of Weeden and Mercy (Comstock) Eldred, of East Greenwich.

CHILDREN

1364. THOMAS ELDRED HAZARD, born Oct. 15, 1830; married *Alice Larkin*.
1365. JONATHAN HAZARD, born March 6, 1832.
1366. MARY ESTHER HAZARD, born Jan., 1834; died June, 1850.
1367. WANTON WILBUR HAZARD, born Sept. 29, 1835.
1368. WILLIAM ARNOLD HAZARD, born April, 1837; married *Caroline Cole*.
1369. JOB HAZARD, born 1841; died Dec. 17, 1862.

§ 772. NANCY HAZARD, 7 (Jonathan, 6; Thomas, 5; Jonathan, 4; Thomas, 3; Robert, 2; Thomas, 1), was born March 30, 1798; she married William T. Gardiner. She died May 20, 1850.

CHILDREN

1370. STEPHEN ARNOLD GARDINER, born April 24, 1823; married —— *Northup*.
1371. ABBY BROWN GARDINER, born April 24, 1823; died Dec. 12, 1881; married *James Busbee*.
1372. GEORGE HAZARD GARDINER, born May 17, 1825; married *Abby Jane Chapman*.
1373. SAMUEL WATSON GARDINER, born June 19, 1828; died Oct. 10, 1885.
1374. ALBERT CLARKE GARDINER, born April 8, 1830.
1375. MARY ESTHER GARDINER, born Jan. 9, 1833; died April 10, 1843.
1376. WILLIAM EMERSON GARDINER, born Aug. 27, 1835; died May 19, 1887.

§ 775. ABIGAIL WATSON, 7 (Abigail Hazard, 6; Thomas, 5; Jonathan, 4; Thomas, 3; Robert, 2; Thomas, 1), was born January 22, 1792; died March 31, 1843; married September 3, 1809, Wilkins Updike, son of Lodowick and Abigail (Gardiner) Updike. He was born January 8, 1784, at Cocumscussuc, or as it was sometimes called, Smith's Castle, an estate which had belonged to the family since the first settlement of the Narragansett country. This settlement was made by an ancestor, Richard Smith or Smythe of Gloucestershire, a man of some fortune, whose family or relations lived at North Nibley in the Cotswold Hills, a few miles from Berkeley Castle. Richard Smith, on arriving in this country, lived for a few
months

months at Taunton, and then removed to New Amsterdam, where his daughter Catharine married Gysbert op ten Dyck or op Dyck, of an old family at Wesel, in Westphalia, where owing to a sort of hereditary burgomastership, the records of their genealogy are traceable in the records of the town, from father to son since the fifteenth century. Smith subsequently removed to Narragansett, and died there, and the estate acquired by him passed into the hands of the Updikes, and remained in the family for about two hundred years. The town of Wickford was at one time known as Updike's New Town, and is so inscribed in old maps. Mr. Updike came of a race of lawyers, his grandfather having been for twenty-five years Attorney-General of the Colony, and one of the first lawyers of the Colony; and his elder brother enjoying the same office. His father, however, lived a life of leisure. Mr. Updike was educated first at home, afterward at the Academy in Plainfield, Connecticut, which in those days had great vogue as a classical school. After leaving the Academy he studied law in the office of James Lanman, afterward Senator from Connecticut, and later in the offices of the Honorable William Hunter, and the Honorable Asher Robbins and Elisha R. Potter. He was admitted to the Bar in 1808. He married September 23, 1809, and lived at Tower Hill, and later at Cocumscussuc, which his father gave him. Owing to becoming security for his brother Lodowick, he lost this property in 1814; a loss about which he felt so strongly that until the end of his life he avoided passing it, or speaking of it. And the name Lodowick, which had alternated with that of Daniel for many generations, has not since been used in the family.

Occupied for many years in politics and the practice of law, and sitting for a long period in the Legislature, he still found time to collect the materials for a volume of sketches of lawyers of an earlier day, which he published in 1842, under the title of *Memoirs of the Rhode Island Bar*. He also amused his leisure hours by collecting the materials for the history of the Episcopal Church in the Narragansett country, in which for many reasons he was interested. His family had always been Churchmen, and benefactors of S. Paul's parish, in which Cocumscussuc lay. The Rev. James MacSparran an S. P. G. missionary to S. Paul's Church, Wickford, married his aunt, and many of his papers were in his possession; Bishop Berkeley had been the intimate friend of his grandfather, and was a connection of his family, as was also Seabury, Bishop of Connecticut. This and his love for the history of men and families, his knowledge of the older state of society, in which he had been brought up and of which he was a part, enabled him to do this work with real interest, and to do it as perhaps no one else could. The book was issued in 1847 under the title of *History of the Episcopal Church in Narragansett*. It has long been a bibliographical rarity.

Mr. Updike possessed a large and very curious library which had been the accumulation of generations at Cocumscussuc. It contained some superb editions of the Greek and Latin classics, an enormous quantity of Anglican theological treatises, chiefly aimed against Methodists, Socinians and the Church of Rome, political pamphlets, law books, and a very interesting accumulation of letters and papers.

papers. The pamphlets and a collection of papers illustrative of the history of the State, forms a special collection in the Public Library in Providence, having been placed there in his memory by his grandson.

There is, says Mr. Abraham Payne in a paper written at the time of Mr. Updike's death, a portrait of Mr. Updike by Lincoln, excellent both as a picture and as a likeness, when he was in the full maturity of his physical and mental powers. It is a radiant face, suggestive of strength and enjoyment. If it were hung in a gallery of portraits of men who have made a mark in the world, it would at once arrest attention and provoke inquiry about the original. As the picture, so the man. In whatever company Mr. Updike was, he was a centre of attraction, not because he asserted himself, but because he was alive in every part of his nature. He enjoyed himself, and so was a source of joy to all around him. He loved to eat, and drink, and laugh, and work. What was worth seeing he saw, what was worth knowing he knew.

I first saw Mr. Updike in General Carpenter's office, when he came to see his son Walter, then a student at law. It is as true of most men as it is of most women, that they " have no characters " at all. But General Carpenter had one, and so Mr. Updike was his friend. If there was anything either good or bad in a man, Mr. Updike paid attention to him. The common sort of people who conform to established rules, and in themselves are neither one thing or another, he passed by. If there was sufficient originality about a man to enable him now and then to make a fool of himself, Mr. Updike at once took a fancy to him, and proceeded to point out to all bystanders what he had discovered in his friend. This gave his ordinary conversation a tone of *banter* which made shallow people call him a trifler. But no man was ever more in earnest. The real triflers are your solemn people, who make no distinctions; to whom all things are equally important; who can not discern absurdity and therefore can neither make nor enjoy fun.

It was about the time of the suffrage movement that I first saw Mr. Updike. This subject presented itself to different minds in a variety of aspects. Mr. Ames said it was a tempest in a teapot. To Mr. Dorr it was an attempt to apply the Declaration of Independence and democratic principles to the government of the State. To Judge Durfee it furnished occasion for uttering, in his modest way, some of the profoundest political philosophy of the time. To Mr. Updike it was an ordinary electioneering rumpus; a mere question whether the "ins" should go out. The old charter was well enough. More people could vote under it than knew how to vote. That was his view of the matter, and so he laughed at the long procession and the roasted ox, and Mr. Dorr's elaborate speeches, until there was a prospect of a fight, and then his wrath was kindled, and he was what Mr. Whipple said every Rhode Island man should be, — a tiger in his den. To Mr. Updike, more than to any other man, we owe a very good judicial system. His judicial reforms were practical, and consisted mainly in diminishing the number of courts and judges. The old Common Pleas with its twenty-five

judges,

judges, fast anchored in the affections of local politicians, drifted and disappeared on the tide of ridicule raised by Mr. Updike.

He did another good work in pushing through the "Married Woman" act. Here he had to encounter a dead-weight of prejudice, and he overcame it. He labored incessantly in the cause of popular education, and his great and valuable services therein have deserved and received ample acknowledgment. This is a good record. But let us come a little nearer to Mr. Updike, for after all what a man *is* and not what he does is the main thing. He was first of all an orator. He worked, not by moving masses of capital, for he was not rich, nor by running party machinery, for in this he had no skill, but by direct action on the minds and hearts of men by means of speech. No formal orations, but talk ; not in mass meetings, but wherever men and women were gathered together, — at dinner tables, in railroad cars, in taverns, in court-houses, and above all in the General Assembly. It is the fashion now to decry mere speakers, and fools have much to say in praise of practical men. For two generations there was no contest in Rhode Island in which the tongue of Mr. Updike could be safely counted out.

But how did he speak? Since his death there have been friendly notices of him, and some of them say he was not logical. If that means anything, it means that he was not stupid. I think the popular idea of logic is methodical stupidity, and in this sense, Mr. Updike certainly was not logical. Nor did he make much display of argumentative tools. He reasoned very much as lightning moves. He went right at his mark, and left the result to show the force of the blow. In the dreary work of reporting the proceedings of the General Assembly, it has been my duty to hear many excellent speeches, to listen to which was a discipline and a toil. Listening was a necessity when Mr. Updike was talking. You might agree with him or differ from him, but you must listen to him. It is easy to talk about his sarcasm, his ridicule, and this and that, after the usual manner of those who must say something and don't know what to say. It is not easy to reproduce Mr. Updike as he was ; like all *living* things he dies in the process of analysis. You may retain what he was made of, but you have lost him. He was always in earnest. If he urged a measure, it was because he thought it ought to pass. If he abused a man it was because he thought he ought to be abused. If he raised a laugh against a man in debate, it was with the zeal of a man in the discharge of a religious duty. Perhaps there was never on the whole a more favorable exhibition of his powers than in the discussions on the old State debt. He did not think that the farmers ought to be taxed to pay that debt. I do not know whether it ought to have been paid or not. Having made up his mind to oppose its payment, Mr. Updike did not waste his power in answering the learned and logical and historical arguments in its favor. He went right at the practical purpose of making the members of the General Assembly vote against it. He had to deal with the history of the State, with all the leading men he had known. His blows were all hard, some I doubt not fell on innocent shoulders, but they all told. One

reason

reason that he gave why the scrip was valueless was, that a certain man had given some of it away, which he would not have done if it had been worth anything. Another was that one of the holders had a squeaking voice, which he mimicked till the house was in a roar. These things made many people mad, but they told on the final vote. They were low arts perhaps, but they have been used by Thaddeus Stevens and Benton and Palmerston and Charles James Fox and Demosthenes, and all robust men who have wielded at will popular assemblies. Right or wrong, they killed the old State debt.

A very good member of the General Assembly once moved to translate all the Latin phrases in the statute, so that the common people could understand them. The exquisite folly of such a measure was by no means obvious to the great body of the Assembly. It was quite as likely to pass as not. A good solid argument against it would probably have carried it through. Mr. Updike took the ground that it was of no advantage to have the people understand the laws. They were not afraid of anything which they understood. It was these Latin words that they were afraid of. " Mr. Speaker, there was a man in South Kingstown about twenty years ago, a perfect nuisance, and nobody knew how to get rid of him. One day he was hoeing corn and he saw the sheriff coming with a paper, and he asked what it was. Now if he had told him it was a writ, what would he have cared? but he told him it was a *capias ad satisfaciendum*, and the man dropped his hoe and ran, *and has not been heard of since.*" Nor has the proposition to translate the Latin words in the statutes. But such sallies of wit do not give a man any permanent influence. A mere joker is almost as tiresome as a man who never jokes at all. Under all this play of his faculties, Mr. Updike had the solid basis of common sense and thorough earnest work towards practical and worthy ends. And these made him a power in the General Assembly for many years.

Mr. Updike had strong convictions, formed from his own observations more than from reading the thoughts of other men. Mr. Whipple thought and read much about Athens. Mr. Atwell was much exercised about the doings of the Barons of Runnymede. For anything that Mr. Updike cared, the human race might have had its origin in South Kingstown. He gave Roger Williams credit for his doctrine of soul-liberty, but he did not like the man, and had a contempt for what he called his notions of equality. Mr. Updike's idea of a well ordered society, was a strong government, supported by the Episcopal Church, with the different classes of society pretty distinct, and each minding its own business.

He loved to study individual character. He knew the exact measure of the men he came in contact with. He believed in blood, and loved to explore the history of families.

He loved to be known as a churchman. But he treated the Church as he did his friends. He cherished her substance and made fun of her shams. Who that ever heard can forget his account of the revival which, as he said, " He and Elder White made in South Kingstown," or his explanation to a friend, who was
shocked

shocked by a professor who played cards and was a little profane — that "Mr. —— was a *high* churchman." He revered all good men and all sacred things, but no amount of solemnity, nor any vestments of any sort could conceal a humbug from him.

He was as zealous a friend of temperance as Neal Dow, and labored in his way in the General Assembly, and among his neighbors, to cure the evil of intemperance. But he made a distinction between temperance and abstinence, which some of the friends of this cause did not perceive.

He was a nobleman in personal appearance and in the generous humanity of his nature. In the House of Lords, he would have been among his peers. But he did not need titles nor broad acres. Wherever he sat was the head of the table. He was a gentleman, — scrupulously neat in all his habits, and always considerate of the happiness of those around him. He was seized with the illness from which he never fully recovered, some six years since, on the morning of the day when he had invited some friends to dine with him. He insisted that the dinner should go on, and concealed his condition as well as he could, and only after the company had gone was it known how sick he was. To the last he made his daily toilet as carefully as when a young man, and was only confined to his bed for a day or two, and his mind was unclouded to the end.

But I must pause, though the half has not been said which crowds upon the memory. Dr. Wayland said, speaking of the death of Mr. Webster, "The doors of eternity seemed to stand open, and he walked right in." Such, to his friends, seemed the close of the long life of Mr. Updike.

CHILDREN

1377. THOMAS BOWDOIN UPDIKE, born 1810 ; died 1892 ; married *Esther Stockton.*
1378. ISABELLA WATSON UPDIKE, born Feb. 28, 1812 ; married *Richard Kidder Randolph.*
1379. ABBY ANTONIA UPDIKE, born July 20, 1813 ; died 1892 ; married *Henry A. Hidden.*
1380. MARY ANSTIS UPDIKE, born July 20, 1814 ; died 1886 ; married, Feb. 15, 1854, *Samuel Rodman.*
1381. WALTER WATSON UPDIKE, born Apr. 17, 1817 ; died 1861 ; married *Prudence Page.*
1382. ARITIS TAYLOR UPDIKE, born Jan., 1819 ; died 1875 ; unmarried.
1383. ANGELINA UPDIKE, born Aug. 1820 ; died 1877 ; married *John F. Greene,* of Warwick.
1384. ELIZABETH TOWNSEND UPDIKE, born 1823 ; died 1841 ; unmarried.
1385. CÆSAR AUGUSTUS UPDIKE, born 1824 ; died 1877 ; married *Elizabeth Bigelow Adams.* Born at South Kingstown, R. I., March 7, 1824. Graduated at Brown University, Providence, R. I., in the class of 1849 ; admitted to the Rhode Island Bar in 1851. He was presiding judge of the Court of Magistrates for several years ; member of Common Council from 1859 to 1863 ; member of the Legislature from 1860 to 1864 ; speaker of the House of Representatives from 1860 to 1862, and Assistant Judge Advocate of the Marine Corps of Artillery, Providence, to his death. He left one son, *Daniel Berkeley Updike.*
1386. CAROLINE MATILDA UPDIKE, born 1826 ; married *John Eddy.*
1387. DANIEL UPDIKE, born 1833 ; died 1842 ; unmarried.
Also a daughter ALICE who died in infancy.


§ 777. ANN COLE, 7 (Mary Hazard, 6; Thomas, 5 ; Jonathan, 4 ; Thomas, 3 ; Robert, 2 ; Thomas, 1), was born 1785 ; she died August 27, 1874 ; she married,
January

January 5, 1806, Elisha Watson ; he was born October 1, 1776, and died July 7, 1847.

CHILDREN

1388.  ABBY WATSON, born Feb. 2, 1807 ; unmarried.
1389.  ELISHA WATSON, born Oct. 7, 1808, died May 31, 1877 ; married, 1st, Dec. 20, 1831, *Mary*, daughter of *John* and *Mary Watson* ; 2d, Dec. 15, 1834, *Hannah*, daughter of *Benjamin* and *Elizabeth Robinson* ; 3d, Nov. 23, 1840, *Hannah Reynolds Hazard* ; 4th, *Rebecca Gorham.*
1390.  MARY ANN WATSON, born May 15, 1810 ; died Aug. 3, 1883 ; married, Nov., 1829, *John Cross.*
1391.  WILLIAM WATSON, born Nov. 6, 1811 ; died June 29, 1874 ; married *Ann Arnold.*
1392.  ELIZA WATSON, born March 3, 1813 ; married *Carder Hazard.* For children, see *No. 945.*
1393.  HARRIET WATSON, born 1815.
1394.  JULIA WATSON, born 1822 ; died Feb. 19, 1845 ; married, 1841, *Stephen Van Rensselaer Watson.*
1395.  LAURA WATSON, married, May 20, 1848, *Robert Dunbar Watson.*
1396.  THOMAS JEFFERSON WATSON, married, 1st, *Mary*, daughter of *Willard Hazard* ; 2d, *Mary Cole.*

§ 780.  WILLIAM COLE, 7 (Mary Hazard, 6 ; Thomas, 5 ; Jonathan, 4 ; Thomas, 3 ; Robert, 2 ; Thomas, 1). He married Lydia Gerry.

CHILDREN

1397.  MARY COLE.
1398.  ANSTIS COLE.
1399.  ABBY COLE.
1400.  ELIZA COLE.
1401.  CAROLINE COLE, married *William Hazard,* son of *Samuel Hazard.*
1402.  GEORGE COLE.
1403.  WILLIAM COLE.
1404.  THOMAS COLE, married *Olive Eaton.*

§ 781.  MARY COLE, 7 (Mary Hazard, 6 ; Thomas, 5 ; Jonathan, 4 ; Thomas, 3 ; Robert, 2 ; Thomas, 1). She married William Watson, son of Elisha and Miriam Watson ; he was born January, 1783, and died November 8, 1870.

CHILDREN

1405-6.  MIRIAM WATSON, born 1827.
1407.  SARAH WATSON, born 1829.
1408.  WILLIAM H. WATSON, born February, 1831.

§ 782.  JAMES DOUGLAS HASZARD, 7 (Thomas Rhodes, 6 ; Thomas, 5 ; Jonathan, 4 ; Thomas, 3 ; Robert, 2 ; Thomas, 1), was born June 27, 1797 ; he died August 17, 1875 ; he married, first, January 27, 1825, Sarah Sophia Gardiner, who died September 27, 1827 ; he married, second, October 29, 1835, Susanna Jane Nelmes, of Bermuda. Mr. Haszard was Queen's printer for the Colony of Prince Edward Island for many years, and was also a bookseller and stationer. For about ten years he was Secretary and Treasurer of the Royal Agricultural Society of the Colony. Mr. Haszard was Lieutenant-Colonel in the Provincial Militia.

CHILDREN

CHILDREN OF FIRST MARRIAGE

1409. GEORGE THOMAS HASZARD, born Feb. 13, 1826; married, May 14, 1850, *Margaret*, daughter of *Thomas Owen*, Esq., Postmaster-General of the Island. He died May 10, 1881.

1410. JOHN JAMES HASZARD, born 1827; died in infancy.

CHILDREN OF SECOND MARRIAGE

1411. JAMES HENRY HASZARD, born Feb. 23, 1837; he died, March 12, 1855. He was a medical student at Harvard University, and while on his way home, in attempting to cross the Straits of Northumberland in an open ice-boat, he perished from exposure.

1412. CHARLES ALBERT HASZARD, born Feb. 8, 1838; died June 10, 1886; he married *Amelia Jones Haszard*, his second cousin.

1413. JANE LIGHTBOURN HASZARD, born Feb. 10, 1841; married, 1st, April 12, 1860, Captain *Adolphus Daniel Smith*; 2d, Sept. 4, 1877, *Charles H. Robinson*.

1414. FREDERICK SAMUEL WILSON HASZARD, born June 7, 1843; died Aug. 27, 1843.

1415. SAMUEL ERNEST HASZARD, born Aug. 6, 1844; died Nov. 29, 1844.

1416. EDWARD RUPERT HASZARD, born Aug. 30, 1845. He was mate of the Brigantine " Helen Davies," which cleared at Charlottetown for Barbadoes, Dec. 7, 1868 ; neither he nor the vessel were ever heard of afterwards.

1417. CLARA AUGUSTA HASZARD, born Nov. 4, 1846; died Aug. 8, 1847.

1418. DONALD DOUGLAS HASZARD, born June 6, 1848; died June 19, 1849.

1419. ARTHUR DEWAND HASZARD, born May 8, 1850.

1420. CLAUDIA FRANCES HASZARD, born June 16, 1851; died Sept. 20, 1851.

1421. HAMILTON GRAY HASZARD, born Sept. 1, 1852; died Sept. 15, 1852.

1422a. JESSIE HENRIETTA HASZARD, born Oct. 9, 1856; married, June 19, 1879, *Thomas J. Harris*.

1422c. ROBERT HASZARD, lives in Auckland, New Zealand; has four sons and two daughters. He is possibly an elder son.

§ 786. CHARLOTTE JOANNA HASZARD, 7 (Thomas R., 6 ; Thomas, 5 ; Jonathan, 4 ; Thomas, 3 ; Robert, 2 ; Thomas, 1), was born July 20, 1807 ; she died July 1, 1890; she married, February 21, 1843, Robert Blake Irving.

CHILDREN

1423. JAMES DOUGLAS IRVING, born Feb. 12, 1844. He lived in Prince Edward Island until 1893, when he removed to Halifax, Nova Scotia, in consequence of his appointment to the position of Deputy Adjutant-General, Commanding Military District No. 9, of that Province. General Irving, early in life, entered the office of Mr. Daniel Hodgson, Prothonotary of the Supreme Court of Prince Edward Island. From March 1, 1871, to April 1, 1885, he was Registrar of the Court of Chancery, and of Vice-Admiralty from March 28, 1876, to April 1, 1885, and Clerk of the Crown, from August 1, 1883 to April 1, 1888; this position he resigned, on being at that date appointed to the staff of the Canadian Militia, as Brigade Major for Military District No. 12, which comprised the Province of Prince Edward Island. His military history is as follows : In 1861 he joined the Charlottetown Artillery and Rifle Volunteers as a gunner. On the 26th of March, 1867, he received his first commission as lieutenant in the active militia of the colony, and shortly after, was promoted to the rank of Captain. On the Island becoming a Province of the Dominion of Canada, the Officers then existing were placed on the Island list *en bloc*, and those who were reappointed under the new order of things commenced their career anew. Gen. Irving was amongst those who then received commissions in the Canadian Militia, being on July 2, 1875, gazetted second Lieutenant in his old company, then known as Battery No. 2, Prince Edward Island Garrison of Artillery. He was promoted to Lieutenant, January 17, 1879; Captain, September 4, 1880; and Major Commanding, March 31, 1882. On April 1, 1885, he was appointed to a position on the District Staff, as Brigade-Major, Military District No. 12. He was

was promoted to the rank of Lieutenant-Colonel, Oct. 7, 1887, and on April 14, 1893, was appointed Deputy-Adjutant-General, Commanding Military District No. 9, Province of Nova Scotia.  Gen. Irving was President of the Caledonian Club of Prince Edward Island for several years.

1424.  MARY JANE SUSANNAH IRVING, born Nov. 27, 1846.

1425.  ROLLA JEAN IRVING, born July 4, 1853.

§ 792. JOHN RHODES GARDINER, 7 (Eunice Haszard, 6; Thomas, 5; Jonathan, 4; Thomas, 3; Robert, 2; Thomas, 1), was born April 24, 1798. When about twenty years of age, Mr. Gardiner visited his relatives in Rhode Island, many of those whom his father and mother left behind, when they went to Prince Edward Island in 1786, being then still living. There he met his first cousin, Mary Gardiner, whom he married on May 29, 1822. Shortly after his marriage, he returned to his native place, North River, Prince Edward Island. After a residence there of three years, he moved to Bedeque. In 1836, he purchased the Gordon Grove property of three hundred and fifty acres, situated in the same settlement. He then became an extensive and prosperous tiller of the soil and remained on the farm until 1866, when he removed to the town of Summerside. There he lived until his death on the 10th of September, 1874. The *Summerside Journal* noticed his death as follows : " This week we have to record the death of the Honorable John Rhodes Gardiner, of this Town, whose name is familiar to most of our readers. In the course of his eminently successful and useful career, he occupied some of the most prominent and honorable positions in this colony. He was appointed by the Crown a Legislative Councillor for Prince Edward Island in 1860, a position which he held for three years. In 1864 he was High Sheriff for this (Prince) County and President of the Summerside Bank from 1866 to 1869." He was also Justice of the Peace for the County and a Commissioner of small debts for Bedeque, &c. After his marriage with his first wife, Mr. Gardiner made frequent trips to Rhode Island to visit his relatives and friends. His last visit was made in the summer of 1874.

He married, first, May 29, 1822, Mary Gardiner of Rhode Island. She died at Bedeque, Prince Edward Island, February 15, 1830, aged twenty-six years. He married, second, March 9, 1831, Mary Hooper, daughter of Major Hooper, a Loyalist, from New Jersey, United States. She was born September 18, 1802, at Bedeque, and died January 25, 1890.

CHILDREN OF FIRST MARRIAGE

1426.  MARGARET JULIA GARDINER, born at Potosi Grove, March 24, 1823, married Dec. 25, 1846, *John Todd.* He died in California.  Mrs. Todd lives in Danville, California (1893).

1427.  CHARLOTTE ELIZA GARDINER, born at Potosi Grove, Jan. 12, 1825; died at Gordon Grove, Bedeque, Feb. 25, 1845.

1428.  JAMES ALFRED GARDINER, born at Centreville, Bedeque, April 15, 1827, married, May, 1851, *Mary Barnes,* of Boston, U. S. A. ; died at Baton Rouge, Louisiana, U. S. A., during the Civil War.

1429.  GEORGE HENRY GARDINER, born at Centreville, Bedeque, May 25, 1829, died July 13, 1830.

CHILDREN

CHILDREN OF SECOND MARRIAGE

1430. GEORGE HENRY GARDINER, born at Centreville, Bedeque, Jan. 1, 1832; married at Crapaud, Jan. 1, 1857, *Sarah Reid.*

1431. ADELAIDE GARDINER, born at Centreville, Sept. 27, 1833, married, Nov. 24, 1859, *Charles B. McNeill.* They live in Summerside, P. E. I. (1895).

1432. CHARLES COLSON GARDINER, born at Centreville, Sept. 10, 1835; married, 1st, Sept. 22, 1868, *Martha Cox,* daughter of the late J. B. Cox. She died June 29, 1869. He married, 2d, Nov. 25, 1873, *Lucy G. Narraway,* of Pictou, Nova Scotia.

1433. MARY SOPHIA GARDINER, born at Gordon Grove, Bedeque, July 18, 1837; she lives at Summerside, P. E. I.

1434. ELIZA JANE GARDINER, born at Gordon Grove, Bedeque, Aug. 3, 1839 ; married, Oct. 14, 1864, *James Butcher* of Charlottetown. They live at Denver, Colorado (1893).

1435. CATHARINE GARDINER, born at Gordon Grove, Feb. 20, 1842, married, Nov. 20, 1868, *J. E. Price,* M. D., of Summerside. They live at Hartford, Conn., U.S.A. (1895).

1436. SARAH CHARLOTTE GARDINER, born at Gordon Grove, May 3, 1843 ; died Dec. 9, 1847.


§ 797. HARRIET CLARISSA HASZARD, 7 (William, 6; Thomas, 5; Jonathan, 4; Thomas 3; Robert, 2; Thomas, 1), was born September 28, 1798, at Bellevue, Prince Edward Island; she died at Charlottetown, February 4, 1841; she married, February 6, 1827, William Spencer Compton, merchant. Mr. Compton died November 6, 1847, at Charlottetown.

CHILDREN

1437. ERNEST FREDERICK COMPTON, born March 8, 1828. He removed to Melbourne, Victoria, and embarked in business. About the year 1872, he settled in Auckland, New Zealand, where he erected the substantial buildings in which he carried on business until his death. He was managing director of the Auckland Tug Company, and was for several years a member of the Harbor Board, and Chairman in 1881 and 1882. Died June 23, 1890, leaving a widow, two sons, and a daughter.

1438. CHARLES COMPTON, born May 31, 1829 ; died Sept. 19, 1884; married, 1st, March 8, 1854, *Leila,* daughter of Major *Compton* ; she died Jan. 14, 1861 ; 2d, *Emily McFadyen,* daughter of *John McFadyen.* Mr. *Compton* was a merchant of St. Eleanors, P.E.I. He emigrated with his family to Nebraska in August, 1880, and died there Sept. 19, 1884.

1439. WILLIAM THOMAS COMPTON, born Nov. 29, 1830 ; unmarried ; lost at sea, Jan. 21, 1859.

1440. LOUIS COMPTON, born March 16, 1833 ; died July 11, 1877 ; unmarried.

1441. ANNE FARRANT COMPTON, born March 16, 1833 ; married, June 29, 1855, *William Eddison Dawson ;* died March 12, 1880.

1442. GEORGE COMPTON, born June 25, 1835 ; married, March 11, 1858, *Eliza P. Compton,* daughter of Major *Compton* of St. Eleanors, P.E.I. Mrs. *Compton* died Aug. 27, 1890 ; her husband, four sons, and five daughters survived her.

1443. EDWARD COMPTON, born March 8, 1837 ; died in infancy.


§ 798. SARAH LOUISA HASZARD, 7 (William, 6; Thomas, 5; Jonathan, 4 ; Thomas, 3; Robert, 2; Thomas, 1), was born at Bellevue, Prince Edward Island, May 20, 1800; she married, September 22, 1831, William Cundall, formerly of Richmond, Surrey, England. She died January 18, 1871; Mr. Cundall died May 13, 1876.

Sarah Louisa Haszard Cundall, was the daughter and grand-daughter of devoted New England loyalists. Brought up in her parents' hospitable home, at the beginning

ginning of the present century, she early learned the details of house-keeping, and was equally at home whether entertaining her guests, or ministering to the necessities of her family in sickness or in health. She was a constant attendant and firm supporter of S. Paul's Church, Charlottetown.

Mr. Cundall was the son of Robert William Cundall and Penelope Bassett. He was born at Richmond, Surrey, England, on the 6th of March, 1805, and went to Prince Edward Island in 1828. In 1830 he resided among his tenants at Park Corner, New London. He removed to Charlottetown in 1835. In May, 1842, he was appointed High Sheriff for Queen's County, and held the position till May, 1847. He then became Head Master in the Central Academy, the chief educational institution in the Province. In 1856 the Bank of Prince Edward Island was established, and Mr. Cundall was chosen manager. Soon after his arrival in Prince Edward Island he was made Justice of the Peace for Queens County, and continued in that capacity till his death. Of strong religious convictions, he was a prominent and useful member of the Church of England. Religion, as it influenced his actions, was a strong principle, bearing fruit in the noble virtues of a manly life.

CHILDREN

1444.  HENRY JONES CUNDALL, born at Park Corner, New London, P. E. I., January 13, 1833. In 1835 the family removed to Charlottetown. After a careful education he entered, in 1848, the land office of Messrs. Samuel and Edward Cunard, who at that time owned about two hundred and twenty thousand acres in the Island. In March, 1853, he became Land Surveyor of the Cunard Estates. On February 13, 1854, he received from the Surveyor-General a certificate of competency as a Land Surveyor, and was shortly afterwards sworn in as such. In 1859 he joined the Volunteer Militia and became a member of the " Prince of Wales Company," which, with a company of the 62d Regiment of Her Majesty's Troops, formed the Prince's Guard of Honor, on his arrival in the Island, August 9, 1860. On the following day, at the Levee, Government House, he was presented to His Royal Highness. Having considerable business of his own to attend to, he resigned the position which he had held in Messrs. Cunard's Estate Office since October, 1848, and removed to his own office May 27, 1863. (The Cunard Estates were sold to the Government in 1866.) Having continued in the Volunteer Militia Service, he received, March 26, 1867, from the Commander-in-Chief of the Province, his commission as Captain in the First Queens County Regiment of Militia. From 1871 to 1874 he was largely occupied with the survey of the Prince Edward Island (Government) Railway, and in drawing plans, preliminary to the valuation of the land damages. From May, 1872, to July, 1886, he was Chief Observer at Charlottetown (a reporting telegraph and storm-signal station) in connection with the Meteorological Service of the Dominion of Canada. In the years 1875 and 1876, he was employed in conducting cases before the Commissioners appointed under the " Land Purchase Act, 1875," to value and purchase the lands of all proprietors holding more than five hundred acres in the Island, and in obtaining the amount of the awards from the Provincial Treasurer. About 1877, an offer of the Commissionership of Public Lands was made to him; this he did not accept. On May 22, 1890, he was appointed, by the Administrator of the Government in Council, a member of the Board of Examiners of Candidates for admission to practise as Land Surveyors for the Province. In March, 1893, he was elected President of the " Telephone Company of Prince Edward Island," and was re-elected in March, 1894. He has sat upon many important arbitrations, in the interests of both Government and individuals. Identified with S. Paul's Church (Church of England) and its Sunday School since his childhood

childhood, he is now (1893) Church Warden of the former and Superintendent of the latter. He has frequently represented his church in the Diocesan Synod of Nova Scotia, and in 1892 was elected by the latter body a Delegate to both the Provincial and General Synods of Canada.

1445. MILLICENT CUNDALL, born at same place, June 6, 1834; died May 6, 1888; unmarried.

1446. PENELOPE ANNE CUNDALL, born at Charlottetown, Jan. 19, 1836.

1447. SARAH CUNDALL, born at Charlottetown, March 2, 1838; died Feb. 12, 1843.

1448. THERESA CUNDALL, born at Charlottetown, P. E. I., May 25, 1840, was for many years an active and consistent member of the Church of England. After the death of her father in 1876, she felt at liberty to carry out a long cherished desire, of devoting herself more entirely to a religious life and work. Accordingly she left her home in Charlottetown for England, August 18, 1877, and after a few months' residence in London, on December 11, 1877, she was admitted as a Postulant to the Clewer Sisterhood of S. John Baptist. At Whitsuntide, 1878, she entered the novitiate, and finally, on July 21, 1880, she made her profession, taking the vows, and was set apart as a professed or full sister by the Bishop of Oxford. She has served in several of the branch houses in England, and is now (1893) "Sister in charge" of a young women's reformatory, S. Mary's Home, Salisbury, England, which position she has filled for some years.

§ 800. MILLICENT CASTLE HASZARD, 7 (William, 6; Thomas, 5; Jonathan, 4; Thomas, 3; Robert, 2; Thomas, 1), was born at Bellevue, Prince Edward Island, August 10, 1803. She married, January 18, 1827, William Hodges of Cymbria Lodge, Rustico, Prince Edward Island, formerly of Monmouthshire, England. He was Estate Agent, and gentleman farmer, and for some time High Sheriff for Queens County, Justice of the Peace for the same County, and Commissioner for small debts. He died January 26, 1857, and was buried beside his wife, in the old burying-ground, Malpeque Road, Charlottetown. She died at St. John, New Brunswick, where she went for the benefit of her health, on May 8, 1855, in her fifty-second year. Her remains were brought to the Island by her brother Charles Hazard, and laid to rest in the old burying-ground, Malpeque Road.

She was a gentle Christian woman, and blessed with a cheerful disposition, generous to the poor, and hospitable to all. To do a kindness to any afflicted one was to her a pleasure. Forgetting her own weakness, she frequently went beyond her strength in endeavoring to bring consolation and comfort to others.[1]

CHILDREN

1449. CLARA AMELIA HODGES, born Nov. 17, 1830; married, Jan. 14, 1852, *David Mutch;* died Jan. 23, 1890; they had eleven children.

1450. ANNE ELIZABETH HODGES, born July 14, 1833; married, 1st, August 13, 1855, *Henry Winsloe,* formerly of Monmouthshire, England, Land Proprietor. He was drowned whilst swimming in a creek adjoining his farm, August 2, 1863; married, 2d, *Duncan McMillan,* October 30, 1872.

§ 802. WILLIAM JONES HASZARD, 7 (William, 6; Thomas, 5; Jonathan, 4; Thomas, 3; Robert, 2; Thomas, 1), was born at Bellevue, Prince Edward Island, July 12, 1808. The earlier part of his life was spent on his farm,—

---

[1] Contributed by Henry Jones Cundall.

part

part of the Bellevue property given to him by his father. He married Louisa Hayden. In company with several others, he and all his family emigrated to New Zealand, in the Brig *Prince Edward*, which sailed from Charlottetown, November 30, 1858. After a residence in that country of nearly eighteen years, he returned alone to his native land, arriving November 21, 1876. Broken in health, he lived for some time at his old home, near the Harbor's Mouth, and died there, April 18, 1879. His remains lie in the burying ground of the Episcopal Church, Southport.

CHILDREN

1451. HARRIET HASZARD, married, 1st, —— *Richards;* married, 2d, —— *Sinclair.*
1452. AMELIA J. HASZARD, married in New Zealand, *Charles Albert Haszard,* her second cousin, son of *James D. Haszard.*
1453. ALEXANDER HASZARD, married, and has a family.
1454. ELIZABETH DOUGLAS HASZARD.
1455. WILLIAM CUNDALL HASZARD, born Dec. 28, 1848; married, and has children.
1456. SARAH LOUISA HASZARD, married —— *Murray.*
1457. ANNA MARIA HASZARD, married —— *Andrews.*
1458. SYDNEY HASZARD, married.

§ 803. CHARLES HASZARD, 7 (William, 6; Thomas, 5; Jonathan, 4; Thomas, 3; Robert, 2; Thomas, 1), was born at Bellevue, Prince Edward Island, February 29, 1812; he died June 4, 1862. At the time of his death he was a member of the Legislative Council (the Upper House) of the Province, and for a quarter of a century previously, had been one of the most active magistrates in Queens County. He was also a Commissioner of small debts, and for a term filled the office of High Sheriff of his County. As one of the leading agriculturists of the County for many years, he took an active part in the affairs of the "Royal Agricultural Society," and was at different times its President and Vice-President. Having a natural aptitude and skill in the management of the sick, and success in curing diseases, he for some years practiced medicine, and his premature death was in some measure attributed to his exposing himself both night and day to the inclemency of the weather. Few men have departed this life more generally esteemed and regretted. He resided at Bellevue and died there. He is buried in the churchyard of the Episcopal Church, Southport. He married, November 28, 1843, at Eska, Margaret, daughter of Francis Longworth; she died August 29, 1881.

CHILDREN

1459. CHARLES JOHN HASZARD, born Feb. 19, 1845; died at Bellevue, Feb. 17, 1889; unmarried.
1460. ANNA ISABELLA HASZARD, born Feb. 16, 1847; married, Jan. 23, 1883, *John Stewart* of Southport, Prince Edward Island.
1461. FRANCIS LONGWORTH HASZARD, born Nov. 20, 1849; married, Oct. 12, 1876, *Elizabeth Des Brisay.*
1462. MARGARET BEATRICE HASZARD, born Nov. 9, 1852; married, Sept. 26, 1872, *John Stewart;* she died Oct. 24, 1876.

§ 804. HENRY BOWDOIN HASZARD, 7 (William, 6; Thomas, 5; Jonathan, 4; Thomas, 3; Robert, 2; Thomas, 1), was born at Bellevue, Prince Edward

ward Island, December 8, 1813; died November 24, 1872. Mr. Haszard, though fully up to the average stature and weight, was in those respects the least of his four brothers. The others stood over six feet in height, and were broad in proportion. From about the year 1841, he for many years carried on business as a merchant in Charlottetown. He was Justice of the Peace for Queens County, a Commissioner for issuing (Government) Treasury Notes, and was for a time Auditor of Public Accounts of the Province. On April 11, 1859, he was appointed Colonial Secretary of the Island. This appointment was confirmed by the Queen, June 2, 1859. At the time of his death he was Surveyor of Shipping for the Province. He was also a prominent promoter of many of the companies and institutions which came into existence between the years 1847 and 1864.

An active and zealous member of the Church of England, he was for many years the efficient warden of S. Paul's Church. He was very desirous that his native Island should have the advantage of a resident Bishop instead of depending on the occasional visits of the Bishop of Nova Scotia. His sudden death at the comparatively early age of fifty-nine years, prevented the carrying out of his plans, and, as he left no successor sufficiently enthusiastic on the subject, the Bishopric still remains in abeyance.

He married, February 10, 1846, Hannah Catharine Cameron, daughter of —— Cameron, M. P. P., of Charlottetown. She was born November 14, 1817, and died June 20, 1889.

CHILDREN

1463. JANE CAMERON HASZARD, born Dec. 10, 1846.

1464. HENRY FENWICK HASZARD, born July 29, 1848; married *Grace C. Webber*, daughter of *Felix Webber, Esq.*, of Glym-dderwin, South Wales, Jan. 24, 1891. He is Commander, late in charge of H. M. Coast Guard service, Mumbles, near Swansea, South Wales.

1465. WILLIAM DOUGLAS HASZARD, born April 3, 1850, Barrister at Law.

1466. JOHN ERNEST HASZARD, born March 26, 1852; died at Montreal, Feb. 19, 1889.

1467. HORACE HASZARD, born Nov. 2, 1853.

1468. DAVID FITZGERALD HASZARD, born Aug. 31, 1855. He emigrated to New Zealand in 1879; married, in *Auckland, Kate*, daughter of *H. D. Morpeth, Esq.* He now (1893) lives in Auckland.

1469. A SON, born Feb. 24, 1857; died Feb. 25.

1470. LOUIS CHARLES HASZARD, born May 10, 1859; died Dec. 19, 1859.

1471. A SON, born Feb. 1, 1861, died in infancy.

§ 805. JOHN HASZARD, 7 (William, 6; Thomas, 5; Jonathan, 4; Thomas, 3; Robert, 2; Thomas, 1), born at Bellevue, Prince Edward Island, March 4, 1816. Mr. Haszard was the tallest of his family, being about six feet two inches in height, and correspondingly broad. He did a successful business at St. Eleanors for several years, until the finding of gold in Australia held out to the world its alluring prospects of quickly acquired wealth. He then closed his business, and left the Island, September 9, 1852, joining the bark *Aurora* at Halifax, Nova Scotia, bound for Melbourne, Australia. On the arrival of the ship at her destination, Mr. Haszard went to the gold-fields; but on December 4, 1853, he returned to Prince Edward Island and resumed business at St. Eleanors, and
engaged

engaged to some extent in shipbuilding. He filled the following positions for longer or shorter periods ; viz. : — Justice of the Peace for Prince County, and a Commissioner of small debts for St. Eleanors ; Captain of the Queen's Rifles (volunteers), St. Eleanors ; Director of the Summerside Bank and a church-warden of S. John's Episcopal Church at St. Eleanors. On the death of his brother Henry Haszard, in 1872, he succeeded him as Surveyor of Shipping for the Province, which office he held at his death, which occurred May 8, 1878.

Mr. Haszard married, March 20, 1856, Amelia, daughter of the Hon. P. S. McNutt of Darnley, Prince County. She died at Lynwood, April 6, 1860. He married secondly, Jane Davenport, daughter of the late Nathan Davies, of Charlottetown, February 11, 1869.

CHILD OF FIRST MARRIAGE

1472. WILLIAM HENRY HASZARD, born at St. Eleanors, Prince Edward Island, Oct. 13, 1859; married, *Caroline Rogers*, daughter of *Benjamin Rogers* of Charlottetown, Sept. 21, 1892.

§ 806. ANN FARRANT HASZARD, 7 (William, 6 ; Thomas, 5 ; Jonathan, 4 ; Thomas, 3 ; Robert, 2 ; Thomas, 1), born at Bellevue, Prince Edward Island, January 29, 1823 ; she married, first, January 22, 1857, Rev. Andrew Lockhead, formerly of Paisley, Scotland, for some time minister of S. David's Presbyterian Church, Georgetown, Prince Edward Island. He died at Paisley, January 12, 1864. She married, second, at Lynwood, St. Eleanors, March 31, 1868, Rev. William Ross Frame, formerly of Colchester, Nova Scotia, Presbyterian minister at Richmond Bay, East, and Summerside ; and afterwards of Mount Stewart, Prince Edward Island. He died at Charlottetown, June 30, 1888, aged fifty-three.

In 1885 Mr. Frame settled in Charlottetown. In the following year, he was engaged as editor of the *Protestant Union* and shortly afterwards he formed a joint stock company, incorporated as " The Island Guardian Publishing Company," which purchased the plant of the *Protestant Union.* The *Island Guardian* was devoted to the cause of morality and religion, and was independent in its politics. Mr. Frame was its editor until his death, which was a great loss to the Province. He was an able and faithful preacher, and was highly esteemed for his readiness to take part in every good work.

Mrs. Frame has led a useful and busy life, and is now (1894) beyond the allotted three-score years and ten.

CHILDREN OF THE FIRST MARRIAGE

1473. WILLIAM HENRY LOCKHEAD, born at Charlottetown, May 10, 1858 ; married, Feb., 1885, *Mabel Bourke.* They live at the Dalles, Oregon.

1474. ANNE AMELIA LOCKHEAD, born at Georgetown, Prince Edward Island, May 30, 1860 ; married, July 2, 1884, *Daniel Davies*, Jr. They live in St. Paul, Minnesota, and have five children.

§ 820. PATIENCE HAZARD, 7 (Griffen B., 6 ; Jonathan J., 5 ; Jonathan, 4 ; Thomas, 3 ; Robert, 2 ; Thomas, 1), was born in 1795 ; she married, first, John
Walton

Walton; he died in 1824; she married, second, Nicholas Yost. He died in 1862.

CHILDREN OF FIRST MARRIAGE
1475. WILLIAM H. WALTON.
1476. GRIFFEN BARNEY WALTON.

CHILDREN OF SECOND MARRIAGE
1477. ELIZABETH YOST.
1478. NICHOLAS YOST.

§ 822. JONATHAN J. HAZARD, 7 (Griffen B., 6; Jonathan J., 5; Jonathan, 4; Thomas, 3; Robert, 2; Thomas, 1), was born in 1799. He lived several years on Lot 52 of Gurnsey survey, Jerusalem, New York. He married Elizabeth Lake; she died in 1868, aged sixty-one. He died in 1876, at the home of his daughter Catharine.

CHILDREN
1479. GRIFFEN BARNEY HAZARD; married, 1st, *Adelaide Hart*; married, 2d, *Mary Ann*, daughter of *Thomas H. Norris*.
1480. CATHARINE HAZARD; married, 1st, *George Dusenbury*; married, 2d, *Hon. Andrew Oliver*, Judge and Surrogate for Yates County, New York.

§ 823. GEORGE W. HAZARD, 7 (Griffen B., 6; Jonathan J., 5; Jonathan, 4; Thomas, 3; Robert, 2; Thomas, 1), was born in 1801; he married, in 1822, Sarah Card, and settled near City Hill. In 1840 he sold this property to George W. Gardiner, and occupied two hundred and forty acres of the old Stephen Card farm, near Himrods, New York, where he died in 1844. His wife survives him, and is now ninety-three.

CHILDREN
1481. HANNAH HAZARD, married *William A. Keadman*.
1482. ESTHER HAZARD, died 1882.
1483. EMMETT HAZARD; unmarried, and lives in Penn Yan, New York.
1484. MARY P. HAZARD, died 1856; married, *E. Darwin Tuthill* (first wife).
1485. SARAH HAZARD; married *John W. Norris*.
1486. GEORGE W. HAZARD; married *Sylvia Miller*.
1487. JAMES HAZARD; unmarried.
1488. JONATHAN J. HAZARD; died young.

§ 824. ELIZABETH HAZARD, 7 (Griffen B., 6; Jonathan J., 5; Jonathan, 4; Thomas, 3; Robert, 2; Thomas, 1), married George S. Wheeler.

CHILDREN
1489. A DAUGHTER; married *W. S. Crane*, M. D.
1490-9. SUSAN WHEELER; married *Charles R. Herrick*, of Edge Water, Bergen County, New Jersey.

§ 826. THOMAS JEFFERSON HAZARD, 7 (Griffen B., 6; Jonathan J., 5; Jonathan, 4; Thomas, 3; Robert, 2; Thomas, 1), was born in 1807; he married, in 1825, Susannah, daughter of Jeffrey Champlin. They first lived on
the

the homestead farm of his father, Griffen B. Hazard, at Eddytown, and moving thence to City Hill, afterwards to Bath, New Jersey, and from thence to Michigan. He died at Alpine, Schuyler County, New York.

CHILDREN

1500. JONATHAN HAZARD.
1501. THOMAS HAZARD.
1502. ELDRED HAZARD.
1503. JAMES HAZARD.
1504. ANDREW WASHINGTON HAZARD, born May 27, 1849; married *Emma Coffin Tucker.*
1505. MARY HAZARD.
1506. EMILY HAZARD.

§ 830. DANIEL WILLIAMS HAZARD, 7 (Joseph Hoxsie, 6; Jonathan J., 5; Jonathan, 4; Thomas, 3; Robert, 2; Thomas, 1), was born February 29, 1812, in Rome, New York; he died June 27, 1888. He always lived on the same farm, a part of which he inherited from his father. The following notice shows the estimation in which he was held by his townsmen: "No man in this vicinity was better known or more respected than he, as was attested by the very large attendance at his funeral. Mr. Hazard was strictly honest in all his transactions, and too generous to be hemmed in by creed or party. He was a successful farmer for years, and acquired a competence by his business. A man of cultured intellect and generous heart, Mr. Hazard will be long remembered for his kindness to all. He was a devoted husband and a most indulgent father."
He married, November 13, 1837, Ann E. Dyre, daughter of Christopher C. Dyre, and granddaughter of Mary Hazard and Colonel Charles Dyre.

CHILDREN

1507. JOSEPH DYRE HAZARD; died young.
1508. MARY JANE HAZARD; married, Dec. 6, 1864, *Albert B. Brown.*
1509. GEORGE HAZARD; died young.
1510. ANNIE E. HAZARD.

§ 831. JOSEPH HAZARD, 7 (Joseph Hoxsie, 6; Jonathan J., 5; Jonathan, 4; Thomas, 3; Robert, 2; Thomas, 1). He removed to Texas many years ago. It is said of him that he would suffer almost any inconvenience, and even personal pain, for the sake of fun. He greatly disliked to see any one wrongfully used. He came justly by his strength and size, as he was a grandson of Patience, daughter of "Stout Jeffrey" Hazard. He married Susan White.

CHILDREN

1511. AMEY SUSAN HAZARD; married ―― *Wilson.*
1512. JOSEPH GOURNEY HAZARD.
1513. ANNA HAZARD.

§ 846. ELIZABETH STARR, 7 (Abigail Hazard, 6; Doctor Robert, 5; Caleb, 4; George, 3; Robert, 2; Thomas, 1), was born June 23, 1791; she died October 20, 1861; she married Gilbert Saltonstall.

CHILDREN

CHILDREN
1514. HARRIET SALTONSTALL, born Oct. 4, 1816; died April 5, 1865.
1515. GURDON SALTONSTALL, born Sept. 17, 1821; died July 30, 1865.
1516. MARY ELIZABETH SALTONSTALL, born Jan. 14, 1824.
1517. GEORGE STARR SALTONSTALL, born April 25, 1830; died Sept. 9, 1831.
1518. GILBERT DUDLEY SALTONSTALL, born July 19, 1836; died Sept. 29, 18—.

§ 850. MARY NILES, 7 (Esther Hazard, 6; Doctor Robert, 5; Caleb, 4; George, 3; Robert, 2; Thomas, 1), was born January 13, 1779; she died in 1868; she married Ezekiel Watson Gardiner.

CHILDREN
1519. PELEG GARDINER, born Nov. 27, 1808; died Jan. 15, 1880; married, 1838, ——.
1520. JOHN GARDINER, born Aug. 19, 1810; died Nov. 6, 1876; married *Sarah Whalen.*
1521. ELIZABETH NILES GARDINER; died July 22, 1857; married *John Underwood,* of Yatesville, New York.
1522. MARY GARDINER; married, after her sister's death, *John Underwood.*

§ 853. CHARLES NILES, 7 (Esther Hazard, 6; Doctor Robert, 5; Caleb, 4; George, 3; Robert, 2; Thomas, 1), was born June 20, 1786; he died June 30, 1855; he married —— Wade of Humphrysboro, Ruthford County, Tennessee, where he lived until 1836, when he moved to Holly Springs, Mississippi, where he died. His wife died at Jackson, Tennessee, in 1877, aged eighty-six.

CHILDREN
1523. ELIZABETH NILES; married *James Elder,* a banker; she died in 1885.
1524. MARY NILES.
1525. ISABELLA NILES; married *Robert Elder,* brother to *James.*
1526. MARTHA NILES.

§ 857. HENRY S. HAZARD, 7 (Sylvester G., 6; Doctor Robert, 5; Caleb, 4; George, 3; Robert, 2; Thomas, 1), was born in April, 1792; he died in 1871; he married, May 12, 1812, Eliza Essex; she was born May 25, 1790; she died in 1851.

CHILDREN
1527. MARY ANN HAZARD, born May 24, 1813; married, Feb. 14, 1829, *Josiah Everett.*
1528. RICHARD GREENE HAZARD, born Sept. 25, 1814; married, Dec. 22, 1845, *Martha Billings.*
1529. ELIZABETH GREENE HAZARD, born Oct. 4, 1816; married, May 2, 1855, *John S. Snow,* who died April 7, 1877.
1530. EMMA ESSEX HAZARD, born Sept. 5, 1818; died Feb. 10, 1852; married *Anson Lewis.*
1531. SYLVESTER GARDINER HAZARD, born Sept. 20, 1820; died Dec. 15, 1862, married, 1st, *Maria Allen;* married, 2d, *Martha Allen;* married, 3d, *Mary F.* ——, who died June 12, 1860.
1532. HENRY S. HAZARD, born May 18, 1822; died Oct. 13, 1859.
1533. A CHILD.
1534. JARED STARR HAZARD, born Dec. 24, 1825.
1535. AMANDA M. HAZARD, born April 17, 1828.
1536. JOHN HAZARD, born Sept. 23, 1830; died Dec. 12, 1856.
1537. LUCINDA LEWIS HAZARD, born April 21, 1833.
1538. ANSON LEWIS HAZARD, died May 25, 1874.

§ 860

§ 860. LUKE HAZARD, 7 (Sylvester G., 6 ; Dr. Robert, 5 ; Caleb, 4 ; George, 3 ; Robert, 2 ; Thomas, 1), was born October 20, 1797 ; he died June 9, 1878 ; he married Julia Miller ; she died June 15, 1835, at East Greenwich, R. I., aged thirty-four.

CHILD
1539. JULIA ELIZABETH HAZARD, died Aug. 23, 1848.

§ 869. ABBY HAZARD, 7 (Charles, 6 ; Dr. Robert, 5 ; Caleb, 4 ; George, 3 ; Robert, 2 ; Thomas, 1), was born October 3, 1804 ; married Henry Snow of Alabama.

CHILDREN
1540. HENRY SNOW, born Aug. 4, 1831 ; died Jan. 6, 1860.
1541. CAROLINE SNOW, born June 15, 1834 ; married, Nov. 10, 1857, *A. P. Hogan.*
1542. MARY A. SNOW, born Jan. 11, 1837 ; married, June 11, 1858, Dr. *J. F. Ormond.*
1543. GEORGE H. SNOW, born March 26, 1839 ; died March 16, 1840.
1544. ABBY MYRA SNOW, born March 15, 1843 ; died Nov. 21, 1848.
1545. EDWARD N. C. SNOW, born Oct. 16, 1845 ; married, Nov. 12, 1872, *Caroline M. Duter.*

§ 870. CAROLINE HAZARD, 7 (Charles, 6 ; Dr. Robert, 5 ; Caleb, 4 ; George, 3; Robert, 2; Thomas, 1), was born November 3, 1806; she died January 20, 1866; she married Zabiel Snow, brother to Henry Snow.

CHILDREN
1546. GEORGE HENRY SNOW, born Aug. 25, 1835; died Sept. 21, 1836.
1547. CHARLES COURTLANDT SNOW, born Feb. 7, 1837; died July 19, 1884.
1548. JOHN BOYLSTON SNOW, born Dec. 24, 1838; died Oct. 23, 1839.

§ 877. GEORGE STARR HAZARD, 7 (Francis, 6; Dr. Robert, 5; Caleb, 4; George, 3; Robert, 2; Thomas, 1), was born December 5, 1809, in New London, Conn.; his father died when he was six years old, his mother a few years afterwards; before her death, she gave her young son to Mrs. Robertson of New London, who gave him the best education that the town afforded. At the age of fifteen he became clerk in a mercantile house, where he served faithfully for eleven years, with frequent promotions. In 1835, Mr. Hazard established himself in Maumee, Ohio, and for nine years was identified with its fortunes. He entered at once into business as a forwarding and commission merchant, and was successful in establishing a large connection.

Mr. Hazard was not only prominent as a merchant, but as a projector of local improvement, and a public man of large views. In 1845, his enterprises necessitating the change, he moved to Toledo for superior facilities of transportation, but remained there only a year, finally locating himself at Buffalo, where he still resides (1895). During Mr. Hazard's residence at Maumee City, the conveyance of freight was a matter of great difficulty. Not until the Wabash and Erie Canal opened did the local trade have any direct outlet to the East, and even then, some time elapsed before the shippers were persuaded of the facilities of the new route

677
GEORGE STARR HAZARD.

route. The first boat loaded with general merchandise, arriving at Maumee City on the completion of the canal was consigned to Mr. Hazard.

During Mr. Hazard's residence in Buffalo, up to his assumption of the important duties of the Bank of Attica, he was as a merchant and member of trade associations, identified with the commercial interests of the place. As early as 1856, and during the extraordinary period of 1861, '62, '63 and '64, he was President of the Board of Trade. In the organization and support of the celebrated One Hundredth New York, known as the "Board of Trade" Regiment, his activity and earnestness, both in his official position, and as an individual patriot, were most prominent.

In 1870, appreciating the completion and dangerous antagonism of the railroad to the Erie Canal, Mr. Hazard with Alonzo Richmond, Esq., prevailed upon the Canal Board to reduce the rates fifty per cent, and thus initiated the more liberal policy which, it is believed, has saved the commerce of that great water-way to the country.

As a writer, Mr. Hazard is nervous and incisive. His "Report on Cereals," made to the Government as one of the Commissioners to the Paris Exposition of 1867, is an exceptionally thorough investigation of the grain producing capacities of different countries. In addition to the Presidency of the Bank of Attica, Mr. Hazard is officially connected with other local institutions. He is a liberal patron of art culture, and was influential in the establishment of the Buffalo Academy of Fine Arts, being its President the second year of its organization.

Soon after the close of the Civil War, Mr. Hazard feeling his health impaired by his long continued labor in the interests of his petted 100th New York Regiment, combined with his enormous and increasing business, commenced a long and extended tour in Europe, and spent several years abroad. On his return to America he resumed his business relations.

While in Europe he studied carefully the system of weather signals then in use in France, and in 1870 he submitted to the "Board of Trade" a report in behalf of the appointment of a Special Committee, looking to the establishment of a system of meteorological observation, in the interest of lake and seaward navigation.

Mr. Hazard married Sarah, daughter of Rev. Archibald Mercer, of New London, Conn., where she was born, April 24, 1815. She was born and reared a daughter of the Church, and to its faith was given her lifelong adherence, to its holy offices and worship her reverent and constant attention. These made her chief support in hours of trial, and also in later years when bodily weakness and infirmity had shaken "this trembling house of clay." With her, death was indeed but "the sweet closing of an eye," and amid the peace and stillness of that nature which she so loved, she slept, July 5, 1866.

CHILDREN

1549. CHARLOTTE MORGAN HAZARD, born March 4, 1834; married *Frank W. Fiske*.
1550. JOHN ROBERTSON HAZARD, born Feb., 1838; married, 1862, *Jane Howel* of Canandaigua.
1551. ARCHIBALD MERCER HAZARD, born August 8, 1844.

§ 878.

§ **878.** WILLIAM SYLVESTER HAZARD, 7 (Francis, 6; Dr. Robert, 5; Caleb, 4; George, 3; Robert 2; Thomas, 1), was born 1812; he died 1890; married Marion, daughter of Colonel Snelling, U. S. A., who built the fort of that name in Minnesota, in 1819. She died in 1881, in Cincinnati.

CHILDREN

1552. JAMES HENRY HAZARD, born March, 1846; he is a physician.
1553. GEORGE STARR HAZARD, born Dec., 1853; unmarried.
1554. FRANCES HASTINGS HAZARD, born April, 1858; married *William Hall.*
1555. ABBY SNELLING HAZARD, born March, 1859.
1556. EDWIN HAZARD, born 1863.

§ **879.** SARAH PECKHAM, 7 (George Hazard Peckham, 6; Mary Hazard, 5; Governor George, 4; George, 3; Robert, 2; Thomas, 1), was born in South Kingstown, Rhode Island; she married Wheeler Watson, and soon afterwards they moved to Rensselaerville, New York.

CHILDREN

1557. HARRIET WATSON, married *Dr. Clarke.*
1558. REBECCA WATSON, married *Lyman Dwight.*
1559. MALBONE WATSON, married —— *Hitchcock.*
1560. JOHN WATSON, married *Mary Watson,* daughter of *John Watson.*
1561. ABIGAIL WATSON, married Col. *Zadock Pratt* of Prattsville, N. Y.
1562. MARY WATSON, married, after the death of her sister, *Zadock Pratt.*
1563. ELIZAETTE WATSON, married —— *Sandford.*
1564. GEORGE WATSON, died young, unmarried.

§ **882.** BENJAMIN TAYLOR PECKHAM, 7 (George Hazard Peckham, 6; Mary Hazard, 5; Gov. George, 4; George, 3; Robert, 2; Thomas, 1), was born October 22, 1773; he died December 16, 1853; married, January 28, 1799, Abigail, daughter of Benedict and Betsey (Ladd) Oatley. She was born July 7, 1767, and died November 9, 1831.

CHILDREN

1565. SARAH PECKHAM, born April 21, 1800; married, Feb. 13, 1817, *James Dixon.*
1566. ELIZABETH PECKHAM, born Nov., 1801; married *Reuben Eaton.*
1567. MARY PECKHAM, born Sept. 25, 1803; died Feb. 16, 1853; married *Samuel Rodman.* (For children see *No. 1084.*)
1568. GEORGE HAZARD PECKHAM, born April 1, 1806; died July 6, 1808.
1569. SUSAN PECKHAM, born Sept. 1, 1810; married *John Gardiner.*

§ **887.** BENJAMIN PECKHAM, 7 (Josephus, 6; Mary Hazard, 5; Governor George, 4; George, 3; Robert, 2; Thomas, 1), was born March 2, 1777; he married, December 5, 1799, Mary Waud.

CHILDREN

1570. CARDER PECKHAM, born Jan. 22, 1801.
1571. HENRY WAUD PECKHAM, born July 22, 1804.
1572. RENEWED PECKHAM, born June 19, 1805.

§ 889.

§ 889. JOSEPHUS PECKHAM, 7 (Josephus, 6; Mary Hazard, 5; Governor George, 4; George, 3; Robert, 2; Thomas, 1), was born May 26, 1788; he married Mary Champlin; he died November 19, 1877; she died December 5, 1877. They had one son.

§ 890. GEORGE PECKHAM, 7 (Josephus, 6; Mary Hazard, 5; Gov. George, 4; George, 3; Robert, 2; Thomas, 1), was born February 15, 1775; he married, November 14, 1805, Elizabeth Cornell. She was born November 23, 1785, died September 5, 1840.

CHILDREN

1573. GEORGE HAZARD PECKHAM, born Nov. 13, 1806; died Dec. 26, 1857; married, Feb. 19, 1829, *Elizabeth Allen.*
1574. EDWARD HAZARD PECKHAM, born Jan. 2, 1809.
1575. ROBERT CORNELL PECKHAM, born March 19, 1817; died Oct. 1, 1817.
1576. ROBERT CORNELL PECKHAM, born June 10, 1819.
1577. RUTH CORNELL PECKHAM, died July 20, 1843.

§ 893. BENJAMIN ROBINSON, 7 (Sarah Peckham, 6; Mary Hazard, 5; Governor George, 4; George, 3; Robert, 2; Thomas, 1), was born August 5, 1763; he died 1830; he married, 1791, Elizabeth, daughter of Deputy Governor George Brown, and of Hannah Robinson his wife. She was born in 1771, and died in 1855. Benjamin Robinson was born in the house at Narragansett Pier, now owned by Miss Mary Watson, and called the "Mansion House." He lived there all his life. His father gave him by will a part of the homestead farm with the house; he bought out his sister's and brothers' right.

CHILDREN

1578. GEORGE ROBINSON, born 1792; died July 17, 1795, aged three years and four days.
1579. JOHN ROBINSON, born Nov. 1, 1794; died Sept. 28, 1841; married *Rubama,* daughter of *Christopher Robinson.*
1580. GEORGE BROWN ROBINSON, born 1796; died 1872; married, 1st, *Mary Wells,* she died 1838, aged twenty-seven; married, 2d, 1839, *Julianna Wells,* aunt to his first wife.
1581. SYLVESTER ROBINSON, born July 16, 1798; died Jan., 1867; married *Eliza Noyes.*
1582. WILLIAM BROWN ROBINSON, born 1800; died 1875; married, 1st, *Harriet,* daughter of *Christopher Robinson;* married, 2d, *Eliza* daughter of *Christopher Robinson.*
1583. HANNAH BROWN ROBINSON, born Feb. 1, 1802; died Nov. 1838; married *Elisha Watson,* Jr., Dec. 15, 1834. (For children see *No. 1389.*)
1584. BENJAMIN ROBINSON, born 1804; died Nov. 29, 1823.
1585. PHILIP WANTON ROBINSON, born 1809; died Aug. 12, 1830.

§ 894. SARAH ROBINSON, 7 (Sarah Peckham, 6; Mary Hazard, 5; Governor George, 4; George, 3; Robert, 2; Thomas, 1), was born December 10, 1764; she married, February 14, 1782, Samuel Tabor, of Waterford, Connecticut; he was born October 29, 1750, and died September 6, 1798.

CHILDREN

CHILDREN
1586. SARAH TABOR, born Nov. 17, 1782 ; married *William Miller.*
1587. SAMUEL WESTCOTT TABOR, born June 30, 1784; unmarried. He died at Buenos Ayres, South America. He was brigadier general in the army, and translated the Constitution into Spanish for the use of the United States Government. His death was the result of a severe cold taken while crossing the Andes from Chili to establish a treaty. His life was one of adventure.
1588. FRANCES TABOR, married *Thomas Hubbard.*
1589. ANNE MARIA TABOR ; married *Gurdon Miller.*
1590. ELIZA SULLIVAN TABOR, married (second wife) *Thomas Hubbard.*
1591. JOHN ROBINSON TABOR, married —— *Creagh.*
1592. WILLIAM ROBINSON TABOR, married —— *Smith* of Charleston, S. C.
1593. SYLVESTER TABOR, died young.

§ 895. WILLIAM ROBINSON, 7 (Sarah Peckham, 6 ; Mary Hazard, 5 ; Governor George, 4 ; George, 3 ; Robert, 2 ; Thomas, 1), was born April 25, 1766 ; he married, March, 1802, Phebe Dennison, of Stonington, Conn.
CHILDREN
1594. MATILDA CAROLINE ROBINSON.
1595. WILLIAM DENNISON ROBINSON.
1596. ELIZABETH DENNISON ROBINSON.
1597. PHEBE ROBINSON.
1598. MARY ROBINSON.
1599. ELIZA DENNISON ROBINSON.
1600. SAMUEL DENNISON ROBINSON.
1601. JULIA GORHAM ROBINSON.
1602. EMMA ROBINSON.

§ 896. JOHN ROBINSON, 7 (Sarah Peckham, 6 ; Mary Hazard, 5 ; Gov. George, 4 ; George, 3 ; Robert, 2 ; Thomas, 1), was born December 16, 1767 ; he died 1831 ; he married Abigail, daughter of James and Ann (Rodman) Robinson. They were first cousins. He married, second, Ruth, daughter of Judge Gardiner. His first wife died 1805, aged thirty-seven.
CHILDREN BY FIRST MARRIAGE
1603. JAMES ROBINSON.
1604. MARIAN ROBINSON.
CHILDREN OF SECOND MARRIAGE
1605. EMILY ROBINSON.
1606. ELIZABETH ROBINSON.
1607. ALBERT ROBINSON.
1608. EDWIN ROBINSON.
1609. CORNELIA ROBINSON.

§ 897. SYLVESTER ROBINSON, 7 (Sarah Peckham, 6 ; Mary Hazard, 5 ; Governor George, 4 ; George, 3 ; Robert, 2 ; Thomas, 1), was born July 12, 1769 ; he died 1807 ; married Eliza, daughter of John and Marcia (Pell) Rodman, of Pelham Manor, Westchester County, New York.
CHILDREN

CHILDREN

1610. ISABELLA ROBINSON, died 1844.
1611. HARRIET ROBINSON, died 1855; married *Cornelius Prall McIlvain.*
1612. JOHN MOWATT ROBINSON, died 1843; he lived in Florida.
1613. FREDERICK DE PEYSTER ROBINSON, died 1855.
1614. CHARLOTTE MOWATT ROBINSON, born about 1818; married *James Bowne Townsend,* of New York.
1615. ELIZA ROBINSON, married *George Buttler,* of New York.
1616. EDWARD ROBINSON, died Oct. 28, 1821, at St. Augustine, Florida.
1617. SYLVESTER ROBINSON, died young.
1618–20. ROWLAND ROBINSON, died young.

§ 900. SARAH PECKHAM, 7 (William Peckham, 6; Mary Hazard, 5; Governor George, 4; Colonel George, 3; Robert, 2; Thomas, 1), was born November 28, 1777; she died May 22, 1859; she married, February 12, 1794, Acors Rathbun. He was born January 23, 1772, and died September 9, 1855.

CHILDREN

1621. JOSHUA RATHBUN, born Nov. 25, 1794; died in infancy.
1622. WILLIAM RATHBUN, born Feb. 18, 1796; died May 4, 1838; married, Sept. 22, 1819, *Bathsheba Pound.*
1623. SARAH RATHBUN, born Nov. 11, 1797; died March 16, 1888; married, Nov. 9, 1820, *Daniel Morey.*
1624. SOLOMON RATHBUN, born June 30, 1799; died Nov. 9, 1861; married, March 3, 1824, *Hannah Quimby.*
1625. WELLS RATHBUN, born Feb. 12, 1801; died May 9, 1873, married, Sept. 21, 1826, *Amy Otis.*
1626. PECKHAM RATHBUN, born Jan. 15, 1802; died Sept. 3, 1883; married, 1st, Dec. 29, 1825, *Nancy Allen;* married, 2d, March 27, 1833, *Mary G. Howland.*
1627. JOSHUA RATHBUN, born Oct. 7, 1803; died Nov. 15, 1887; married, 1st, Oct. 23, 1832, *Sarah Coehaven;* married, 2d, Oct. 26, 1876, *Evelyn B. Nelson.*
1628. MERCY RATHBUN, born Sept. 6, 1806; died Feb. 13, 1889; married, Oct. 15, 1829, *James Hallock.*
1629. DORCAS RATHBUN, born April 28, 1809; married, 1st, Jan. 30, 1852, *Richard Searing;* married, 2d, Nov. 13, 1861, *Henry Wells.*
1630. PERRY RATHBUN, born July 22, 1811; died July 27, 1890; married, Dec. 15, 1837, *Lydia W. Hull.*
1631. BENJAMIN RATHBUN, born Aug. 23, 1813; died Feb. 15, 1889; unmarried.
1632. MARY ANN RATHBUN, born Dec. 20, 1815; died May 6, 1893; married, Nov. 10, 1830, *John G. Barr.*
1633. ROWLAND RATHBUN, born Aug. 17, 1817; married, 1st, Jan. 5, 1831, *Eliza A. Mosely;* married, 2d, Oct. 26, 1851, *Harriet Mosely;* married, 3d, Oct. 17, 1860, *Josephine Smith.*
1634. JAMES RATHBUN, born May 3, 1821.

§ 901. ALICE PECKHAM, 7 (William Peckham, 6; Mary Hazard, 5; Governor George, 4; Colonel George, 3; Robert, 2; Thomas, 1), was born January 19, 1780; she died in Belgrade, Maine, September 9, 1845. She married Rowland Robinson Rathbun, October 14, 1801, and soon after her marriage moved to Smithfield, Rhode Island, where they lived until 1837, when they removed to Blackstone, Massachusetts, where she passed the remainder of her life.

Soon

Soon after her marriage she became a recognized Minister in the New England Yearly Meeting of the Society of Friends, and during her subsequent life was regarded as one of the most distinguished preachers in that religious sect. Her labors in behalf of the gospel of peace and good-will were not confined to her immediate surroundings, but her sweet and eloquent voice was heard by thousands throughout the hills and valleys of New England. Her gentle but living words in reproval of sin and wrong doing, moved her hearers without distinction of sect or belief. She fulfilled her mission as perfectly as it is in the power of finite beings to accomplish the full measure of their work.

While making preparations for her last ministering visit to distant Friends, she felt a premonition that this would be her last, and made full preparations for her death and burial, taking, it is said, even her burial clothes with her. The warning of the "inward light" proved a true warning, for she died soon after her arrival in Belgrade, Maine, September 9, 1845, aged sixty-five.

CHILDREN

1635. LYDIA RATHBUN, born July 13, 1803; married, May 6, 1830, *Eli Kelly.*
1636. MERCY PECKHAM RATHBUN, born April 2, 1805; married *William Osborne,* died Nov. 13, 1881.
1637. MARY RATHBUN, born Oct. 1, 1806; married *Charles Hadwin.*
1638. EDWARD BURROUGH RATHBUN, born Oct. 7, 1809; unmarried.
1639. FRANCIS HOWGILL RATHBUN, born Aug. 19, 1811; married *Susan Brown,* died Nov. 12, 1855.
1640. WILLIAM PECKHAM RATHBUN, born Oct. 18, 1814; married *Eliza Van Slyck.*
1641. ELIZABETH RATHBUN, born Dec. 27, 1818; married —— *Gordon.*

§ 902. WILLIAM PECKHAM, 7 (William Peckham, 6; Mary Hazard, 5; Governor George, 4; Colonel George, 3; Robert, 2; Thomas, 1), was born November 11, 1781; he died November 7, 1863. His boyhood was passed at home, where he acquired his limited education; he attended school four months. His parents were prominent members of the Society of Friends, and his early religious instructions were on a line with that simple faith, guided by the "light within." He continued "a birth-right member" of that sect until February 2, 1803, when he married Susannah Stanton. She not being a member of the Society, he forfeited his right of membership; but both he and his wife continued to worship with the Society during their lives.

In early life he took a deep interest in public affairs, and observed closely the political aspect of the times. In 1810 he was elected to the State Senate, and from that time until late in life he held many offices of trust. In 1814, during the last war with Great Britain, Governor William Jones gave him a commission as Captain of the second Company of Infantry, of the town of South Kingstown, and he was called out to defend the old sloop Wampum, which was chased and driven ashore on Matunuck beach by a British cruiser. This duty he performed much to the annoyance of his good peace-loving Quaker friends.

From 1822, to 1827, he was one of the associate Judges of the Court of Common

Pleas

Pleas of Washington County, and from 1835 to 1841, he was Chief Justice of the same County. He was also one of the State Bank Commissioners from 1838 to 1841. In 1828–29–30–31–32, he was Sheriff of Washington County, elected by the Legislature, according to the law at that time. About 1839, he was appointed by the State of Rhode Island one of the Commissioners (his associates being the late Judge Elisha R. Potter of South Kingstown, and Judge George D. Cross of Westerly, together with Moses B. Lockwood of Providence) as surveyors, to meet a like Commission from Connecticut, to survey and adjust the boundary line between the two States, which had been in dispute for a number of years. In 1844, he was elected a member of the State Legislature, and was chairman of the Committee on Resolutions, to which were referred the resolutions passed by that honorable body, in opposition to the annexation of Texas. In 1835, he was appointed by Governor William Hoppin, a commissioner "to superintend the organization of the Richmond Bank."

He was strongly opposed to slavery and believed in the free public discussion of that question ; hence his house was the refuge of the most radical abolitionists, and he often defended in public their right to the freedom of speech ; sometimes at the risk of personal safety, for in those days to harbor or entertain at one's house an abolitionist, subjected the offender to social ostracism and public indignity, even in liberty-loving New England. But Judge Peckham was strictly a " Law and Order," man ; he believed in the peaceful, political attainment of good wholesome laws, and their rigid enforcement by public officials supported by all good citizens.

He was associated politically with such congenial friends as Nathan F. Dixon, Lemuel H. Arnold, Tristam Burgess, Nehemiah R. Knight, Asher Robbins, James F. Simmons, Henry Y. and Robert B. Cranston, and a number of other men who figured conspicuously in Rhode Island's political history at that time. His association with these men strongly confirmed him in that native sturdiness and independence which was a striking characteristic of the representative men of those days. When the change in the organic law of the State, from the Old Charter, granted by Charles II, in 1663, under which Rhode Island came into the Union as a State, and which she continued to recognize as her fundamental law until 1842, was agitated, he was a strong advocate of the change. He also advocated a more equal apportionment of representatives in the Legislature, and a liberal extension of suffrage. He was once indeed a candidate for Governor on the " Free Suffrage" ticket ; but when Thomas W. Dorr and the more radical friends of the movement purposed to resort to forcible means to attain the end desired, he promptly notified Mr. Dorr and his adherents that, "while he recognized the necessity of the change for which they contended, and was ready to resort to all peaceful and lawful means to secure it, he was not ready to take arms against the existing government to redress a wrong which he believed could be accomplished under recognized lawful authority." In pursuance of that resolution, when the Governor called for volunteers to support the state authority he
appeared

appeared on Market Square in Providence, with five sons, armed and equipped
for that service.

Thus for more than half a century, Judge Peckham was known to the people of
Rhode Island ; known personally and politically to a very large proportion of
the people ; and acting in a public capacity nearly all his life ; and always upright
and honorable amid responsibilities and duties.

Judge William Peckham married, February 13, 1803, Susannah, daughter of
Joseph Stanton.

CHILDREN

1642. SUSANNAH PECKHAM, born Jan. 3, 1804; married *Frank B. Seager*.
1643. SARAH PECKHAM, born June 23, 1805; married *Samuel Tucker*.
1644. BENJAMIN PECKHAM, born Nov. 18, 1806; married *Mary*, daughter of *John* and *Eliza Hoxsie*.
1645. WILLIAM PECKHAM, born Sept. 22, 1808; married *Eliza Hoxsie*.
1646. MERCY PECKHAM, born April 29, 1810; married *William Augustus Weeden;* died 1894.
1647. DORCAS PECKHAM, born June 8, 1812.
1648. JANE HAZARD PECKHAM, born June 8, 1814; unmarried.
1649. GEORGE HAZARD PECKHAM, born Feb. 18, 1816, married *Frances Pennego.*
1650. JAMES PERRY PECKHAM, born March 25, 1819; married *Almira Sheffield*.
1651. EDWIN ALEXANDER PECKHAM, born Dec. 10, 1820; died 1894; married, May 13, 1849, *Mary*,
daughter of *Asa* and *Mary Dye*.
1652. JOHN CROSS PECKHAM, born Nov. 30, 1822; died 1893; married, 1st, *Sarah Austin*; married,
2d, ——
1653. ALICE RATHBUN PECKHAM, born March 8, 1826.

§ 903. MERCY PECKHAM, 7 (William, 6 ; Mary Hazard, 5 ; Governor
George, 4 ; George, 3 ; Robert, 2 ; Thomas, 1), was born July 11, 1783 ; she died
November 29, 1850 ; she married, November 8, 1809, John Bigland Dockray.

CHILDREN

1654. JOHN BIGLAND DOCKRAY, born April 24, 1813; died 1893; married *Susannah Curtis.*
1655. WILLIAM PECKHAM DOCKRAY, born Jan. 14, 1815.
1656. MERCY DOCKRAY, born Oct. 23, 1817; married, June 6, 1843, *Elisha F. Watson.*
1657. JAMES PERRY DOCKRAY, born May 18, 1820; married *Abby Lawton.*

§ 904. PERRY PECKHAM, 7 (William, 6 ; Mary Hazard, 5 ; Governor
George, 4 ; George, 3 ; Robert, 2 ; Thomas, 1), was born June 30, 1789 ; he was
drowned off Point Judith, December 25, 1817 ; he married Sarah —— .

CHILDREN

1658. JAMES PERRY PECKHAM, born Dec. 24, 1814; died July 5, 1863.
1659. MERCY PECKHAM, born Sept. 4, 1816; married *Benjamin Hadwin;* died March 27, 1869.
1660. ELIZABETH PECKHAM, born July, 1817; died Oct. 15, 1828.

§ 907. DORCAS PECKHAM, 7 (William, 6 ; Mary Hazard, 5 ; Governor
George, 4 ; George, 3 ; Robert, 2 ; Thomas, 1), was born February 7, 1787 ; died
October 22, 1859 ; she married, January 28, 1813, Hezekiah Babcock (son of
Caleb and Waite Babcock) of South Kingstown.

CHILDREN

CHILDREN

1661. DORCAS GARDINER BABCOCK, born Feb. 26, 1816; unmarried.
1662. WILLIAM PECKHAM BABCOCK, born April 28, 1818.
1663. HEZEKIAH BABCOCK, born Oct. 31, 1820; married *Hannah*, daughter of *Richard Ward Hazard*.
1664. ADAM BABCOCK, born Dec. 24, 1822; died Oct. 26, 1872; married.
1665. JOHN BABCOCK, born May 23, 1831; married, Sept. 23, 1856, *Mary Perry*.

§ 908. SARAH PERRY, 7 (Mary Peckham, 6 ; Mary Hazard, 5 ; Governor George, 4 ; George, 3 ; Robert, 2 ; Thomas, 1), married Dr. Joseph Comstock.

CHILDREN

1666. JOSHUA PERRY COMSTOCK, died young.
1667. MARY COMSTOCK, unmarried.
1668. ELIZABETH COMSTOCK, unmarried.
1669. JOSEPH COMSTOCK, married *Elizabeth Comstock*.
1670. ESTHER COMSTOCK, unmarried.

§ 909. ABBY PERRY, 7 (Mary Peckham, 6 ; Mary Hazard, 5 ; Governor George, 4 ; George, 3 ; Robert, 2 ; Thomas, 1), she married Thomas Rose. He died young. His children were brought up in their grandfather's house. This house was the original old Hazard "mansion-house," built by Robert Hazard in the seventeenth century. It was standing in the present century.

CHILDREN

1671. JOHN ROSE, M.D., born Feb. 17, 1801; died Nov. 18, 1885; married, July 6, 1837, *Juliette Amanda Carter*.
1672. MARY ROSE, born March, 1802; died 1861; unmarried.
1673. ABBY CONGDON ROSE, born about 1803; died 1880; unmarried.
1674. ELIZABETH BOSS ROSE, born about 1806; died Jan. 25, 1884; unmarried.
1675. ORPHA SWEET ROSE, born Oct. 9, 1810; died Aug., 1889; unmarried.

§ 911. MARTHA PERRY, 7 (Mary Peckham, 6 ; Mary Hazard, 5 ; Governor George, 4 ; George, 3 ; Robert, 2 ; Thomas, 1), married Joshua Barker.

CHILDREN

1676. JOSHUA BARKER.
1677. JAMES BARKER.
1678. ELIZABETH BARKER, married —— *Hale*.

§ 914. PELEG BENJAMIN PECKHAM, 7 (Peleg, 6 ; Mary Hazard, 5 ; Governor George, 4 ; Colonel George, 3 ; Robert, 2 ; Thomas, 1), was born in Rhode Island, July 17, 1792. He removed to Utica, New York, and married, October 4, 1814, Laura Griggs.

CHILDREN

1679. ELIJAH GRIGGS PECKHAM, born Oct. 13, 1815, in Cooperstown, New York; married, Sept. 1, 1837, *Harriet Maria White*, of Utica, New York.
1680. FANNIE PECKHAM, born June 15, 1835, at Utica, New York; married *S. S. Thorn*, M.D., of Utica.

§ 915.

§ 915. GEORGE WILLIAMS PECKHAM, 7 (Peleg, 6 ; Mary Hazard, 5 ;
Governor George, 4 ; Colonel George, 3 ; Robert, 2 ; Thomas, 1), was born in
Rhode Island, February 24, 1796 ; he married Mary, daughter of John Watson,
of Rhode Island. He died 1873.

CHILDREN
1681. HENRY PECKHAM, born March 19, 1831; died Aug. 22, 1834.
1682. GEORGE WILLIAMS PECKHAM, born Aug. 10, 1832; died Aug. 4, 1833.
1683. MARY PECKHAM, born June 20, 1835; died May 5, 1840.
1684. ISABELLA PECKHAM, born March 7, 1838; died June 11, 1864.
1685. MARY PECKHAM, born Dec. 14, 1841; died March 14, 1843.
1686. ELIZA PECKHAM, born Feb. 8, 1843; died Oct. 10, 1871.
1687. GEORGE WILLIAMS PECKHAM, born March 23, 1845; married *Elizabeth Gifford.*
1688. WILLIAM HENRY PECKHAM, born Jan. 19, 1847.

§ 917. WALTON HAZARD PECKHAM, M.D., 7 (Peleg, 6 ; Mary Haz-
ard, 5 ; Governor George, 4 ; Colonel George, 3 ; Robert, 2 ; Thomas, 1), was
born in Rensselaerville, New York; he married Margaret A. Milderburger, widow
of Robert Stuyvesant. He was a physican and practiced in New York City.

CHILDREN
1689. MARGARET AUGUSTA PECKHAM, born Aug. 1840; married *Gabriel Mead Tooker.*
1690. WALTON MILDERBURGER PECKHAM, born April 28, 1842; married, Jan. 18, 1876, *M. Louise Chesebrough.*

§ 918. RUFUS W. PECKHAM, 7 (Peleg, 6 ; Mary Hazard, 5 ; Gov. George,
4 ; Colonel George, 3 ; Robert, 2 ; Thomas, 1), was born in Rensselaerville,
N.Y., December 20, 1809. Soon after, his father removed to Otsego County. He
was early sent to Hartwick Seminary in the same county, and in 1825 entered
Union College ; he graduated in 1827. Mr. Peckham went to Utica on leaving
college, and entered the office of Bronson and Beardsley as a law student. He was
admitted to the bar in 1830, and opened a law-office in Albany. He was engaged
as counsel in a large portion of the cases tried at the circuit, and having for his
competitors such men as Samuel Stevens, Marcus T. Reynolds and Henry G.
Wheaton, it is evident that it was no easy task to acquire prominence among
them. In 1838, when twenty-nine years of age, he was appointed by Gov. Marcy,
District Attorney for the city and county of Albany. The duties of this office,
he discharged both faithfully and ably. He continued in the office of District
Attorney until 1841, when the office was bestowed by Governor Seward on Henry
G. Wheaton. In 1845 he was a candidate before the legislature, which then had
the appointment, for Attorney-General of the State. He had a formidable opponent in John Van Buren, and after a sharp contest was beaten by a single vote.
In the autumn of 1852, he was returned by the city and county of Albany as
representative to the Thirty-third Congress of the United States.
On the expiration of his congressional term he resumed the active practice of
his profession at Albany, having previously associated with him, as a partner,
Lyman Tremain. In the spring of 1859, with health somewhat impaired, he made
a visit

a visit to Europe. On his return he was immediately nominated and soon after elected a Justice of the Supreme Court, by a decided majority over his very able and popular opponent. He brought to the bench excellent qualities. Well read in the law and familiar with the practice of his profession, he dispatched the business of the circuits with rapidity and ability. But more, and most of all, he brought there an ingrained honesty of purpose, — a determination to mete out, without fear or favor, equal and exact justice to all men. At the close of his first judicial term of eight years, Judge Peckham was re-elected without opposition, no candidate being named against him. Before the close of his second term he was elected a member of the Court of Appeals. Thus, after his first elevation to the bench, his life flowed on in a smooth, unbroken current to its sudden close.

Judge Peckham's true individuality, aside from his intellectual life, was exhibited in the warmth and intensity of his affections, and his genius for making himself beloved by all. His friendships were not only strong and enduring, but they were the genuine outgrowth of a generous nature.[1]

Judge Peckham was lost with his wife, in the steamer Ville de Havre, on the 21st of November, 1873.

He married, first, Isabella, daughter of the Rev. Dr. Lacey, rector of S. Peter's Church, Albany. She died young, leaving two sons. His second wife, Mary Foote, was with him on the Ville de Havre. They had no children.

CHILDREN OF THE FIRST MARRIAGE

1691. WHEELER HAZARD PECKHAM, married *Annie Keasby*.
1692. RUFUS W. PECKHAM, married *Harriet Arnold* of New York.[2]
1693. HENRY PECKHAM, died young.


§ 926. MARTHA HAZARD, 7 (George, 6; Mayor George, 5; Governor George, 4; George, 3; Robert, 2; Thomas, 1), was born January 25, 1782; married Marlborough Stanton. He died December 2, 1835.

CHILDREN

1694. GEORGE STANTON.
1695. ALBERT STANTON.


§ 927. BRENTON HAZARD, 7 (George, 6; Mayor George, 5; Governor George, 4; George, 3; Robert, 2; Thomas, 1), was born January 15, 1784; he married Ann G. Childs, of Bristol, Rhode Island.

CHILDREN

1696. WILLIAM WANTON HAZARD, born March 11, 1810; died 1837.
1697. MARTHA B. HAZARD, born April 26, 1812; died *circa* 1880; married, Sept. 25, 1842, *Charles Crosse*.
1698. ELIZA HAZARD, born June 7, 1816; married —— *Wilbor*.
1699. MARY STANTON HAZARD, born May 7, 1829; died 1850; unmarried.

---

[1] Condensed from, "In Memory of Rufus W. Peckham," prepared by a committee of the Bar of the State of New York.
[2] Rufus W. Peckham is now (1894) Judge of the Court of Appeals in Albany, N. Y.

§ 928.

§ 928. GEORGE CHAMPLIN HAZARD, 7 (George, 6; Mayor George, 5; Governor George, 4; George, 3; Robert, 2; Thomas, 1), was born July 4, 1787; he married Eliza Butter.

CHILDREN

1700. GEORGE HAZARD.
1701. ELIZA BUTTER HAZARD.
1702. JEANNETTE HAZARD.
1703. JOHN HAZARD.
1704. CAROLINE HAZARD.
1705. EDWARD HAZARD.

§ 929. JULIA HAZARD, 7 (Carder, 6; Mayor George, 5; Governor George, 4; George, 3; Robert, 2; Thomas 1), was born in Middletown, Rhode Island, February 6, 1806; died September 24, 1878; she married, Sunday, February 3, 1828, Abial Sherman; he died March 12, 1885.

CHILDREN

1706. WILLIAM CARDER HAZARD SHERMAN, born in Norwich, Conn., June 28, 1829; died in Norwich, July 20, 1882; married *Amelia Kimball Taft.*
1707. JOSEPHINE HAZARD SHERMAN, born October 9, 1830; married, Aug. 16, 1854, *Daniel Thomas.*
1708. ELIZABETH LUCY SHERMAN, born Aug. 19, 1832.
1709. JOANNA ROSALINE SHERMAN, born Feb. 28, 1834; died Sept. 6, 1835.

§ 930. ANGELINE M. HAZARD, 7 (Carder, 6; Mayor George, 5; Governor George, 4; George, 3; Robert, 2; Thomas, 1) was born in Norwich, Connecticut, January 3, 1810; she married, May 27, 1831, Elijah A. Bill.

CHILDREN

1710. ELIZABETH DWIGHT BILL, born in Norwich, Conn., Saturday, Dec. 29, 1832; married, Feb. 24, 1859, *James Lewis.*
1711. SARAH HAZARD BILL, born in Norwich, Monday, April 17, 1837.
1712. JULIA ALMIRA BILL, born Saturday, Oct. 31, 1840.
1713. MARY HANNAH BILL, born Tuesday, Sept. 14, 1847.
1714. BENJAMIN LEIGHTON BILL, born Thursday, March 25, 1852; died June 21, 1885.

§ 936. SAMUEL FALES HAZARD, 7 (Nathaniel, 6; Mayor George, 5; Governor George, 4; George, 3; Robert, 2; Thomas, 1), was born February 29, 1804, at Taunton, Mass. He entered the Navy as midshipman, January, 1823. He served in the war with Mexico, and in the war of the Rebellion, being with Admiral Foote on the Mississipi River at the taking of Island No. 10 and was attached to the staff of General Burnside, commanding the naval forces, in the expedition against Newbern and Roanoke Island. It was owing to the exposure during this service that he contracted the disease which finally ended his life, January 15, 1867. Of his forty-four years in the service, twenty years and seven months were spent at sea, thirteen years and two months on shore duty, only ten years and two months being unemployed. He married, August 10, 1841, Martha, daughter of Charles and Mary DeWolfe.

CHILDREN

CHILDREN

1715. VIRGINIA HAZARD, died at five years.
1716. MARTHA DeWOLFE HAZARD, married *Frederick Russell Sturgis*, of New York.

§ 941. JOSEPH HAZARD, 7 (Thomas C., 6; Judge Carder, 5; Governor George, 4; George, 3; Robert, 2; Thomas, 1), married Ruhamah Champlin, October, 1823.

CHILDREN

1717. CARDER HAZARD, married, Dec. 10, 1848, *Susan*, daughter of *Benjamin Knowles*. She was a deaf-mute.
1718. PETER HAZARD.
1719. JOHN HAZARD.
1720. SUSAN HAZARD, married —— *Tuttle*.
1721. MARIAN HAZARD, married *Jeremiah Cranston*.
1722. THANKFUL HAZARD.
1723. RUHAMAH HAZARD.

§ 944. WILLIAM HENRY HAZARD, M.D., 7 (Doctor George, 6; Carder, 5; Governor George, 4; George, 3; Robert, 2; Thomas, 1), was born in South Kingstown, at Matunuck, in the house owned by his father, Doctor George Hazard. This house is still standing, but with the large ell removed, the great barn being replaced by a modern building, the apothecary's shop, the ice-house and other out-buildings that once gave the place the semblance of a small village rather than a private residence, being also taken down. After a few years spent at home and attendance in the public schools, he was sent to Plainfield, Connecticut, for further and better advantages of education. He then attended lectures in Boston under Doctor Warren and Doctor Webster, both well known and prominent physicians — the latter notorious afterward as the murderer of Dr. Parkman. After finishing this course in Boston, Dr. Hazard entered the office of Dr. Daniel Turner, of Newport, remaining there several years. About 1830, he came back to Wakefield and commenced the practice of medicine, continuing there for over fifty years. His success was owing in part to the fact of his quick intuitions and rapid judgment, and partly it may be to the fact, that he gave *very* little medicine. In 1853 he was brought into immediate contact with Dr. Okie, a well-known homeopathic physician of Providence. After a careful study of the principles of homeopathy, he adopted its theory with great success.

When about eighty years of age his eyesight failed, and though still in vigorous health and capable of sustaining easily all the demands made upon the strength of a country physician, he gave up his practice; not without regret, however. He often said that he felt his judgments more sure, and his knowledge greater than ever before.

In his early manhood Dr. Hazard was an enthusiastic politician, although not seeking office for himself, and never accepting a nomination with but one exception, namely in 1838. Elisha R. Potter of Kingston, being dead, it was supposed that

that his place in the General Assembly would fall to his son Elisha R. Potter, Jr., whose party built great hopes upon the prestige of his father's name. It was said that there was but one man in the town that could be successfully opposed to him, and that man was Doctor Hazard, and he was persuaded to accept the nomination, and was elected by a small majority. He was re-elected again in the autumn, for at this time the members of the General Assembly of Rhode Island were elected twice a year, but his increasing practice, which he would not sacrifice, prevented him from accepting a nomination again. This did not prevent him from being a strong factor in his party and a great worker, politically, for his friends. He was also a great worker in his profession. His splendid physique was like well-tempered steel, elastic after his most exhausting days of labor. Dr. Hazard was a most hospitable man, Mrs. Hazard being peculiarly fitted by her experience in her father's house, to aid him in making her own house attractive to all guests. There is no house in the town around which such pleasant memories linger of good cheer, and good company. Doctor Hazard had a keen sense of humor, and his large experience in his profession, which brought him in contact with "all sorts and conditions of men," gave him a fund of amusing stories, of which his own hearty appreciation added much to the enjoyment of the listener. A sketch of Doctor Hazard would be incomplete, if his liberality was not mentioned. When his practice was at its maximum it amounted to ten thousand dollars a year, but perhaps more than one-half of this was given away in charity. He never refused to attend a patient no matter how great the patient's poverty ; and not only did he give his attention and medicines, but food and clothing were often added. It was no uncommon sight to see his wagon filled with baskets and boxes for the sick heaped up with the products of his farm, for like a true country physician he was also a farmer, and took much pleasure in his fine herd of Jerseys. In his charities he was ably supported by his friend and kinsman, Rowland Gibson Hazard of Peacedale, whose directions were, "don't let your poor sick patients suffer while I have the means to help them." Doctor Hazard was the true type of the country doctor and country gentleman, for his courtesy came from his native kindness of heart, and from the spirit of " noblesse oblige." He married, March 15, 1840, Louisa, daughter of Governor Lemuel Hastings and Sally (Lyman) Arnold. She came from a line of good old families, and was justly proud of her beautiful grandmother, the daughter of John Wanton of Newport, the " toast " of the officers of the Revolution. They had no children.

§ 945. CARDER HAZARD, 7 (Doctor George, 6; Judge Carder, 5; Governor George, 4; George, 3; Robert, 2; Thomas, 1), was born August 20, 1809; he died July 3, 1863. He married, March 3, 1834, Eliza, daughter of Elisha and Ann (Cole) Watson.

CHILDREN

1724. CHARLES HENRY HAZARD, born March 5, 1835; married *Susan*, daughter of *Elisha* and *Hannah* (*Robinson*) *Watson*. For children see *No. 1384.*

1725.

1725. ANN ELIZA HAZARD, born June 6, 1837; married *Jedediah Huntington*.
1726. JULIA HAZARD, born 1844; married *George Durfee*, April 18, 1867.

§ 947. GEORGE HAZARD, 7 (Doctor George, 6; Carder 5; Governor George, 4; George, 3; Robert, 2; Thomas, 1), was born August 25, 1813; he died February 12, 1864; he married ———.

CHILDREN
1727. ELIZA STOCKFORD HAZARD, married *Josiah Crooker*.
1728. CLARE HAZARD.
1729. JANE MARIA HAZARD.

§ 949. MARY HOXSIE HAZARD, 7 (Doctor George, 6; Judge Carder, 5; Governor George, 4; Colonel George, 3; Robert, 2; Thomas, 1), was born March 10, 1815, at South Kingstown, Rhode Island. She married, June 16, 1847, Reverend James Carpenter; he died February 18, 1881. Her brothers often declared that she had never consciously done a wrong to herself or to others; combined with her gentle manner and soft voice, was a keen sense of humor. The quaint stories, recollections of her old home on her father's farm, and her early married life in the old Willett homestead in Boston Neck, were told with a charming grace and thorough appreciation. Always of a delicate constitution, she was for the greater part of her life a confirmed invalid and "mother's room and invalid chair" became the centre round which clustered every thought of the household, and the devotion of her three daughters. A more united, unselfish household it would be difficult to find. "Thine ease, not mine" was the watchword.

Mr. Carpenter at the early age of fifteen went to Providence, Rhode Island, and entered on a business training, remaining there eleven years. His fine moral sense soon developed into a strong religious faith, under the influence of the Rev. John A. Clark, the devoted rector of Grace Church, and he was confirmed at the age of twenty-five. Entering upon his new responsibilities with the quiet faithfulness which characterized him, he ably assisted Mr. Clark in parish work.

His decision to enter the priesthood was made at a sacrifice of the most promising prospects of success in business life. But one of his singular purity of nature could set but small value upon material gains. He pursued his studies at the General Theological Seminary, New York, from 1838 to 1842, providing for his simple wants by his own industry. He was ordained deacon, 1842, at Gardiner, Maine, by the venerable Bishop Griswold, and was ordained priest by Bishop Henshaw, always one of the truest and warmest of his personal friends. His parochial charges as missionary, were in Providence and Cumberland, and those held by him as rector, in Manville and Wakefield, Rhode Island. His sermons were composed with singular zeal and diligence, were systematic in thought, pointed in style, and deeply devout in spirit. As parish priest he was faithful and gentle in his relations with his people. His ministrations in houses of mourning are still cherished in grateful remembrance; and his watchfulness over the young was touchingly illustrated in the revival of old associations at his funeral.

For

For the last thirteen years of his life, his home was in Wakefield. Here he fo.-lowed the congenial occupation of teaching, greatly enjoying the kindly inter-course with his attached pupils. . . . He had very lately been employed on a "History of Washington County, Rhode Island," which was included in a "History of the New England States," published in Boston. His last public act was on the occasion of the late presidential election, when rallying his last failing strength for an effort of duty, he went to the polls in the care of a young clerical brother, and leaning on the faithful arm of his young companion, cast his vote for the perpetuating of those principles of freedom and nationality to which he had ever been consistently, though unobtrusively devoted. It was evidently at this time that he received some intimation that it was in vain to expect a return of health, for he spoke to his friend in terms similar to those which he afterwards used in his family, to the effect that God's time was the rightful one ; and that to have lived as long as He ordained was long enough to satisfy a submissive spirit. There was a touching gentleness of resignation in the greatness of soul thus un-consciously manifested by one who cherished an innocent love of life, and always found something to enjoy, something for which to give thanks, even under hard conditions.[1]

" The Reverend James Helme Carpenter passed to his rest by slow and sensible degrees, and, after a protracted and wearisome illness, meekly and submissively rendered back his spirit to the God who gave him life. He was a man without guile, transparent and simple as a child, always accepting his lot as the ordering of One who knew what was the discipline which he most needed. Mr. Carpenter was a studious and thoughtful man. He did the work that was given him to do, thoroughly and to his best ability ; and when his public career was over, he con-tinued to benefit those around him by his pure and unspotted life, and absolute resignation to the will of God." [2]

Esther Bernon Carpenter, the first child that came to bless the parents' home with her presence, was rarely gifted by nature, and highly cultivated by her ar-dent love for study. She was educated in her father's house, passing a few years only at S. Mary's Hall, in New Jersey. Few children, however, have had the careful training and instruction that she received from her father ; at eleven years of age she was reading with him, Shakespeare's plays, enjoying and possi-bly appreciating them more than many older persons. Leaving school did not mean, for her, giving up study, but on the contrary, a continuance and constant advancement. She was fond of the study of languages, and had a good working knowledge of Latin, German, French and Spanish. With the exception of Latin, which she studied at school and under her father, she was almost entirely self-taught. Her reading was, like her memory, marvellous, and she was thoroughly well informed on all intellectual subjects, and was rarely at fault in a quotation

[1] A Memorial of the late James H. Carpenter. By his daughter, Esther Bernon Carpenter.
[2] From the Address of Rt. Rev. Thomas M. Clarke, at the Ninety-first Annual Convention of the Diocese of Rhode Island, June 14th, 1881.

from

from the classics or modern poets. For many years she was a contributor to historical papers, newspapers and periodicals, and she published a number of her short stories in a little volume called *South County Neighbors*. Many of these stories embodied the old traditions and quaint recollections of her mother. She died at Wakefield, October 22, 1893, and a tablet to her memory is placed in the Hazard Memorial Hall at Peacedale.

CHILDREN

1730. ESTHER BERNON CARPENTER, born April 4, 1848; died Oct. 22, 1893.
1731. BETSEY CARPENTER, born Dec. 17, 1849; died in infancy.
1732. LAURA HAZARD CARPENTER, born Sept. 19, 1852.
1733. MARY CARPENTER, born Feb. 22, 1856.
1734. JAMES WILLET CARPENTER, born April 13, 1857; died in infancy.

§ 950. LAURA HAZARD, 7 (Doctor George, 6; Judge Carder, 5; Governor George, 4; George, 3; Robert, 2; Thomas, 1), was born November 4, 1819; she married, March 17, 1841, Attmore Robinson, son of James and Mary (Attmore) Robinson; they were married at the Church of the Ascension, in Wakefield, Rhode Island, by the Reverend W. H. Newman.

CHILDREN

1735. JAMES ATTMORE ROBINSON, born Tuesday, Jan. 13, 1842; married, 1st, *Lizzie Alger*; married, 2d, *Mary Ring*.
1736. JANE HULL ROBINSON, born Monday, Aug. 21, 1843.
1737. SYLVESTER C. ROBINSON, born Friday, May 16, 1845.
1738. GEORGE HAZARD ROBINSON, born Tuesday, March 22, 1847; married *Sarah Delamater*.
1739. ANNIE CHASE ROBINSON, born Tuesday, March 22, 1849.
1740. WILLIAM HENRY ROBINSON, born Saturday, April 9, 1853; married *Sally Crosier*.

§ 964. MARY HAZARD, 7 (Richard Ward, 6; Judge Carder, 5; Governor George, 4; George, 3; Robert, 2; Thomas, 1). She married John Nichols.

CHILD

1741. JOHN NICHOLS.

§ 965. JOSEPH HAZARD, 7 (Richard Ward, 6; Judge Carder, 5; Governor George, 4; George, 3; Robert, 2; Thomas, 1), was born September 14, 1814; he died May 25, 1875; he married, January 17, 1847, Susan R., daughter of Benjamin Congdon. Mr. Hazard moved to New York State early in life.

CHILDREN

1742. MARY JANE HAZARD, born April 5, 1848; died Sept. 11, 1848.
1743. GEORGE CARDER HAZARD, born Sept. 2, 1849; died Aug. 12, 1861.
1744. CHARLES BENJAMIN HAZARD, born July 24, 1852; died July 11, 1861.
1745. JOSEPH EDWARD HAZARD, born Sept. 10, 1855; married, Oct. 1, 1877, *Ada*, daughter of *Orray Snow*.
1746. DANIEL ARTHUR HAZARD, born Nov. 15, 1858; married, Oct. 8, 1879, *Ida E.*, daughter of *Eben Sibley*.
1747. THEODORE LINCOLN HAZARD, born Sept. 9, 1860; married, Jan. 3, 1883, *Clara C.*, daughter of *Archibald Merrill*.

1748.

1748. WILLIAM HENRY HAZARD, born Aug. 22, 1866; married, June 24, 1890, *Emma*, daughter of *Charles D. Brown.*

§ 969. HANNAH HAZARD, 7 (Richard Ward, 6; Judge Carder, 5; Governor George, 3; Robert, 2; Thomas, 1), was born October, 1827; she married, first, Hezekiah Babcock; she married, second, Jonathan Allen, her brother-in-law.

CHILDREN OF FIRST MARRIAGE

1749. GEORGE HAZARD BABCOCK, born Aug. 10, 1845; married *Alice House.*
1750. MARY DORCAS BABCOCK, born July 4, 1849; married *George Sherman.*

§ 973. CARDER CLARKE, 7 (Sarah Hazard, 6; Judge Carder, 5; Governor George, 4; George, 3; Robert, 2; Thomas, 1), was born July 21, 1811; he died August 28, 1892; he married, June 16, 1846, Hannah Allen; they were married by Reverend Wilson Coggeshall; she died May 18, 1889.

CHILDREN

1751. SARAH ALICE CLARKE, born April 11, 1847; married, March 9, 1885, *Richard A. Harrall.*
1752. HANNAH EMMELINE CLARKE, born July 6, 1849; married, October 29, 1873, *Stephen B. Gardiner.*
1753. JULIA HAZARD CLARKE, born June 11, 1854; married, Nov. 13, 1873, *Charles H. Knowles.*
1754. MARY ELLA CLARKE, born June 23, 1857; married, Oct. 16, 1878, *Walter A. Nye.*
1755. A CHILD, born and died April 6, 1865.

§ 974. PETER W. CLARKE, 7 (Sarah Hazard, 6; Judge Carder, 5; Governor George, 4; George, 3; Robert, 2; Thomas, 1), was born March 12, 1815; he married, February 1, 1843, Martha Browning; she died May 25, 1851, aged thirty-four. He married, second, Elizabeth ——, February 28, 1853.

CHILDREN OF FIRST MARRIAGE

1756. JAMES N. CLARKE, born Aug. 12, 1845; died Feb. 7, 1848.
1757. JAMES F. CLARKE, born Oct. 25, 1848; died June 25, 1850.
1758. PETER B. CLARKE, born May 25, 1851.

CHILDREN OF SECOND MARRIAGE

1759. MARTHA CLARKE, born Dec. 21, 1856; died April 14, 1859.
1760*a*. LUCY A. CLARKE, born Nov. 16, 1860.

§ 978. OLIVER HAZARD PERRY, 7 (Christopher Raymond, 6; Mercy Hazard, 5; Oliver, 4; George, 3; Robert, 2; Thomas, 1), was born in the village of Rocky Brook, South Kingstown, August 23, 1785; he died August 23, 1819. He entered the United States Navy as midshipman, April 7, 1799; cruised with his father, a naval officer, in the West Indies, 1799–1800; was engaged in the war against Tripoli 1804–5; became lieutenant, January 15, 1807, and at the outbreak of the War of 1812 was in command of a flotilla of gunboats on the Atlantic coast, when in February, 1813, he was transferred at his own request to serve under Commodore Isaac Chauncey on Lake Ontario.

He took an active part in the attack upon Fort George; was appointed to fit out a squadron upon Lake Erie, which he successfully accomplished at Presque Isle

978
OLIVER HAZARD PERRY.

Isle (now Erie), Pennsylvania ; and having equipped nine small vessels, attacked and captured the British fleet near Put-in-Bay, Ohio, Sept. 10, 1813. This action, known as the "battle of Lake Erie," or more commonly as "Perry's Victory," obtained him an immense popularity, partly attributable to the manner in which it was announced by the famous dispatch, "We have met the enemy and they are ours." Congress rewarded him with a vote of thanks, a medal, and the rank of captain. Perry co-operated with Gen. Harrison in his operations at Detroit and at the battle of the Thames, October 5, 1813, and in the following year was employed upon the Potomac and in the defense of Baltimore. He commanded the *Java* in Decatur's squadron in the Mediterranean, in 1815 ; was sent to the Spanish Main in command of a squadron, June, 1819 ; ascended the Orinoco to Angostura in July ; was seized with yellow fever, and died at Port Spain, on the island of Trinidad, the day of his arrival there, August 23, 1819. His remains were removed to Newport in a ship of war, by order of Congress, and buried in the cemetery of that city, December 4, 1826, where an imposing obelisk was erected by the State of Rhode Island. In September, 1860, a marble statue of Commodore Perry was erected at Cleveland, Ohio, and on September 10, 1885, a fine bronze statue was unveiled at Newport, Rhode Island.[1]
He married, May 5, 1811, Elizabeth Champlin Mason. There are no descendants in the male line from Commodore Oliver Hazard Perry living to-day.

CHILDREN

1760b. CHRISTOPHER GRANT PERRY, born April 2, 1812 ; married, May 31, 1838, *Fanny Sargent*, of Philadelphia.
1760c. OLIVER HAZARD PERRY, born Feb. 23, 1813 ; died March 4, 1814.
1761. OLIVER HAZARD PERRY, born Feb. 23, 1815 ; died Aug. 30, 1878 ; married, 1st, Sept. 24, 1837, *Elizabeth Ann*, daughter of Hon. *Kidder Randolph*; she died Aug. 3, 1847 ; he married, 2d, *Mary Ann Morely*, of Newburyport, Mass. He was a Lieutenant in the U. S. Navy, and resigned, July 23, 1848.
1762. CHRISTOPHER RAYMOND PERRY, born June 29, 1816 ; died Oct. 8, 1848. He graduated at the U. S. Military Academy and entered the U. S. Army.
1763. ELIZABETH MASON PERRY, born Sept. 15, 1819 ; died 1842 ; married Nov. 2, 1841, Rev. *Francis Vinton*, D.D.

§ 979. RAYMOND HENRY JONES PERRY, 7 (Christopher Raymond, 6 ; Mercy Hazard, 5 ; Oliver, 4 ; George, 3 ; Robert, 2 ; Thomas, 1), was born February 11, 1789 ; he died March 12, 1826 ; he married May 16, 1814, Mary Ann DeWolfe, daughter of James DeWolfe of Bristol, Rhode Island. He was a lieutenant in the United States Navy.

CHILDREN

1764. JAMES DEWOLFE PERRY, born Sept. 2, 1815 ; died Sept. 9, 1876 ; married *Julia Sophia Jones*, March 3, 1836.
1765a. RAYMOND HENRY PERRY, born June 25, 1817 ; died July 2, 1817.
1765b. NANCY BRADFORD PERRY, born Jan. 13, 1819 ; died July 12, 1883 ; married *Robert Lay*, Aug. 29, 1847.

[1] See Life by Captain Alexander S. Mackenzie (N.Y.,1843); also Johnson's Universal Cyclopædia, Vol. VI., p. 533.
1766.

1766. ALEXANDER PERRY, born May 4, 1822; died Nov. 9, 1888; married *Lavinia Cady Howe*, May 6, 1847.

§ 981. MATHEW CALBRAITH PERRY, 7 (Christopher Raymond, 6; Mercy Hazard, 5; Oliver, 4; George, 3; Robert, 2; Thomas, 1), was born in Newport, Rhode Island, April 10, 1794; he died March 4, 1858. He entered the Navy, 1809; was made lieutenant in 1813. In 1819, while cruising, he settled the question of the location of the first occupation of Liberia. In 1821–24, in command of the schooner *Shark*, he captured several pirates near the West India Islands. In 1833, after a three years' cruise in the Mediterranean, he became the superintendent of a school for gun practice in the Brooklyn Navy Yard, and superintended the application of steam to war vessels. In 1837 he was made captain, and in 1838 went abroad to visit the dock-yards, and inspect the danger signals on the coasts. In 1839–41 he was commandant at the Brooklyn navy-yard, afterwards of the African squadron and the Gulf squadron, and gallantly co-operated with the land forces at the battle of Vera Cruz. In 1852–54 he went on an expedition to Japan. He was one of the first public men in this country who looked for the peaceful opening of Japan, and long before he was appointed to command the fleet, March 1852, he had carefully studied the land, the people, and the problem from every side. He arrived off Uraga in the bay of Yeddo, July 7, 1853, and after leaving letters for the Tycoon, sailed away July 17, and returned in February, 1854. On March 8, the formal articles of convention between the United States and Japan were exchanged at Yokohama, on the spot now occupied by the Union Christian Church. Perry's one mistake was in not treating with the true sovereign, the Mikado, from Osaka, instead of with his lieutenant, the Tycoon. Commodore Perry was a cultivated scholar and the *Narrative of the Expedition of an American Squadron to the China Seas and Japan*, though nominally edited by Dr. Francis L. Hawks, is, in the main, an exact reprint of Perry's diary and autograph narrative. He died in New York.
A superb bronze statue of Commodore M. C. Perry, with four bas-reliefs in bronze illustrating scenes in his public life, by J. Q. A. Ward, stands in Truro Park, Newport, Rhode Island, erected by his son-in-law, August Belmont, of New York.[1]
He married, October 24, 1819, Jane Slidell, daughter of John Slidell, of New York. She was born in New York, February 29, 1797, and died at Newport, January 14, 1879.
CHILDREN
1767*a*. JOHN SLIDELL PERRY, died March 24, 1817.
1767*b*. SARAH PERRY; married, Dec. 15, 1841, Col. *Robert S. Rodgers* (brother of Rear-Admiral *John Rodgers*, U. S. N.), at Navy Yard, Brooklyn, New York.
1767*c*. JANE HAZARD PERRY; married, Oct. 20, 1841, *John Hone*, of New York; died Dec. 24, 1882.

[1] The International Cyclopædia, Vol. II., p. 529.

*901*
MATTHEW CALBRAITH PERRY.

1768a. Matthew Calbraith Perry; midshipman, June 1, 1835; lieutenant, April 3, 1848; later, captain; married, April 26, 1853, *Harriet Taylor*, of Brooklyn; died Nov. 16, 1873.
1768b. Susan Murgatroyd Perry, died Aug. 15, 1825.
1769. Oliver Hazard Perry; appointed lieutenant U. S. Marine Corps, Feb. 25, 1841; was in the Mexican War, rising, July 23, 1849; later appointed U. S. Consul at Hong Kong; died in London, 1870, unmarried.
1770a. William Frederick Perry, died March 18, 1884.
1770b. Caroline Slidell Perry; married, Nov. 7, 1849, Hon. *August Belmont ;* died 189—. *August Belmont* was born in Alzei, Hesse-Darmstadt, his father being a small landed proprietor in the Rhenish Palatinate. Early in life he obtained a position in the office of the Rothschilds, and before the age of twenty found himself entrusted with the management of negotiations between his employers and various Continental governments. In 1837 he came to New York to represent the Rothschilds in this country. In 1844 he was appointed as Consul-General of Austria to New York, which position he held until 1850. He was later appointed American Minister to the Netherlands, and, through his influence with the Rothschilds, he succeeded in sustaining the credit of the United States Government during the Civil War ; and to his efforts has also been attributed the non-recognition of the Confederacy by England and France. Mrs. *Belmont* was for a great many years one of the most conspicuous figures in the society of New York. There were six children, four of whom survived her: *Perry Belmont*, for eight years a member of Congress, and subsequently United States Minister to Spain; *August Belmont*, the head of the firm of *August Belmont & Company*, bankers; *Frederica Belmont*, wife of Mr. *S. S. Howland; Oliver Hazard Perry Belmont ; Jennie*, who died at the age of seventeen; and *Raymond Rogers*, who was killed by the accidental discharge of a pistol.
1770c. Isabella Bolton Perry; married, Aug. 17, 1864, *George Tiffany*, of New York.

§ 986. MERCY CHAMPLIN, 7 (Elizabeth Perry, 6; Mercy Hazard, 5; Oliver, 4; George, 3; Robert, 2; Thomas, 1), was born September 19, 1783; she died August 14, 1857; she married, in 1806, Rev. James Rogers, a Baptist clergyman of Wheatland, New York; they removed to Palmyra, New York.

Children
1771. Ruth Hayward Rogers, born May 13, 1809; married, April 27, 1836, *Elisha Harmon*.
1772. Joshua Perry Rogers; married *Electa Baldwin.*
1773. Caroline Hayward Rogers; married Rev. —— *Tucker.*
1774. Elizabeth Rogers; married *Robert Pomeroy.*
1775. Erenah R. Rogers; married *John Keeney.*
1776. Ryland J. Rogers; married, 1st, *Eliza Pomeroy ;* married, 2d, *Eunice Goddard.*

§ 987. WILLIAM BROWNING CHAMPLIN, 7 (Elizabeth Perry, 6; Mercy Hazard, 5; Oliver, 4; George, 3; Robert, 2; Thomas, 1), was born February 13, 1785; he removed to Northumberland, Pennsylvania, where he died in 1853; he married, in 1811, Olive Manning.

Children
1777. Elizabeth Champlin.
1778. Manning Champlin.
1779. Rhoda Champlin; married —— *Mitchel.*
1780. Olive Champlin; married —— *Mitchel.*

§ 989. ELIZABETH CHAMPLIN, 7 (Elizabeth Perry, 6; Mercy Hazard, 5; Oliver, 4; George, 3; Robert, 2; Thomas, 1), was born in South Kingstown, December

December 2, 1786; she died at Northumberland, Pennsylvania, in 1820; she married Sherman Loomis. He was born in Lebanon, Connecticut, in 1786.

CHILDREN

1781. ISAIAH C. LOOMIS, born 1811, in Lebanon, Connecticut; died in Carlisle, Pa.
1782. STEPHEN CHAMPLIN LOOMIS, born 1813; he lives in Emporia, Kansas.
1783. WILLIAM WALLACE LOOMIS, born 1815, in Lebanon, Conn.
1784. ELIZABETH RAYMOND LOOMIS, born 1817, in Northumberland, Pa.

§ 990. STEPHEN CHAMPLIN, 7 (Elizabeth Perry, 6; Mercy Hazard, 5; Oliver, 4; George, 3; Robert, 2; Thomas, 1), was born in South Kingstown, November 17, 1789; he died in Buffalo, New York, February 20, 1870. He was a commodore in the United States Navy, and fired the first and the last shot in the war of 1812. He married, January 5, 1817, Minerva Pomeroy; she was born in Vermont, and died in Buffalo, June 8, 1857, aged sixty.

CHILDREN

1785. OLIVER HAZARD PERRY CHAMPLIN, born at Lebanon, Connecticut, Nov. 25, 1818; married, in Newport, Rhode Island, Oct. 1, 1856, *Ruth Tilley*.
1786. JANE ELIZABETH CHAMPLIN, born in Lebanon, Connecticut, Jan. 11, 1821; died Feb. 24, 1870; married, April 22, 1839, *James H. Simpson*.
1787. STEPHEN RAYMOND CHAMPLIN, born in Lebanon, Connecticut, April 14, 1823; died in St. Paul, Minnesota.
1788. LYDIA MINERVA CHAMPLIN, born in Lebanon, Connecticut, Aug., 1825; married, Aug. 14, 1843, *Charles L. Emerson*, of Buffalo, New York.
1789. ELIZA ELLEN CHAMPLIN, born in Lebanon, Connecticut, Sept. 11, 1827; married, Aug. 30, 1853, *John B. Cook*, of Erie, Pennsylvania.
1790. THOMAS A. P. CHAMPLIN, born in Lebanon, Connecticut, Aug. 17, 1829; married, Dec. 22, 1852, *Jennie Howell*, of Canandaigua, New York.
1791. WILLIAM BROWNING CHAMPLIN, born in Lebanon, Connecticut, June 24, 1831; married *Sophia Riley*, of Aurora, New York.
1792. JAMES HARVEY CHAMPLIN, born in Buffalo, New York, Nov. 1839; died 1841.

§ 991. MARY PERRY CHAMPLIN, 7 (Elizabeth Perry, 6; Mercy Hazard, 5; Oliver, 4; George, 3; Robert, 2; Thomas, 1), was born in South Kingstown February 7, 1793; she married, in Lebanon, Connecticut, November 27, 1820, Gordon Bailey; he was born February 7, 1793.

CHILDREN

1793. SAMUEL G. BAILEY, born Aug. 1, 1821; married *Isabella Sinclair*, of Milwaukee, Wis.
1794. ELIZABETH PERRY BAILEY, born Aug. 9, 1823; married *Joseph Eckley*.
1795. LYDIA C. BAILEY, born April 7, 1825.
1796. MARY JEANNETTE BAILEY, born May 13, 1828; married *Thomas C. Rayburn*.
1797. JOHN C. BAILEY, born April 13, 1830; married *Anna Grant*.
1798. JULIA A. BAILEY, born Jan. 9, 1832; married *Philo DuBois*.
1799. LUCIAN CHAMPLIN BAILEY, born Nov. 30, 1836; married *Helen Hayden*, of Haydenville, Massachusetts.

§ 993. FREEMAN PERRY WATSON, 7 (Susan Perry, 6; Mercy Hazard, 5; Oliver, 4; Colonel George, 3; Robert, 2; Thomas, 1), was born May 16, 1787;

1787; he married, December 13, 1811, Phebe Watson, daughter of Job and Phebe (Weeden) Watson.

CHILDREN

1800. JOB WEEDEN WATSON, born Feb. 9, 1813; died Feb. 7, 1875.
1801. ELISHA FREEMAN WATSON, born March 28, 1814; married, June 6, 1843, *Mary*, daughter of *John Dockray*.
1802. FREEMAN PERRY WATSON, born March 1, 1819; died June 12, 1890; married, 1st, *Mary*, daughter of *Daniel* and *Mary (Congdon) Watson;* 2d, *Abby*, daughter of *Benjamin Hull*.
1803. PHEBE WEEDEN WATSON, born 1825; married, Jan. 23, 1849, *Stephen H. Tefft*.

§ 994. SUSANNAH WATSON, 7 (Susan Perry, 6; Mercy Hazard, 5; Oliver, 4; Colonel George, 3; Robert, 2; Thomas, 1), was born March 13, 1789; she married George, son of John Watson.

CHILDREN

1804. ELLEN WATSON.
1805. GEORGE WATSON.

§ 995. ELIZABETH WATSON, 7 (Susan Perry, 6; Mercy Hazard, 5; Oliver, 4; Colonel George, 3; Robert, 2; Thomas, 1), was born June 24, 1790; she married Benjamin Brown.

CHILDREN

1806. JEREMIAH BROWN.
1807. JOHN L. BROWN.
1808. ELIZA BROWN.
1809. ELEANORA BROWN; died young.

§ 996. MIRIAM WATSON, 7 (Susan Perry, 6; Mercy Hazard, 5; Oliver, 4; George, 3; Robert, 2; Thomas, 1), was born October 30, 1793; she married Stephen Browning.

CHILDREN

1810. GEORGE W. BROWNING, born Oct. 6, 1822.
1811. STEPHEN BROWNING.
1812. MIRIAM BROWNING; married —— *Knox*, of Brookfield, ——.
1813. FRANCES BROWNING; married *John Eddy*.
1814. ELIZABETH BROWNING; married *Rowland F. Gardiner*.
1815. SUSAN BROWNING; married *Jeremiah*, son of *Arnold Hazard*.
1816. ELISHA WATSON BROWNING; married *Susan Watson*, daughter of *George* and *Susannah*.

§ 1003. JONATHAN NICHOLS HAZARD, 7 (Jonathan, 6; Stephen, 5; Stephen, 4; Stephen, 3; Robert, 2; Thomas, 1), was born January 16, 1795. He was sometimes called, by way of distinction, "Squire Hazard." His father died when he was but seven years of age, leaving his mother with six small children. Her means for the support of the helpless little family were not large, as a relative had taken advantage of her unprotected condition to defraud her of the patrimony left to her by her grandfather, James Perry. She herself taught school for a time, to help feed her little brood, and her sons were taught serviceable trades. Jonathan, her third son, learned the carpenter's trade. About 1820 he commenced

commenced manufacturing coarse woolen goods, in company with Isaac Peace Hazard, at a place called Brushy Brook, in the western part of the town. This enterprise was very successful for a few years. Mr. Hazard then moved to Rocky Brook, and operated Thomas R. Hazard's mills, in that place; here he was successful. Thomas R. Hazard was enabled to retire from business a few years afterwards, with what was at that time considered a fortune.

Jonathan Hazard then bought one of the mills on his own account, which he run until about 1837, when he gave up the manufacturing business; and after one year spent in Newport, he bought one-half of a property in Narragansett Pier. At this time he ran a line of sloops to Providence, Newport and New York; the sloop *Washington* made three trips a week to Providence and Newport; the *Point Judith* and *Pettasquamscutt* sailed one each week to New York. These sloops were built and launched at the "Pier," near where the Casino now stands, and were built by Captain John Saunders.

Mr. Hazard was an exceedingly quick-tempered, but also an exceedingly kind-hearted and sympathetic man. While scolding a miserable drunkard for his improvidence and neglect of his family, he would at the same time busy himself in filling a basket with provisions, and to the last denunciatory word he would add, "Come for more when that is gone." He truly understood the meaning of the word "neighbor." On one occasion, seeing a heavy thunder-storm coming up, and also seeing his neighbor's hay, that was well cured and ready for the barn in danger of injury, and knowing his friend was away from home, Mr. Hazard called some men from his mill, and, taking his teams, went to the field and gathered the hay into the barn. When thanked for this kind deed, he said, "There is nothing to thank me for; am I not thy neighbor?" His wife was a member of the Society of Friends, and thus his changing fortunes did not prevent his children from being all well educated in the Friends' School in Providence.

Jonathan Hazard married Mary Congdon

CHILDREN

1817. MARY ABIGAIL HAZARD, born April 29, 1828.
1818. ANNA CONGDON HAZARD, born March 19, 1830; died July 10, 1832.
1819. SARAH CONGDON HAZARD, born Dec. 28, 1831; married *Louis Hazard;* for children, see *No. 1290.*
1820. ANNA CONGDON HAZARD, born Jan. 26, 1835; died Oct. 11, 1835.
1821. JOHN CONGDON HAZARD, born March 31, 1836.
1822. ROWLAND N. HAZARD, born April 20, 1838; married *Sarah L. Suydam,* of New York.
1823. WILLIAM HAZARD, born May, 1846.
1824. HERBERT HAZARD, born 1848; married, 1st, *Jennie Hunter;* married, 2d, *Fannie Ross.*

§ 1004. SYLVESTER ROBINSON HAZARD, 7 (Jonathan, 6; Stephen, 5; Stephen, 4; Stephen, 3; Robert, 2; Thomas, 1). He married Alice, daughter of Robert Hull, about 1820.

CHILDREN

1825. JONATHAN HAZARD, born June 23, 1823; married *Elizabeth Pierce;* he died Sept. 12, 1877.
1826. MARY HULL HAZARD, born 1821; died unmarried.

1827.

1827. EDWARD HAZARD, born Oct. 31, 1827; married, 1858, *Louisa,* daughter of *Stephen Fiske;* he died Aug. 16, 1888.
1828. GEORGE HAZARD, born 1829; married *Laura Davis,* of Orange County, New York.
1829. ALICE HAZARD, born 1830; died unmarried.
1830. SYLVESTER HAZARD, born 1834; married *Rubamah Hazard.*

§ 1026. STANTON HAZARD, 7 (Joshua, 6; Judge Joseph, 5; Governor Robert, 4; Stephen, 3; Robert, 2; Thomas, 1), was born April 21, 1809; he died August 16, 1892. He was born in Westerly, Rhode Island. One who was permitted to know him during the last few years of his life only, says — " His whole appearance was impressive, and stamped upon one's memory an undying picture. As he came into the room where I was sitting, I could but think of one of the old patriarchs. His silvery white hair was worn rather long, as though it was a sin to cut away so much beauty, and his soft white beard, also worn quite long, was as beautiful as his hair. His manner was gentle and courteous, and evidenced the true gentleman, not of the " old school " alone, but of the school that is always old, and always new. He had a keen sense of the humorous, and at dinner entertained his guests with many bright anecdotes; his quiet laugh was infectious. In knowing Mrs. Hazard, one could not be surprised at the long continued affection between them and the mutual confidence in, and appreciation of each other. She was a tiny woman, as upright in her carriage as in her character, and although approaching her four-score years, seemed scarcely three-score, so well preserved was she, not only in her personal appearance, but also in her activity — she tripped about the room as lightly as a girl. Mrs. Hazard was of Huguenot descent, and retained, in a measure, the bright spirit of the old French ancestors. In the house were many valuable relics that were brought from France; beautiful pieces of cut glass and china, rare and old, and several statuettes, all in fine preservation. Mr. Hazard had reproduced the statuettes in beautifully carved rosewood.

He had a great love for, and pride in, his ancestry, and had made a valuable and exhaustive collection of family records of his descent from Deputy Governor Robert, and Doctor Robert Hazard. It is from these records that the material has been taken which makes these two lines possibly the most perfect of this book.

He married, March 11, 1834, Bethnia Brattle Aborn; she was born August 14, 1814 (the day the British left Stonington Point); and was daughter of Jonathan Aborn, of Pawtucket, Rhode Island.

CHILDREN

1831. ELIZABETH HAZARD, born May 25, 1835; married *William D. Moss,* eldest son of *Jesse L. Moss;* he was born Aug. 25, 1830.
1832. HARRIET HAZARD, born Nov. 25, 1839; married, June 17, 1864, *Charles H. Rhodes,* he was born 1835; died April 17, 1878.

§ 1027. EVAN MALBONE HAZARD, 7 (Joshua, 6; Judge Joseph, 5; Governor Robert, 4; Stephen, 3; Robert, 2; Thomas, 1), was born October 1,
1811

1811; he married, January 26, 1836, Jane Hume, of Huntsville, Alabama. She was born February 27, 1815.

CHILDREN

1833. CELESTE HAZARD, born July 23, 1837; married, April 28, 1859, *Arius Newton Kingsbury.*
1834. MARY EVELYN HAZARD, born Feb. 1, 1840; married, Dec. 1, 1864, *Darius Kingsbury,* of Carlyle, Ill.
1835. LAURA JANE HAZARD, born March 17, 1842; married, Dec. 25, 1861, *Charles Winstead Holliday,* of Alton, Ill.
1836. WILLIAM PRIME HAZARD, born Jan. 3, 1845; married Feb. 9, 1876, *Celeste Loraine,* of Galena, Ill.
1837. CHARLES PHILLIPS HAZARD, born Nov. 17, 1847; died April 14, 1850.
1838. EVAN MACMASTERS HAZARD, born Sept. 9, 1851.
1839. JOSEPHINE TAYLOR HAZARD, born June 19, 1856.

§ 1028. MARY NILES HAZARD, 7 (Joshua, 6; Joseph, 5; Governor Robert, 4; Stephen, 3; Robert, 2; Thomas, 1), was born October 13, 1813; she died December 24, 1846; she married, November 5, 1831, Ebenezer Dennison.

CHILDREN

1840. JOSHUA HAZARD DENNISON, born Aug. 12, 1833; died July 31, 1865.
1841. JANE ELIZABETH DENNISON, born Aug. 17, 1835; died Nov. 25, 1865.
1842. MARY PHEBE DENNISON, born Aug. 4, 1838; died Oct. 25, 1838.
1843. MARY L. DENNISON, born Feb. 28, 1843; married *Alexis Chappie,* of Jersey Co., Ill.

§ 1030. ESTHER HAZARD, 7 (Joshua, 6; Judge Joseph, 5; Governor Robert, 4; Stephen, 3; Robert, 2; Thomas, 1), was born May 30, 1817; she married Captain Waterman Clift, of Mystic, Connecticut.

CHILDREN

1844. ROBERT HAZARD CLIFT, born April 18, 1838; died Sept. 1, 1868; married Feb. 14, 1864, *Emeline Walton.*   He died from exposure in the Civil War.
1845. CHARLES W. CLIFT, born April 21, 1840; married, Nov. 3, 1862, *Jane Forsith.*
1846. JOHN GARDINER CLIFT, born March 25, 1846; married, July 27, 1871, *Mary Packer.*
1847. WILLIAM CLIFT, born March 25, 1852; died Nov. 22, 1871.
1848a. THANKFUL ALETTA CLIFT, born May 9, 1854; married, Oct. 28, 1880, *Benjamin Holmes.*
1848b. STANTON HAZARD CLIFT, born June 10, 1857; married June 9, 1888.

§ 1033. JOSEPH GRIFFEN, 7 (Hannah Hazard, 6; Joseph, 5; Governor Robert, 4; Stephen, 3; Robert, 2; Thomas, 1), married Abby Hoxsie.   She was born 1818.

CHILDREN

1849a. ABBY HOXSIE GRIFFEN, born June 25, 1829; married, Oct. 5, 1859, *Joseph Lyscent.*
1849b. JOSEPH HAZARD GRIFFEN, born Nov. 24, 1841.
1850. LOUIS PHILLIPS GRIFFEN, born Oct. 7, 1843; married, April 11, 1872, *Emma E. Hinds,* of Vandalia, Ill.

§ 1035. HANNAH GRIFFEN, 7 (Hannah Hazard, 6; Joseph, 5; Governor Robert, 4; Stephen, 3; Robert, 2; Thomas, 1). She married Randall Sisson.

CHILDREN

1851. EVAN HAZARD SISSON, born Sept. 28, 1835.

1852.

1852. JOHN HAZARD SISSON, born May 18, 1837.
1853. RANDALL SISSON, born July 19, 1839.
1854. SARAH A. SISSON, born Jan. 31, 1841.
1855. FRANCES SISSON, born Sept. 7, 1844.
1856. WILLIAM SISSON, born April 4, 1849.
1857. JOB SISSON, born Nov. 27, 1850; died Oct. 24, 1870.

§ 1037. STEPHEN AUGUSTUS GRIFFEN, 7 (Hannah Hazard, 6; Joseph, 5; Governor Robert, 4; Stephen, 3; Robert, 2; Thomas, 1), was born August 21, 1818; he married, July 27, 1856, Eliza Card.

CHILDREN

1858. STEPHEN GRIFFEN.
1859. JOSEPH GRIFFEN.
1860. ANSON GRIFFEN.
1861. JOSHUA GRIFFEN.

§ 1039. JARED STARR BABCOCK, 7 (Robert, 6; Esther Hazard, 5; Governor Robert, 4; Stephen, 3; Robert, 2; Thomas, 1), was born 1763; he died October 16, 1838; he married, December 7, 1817, Diadema Douglass; she died November 18, 1877, aged seventy-seven.

CHILDREN

1862. BENJAMIN DOUGLASS BABCOCK, died in infancy.
1863. JANE ANN BABCOCK, died Sept. 6, 1866, in Chicago, Ill.; unmarried.
1864. ROBERT FULTON BABCOCK, married, Jan. 15, 1849, *Mary S. Gilman.*
1865. LOIS DOUGLASS BABCOCK, married, Oct. 20, 1848, *Jabiel M. Parkes,* of Pittsfield, Ill.
1866. MIRIAM WAIT BABCOCK, died in infancy.

§ 1041. ESTHER BABCOCK, 7 (Robert Babcock, 6; Esther Hazard, 5; Governor Robert, 4; Stephen, 3; Robert, 2; Thomas, 1). There is no record of birth; she married, May 3, 1825, Robert Tripp.

CHILDREN

1867. MARY L. TRIPP.
1868. ALCENOR TRIPP.
1869. MARTHA TRIPP.
1870. SARAH TRIPP.
1871. ESTHER TRIPP.
1872. HELEN TRIPP.

§ 1042. NICHOLS HAZARD BABCOCK, 7 (Robert Babcock, 6; Esther Hazard, 5; Governor Robert, 4; Stephen, 3; Robert, 2; Thomas, 1); he married Maria Hamblin.

CHILDREN

1873. NICHOLS HAMBLIN BABCOCK.
1874. JARED STARR BABCOCK.
1875. ALMIRA BABCOCK.
1876. MARIA BABCOCK.
1877. HELEN V. BABCOCK.
1878. EMMA BABCOCK.

§1068

§ 1068. MARY HAZARD, 7 (Thomas S., 6; Stephen, 5; Thomas, 4; Stephen, 3; Robert, 2; Thomas, 1); she married, January 22, 1807, John, son of Joseph Knowles. .

CHILDREN
1879. MARY ANN KNOWLES.
1880. SALLY KNOWLES.
1881. WILLIAM KNOWLES.
1882. ELIZA KNOWLES.

§ 1069. STEPHEN HAZARD, 7 (Thomas, 6; Stephen, 5; Thomas, 4; Stephen, 3; Robert, 2; Thomas, 1); he married Abby Knowles, daughter of Joseph and Bathsheba (Seager) Knowles.

CHILDREN
1883. JAMES HAZARD.
1884. JOHN HAZARD.
1885. ROWLAND HAZARD.
1886. SARAH HAZARD, born 1818; died Nov. 2, 1842.

§ 1072. STANTON HAZARD, 7 (Thomas S., 6; Stephen, 5; Thomas, 4; Stephen, 3; Robert, 2; Thomas, 1); he married, April 17, 1820, Ann Gridley.

CHILDREN
1887. CHARLES HAZARD, born Oct. 31, 1822.
1888. MARY ANN HAZARD, born Jan. 10, 1825.
1889. GEORGE A. HAZARD, born June 21, 1827.
1890. FRANK HAZARD, born Dec. 21, 1833; died Sept. 10, 1885.
1891. HENRY HAZARD, born March 7, 1836; died Feb. 20, 1881.
1892. HELEN HAZARD, born June 10, 1840.
1893. ADELAIDE HAZARD, born Jan. 4, 1844; died Nov. 25, 1880.

§ 1073. AUGUSTUS GEORGE HAZARD, 7 (Thomas, 6; Stephen, 5; Thomas, 4; Stephen, 3; Robert, 2; Thomas, 1), was born in South Kingstown, April 28, 1802; he died May 7, 1868. His father, Thomas S. Hazard, was a sea-captain, the memory of whose bold and manly character is still treasured on the south shore of Rhode Island; his mother, Silence Hazard, is remembered for strong and generous qualities which marked her among women, and reappeared in her youngest and last surviving of eight children. The family removed in 1808 to Columbia, Connecticut, and the son remained there on the farm until he was fifteen years old.

In 1827, Colonel Hazard, after some adventures in the South, at the age of twenty-five removed to New York and there began the establishment of a commission house; became, by agency and proprietorship, connected with the line of packets sailing between that city and Savannah, a large receiver of southern produce, and the resident purchaser for his own and other commercial houses at the South. Successfully engaged in this large and profitable business, he was overtaken by the unprecedented financial crash of 1837. He passed through that memorable

1073
Augustus George Hazard.

memorable epoch not without serious loss, but paying every dollar of indebted-ness, principal and interest; with credit not only exempt from harm, but strength-ened by the firmness of his integrity, and the gallantry of his conduct.

Colonel Hazard became interested in the manufacture of gunpowder, a business which he subsequently pursued with remarkable results. His exertions in this field of enterprise culminated, in 1843, in his organizing the Hazard Powder Company, a corporation which has become known in all parts of the United States. In 1845, realizing the importance of personal residence in the vicinity of his establishment, he removed to Enfield, Connecticut, where he resided the remainder of his life.

Under his charge and direction the manufactory rose to great proportions. A mill in the town of Canton, another in East Hartford, and a third at Scitico, have been only aids and adjuncts to the main works lying in the secluded and beau-tiful valley of Fair Lawn, in Enfield: the last mentioned extending along the Scantic River, more than a mile in length, and covering an area of five hundred acres; employing a succession of waterfalls, a motive power of thirty water-wheels and four steam-engines, and a variety of machinery whose magnitude is shown by thirty-six cast-iron rollers of eight tons each, separated but acting in unison. Coming to Enfield with a resolute purpose to excel in his sphere of production, he elevated the reputation of his manufacture to a point not sur-passed in this or other countries, as acknowledged especially in the calls for higher grades of powder coming from individuals and governments, of Great Britain as well as of the United States. As an illustration of the great power and unerring exactness which this enterprise attained under his direction, in a single instance during the Crimean war, these works promised to the English Govern-ment, at short notice, ten thousand barrels of rifle and cannon powder, every pound of which was approved and accepted by the British Board of Ordnance.

Colonel Hazard died May 7, 1868. Cordial were the expressions, both far and near, from individuals and the public press, betokening the general sense of loss. Many thousands, comprising persons from all walks of life, assembled at the funeral. In all the long-drawn valley of the Connecticut, studded with the homes of the cultured and the good, rarely has a man passed away whose death has been so keenly felt, and so widely mourned.

Colonel Hazard married in 1822, Salome Merrill, of West Hartford, Connec-ticut. She was born September 12, 1802, and died November 16, 1880. Mrs. Hazard was a worthy helpmeet to her husband. She was a woman of strong common sense and correct judgment, and was of a most charitable disposition, full of kindly thought for all about her. Her influence was improving, elevating, and inspiring, and her daily example was a blessed heritage to her children.

CHILDREN

1894. ELVIRA HAZARD, born May 15, 1824; married Gov. *Alexander Hamilton Bullock* of Wor-cester, Mass.

1895. GEORGIANA HAZARD, born July 29, 1827; married *Joseph Sexton*, of New York.

1896.

1896. FANNY HAZARD, born Oct. 1, 1830; married, Nov. 3, 1869, *Ephraim Ward Bond*, of Springfield, Mass. ; died Dec. 5, 1891.
1897. HORACE HAMILTON HAZARD, born Jan. 1, 1832; died April 4, 1855. He was fatally injured while testing some samples of gunpowder by the *eprouvette;* a premature discharge occurred, shattering his right arm, and otherwise so severely injuring him, that he survived only twelve hours.
1898. EMILY HAZARD, born June 24, 1834; died Sept. 18, 1866; married *Francis E. Dakin*, of Freeport, Ill.
1899. CORDELIA HAZARD, born Oct. 4, 1835; died Nov. 30, 1842.
1900. A DAUGHTER, born March 1, 1842; died March 14, 1842.
1901. SAMUEL DOUGLASS HAZARD, born Aug. 15, 1844; died Dec. 20, 1860.

§ 1175. HANNAH OATLEY, 7 (Mary Hazard, 6; Stephen, 5; Thomas, 4; Stephen, 3; Robert, 2; Thomas, 1), was born November 6, 1781; she married James Rodman Carpenter.

CHILDREN

1902. HANNAH CARPENTER, born 1800; died in infancy.
1903. ANN CARPENTER, born 1802; died in infancy.
1904. JOSEPH CARPENTER, born 1806; died in infancy.
1905. ROWLAND HAZARD CARPENTER, born 1809; died 1869; married *Thankful Rose.*
1906. ROUSE CARPENTER, born 1811; died 1875; married *Ruth Larkin.*
1907. MARY CARPENTER, born 1813; married, 1st, *James Whitford;* married, 2d, *Robinson Perry.*
1908. HANNAH CARPENTER, born 1816; married *Nathaniel Armstrong.*
1909. ELIZABETH CARPENTER, born 1819; married *Robert Armstrong.*
1910. ISAAC HAZARD CARPENTER, born 1821; married *Abby Perry.*

§ 1176. BETSEY OATLEY, 7 (Mary Hazard, 6; Stephen, 5; Thomas, 4; Stephen, 3; Robert, 2; Thomas, 1), was born February 16, 1786; she married, as second wife, Jonathan Carpenter.

CHILDREN

1911. JOSEPH CARPENTER, born April 4, 1804; died 1832, in Cincinnati; married *Eliza Quirrer.*
1912. MERRIAN CARPENTER, born Jan. 3, 1805; married *Harry Tatten.*
1913. HARRIET CARPENTER, born Feb. 3, 1808; married *Eli Knox.*

§ 1077. NANCY OATLEY, 7 (Mary Hazard, 6; Stephen, 5; Thomas, 4; Stephen, 3; Robert, 2; Thomas, 1), was born March 28, 1788; she died May 6, 1873; she married, December 25, 1811, Jonathan Carpenter. When Mr. Carpenter was about eighteen years of age, he shipped on board a merchantman, bound to Spain. The vessel was captured by the Spanish, and he, with the rest of the crew, held as prisoners at Lisbon for six months, having the freedom of the city in the day, but returning to the ship at night. After being released, he went to England, and then, returning to his native land, married Mary Hazard, daughter of Simeon Hazard, who lived but a year. After her death, he again took up a sea-faring life; but after a few voyages married Betsey Oatley, and settled at Narragansett Pier, building a house there. He ran a sloop to Newport, carrying passengers and freight. At the time he built his house at Narragansett Pier, there was but one other, at what is now known as the "Pier" proper. He later removed to Newport, Rhode Island, and finally settled in Springfield, Massachusetts, where he died.

CHILDREN

CHILDREN
1914. BETSEY CARPENTER, born Sept. 16, 1813; married, May 20, 1840, *Walter North.*
1915. ALBERT G. CARPENTER, born March 5, 1815; died April 8, 1850; married *Electa Lyon.*
1916. GEORGE HAZARD CARPENTER, born Dec. 21, 1816; died May 28, 1882; married, 1st, 1841, *Lydia Cowen;* married, 2d, 1854, *Caroline Nutting.*
1917. JONATHAN CARPENTER, born Nov. 15, 1818; died Feb. 7, 1865; married, 1842, *Eliza Patterson.*
1918. JULIA A. CARPENTER, born March 28, 1820; died Feb. 12, 1889; married *Henry Ferra.*
1919. STEPHEN HAZARD CARPENTER, born Jan. 13, 1822; died Sept. 26, 1883; married *Martha Nettleton.*
1920. BENEDICT OATLEY CARPENTER, born Jan. 1, 1824; died April 1, 1882; married *Frances Way.*
1921. SARAH A. CARPENTER, born Oct. 20, 1825; married, 1848, *Frederick S. Smith.*
1922. HANNAH MARIA CARPENTER, born Nov. 5, 1827; died 1830.
1923. SUSAN EMMA CARPENTER, born June 4, 1829; married, May 18, 1849, *Richard N. Allen.*

§ 1079. JOSEPH OATLEY, 7 (Mary Hazard, 6; Stephen, 5; Thomas, 4; Stephen, 3; Robert, 2; Thomas, 1), was born in South Kingstown, Rhode Island, September 13, 1793; he died Jan. 13, 1883; he married, in 1823, Eliza Wells, of West Hartford, Connecticut.

CHILDREN
1924. MARY ELIZA OATLEY, born in Blandford, Massachusetts, July 21, 1824.
1925. CAROLINE FIDELIA OATLEY, born in Blandford, Feb. 6, 1826.
1926. HELEN MARIA OATLEY, born in Blandford, Sept. 27, 1828.
1927. ANGELINE SOPHIA OATLEY, born in Blandford, March 5, 1830.
1928. EMERSON WELLS OATLEY, born in Blandford, Nov. 10, 1831.
1929. SUSAN MARINDA OATLEY, born in Blandford, July 3, 1833.
1930. LAURINDA ROBINSON OATLEY, born in Blandford, March 3, 1835.
1931. RUTH ANN OATLEY, born in Blandford, April 23, 1838.
1932. LOUISA ADELAID OATLEY, born in Blandford, March 9, 1842.

§ 1081. MARY OATLEY, 7 (Mary Hazard, 6; Stephen, 5; Thomas, 4; Stephen, 3; Robert, 2; Thomas, 1), was born in South Kingstown, Rhode Island, August 28, 1798; she married, April 28, 1816, Stephen Congdon.

CHILDREN
1933. JOSEPH CONGDON, born Dec. 17, 1816; died July 7, 1890; married *Emma Miller.*
1934. NANCY CONGDON, born Aug. 25, 1818; died Nov. 28, 1820.
1935. CHRISTOPHER CONGDON, born Dec. 17, 1820; died Oct. 24, 1838.
1936. MARY CONGDON, born April 24, 1823; died April, 1831.
1937. ALBERT CONGDON, born Dec. 29, 1824; died March, 1890; married, 1st, *Amanda Gasset;* married, 2d, *Adelaide Grover.*
1938. ROMANTA S. CONGDON, born Dec. 27, 1826; married, 1st, *Ann Taylor;* married, 2d, *Hannah Prescott.*
1939. CHARITY E. CONGDON, born March 1, 1829; married, May 28, 1848, *Edward Pitsinger.*
1940. WILLIAM W. CONGDON, born Jan. 31, 1831; married, 1st, *Abby Ladd;* married, 2d, *Annette Glass.*
1941. ISAAC H. CONGDON, born June 1, 1833; married, 1st, *Caroline E. Hilton;* married, 2d, *Julia E. Niles.*
1942. HANNAH M. CONGDON, born Oct. 13, 1835; died Nov. 26, 1838.
1943. MARY ELIZA CONGDON, born June 18, 1838; died Nov. 8, 1841.

1944.

1944. SUSAN JEANNETTE CONGDON, born July 22, 1840; married *Lovell O. Gassett.*
1945. GEORGE WHITFIELD CONGDON, born March 25, 1847.

§ 1082. SUSAN OATLEY, 7 (Mary Hazard, 6; Stephen, 5; Thomas, 4; Stephen, 3; Robert, 2; Thomas, 1), was born May 2, 1803; she married, May 21, 1821, Davis Mumford, who lived but a few years after his marriage. She married, second, Isaac T. Hopkins, January 13, 1828. She is now living (January 18, 1894).

CHILDREN OF FIRST MARRIAGE
1946. MARY ELIZA MUMFORD, born May 26, 1822; married, Oct. 18, 1841, *Joseph B. Potter.* She died March 12, 1885.
1947. HARRIET MUMFORD, born Aug. 1, 1824; died Oct., 1824.

CHILDREN OF SECOND MARRIAGE
1948. SARAH A. HOPKINS, born Oct. 16, 1828; died July 13, 1841.
1949. LOUISA W. HOPKINS, born March 1, 1830; died June 22, 1841.
1950. JOHN J. HOPKINS, born Jan. 14, 1833; he married, Jan. 22, 1873, *Martha C. Greene.*
1951. SUSAN LOUISA HOPKINS, born Oct. 30, 1841; married, Oct. 17, 1862, *John S. Potter.*

§ 1084. SAMUEL RODMAN, 7 (Elizabeth Hazard, 6; Stephen, 5; Thomas, 4; Stephen, 3; Robert, 2; Thomas, 1), was born in South Kingstown, May 3, 1800. Both in personal appearance and in character he was said to resemble his great-grandfather, Samuel Rodman, while he inherited from his mother a strain of the Hazard blood, and with it the will and energy necessary to success. He was born in the house that his great-uncle, William Rodman, built, and in the great west chamber that had been made historic as being also the birthplace of Oliver Hazard Perry, the hero of Lake Erie.

About 1830 he leased the Peacedale mills from Isaac Hazard, and began manufacturing; and in 1835, with Attmore Robinson, he bought the tract of land with the wharf at Narragansett Pier, since called the " Old Pier," where a breakwater was afterwards built. Its builders, like those, as it is said, of the second Eddystone lighthouse, defied Almighty God to overthrow the work; but it was partly destroyed in the first great storm after its completion. During the progress of the work on the breakwater, an accomplished French engineer, on examining it, said that it was built on a wrong principle, and that the dock would fill with sand. Time has proved the truth of this prediction, for children now play on the sands where was once from fifteen to twenty feet of water.

In 1838, Samuel Rodman sold his rights in the " Pier " property, and bought of Thomas R. Hazard "one hundred and twenty-five or thirty" acres in the village of Rocky Brook; and in the same year he built the homestead, where seven of his children were born. There were on the property at the time four small houses, and a small mill containing one or two sets of machinery. In this mill he began the manufacture of woolen goods. During the following year (1839) he bought thirty acres, on a part of which stood the old Rodman mansion-house, and a woolen mill. In 1853 he bought thirty acres more with several houses and a woolen mill and about the same time he added to his own farm the Freeman Watson

*1084*
SAMUEL RODMAN.

Watson farm adjoining it.  This farm once belonged to his great-uncle, William Rodman, who in the last century had built the house already mentioned as the one in which Samuel Rodman was born. The small mills on the Rocky Brook estate Mr. Rodman soon replaced by substantial stone buildings, taking all the stone that he used from his own meadows, which were well named "Rocky." His success as a manufacturer was uninterrupted until the war of 1862, and he became one of the richest mill-owners in the State, owning, in addition to the Rocky Brook property, mills in Wakefield and in Newport.

Mr. Rodman represented his town several times in the General Assembly. In 1854, when a nomination was equivalent to an election, he was asked to take the nomination for lieutenant-governor, but he declined it. He was never defeated, with the exception of once, in any election for which he stood as candidate. In 1841 he entered enthusiastically upon the total abstinence reform, and its measure of success in his own and the neighboring villages was largely attributable to his zeal.

For over forty years Samuel Rodman was a member of the Baptist Church, and an honor to his communion. He contributed largely toward the building of the new Baptist house of worship in Wakefield in 1852, and was one of its chief benefactors. He aided, by liberal contributions, in the building of no less than twenty-six other churches; nor did he confine his benevolence to his own denomination.

His character was of great natural energy, yet there were no hard lines in it. He had a certain gentleness of manner, combined with decision, which made him greatly beloved and trusted by all who came in contact with him, especially by his employees, who, during his last illness, came to the house in numbers, begging to be allowed the privilege of watching through the nights with him. No "strike" was ever thought of in his mills. The relations between them were those of mutual confidence. He perceived that the truest method of elevating the laborer was to make him independent, and to this end, by the sale of lands to them at nominal prices, he encouraged his laborers to become landowners.

A friend writing to his widow after his death, said, "Mr. Rodman was the most generous man I ever knew, and I have reason to know how generous. He conferred a favor in such a way that the recipient might well question whether he had received or conferred the obligation."

Samuel Rodman married Mary, daughter of Benjamin and Abigail (Oatley) Peckham, who was a descendant of Deputy-Governor George Hazard. She was the mother of all his children. The influence of her character and teaching was seen clearly in her eldest son, General Isaac Peace Rodman. To her husband she was truly a helpmeet, not only in forming the character of the older children, who came especially under her influence, but as a wise and faithful counsellor in all his business relations. He took no important step without her advice. She was born September 25, 1803, and died February 16, 1853; married July 15, 1821. He married, second, February 15, 1854, Mary Anstis, daughter of Wilkins Updike, Esq'., of South Kingstown, also a descendant of the Hazard family.

CHILDREN

CHILDREN OF FIRST MARRIAGE

1952. ISAAC PEACE RODMAN, born Aug. 18, 1822; died Sept. 30, 1862; married *Sally*, daughter of *Lemuel H.* and *Sally (Lyman) Arnold.*
1953. BENJAMIN PECKHAM RODMAN, born Aug. 18, 1824; died June 18, 1825.
1954. LOUISA HAZARD RODMAN, born March 26, 1826; died May 2, 1854; married Col. *Daniel Chase Hiscox.*
1955. ROWLAND G. RODMAN, born Jan. 10, 1828; married, Sept. 24, 1856, *Mary*, daughter of *Nathaniel* and *Harriot (Greene) Durfee.*
1956. EDWARD FRANCIS RODMAN, born 1830; died 1833.
1957. JULIA MARIA RODMAN, born Sept. 7, 1831; died Sept. 27, 1891; married *John Thompson*, of San Francisco, California.
1958. CAROLINE ELIZABETH RODMAN, born July 4, 1833; married, Nov. 20, 1854, *Benjamin F. Robinson.*
1959. EDWARD FRANCIS RODMAN, born May 7, 1835; died Aug., 1835.
1960. MARY HAZARD RODMAN, born Sept. 20, 1836; died Feb. 23, 1837.
1961. MARY PECKHAM RODMAN, born Nov. 12, 1838; married *William H. Baldwin.*
1962. SARAH ABIGAIL RODMAN, born Sept. 15, 1840; married *William Woodward.*
1963. SAMUEL RODMAN, born Nov. 4, 1842; died 1890; married *Mary McDaniel.*
1964. RICHARD SHERMAN RODMAN, born Dec. 14, 1844; died Oct. 31, 1892; unmarried.
1965. EDWARD RODMAN, born Dec. 14, 1845; married *Hannah C. Perry.*
1966. JAMES CLARKE RODMAN, born Sept., 1847; died Sept. 15, 1848.
1967. JAMES RODMAN, born Sept. 11, 1849; unmarried.

§ 1085. ELIZABETH RODMAN, 7 (Elizabeth Hazard, 6; Stephen, 5; Thomas, 4; Stephen, 3; Robert, 2; Thomas, 1), was born July, 1801; married Henry Money.

CHILDREN

1968. LYDIA MONEY, born 1827; unmarried.
1969. ABBY MONEY, born 1829.
1970. BENJAMIN MONEY, born 1830.
1971. MARIA MONEY, born 1832.
1972. MARY MONEY, born 1834.
1973. GEORGIANA MONEY, born 1843.
1974. SUSAN MONEY, born 1845.

§ 1086. ABBY RODMAN, 7 (Elizabeth Hazard, 6; Stephen, 5; Thomas, 4; Stephen, 3; Robert, 2; Thomas, 1), was born May 21, 1804; she died May 31, 1829; she married Thomas, son of Thomas and Susan (Chase) Hiscox.

CHILDREN

1975. ELIZA CHASE HISCOX, born Sept. 18, 1826; died 1861; married *Daniel Wall.*
1976. SUSAN WARD HISCOX, born Aug. 22, 1827; died 1827.
1977. SUSAN WARD HISCOX, born Feb. 3, 1829; died Oct. 14, 1832.

§ 1087. SARAH RODMAN, 7 (Elizabeth Hazard, 6; Stephen, 5; Thomas, 4; Stephen, 3; Robert, 2; Thomas, 1), was born September 19, 1805; she died August 10, 1845; she married William, son of Daniel and Sarah Knowles.

CHILDREN

1978. SUSAN KNOWLES, born Nov. 23, 1829; died July 25, 1850; married *Thomas J. Gould.*
1979. GEORGE P. KNOWLES, born July 1, 1833; married *Hannah F. Browning.*

1980.

1980. MARY KNOWLES, born May 10, 1836; unmarried.
1981. ALFRED KNOWLES, born Nov. 2, 1838; married *Ellen Howard.*
1982. WARREN KNOWLES, born Nov. 2, 1838; married *Susan Harvey.*

§ 1088. AMOS PEASELEY RODMAN, 7 (Elizabeth Hazard, 6; Stephen, 5; Thomas, 4; Stephen, 3; Robert, 2; Thomas, 1), was born in 1806; he married Clarissa Allen.

CHILDREN

1983. SAMUEL RODMAN, born 1834; died 1836.
1984. LAURA HAZARD RODMAN, born 1836; married *Samuel Coney Barton,* of La Crosse, Wis.
1985. AMOS PEASELEY RODMAN, born 1838; died 1856.
1986. ERASMUS CAMPBELL RODMAN, born 1842. He was a member of a Wisconsin company of volunteers during the Civil War, and was mortally wounded at the siege of Vicksburg.
1987. SUSAN RODMAN, born 1845; died 1846.
1988. CHARLES RODMAN, born 1849; married *Isabella Fisher,* of La Crosse, Wis.
1989. ROWLAND HAZARD RODMAN, born 1852; married *Minnie M. Hubbard.*
1990. HOWARD MALCOM RODMAN, born 1854; married, 1879, *Isabella Cusbin,* of La Crosse, Wis.

§ 1089. PENELOPE RODMAN, 7 (Elizabeth Hazard, 6; Stephen, 5; Thomas, 4; Stephen, 3; Robert, 2; Thomas, 1), was born March 24, 1807; she died May 1, 1856; she married Daniel Gould.

CHILDREN

1991. MARY ELIZABETH GOULD, born Sept., 1842; married, 1st, Dr. *Jonathan Sweet;* married, 2d, *Ezekiel H. Browning.*
1992. JULIA GOULD, born Jan. 19, 1844; married *Peleg Brown.*
1993. SARAH RODMAN GOULD, born Sept. 11, 1847; married *Lorenzo Chase.*
1994. LYDIA ANN GOULD, born April 27, 1849; died Dec. 3, 1880; married *George Fitzgerald.*
1995. DANIEL AMOS GOULD, born May 30, 1851.

§ 1090. BENJAMIN RODMAN, 7 (Elizabeth Hazard, 6; Stephen, 5; Thomas, 4; Stephen, 3; Robert, 2; Thomas, 1), was born at South Kingstown, September 13, 1808; he died April 15, 1860; he married, August 10, 1836, Hannah, daughter of John and Mary (Robinson) Brown; she was born August 13, 1817, and died January 22, 1876.

CHILDREN

1996. HARRIET NEWELL RODMAN, born July 31, 1837; married *Peleg F. Pierce.*
1997. JOHN BROWN RODMAN, born Feb. 15, 1839; married *Sarah E. Babcock.*
1998. ROUSE BABCOCK RODMAN, born June 13, 1842; died Nov. 23, 1866; unmarried.

§ 1091. HANNAH RODMAN, 7 (Elizabeth Hazard, 6; Stephen, 5; Thomas, 4; Stephen, 3; Robert, 2; Thomas, 1), was born at South Kingstown in 1815; she married, in 1833, Erasmus D. Campbell.

CHILDREN

1999. ROWENA HAZARD CAMPBELL, born 1834; married, 1854, *Stephen Crary.*
2000. JAMES HAZARD CAMPBELL, born 1835; died 1861; married *Mary Lord.*
2001. SAMUEL RODMAN CAMPBELL, born 1837; married *Lucy Marsh.*
2002. OLIVE W. CAMPBELL, born 1839; died 1844.
2003. ABBY JANE CAMPBELL, born 1840.

2004.

2004. COLIN CAMPBELL, born 1841; died 1890.
2005. ELLA D. CAMPBELL, born 1852; died 1857.
2006. ANNIE E. CAMPBELL, born 1858; died 1859.
2007. ZAIDEE CAMPBELL, born 1860.

§ 1092. ANN RODMAN, 7 (Elizabeth Hazard, 6; Stephen, 5; Thomas, 4; Stephen, 3; Robert, 2; Thomas, 1), was born in 1822; she married Lorenzo Hall.

CHILDREN
2008. SARAH HALL; died young.
2009. OLIVE HALL; married *Chester Allen.*
2010. MARY ELIZA HALL.
2011. ISAAC HALL; married *Eva Pierce.*
2012. CLARA HALL; married —— *Wilkinson.*
2013. AMANDA HALL; married *Elisha Bucklin.*

§ 1093. ROBERT RODMAN, 7 (Elizabeth Hazard, 6; Stephen, 5; Thomas, 4; Stephen, 3; Robert, 2; Thomas, 1), was born in 1820; he died in 1870; he married Mary Gardiner.

CHILDREN
2014. SARAH RODMAN, married —— *Shippee.*
2015. ELISHA RODMAN.
2016. ROBERT RODMAN.
2017. LOUISA RODMAN.
2018. MARY RODMAN.
2019. BENJAMIN RODMAN.

§ 1095. ARNOLD HAZARD, 7 (Thomas, 6; Jeremiah, 5; Jeffrey, 4; Robert, 2; Thomas, 1), was born in 1792; he died March 19, 1856; he married Hannah, daughter of Job and Phebe (Weeden) Watson. She was born August 1, 1792, and died April 25, 1885.

CHILDREN
2020. LUCY HAZARD, born Sept., 1810; died Nov., 1816.
2021. JEREMIAH HAZARD, born 1812; died Aug. 27, 1872; married *Susan Browning.*
2022. THOMAS ARNOLD HAZARD, born 1813; died Dec. 8, 1886; unmarried. He was a physician, and practiced with success in South Kingstown for nearly fifty years.
2023. JOB WATSON HAZARD, born 1816; died Aug. 4, 1884; married, 1st, *Ann Eliza,* daughter of *John* and *Ann Weeden;* married, 2d, *Sarah Ann* ——.
2024. DANIEL WATSON HAZARD, born 1820; died Sept. 18, 1848.

§ 1101. JEREMIAH B. HAZARD, 7 (Robert, 6; Robert, 5; Jeffrey, 4; Robert, 3; Robert, 2; Thomas, 1). He died in 1883; he married Hannah ——; she died March 18, 1861, aged fifty-two.

CHILDREN
2025. JOSEPH HOXSIE HAZARD, born Jan. 5, 1838.
2026. MARY ARMOR HAZARD, born Aug. 15, 1829.
2027. ELIZA ANN HAZARD, born Nov. 20, 1835; died Oct. 17, 1855.
2028. ABBY ALICE HAZARD, born Jan. 1, 1840.

2029.

2029. Jane Hazard, born Sept. 8, 1843; died May 25, 1876.
2030. John Hazard, born Nov. 26, 1848.

§ 1106. ROBERT HAZARD, 7 (John, 6; Robert, 5; Robert, 4; Robert, 3; Robert, 2; Thomas, 1), was born June 26, 1790; he died March 19, 1871; he married, December 21, 1815, Amey, daughter of Governor Jeffrey Hazard.

Children

2031. James Monroe Hazard, born Aug., 1817; died Dec., 1877; married *Sabre*, daughter of *Josiah Greene*.
2032. John Randolph Hazard, born March 3, 1820; married, 1847, —— daughter of *Welcome Burdick*, of Charlestown, R. I.
2033. Charles Stone Hazard, born 1822; died July 27, 1858.

§ 1107. THOMAS T. HAZARD, 7 (John, 6; Robert, 5; Robert, 4; Robert, 3; Robert, 2; Thomas, 1), was born March 2, 1792; he died August 2, 1874; he married, December 8, 1818, Esther, daughter of Thomas Tillinghast. She was born December 11, 1798, and died November 5, 1865.

Children

2034. Jason P. Hazard, born Feb. 21, 1823; married, March 15, 1847, *Betsey Lewis*, of Exeter, R. I.
2035. Robert Jeremiah Hazard, born Aug. 1, 1826.
2036. Alexander S. Hazard, born Jan. 25, 1836.

§ 1109. PHEBE HAZARD, 7 (John, 6; Robert, 5; Robert, 4; Robert, 3; Robert, 2; Thomas, 1), was born November 21, 1796; she married Easton Lewis.

Children

2037. Amey Lewis, married *Stafford Greene*.
2038. Ann Lewis, married *Benjamin Tillinghast*.

§ 1113. WILLARD HAZARD, 7 (Governor Jeffrey, 6; Jeremiah, 5; Robert, 4; Robert, 3; Robert, 2; Thomas, 1), married, April 4, 1826, Mary, daughter of George W. Hazard.

Children

2039. Mary Ann Hazard, married *Thomas Watson*.
2040. Jeffrey Hazard.

§ 1114. JOHN HAZARD, 7 (Governor Jeffrey, 6; Jeremiah, 5; Robert, 4; Robert, 3; Robert, 2; Thomas, 1); he married Margaret Crandall.

Children

2041. John G. Hazard, born April 15, 1832.
2042. Jeffrey Hazard, born 1835; married *Annie Hartwell*.

§ 1115. PHEBE HAZARD, 7 (Governor Jeffrey, 6; Jeremiah, 5; Robert, 4; Robert, 3; Robert, 2; Thomas, 1), married Reuben Brown.

Children

2043. Jason P. S. Brown.

2044.

2044. Willard Brown.
2045. Amelia Brown.

§ 1117. JOHN BOSS HAZARD, 7 (John, 6; Jeremiah, 5; Robert, 4; Jeremiah, 3; Robert, 2; Thomas, 1), was born February 17, 1778; he died May 28, 1848; he married Mary Potter, of Warwick. She was born August 31, 1774, and died October 21, 1838.

Children
2046. George Potter Hazard, born Oct. 19, 1809; died Sept. 18, 1887; married *Rachel*, daughter of *Samuel* and *Freelove Joy*.
2047. Anthony Hazard, born Feb. 6, 1811; died July 21, 1887; unmarried.
2048. John Hazard, born May 22, 1812; married *Isabella*, daughter of *Arthur* and *Zilpha Potter*, of Cranston, R. I.
2049. Robert Hazard, born Aug. 28, 1813; died July, 1886; unmarried.

§ 1124. JEREMIAH HAZARD, 7 (John, 6; Jeremiah, 5; Robert, 4; Jeremiah, 3; Robert, 2; Thomas, 1), was born October 10, 1792; he died October 19, 1878. He was married September, 1814, to Harriet Moore, in Newport. Mr. Hazard was a man of strongly marked character, who fearlessly expressed his opinions, and clung tenaciously to what he conceived to be right. He had no sympathy with shams of any kind. Of sturdy honesty — a self-respecting, but not a self-asserting man — of iron will and indomitable energy, yet extremely modest in his desires, he was contented in an humble course, and of simple tastes. He was happy in his domestic life, and devoted to his family, for whom he toiled industriously early and late, and for whom his self-sacrificing affection was boundless. Deeply religious, he rested securely in an unswerving, child-like confidence in his Heavenly Father.

He was possessed of a wonderfully retentive memory for subjects which interested him, and he could quote from his favorite books with unerring facility. On matters of personal family history he was very entertaining, and his style of presenting facts carried interest, conviction of the truth and reliability. He was a man universally respected by his fellow-townsmen of Newport, who listened with interest, even when they could not agree with his opinions; for his presentation of a case was clear, persistent and emphatic. In personal appearance he was tall, dignified and impressive, with square, forcible chin, prominent nose, firm mouth and high forehead. Even at eighty years his step was strong and elastic, his form straight and unyielding to the weight of years, his eyesight undimmed, his hearing distinct and unimpaired, his voice strong and clear as that of a young man.

Children
2050. James Moore Hazard, born Aug. 4, 1815; died at Gilboa, Schoharie County, N. Y., Sept. 30, 1884.
2051. Harriet Moore Hazard, born July 17, 1817; married, Jan. 23, 1842, *George Hunt Wilson*.

§ 1137. BENJAMIN STANTON HAZARD, 7 (Wilbor, 6; Jeremiah, 5; Robert, 4; Jeremiah, 3; Robert, 2; Thomas, 1), was born August 25, 1812; he
died

died May 12, 1890. He married, March 19, 1840, Charlotte, daughter of Jeremiah and Izett Atwood, of Warwick, Rhode Island. She was born March 6, 1815, and died June 21, 1888.

CHILDREN

2052. IZETT HAZARD, born May 23, 1842; died May 6, 1843.
2053. BENJAMIN STANTON HAZARD, born Feb. 21, 1844; died Feb. 4, 1858.
2054. JEREMIAH ATWOOD HAZARD, born Jan. 14, 1848; died March 4, 1858.
2055. JOHN A. HAZARD, born June 2, 1854.

§ 1138. WILBOR HAZARD, 7 (Wilbor, 6; Jeremiah, 5; Robert, 4; Jeremiah, 3; Robert, 2; Thomas, 1), was born February 27, 1814; he died March 26, 1892.

In the obituary notice of Mr. Hazard it was said, "He was a keen, active man of affairs, of excellent judgment, cautious, yet sure, in laying and developing plans for the advancement of his business interests; an honest man, faithful, jovial, kindly and affectionate." He married, December 25, 1843, Lydia S., daughter of William and Abby Pierce; she died March 29, 1892, surviving her husband but three days. "She was loved by all who knew her, a true helpmeet to her husband for nearly fifty years, zealous in every good work. The example she set as an earnest Christian woman will live in the hearts and lives of many."

CHILDREN

2056. SARAH KNOWLES HAZARD, born Nov. 16, 1844.
2057. WILBOR HAZARD, born April 19, 1846; married *Isabel Carr*.

§ 1142. DANIEL STANTON HAZARD, 7 (Wilbor, 6; Jeremiah, 5; Robert, 4; Jeremiah, 3; Robert, 2; Thomas, 1), was born in North Kingstown, January 26, 1824; he married, June 21, 1847, Hannah Stanton, daughter of Benjamin and Mary Congdon. She was born August 26 1824.

CHILDREN

2058. MARY WILBOR HAZARD, born March 26, 1848; married, Nov. 5, 1879, *William Keyes Reynolds*, of Providence, R. I.
2059. ANNIE COTTRELL HAZARD, born June 1, 1853; married, April 23, 1888, *Walter Kimball Jenks*.
2060. JULIA TALMAN HAZARD, born Feb. 7, 1863.

§ 1151. ROBERTSON HAZARD, 7 (Freeborn, 6; Gideon, 5; Robert, 4; Jeremiah, 3; Robert, 2; Thomas, 1), was born August 27, 1785; he married, December 20, 1816, Elizabeth Marshall. She was daughter of Benjamin and Nancy Marshall. He dwelt in North Kingstown on a part of the farm of his great-great-grandfather, Jeremiah Hazard, about one mile north of Wamsley Hill, on the old post-road. He died August 16, 1871, his widow died December 12, 1883.

CHILDREN

2061. BENJAMIN HAZARD, born Sept. 29, 1819; married. 1st, *Jane Knox*; married, 2d, *Alexandrina Farrier*.

2062.

2062. Louis Hazard, born Oct. 27, 1820; married *Harriet G. Harwood.*
2063. Mary E. Hazard, born June 27, 1829; married *John Q. A. Gardiner.*
2064. Sarah R. Hazard, born Jan. 17, 1839; married *George B. Willis.*

§ 1152. STANTON HAZARD, 7 (Freeborn, 6; Gideon, 5; Robert, 4; Jeremiah, 3; Robert, 2; Thomas, 1), was born August, 1786; he married Phebe Bush.

CHILDREN
2065. George S. Hazard, born Jan. 10, 1810.
2066. Mary A. Hazard, born June 14, 1811; married, 1st, *Harvey Brown;* married, 2d, *Daniel Sherman.*
2067. John W. Hazard, born May 20, 1813; died Sept. 10, 1851.
2068. Albert R. Hazard, born Aug. 18, 1815; died in infancy.
2069. Oliver S. Hazard, born Dec. 29, 1817; married, 1st, *Lucy A. Rice;* married, 2d, *Juliette E. Sholes.*
2070. Brayman R. Hazard, born Dec. 10, 1819; died in infancy.
2071. Phebe A. Hazard, born Nov. 30, 1825; married *Orris Gardiner.*

§ 1153. SUSAN HAZARD, 7 (Freeborn, 6; Gideon, 5; Robert, 4; Jeremiah, 3; Robert, 2; Thomas, 1), was born November 11, 1788; she died March 25, 1859. She married Stephen, son of Robert Hazard.

CHILDREN
2072. Louis Hazard.
2073. William Hazard.
2074. Hannah Hazard.
2075. Rowland Anson Hazard; married *Amanda L. V. Gardiner.*

**End of the Seventh Generation.**

THE

# THE HAZARD FAMILY

## Eighth Generation

ROBERT HAZARD, 8 (Thomas, 7; Robert, 6; Thomas, 5; Robert, 4; Thomas, 3; Robert 2; Thomas 1), married Elizabeth Alexander.

CHILDREN
2076. EZRA HAZARD.
2077. SYLVIA HAZARD.

§ 1165. SENECA HAZARD, 8 (Thomas, 7; Robert, 6; Thomas, 5; Robert, 4; Thomas, 3; Robert. 2; Thomas, 1); he married first, Elizabeth Allen; second, Persis Hoag.

CHILDREN OF FIRST MARRIAGE
2078. ELIZABETH HAZARD.

CHILDREN OF SECOND MARRIAGE
2079. PERSIS HAZARD, died unmarried.
2080. SENECA HAZARD, married *Frances Hand.*
2081. PLINY HAZARD, died unmarried.
2082. RUSSELL HAZARD, died young.

§ 1166. ACHSAH HAZARD, 8 (Thomas, 7; Robert, 6; Thomas, 5; Robert, 4, Thomas, 3; Robert, 2: Thomas, 1), married —— Taber.

CHILD
2083. RICHARD TABER.

§ 1175. WILLIAM B. HAZARD, 8 (William, 7; Robert, 6; Thomas, 5; Robert, 4; Thomas, 3; Robert, 2; Thomas, 1), was born March 20, 1843, at North Ferrisburg, Vermont. He went to the war when nineteen years of age, but exposure in the field brought on paralysis of the legs. This compelled a change in his plans for life, and he studied medicine, first at Monmouth, Illinois, then at Chicago, and finally graduated at Bellevue Hospital, New York City. After graduating, he became assistant physician at the Flatbush (Long Island) Hospital. He went to St. Louis in 1866. For a number of years he was Superintendent of the St. Louis Insane Asylum, and afterward consulting physician at the City Hospital, and a professor at the St. Louis College of Physicians and Surgeons, a position which he resigned in 1887. He was editor of *The Clinic Record* and a contributor for many medical publications. He died March 17, 1888. He married, April 21, 1868, Gertrude M. Holmes, of Charlotte, Vermont. Mr. Hazard died in St. Louis.

CHILDREN

CHILDREN
2084. ROBERT HAZARD, born 1869.
2085. LUCIA GRACE HAZARD, born 1875.

§ 1184. SAMUEL L. HAZARD, 8 (Thomas R., 7; Thomas, 6; Thomas, 5; Robert, 4; Thomas, 3; Robert, 2; Thomas, 1), was born June 16, 1813 ; he married, February 9, 1840, Olive Woodman, of Wilton, Maine.

CHILDREN
2086. OLIVER W. HAZARD, born in Boston, Jan. 10, 1841 ; married, June 27, 1864, *Margaret Fulton*, of Cambridge, Mass.
2087. THOMAS R. HAZARD, born in Boston, April 4, 1843 ; married, May 24, 1868, *Ida Shattuck*.
2088. SAMUEL LISTER HAZARD, born in Cambridge, Sept. 23, 1854.

§ 1185. EDWARD HAZARD, 8 (Thomas R., 7; Thomas, 6; Thomas, 5; Robert, 4; Thomas, 3; Robert, 2; Thomas, 1), was born in 1816; he married, 1849, Mary Anderson, of Delhi Township, Ohio.

CHILDREN
2089. ROBERT HAZARD, born 1840.
2090. MARIA HAZARD, born 1842.
2091. EMMA HAZARD, born 1844.
2092. WILLIAM HAZARD, born 1846.
2093. ELLA HAZARD, born 1848.
2094. ELIZABETH HAZARD, born 1850.
2095. CHARLES HAZARD, born 1852.
2096. MINNIE HAZARD, born 1854.
2097. ALICE HAZARD, born 1855.
2098. THOMAS E. HAZARD, born 1856.

§ 1187. ROBERT P. HAZARD, 8 (Thomas R., 7; Thomas, 6; Thomas, 5; Robert, 4; Thomas, 3; Robert, 2; Thomas, 1), was born in 1821; died in 1865; married, in 1842, Eliza Mixer, of Delhi Township, Ohio.

CHILDREN
2099. THOMAS R. HAZARD, born 1843; died 1861.
2100a. EBEN HAZARD, born 1845.
2100b. ARABEL HAZARD, born 1847.
2100c. CHARLES HAZARD, born 1851.

§ 1189. WILLIAM HAZARD HOWLAND, 8 (Sarah Hazard, 7; Thomas, 6; Thomas, 5; Robert, 4; Thomas, 3; Robert, 2; Thomas, 1), was born at New Bedford, February 3, 1807; he died in New York, March 3, 1865. He married, November 3, 1841, Annie M. West, of South Carolina.

CHILDREN
2101. CORNELIA S. HOWLAND, born in New York, Dec. 6, 1842.
2102 ANNIE ELLIOTT HOWLAND, born in New York, 1844; died 1856.
2103. SARAH CATHARINE HOWLAND, born in New York, May 5, 1846; married, June 10, 1869, *Millen Ford*.

§ 1191.

§ 1191. MARY RODMAN HOWLAND, 8 (Sarah Hazard, 7 ; Thomas, 6 ; Thomas, 5 ; Robert, 4 ; Thomas, 3 ; Robert, 2 ; Thomas, 1), was born in New York City, November 26, 1810 ; she married, March 12, 1830, Morris, son of William Ferris Pell, of New York, and Mary Shipley, of London.

CHILDREN

2104. JOHN HOWLAND PELL, born Dec. 23, 1830; died Oct. 6, 1882; married, 1st, *Cornelia Corse ;* married, 2d, *Caroline E. Hyatt.*

2105. WILLIAM HOWLAND PELL, born Sept. 3, 1833; married, Sept. 30, 1852, *Adelaide Ferris.*


§ 1197. WILLIAM H. BARKER, 8 (Elizabeth Hazard, 7 ; Thomas, 6 ; Thomas, 5 ; Robert, 4 ; Thomas, 3 ; Robert, 2 ; Thomas, 1), was born August 21, 1809 ; he died September 17, 1879 ; he married, November 14, 1832, Jeanette B. James, of Albany, New York. She was born in 1814; died May 8, 1842.

CHILDREN

2106. WILLIAM BARKER, born 1834; died March 2, 1839.

2107. ELIZABETH H. BARKER, born May 23, 1836; married *George Higginson,* Jr.

2108. ROBERT BARKER, born 1840; died Feb. 8, 1868; unmarried,

2109. AUGUSTUS J. BARKER, born April or May, 1842; died Sept. 18, 1863; unmarried.


§ 1199. ANNA HAZARD BARKER, 8 (Elizabeth Hazard, 7 ; Thomas, 6 ; Thomas, 5 ; Robert, 4 : Thomas, 3 ; Robert, 2 ; Thomas, 1), was born October 25, 1813 ; she married, October 3, 1840, Samuel Gray Ward, of Boston, son of Thomas Wren Ward, and Lydia Gray his wife.

CHILDREN

2110. ANNA BARKER WARD, born Sept. 20, 1841; died Nov. 24, 1875; married *Joseph Marie Antoine Thoron.*

2111. LYDIA GRAY WARD, born April 24, 1843; married *Richard Freiherr von Hoffman.*

2112. THOMAS WREN WARD, born Oct. 8, 1844; married *Sophia Read Howard.*

2113. ELIZABETH BARKER WARD, born Sept. 26, 1847; married Baron *Ernst Augustus Schoenberg,* of Roth-Schoenberg, Saxony. He was born Jan. 4, 1850.


§ 1202. ELIZABETH HAZARD BARKER, 8 (Elizabeth Hazard, 7 ; Thomas, 6 ; Thomas, 5 ; Robert, 4 ; Thomas, 3 ; Robert, 2 ; Thomas, 1), was born July 4, 1817 ; she married, first, Baldwin Brower ; married, second, William Thompson Van Zandt, son of Thomas and Mary Underhill Van Zandt ; she married, third, John McCanless, son of John and Ellen Long McCanless.

CHILDREN OF FIRST MARRIAGE

2114. ANNA HAZARD BROWER, born May 20, 1837; died June 10, 1838.

2115. WILLIAM BALDWIN BROWER, born April 29, 1839.

2116. BALDWIN BROWER, born Aug. 6, 1842.

CHILDREN OF SECOND MARRIAGE

2117. EUGENE VAN ZANDT, born Oct. 25, 1847.

2118. SIGOURNEY VAN ZANDT, born Oct. 25, 1847.

2119. ELIZABETH KNEELAND VAN ZANDT, born July 17, 1849.

2120. ERNEST VAN ZANDT, born Dec. 18, 1851.

2121.

2121.  WALTER VAN ZANDT, born Nov. 10, 1855.
2122.  WILLIAM BARKER VAN ZANDT, born Aug. 5, 1857; died Jan. 8, 1858.

§ 1203. SARAH BARKER, 8 (Elizabeth Hazard, 7; Thomas, 6; Thomas, 5; Robert, 4; Thomas, 3; Robert, 2; Thomas, 1), was born July 27, 1819; she married, first, John C. Harrison, of Baltimore, Maryland; she married, second, William H. Hunt, Secretary of the Navy, 1881, and United States Minister to Russia, 1882.

CHILDREN
2123.  JOHN C. HARRISON.
2124.  THOMAS BULLITT HARRISON.
2125.  BARKER HARRISON.
2126.  WILLIAM HARRISON.
2127.  HALL HARRISON.

§ 1204. ABAHAM BARKER, 8 (Elizabeth Hazard, 7; Thomas, 6; Thomas, 5; Robert, 4; Thomas, 3; Robert, 2; Thomas, 1), was born June 3, 1821; he married, first, June 3, 1842, Sarah Wharton, daughter of William Wharton, and Deborah Fisher, his wife; married, second, June 28, 1871, Katharine Crane, daughter of James Crane, of Elizabeth, New Jersey, and Phebe, his wife. He had no children by his second wife.

CHILDREN
2128.  JACOB BARKER, born June 18, 1843; died March 13, 1851.
2129.  WILLIAM BARKER, born July 27, 1844; died Nov. 3, 1844.
2130.  WHARTON BARKER, born May 1, 1846; married *Margaret C. Baker.*
2131.  ABRAHAM BARKER, born Sept. 29, 1849; died June 6, 1851.
2132.  SIGOURNEY BARKER, born May 15, 1852; died March 4, 1882, at San Antonio, Texas; unmarried.
2133.  DEBORAH FISHER BARKER, born Dec. 28, 1854; married *Edward Mellor.*
2134.  ELIZABETH BARKER, born Jan. 4, 1858; died Dec. 6, 1860.
2135.  ANNA FERRIS BARKER, born Oct. 28, 1861.

§ 1207. JOANNA HONE, 8 (Anna Hazard, 7; Thomas, 6; Thomas, 5; Robert, 4; Thomas, 3; Robert, 2; Thomas, 1), was born June 26, 1811; died February 20, 1837; she married, April 29, 1829, Charles Kneeland, of New York. He died December 19, 1881.

CHILDREN
2136.  CHARLES KNEELAND, born March 3, 1830; died May 18, 1866; married *Louise Tainter.*
2137.  GEORGE KNEELAND, born Aug. 4, 1832; died June 13, 1859.
2138.  HENRY KNEELAND, born April 10, 1834; died Nov. 6, 1837.
2139.  ANNA KNEELAND, born Sept. 12, 1836; died Aug. 12, 1858.

§ 1214. ROWLAND HAZARD, 8 (Rowland G., 7; Rowland, 6; Thomas, 5; Robert, 4; Thomas, 3; Robert, 2; Thomas, 1), was born in Newport, Rhode Island, August 16, 1829. His parents moved to Peacedale, Rhode Island, in 1833, and it was in Peacedale that he grew to manhood. In 1845, he went to the Friends' College, at Haverford, and afterward entered Brown University. He

He graduated in 1849, ranking in the first third of the class. In the department of mathematics he gained the first prize for three years, and a second prize the fourth year. He also took the philosophical prize for the best essay in that department.

He has always been active in village and town affairs. In 1854 he organized a Sunday school in the schoolhouse. February 13, 1857, in response to his invitation, thirteen people met at his house, and the Second Congregational Church of South Kingstown was organized. In 1872 he built the present stone church, drawing the plans himself. The large worsted mill was built after his plans in 1872. The weaving shed at a later date, and the picturesque stone bridges about Peacedale are all of his building. One bridge of a single stone arch, with a span of forty feet, is said to be the largest single arch in the State. He was largely instrumental in establishing the Narragansett Library in 1855, and in the organization of the High School — giving the land for the building, and assisting in its maintenance. In the improvement of the village and town he has had an active part. After much study of the distribution of profits and the question of the relation of capital and labor, and after personal inspection of the co-operative establishment of Rochdale, England, and elsewhere, he introduced the system of profit sharing into the Peacedale mills.

Mr. Hazard has always been interested in agriculture and the improvement of breeds of cattle, and is the president of the Washington County Agricultural Society, to which office he was elected at the organization of the society in 1876. Mr. Hazard served the town of South Kingstown as moderator for several years, and the State Legislature as representative in 1863, and as senator in 1867 and 1868. He was the independent candidate for governor in 1875, receiving the plurality of votes, but failed of an election in the Legislature.

Mr. Hazard has been interested in the production of lead, and took charge of Mine La Motte, Missouri, in 1875. His active mind has naturally been awake to all new forms of industry. In 1881 he took steps to introduce the manufacture of soda-ash into this country. Previously nearly the whole supply had been imported. He was instrumental in organizing the Solvay Process Company, of Syracuse, New York, and became its president. The first soda-ash made by the ammonia process in America was produced by this company, January, 1884: Mr. Hazard's large experience and practical wisdom have greatly aided the industry. He married, March 29, 1854, Margaret Ann Rood, of Philadelphia, daughter of Reverend Anson Rood; she died August, 1895.

CHILDREN

2140.  ROWLAND GIBSON HAZARD, born Jan. 22, 1855; married, Nov. 16, 1880, *Mary Pierpont*, daughter of Rev. *George Bushnell*, of Beloit, Wis.

2141.  CAROLINE HAZARD, born June 10, 1856.  Miss *Hazard* inherits her grandfather's intellectual tastes.  She is the editor of a collected edition of his philosophical and economic writings, under the title of *Works of Rowland Gibson Hazard*, in five volumes, and is the author of a biography entitled *Thomas Hazard, son of Robert, call'd College Tom. A Study of Life in Narragansett in the XVIIIth century*, a book full of early Narragansett history ; and of a
volume

volume of poems called *Narragansett Ballads.* She is the author-editor of a volume issued as a memorial of *J. Lewis Diman,* of Brown University. Miss *Hazard* is full of knowledge, and interest in what was best in the Old Narragansett, and helps on all that is best in the new.

2142. FREDERICK ROWLAND HAZARD, born June 14, 1858; married, May 29, 1886, *Dora G. Sedgwick,* daughter of *Charles B. Sedgwick,* of Syracuse, N.Y.

2143. HELEN HAZARD, born Jan. 15, 1861; married, Oct. 6, 1885, *Nathaniel Terry Bacon.*

2144. MARGARET HAZARD, born May 31, 1867; married June 24, 1893, Dr. *Irving Fisher,* of Yale University.

§ 1215. JOHN NEWBOLD HAZARD, 8 (Rowland Gibson Hazard, 7; Rowland, 6; Thomas, 5; Robert, 4; Thomas, 3; Robert, 2; Thomas, 1), was born in Peacedale, Rhode Island, September 11, 1836. He married, first, Hortense DeHuys, in France; he married, second, Augusta G. Gurloff, in Philadelphia.

CHILDREN OF FIRST MARRIAGE
2145. MARIE HAZARD, born in France.
2146. ÉMILE HAZARD, born in France.

CHILDREN OF SECOND MARRIAGE
2147. ERNEST NEWBOLD HAZARD, born June 25, 1869.
2148. ROBERT HAZARD, born 1871; died Nov. 18, 1874.
2149. EDITH HAZARD, born May 27, 1873.
2150. MARY PEACE HAZARD, born July 8, 1874.
2151. MABEL HAZARD, born Sept. 26, 1875; died Oct. 24, 1875.
2152. JOHN GIBSON HAZARD, born Feb., 1877.
2153. ANNA HAZARD, born July 8, 1880.
2154. ISAAC PEACE HAZARD, born 1883.

§ 1216. JOHN WILBUR HAZARD, 8 (William R., 7; Rowland, 6; Thomas, 5; Robert, 4; Thomas, 3; Robert, 2; Thomas, 1), was born at Peacedale, Rhode Island, December 4, 1830; he married, first, September 23, 1857, Adelia Hoag; she died April 14, 1866; he married, second, Sarah Elizabeth Raymond; there were no children by second wife.

CHILDREN OF FIRST MARRIAGE
2155. WILLIAM J. HAZARD, died in infancy.
2156. CHARLES M. HAZARD, born December 6, 1860.

§ 1218. LYDIA C. HAZARD, 8 (William, 7; Rowland, 6; Thomas, 5; Robert, 4; Thomas, 3; Robert, 2; Thomas, 1), was born in Dutchess County, New York, January 17, 1835; she married, September 22, 1858, Franklin E. Hoag. He died April 5, 1865.

CHILDREN
2157. GEORGE F. HOAG, born June 28, 1860; died Feb. 13, 1888; married 1878. He left children.
2158. MARY E. HOAG, born Dec. 10, 1862.

§ 1220. ROWLAND H. HAZARD, 8 (William, 7; Rowland, 6; Thomas, 5; Robert, 4; Thomas, 3; Robert, 2; Thomas, 1), was born February 10, 1839, in Dutchess County, New York. He married April 12, 1865, Phebe Ann Moore.

CHILDREN

CHILDREN
2159. GEORGE HAZARD, died young.
2160. WILLIAM HAZARD, born 1868.

§ 1221. ANNA HAZARD, 8 (William, 7; Rowland, 6; Thomas, 5; Robert, 4; Thomas, 3; Robert, 2; Thomas, 1), was born in Dutchess County, October 2, 1841; she married, April 24, 1867, Thomas Tierney.
CHILDREN
2161. AGNES L. TIERNEY, born Feb. 13, 1868.
2162. JOHN W. TIERNEY, born May 24, 1869.
2163. BERTHA H. TIERNEY, born Jan. 9, 1871.
2164. WILLIAM H. TIERNEY, died in infancy.
2165. GRACE A. TIERNEY, born Oct. 24, 1874.
2166. THOMAS L. TIERNEY, born Feb. 22, 1878.

§ 1222. WILLIAM WILBUR HAZARD, 8 (William, 7; Rowland, 6; Thomas, 5; Robert, 4; Thomas, 3; Robert, 2; Thomas, 1), was born in Dutchess County, New York, September 25, 1843; he married, April 12, 1888, Mary Rebecca Haight. She died February 9, 1889.
CHILDREN
2167. REBECCA HAZARD, born Jan. 27, 1889; died Jan. 15, 1890.
2168. MARY HAZARD, born Jan. 27, 1889.

§ 1223. ISAAC PEACE HAZARD, 8 (William, 7; Rowland, 6; Thomas, 5; Robert, 4; Thomas, 3; Robert, 2; Thomas, 1), was born in Dutchess County, New York, October 27, 1847; he married, March 20, 1871, Elizabeth A. Howland.
CHILDREN
2169. ISAAC PEACE HAZARD, born June 9, 1880.
2170. WILLIAM HAZARD, died young.

§ 1225. FRANCES HAZARD, 8 (John, 7; John, 6; Benjamin, 5; George, 4; Thomas, 3; Robert, 2; Thomas, 1), was born about 1803; she married, first, May 11, 1827, Elnathan Brown; he died in January, 1830; she married, second, Osmus Stillman.
CHILD OF FIRST MARRIAGE
2171. FRANCES BROWN; married *Theophilus Hyde*. They had several children.

§ 1226. WILLIAM R. HAZARD, 8 (Nathan, 7; John, 6; Benjamin, 5; George, 4; Thomas, 3; Robert, 2; Thomas, 1), was born January 11, 1810; he died September 26, 1873; he married Sarah, daughter of Joseph and Mary Norris Potter. He married, second, Alice Burlingame.
CHILD OF FIRST MARRIAGE
2172. WILLIAM EDWIN HAZARD, born June, 1842; died Feb. 12, 1846.

§ 1228. CATHARINE HAZARD, 8 (Nathan G., 7; John, 6; Benjamin, 5; George, 4; Thomas, 3; Robert, 2; Thomas, 1), was born June 2, 1818; she married

married, at Stonington, Connecticut, November 28, 1848, Peleg Noyes. She died January 8, 1894; he died January 11, 1894.

CHILD
2173. ROWLAND N. NOYES, born in Westerly, R. I., Aug. 3, 1852.

§ 1230. GEORGE MUMFORD HAZARD, 8 (Mumford, 7; George, 6; Simeon, 5; George, 4; Thomas, 3; Robert, 2; Thomas, 1), was born March 13, 1822; he married, February 1, 1847, Almira Sweet; she was born June 27, 1823.

CHILDREN
2174. HENRY HOLT HAZARD, born July 11, 1848; died Aug. 27, 1851.
2175. ALBERT ARMSTRONG HAZARD, born July 25, 1850; died March 2, 1852.
2176. FRANK SWEET HAZARD, born Feb. 25, 1852.
2177. HERBERT GOULD HAZARD, born Nov. 15, 1854; married, 1878, *Fannie Packard*.
2178. SIMEON HAZARD, born Jan. 16, 1856.
2179. MARY FRANCES HAZARD, born Nov. 16, 1857; died Sept. 1, 1858.
2180. BENJAMIN I. HAZARD, born March 11, 1860; died Aug. 26, 1860.

§ 1231. CHARLES H. HAZARD, 8 (Mumford, 7; George, 6; Simeon, 5; George, 4; Thomas, 3; Robert, 2; Thomas, 1). He married Mary Smith.
CHILDREN
2181. DANIEL HAZARD.
2182. ISAAC HAZARD.
2183. MARIA HAZARD.
2184. HENRY HAZARD.
2185. EMMA HAZARD.

§ 1232. JAMES T. HAZARD, 8 (Mumford, 7; George, 6; Simeon, 5; George, 4; Thomas, 3; Robert, 2; Thomas, 1), was born May 2, 1828; he married, March 10, 1851, Phebe, daughter of Thomas Gould; she was born June 8, 1828.
CHILDREN
2186. FANNY H. HAZARD, born May 15, 1853; married, 1876, *Gardiner S. Perry*.
2187. ELOISE HAZARD, born June 4, 1858.

§ 1233. BENJAMIN I. HAZARD, 8 (Mumford, 7; George, 6; Simeon, 5; George, 4; Thomas, 3; Robert, 2; Thomas, 1), was born March, 1831; he married Sarah Ingalls, of Taunton, Massachusetts. He lives in Georgetown, South Carolina.
CHILDREN
2188. ALLEN P. HAZARD.
2189. WALTER HAZARD.
2190. BENJAMIN I. HAZARD.
2191. JONATHAN INGALLS HAZARD.
2192. SCHUYLER HAZARD.
2193. LENA MAY HAZARD.
2194. RUTH TILLEY HAZARD.
2195. HATTIE W. HAZARD.

§ 1234.

§ 1234. WILLIAM T. HAZARD, 8 (Mumford, 7; George, 6; Simeon, 5; George, 4; Thomas 3; Robert, 2; Thomas, 1), was born in 1833; he married Mary Ryan. He lives in Randolph, Massachusetts.

CHILDREN
2196. NELLIE HAZARD.
2197. WILLIAM R. HAZARD.
2198. BLANCHE HAZARD.

§ 1236. THOMAS T. HAZARD, 8 (Mumford, 7; George, 6; Simeon, 5; George, 4; Thomas, 3; Robert, 2; Thomas, 1), was born in 1839; he lives in New York. He married Margaret Kellogg.

CHILDREN
2199. LEVERETT K. HAZARD.
2200. NELLIE T. HAZARD.
2201. THOMAS T. HAZARD.
2202. SALLIE T. HAZARD.

§ 1242. GEORGE SULLIVAN HAZARD, 8 (Charles T.,7; George,6; Simeon, 5; George, 4; Thomas, 3; Robert, 2; Thomas, 1), was born May 18, 1827; he married, first, Mary Wilson; he married, second, Annie Wellman.

CHILD OF FIRST MARRIAGE
2203. ANNIE F. HAZARD.

§ 1243. CHARLES GODFREY HAZARD, 8 (Charles, 7; George, 6; Simeon, 5; George, 4; Thomas, 3; Robert, 2; Thomas, 1), was born November 9, 1830; he married Mary Warner.

CHILDREN
2204. CHARLES T. HAZARD.
2205. LOUIS AUGUSTUS HAZARD.

§ 1247. SILAS H. HAZARD, 8 (Charles T., 7; George, 6; Simeon, 5; George, 4; Thomas, 3; Robert, 2; Thomas, 1), was born January 27, 1840. He married Sallie Burdick.

CHILD
2206. FANNIE HAZARD.

§ 1250. GEORGE A. HAZARD, 8 (Arnold, 7; George, 6; Simeon, 5; George, 4; Thomas, 3; Robert, 2; Thomas, 1), was born August 5, 1831; he married Mary Barber.

CHILDREN
2207. SARAH ELLEN HAZARD.
2208. WILLIAM S. HAZARD.
2209. ELIZABETH S. HAZARD.
2210. AMELIA T. HAZARD.

§ 1253. SARAH CONTENT HAZARD, 8 (Arnold, 7; George, 6; Simeon, 5; George, 4; Thomas, 3; Robert, 2; Thomas, 1), was born October 14, 1834; she

she married, first, Jethro C. Carr, December 1, 1852. She married, second, George W. Sandford.

CHILDREN OF FIRST MARRIAGE
2211. GEORGE H. CARR.
2212. FLORENCE T. CARR.
2213. SAMUEL E. CARR.

CHILD OF SECOND MARRIAGE
2214. JAMES HAZARD SANDFORD.

§ 1255. HARRIET A. HAZARD, 8 (Arnold, 7; George, 6; Simeon, 5; George, 4; Thomas, 3; Robert, 2; Thomas, 1), was born June 5, 1838; she married, September 18, 1856, Charles F. Palmer.

CHILD
2215. SARAH J. PALMER.

§ 1259. ISABELLA DONALDSON HAZARD, 8 (William W., 7; George, 6; Simeon, 5; George, 4; Thomas, 3; Robert, 2; Thomas, 1). She married, October 6, 1855, Joseph M. Bokee, of Brooklyn, New York.

CHILDREN
2216. IDA DONALDSON BOKEE.
2217. MARGARET HELENA BOKEE.
2218. JOSEPH ALEXANDER BOKEE.
2219. ARCHER HAZARD BOKEE.

§ 1261. GEORGE ARMSTRONG HAZARD, 8 (William, 7; George, 6; Simeon, 5; George, 4; Thomas, 3; Robert, 2; Thomas, 1). He married, December 18, 1871, Josephine Augusta, daughter of Thomas T. Carr, of Newport, Rhode Island.

CHILD
2220. DUNCAN ARMSTRONG HAZARD, born May, 1875.

§ 1265. WILLIAM ALBERT ARMSTRONG, 8 (Harriet Hazard, 7; George, 6; Simeon, 5; George, 4; Thomas, 3; Robert, 2; Thomas, 1), was born October 11, 1834; he married, 1857, Carrie Lewis.

CHILDREN
2221. MINNIE ARMSTRONG.
2222. GEORGE A. ARMSTRONG.

§ 1268. LEBBEUS ENSWORTH HAZARD, 8 (Henry, 7; George, 6; Simeon, 5; George, 4; Thomas, 3; Robert, 2; Thomas, 1), was born July 3, 1841; he married, August 3, 1865, Amelia J. Ludlum, of New York. She died February 13, 1878, aged thirty-three.

CHILD
2223. LAWRENCE WILBUR HAZARD, born Oct. 17, 1874.

§ 1275. SARAH W. HAZARD, 8 (Simeon, 7; George, 6; Simeon, 5; George, 4;

4; Thomas, 3; Robert, 2; Thomas, 1), was born October 2, 1839; she married, June 27, 1864, Edwin G. Spooner.

CHILDREN

2224. SARAH C. SPOONER, born March 12, 1865.
2225. GEORGE J. SPOONER, born Jan. 1, 1869.

§ 1278. GEORGE S. HAZARD, 8 (Simeon, 7; George, 6; Simeon, 5; George, 4; Thomas, 3; Robert, 2; Thomas, 1), was born June 4, 1846; he married, October 20, 1870, Sarah Amanda Stoddard.

CHILDREN

2226. MAGGIE S. HAZARD, born May 11, 1872.
2227. GEORGE ASHLEY HAZARD, born April 12, 1875.

§ 1281. MARTHA SIMPSON HAZARD, 8 (James Lawrence, 7; George, 6; Simeon, 5; George, 4; Thomas, 3; Robert, 2; Thomas, 1), was born September 30, 1843; she married, May 31, 1866, Eben Godbold.

CHILDREN

2228. EDWARD JOSLYN GODBOLD.
2229. LAWRENCE HAZARD GODBOLD.

§ 1285. CHRISTOPHER GRANT HAZARD, 8 (Sylvester, 7; Thomas A., 6; George, 5; George, 4; Thomas, 3; Robert, 2; Thomas, 1), was born in Newport, Rhode Island. Early in life he entered the chemist's shop of his uncle, Doctor Rowland Hazard, and after attaining his majority, opened a shop on his own account. Later he removed to Brooklyn, New York. Here for many years he dispensed remedies to thousands, and was noted for his conscientious administration of medicine. To the poor and needy he gave freely. He did not leave a fortune to his family, but a name that his children can call blessed. He died May 31, 1888.

He married, December 15, 1846, Eliza Gardiner Coggeshall.

CHILDREN

2230. CLARE GARDINER HAZARD, born April 11, 1848; married *Charles Wiltshire Wood.*
2231. CHRISTOPHER GRANT HAZARD, born May 9, 1852; married *Fannie Seward Post.*
2232. FREDERIC SYLVESTER HAZARD, born March 26, 1856; married *Emily Cook.*
2233. GEORGE ROBINSON HAZARD.

§ 1286. ABBY ROBINSON HAZARD, 8 (Sylvester, 7; Thomas A., 6; George, 5; George, 4; Thomas, 3; Robert, 2; Thomas, 1), was born January 3, 1833; she married, November 19, 1849, William A. Whaley; they were married in Newport, Rhode Island, where they have always lived.

CHILDREN

2234. GULIELMA M. WHALEY, born Dec. 23, 1850; died Sept. 3, 1854.
2235. MARY A. WHALEY, born Sept. 25, 1852; married, Nov. 19, 1874, in Newport, *Ira A. Goff,* of Providence, R. I.
2236. ABBY C. WHALEY, born Nov. 8, 1857; died Sept. 12, 1859.
2237. ANNA COLLINS WHALEY, born Dec. 26, 1867.

§ 1290.

§ 1290. LOUIS L. HAZARD, 8 (George, 7 ; Thomas, 6 ; George, 5 ; George, 4 ; Thomas, 3 ; Robert, 2 ; Thomas, 1). He married Sarah Congdon, daughter of Jonathan and Mary (Congdon) Hazard ; she was born December 28, 1831. He was a captain, and was lost at sea.

CHILDREN
2238. ADA HAZARD; married *Thomas G. Brown.*
2239. HELEN MAUD HAZARD; married *I. Goodwin Hobbs*, U. S. Navy.
2240. GEORGE ROBINSON HAZARD.
2241. SARAH CONGDON HAZARD.
2242. LOUISE HOLYOKE HAZARD, } twins.
2243. JENNIE HUNTER HAZARD,  }

§ 1294. JEREMIAH POTTER ROBINSON, 8 (Mary Niles Potter, 7 ; Sarah Hazard, 6 ; Enoch, 5 ; George, 4 ; Thomas, 3 ; Robert, 2 ; Thomas, 1), was born August 18, 1819, at Tower Hill, in the "Church House" ; he died in Brooklyn, New York, August 26, 1886. Mr. Robinson began life in Newport, Rhode Island. In 1836, at the age of sixteen, he went to New York, where he was employed by the firm of P. & A. Woodruff, and, after a few years, attained a partnership in the business. The name of the firm later was changed to A. Woodruff & Robinson, and then to J. P. & G. C. Robinson. His business desk stood for almost half a century on nearly the same spot, and business is now transacted on what is practically the site of the house which he entered as a boy. About the year 1843, Mr. Robinson began to look with much interest upon the growing city of Brooklyn, and soon purchased large blocks of real estate on the Brooklyn river front, improving them by building upon them warehouses and piers. He was thus among the pioneers of the great warehouse system of that city. A few years later, with William Beard, he became interested in the water front in South Brooklyn, and began the work of planning and constructing the great Erie basin, and the adjoining basins, building piers and warehouses, until at this time there is a wharfage and dockage of several miles where vessels are loaded and unloaded. It is the largest and most comprehensive dock system in the world. Mr. Robinson was ever watchful of the rights of laboring men, and in his business projects much care was taken to pay each laborer liberally for extra service, the result being great faithfulness to the interest of their employer. Mr. Robinson was one of the prominent supporters of the great East River Bridge enterprise, and as a bridge trustee gave intelligent attention to all the details of its progress and management. He honorably filled the position of president of the board of trustees through the most trying period of the work.
Successful for himself, kind, helpful, generous to the poor, and useful in the community, his death was universally regretted. He married, May 23, 1843, Elizabeth DeWitt, of Cranberry, New Jersey ; she was born June 30, 1819, and died November, 1888, in Brooklyn, New York.

CHILDREN
2244. MARY NILES ROBINSON, born March 13, 1844; died July 30, 1845.

2245.

2245. JEREMIAH POTTER ROBINSON, born May 1, 1846, in Brooklyn, N. Y.; married, Nov. 12, 1867, *Margaret Downing Lanman*, daughter of *David Trumbull Lanman*.
2246. ELIZABETH DEWITT ROBINSON, born Aug. 12, 1851; married, Jan. 10, 1870, *Lewis Leonard*.
2247. HARRIET WOODRUFF ROBINSON, born March 11, 1853; married, June 21, 1883, *John E. Leech*.
2248. ISAAC RICH ROBINSON, born July 8, 1856; married, Nov. 21, 1877, *Ellen Louise Pate*.

§ 1297. GEORGE CHAMPLIN ROBINSON, 8 (Mary N. Potter, 7; Sarah Hazard, 6; Enoch, 5; George, 4; Thomas, 3; Robert, 2; Thomas, 1), was born January 26, 1825. He began business in New York with his brother, Jeremiah P. Robinson, and after a few years was taken into the business as partner. He retired about 1880, and since that time he has lived in Wakefield, Rhode Island. He married, May 10, 1852, Mary Lyman, daughter of Governor Lemuel Hastings and Sally (Lyman) Arnold.

CHILDREN
2249. GEORGE CHAMPLIN ROBINSON, born June 14, 1854.
2250. LOUISA LYMAN ROBINSON, born May 24, 1856; married, Oct. 27, 1880, *George F. Weeden*.
2251. MARY NILES ROBINSON, born Sept. 4, 1858; married, April 13, 1880, *Thomas L. Arnold*.
2252. RICHARD ARNOLD ROBINSON, born Aug. 1, 1860; died June 4, 1862.
2253. MARGARET ARNOLD ROBINSON, born April 4, 1864.
2254. ANNA DENNIS ROBINSON, born July 13, 1866.
2255. MAUD ROBINSON, born March 29, 1870; died Sept. 11, 1871.
2256. EDWARD WANTON ROBINSON, born Dec. 19, 1872.

§ 1298. MARY NILES ROBINSON, 8 (Mary Potter, 7; Sarah Hazard, 6; Enoch, 5; George, 4; Thomas, 3; Robert, 2; Thomas, 1), was born April 2, 1827. She married, October 15, 1849, George Griswold Pearse, of Bristol, Rhode Island.

CHILDREN
2257. GEORGE ROBINSON PEARSE, born July 14, 1850; married, Oct. 14, 1880, *Nellie Morse*.
2258. MARY ELIZABETH PEARSE, born July 7, 1852; died Dec. 23, 1859.
2259. JEREMIAH NILES PEARSE, born March 9, 1855.
2260. JOSEPH CHILDS PEARSE, born July 27, 1857.
2261. MARY FRANCES PEARSE, born Jan. 26, 1864; died Aug. 16, 1874.
2262. ELIZABETH EMMA PEARSE, born July 9, 1866; married, Sept. 15, 1892, *Edward D. Depew*.

§ 1299. SARAH FALES POTTER, 8 (Jeremiah N. Potter, 7; Sarah Hazard, 6; Enoch, 5; George, 4; Thomas, 3; Robert, 2; Thomas, 1), was born July 26, 1833; she married, February 20, 1868, Walter Watson, son of Hazard and Frances (Robinson) Watson.

CHILDREN
2263. MARY ROBINSON WATSON, born at Point Judith, South Kingstown, Oct. 7, 1869.
2264. WALTER HAZARD WATSON, born at Point Judith, June 1, 1878.

§ 1310. HARRIET MARIA HAZARD, 8 (William, 7; Thomas G., 6; Thomas, 5; George, 4; Thomas, 3; Robert, 2; Thomas, 1), was born January 16, 1842; she married, September 8, 1869, John G. Clarke. He was born July 4, 1824; died December 7, 1891.

CHILDREN

CHILDREN

2265. MARY CLARKE, born Sept. 13, 1870; died March 23, 1884.
2266. ALMIRA HULL CLARKE, born April 24, 1872.
2267. HARRIET BRENTON CLARKE, born Oct. 5, 1874.
2268. JOHN GIDEON CLARKE, born Dec. 23, 1876.
2269. WILLIAM HAZARD CLARKE, born Aug. 1, 1878.
2270. LATHAM CLARKE, born Dec. 27, 1881.

§ 1317. LIZZIE HAZARD, 8 (George Borden, 7; Thomas G., 6; Thomas, 5; George, 4; Thomas, 3; Robert, 2; Thomas, 1). She married William Cotton.

CHILDREN

2271. WILLIAM COTTON.
2272. MARY COTTON.

§ 1325. CHARLES MASON BROOKS, 8 (Harriet Hazard, 7; Benjamin, 6; Thomas, 5; George, 4; Thomas, 3; Robert, 2; Thomas, 1), was born July 24, 1840; he married, April 19, 1866, Eleanor Williamson MacIntire.

CHILDREN

2273. MARY WILLIAMSON BROOKS, born June 10, 1867; married, Oct. 26, 1891, Dr. *W. Dillinbach*, of Washington, D. C.
2274. DANIEL HAZARD BROOKS, born Jan. 3, 1871.
2275. JOHN MACINTIRE BROOKS, born June 28, 1874; died June 20, 1876.
2276. LYMAN BROOKS, born July 18, 1876; died July, 1878.

§ 1326. HARRIET LYMAN BROOKS, 8 (Harriet Hazard, 7; Benjamin, 6; Thomas, 5; George, 4; Thomas, 3; Robert, 2; Thomas, 1), was born July 18, 1841; she married, October 1, 1863, George Stevens.

CHILDREN

2277a. CHARLES BROOKS STEVENS, born Oct. 11, 1864.
2277b. ELIZABETH LYMAN STEVENS, born June 24, 1866; married, Dec. 28, 1893, *Ernest Dosseter Pawle*, of Reigate, Surrey, England.
2278. GEORGE STEVENS, born Nov. 10, 1867.
2279. MAUD LYMAN STEVENS, born May 16, 1869.

§ 1328. MARY E. BROOKS, 8 (Harriet Hazard, 7; Benjamin, 6; Thomas, 5; George, 4; Thomas, 3; Robert, 2; Thomas, 1), was born April 6, 1847; she married Lieutenant Washburne Maynard, United States Navy, now (1893) Commodore Maynard.

CHILDREN

2280. GEORGE STEVENS MAYNARD, born Jan. 28, 1873.
2281. EDWARD MAYNARD, born Sept. 13, 1875.
2282. ROBERT WASHBURNE MAYNARD, born Oct. 17, 1879.

§ 1332. SUSAN STEVENS, 8 (Margaret L. Hazard, 7; Benjamin, 6; Thomas, 5; George, 4; Thomas, 3; Robert, 2; Thomas, 1), was born November 20, 1846; she married, at Portland, Oregon, October 27, 1870, Captain Richard J. Eskridge, United States Army. Captain Eskridge is now stationed at Fort Sam Houston San Antonio, Texas.

CHILDREN

CHILDREN

2283*a*. MAUD ESKRIDGE, born at Fort Vancouver, Washington, Aug. 21, 1871.
2283*b*. RICHARD STEVENS ESKRIDGE, born at Yuma Depot, Arizona, Oct. 24, 1872; he is a student at Harvard University Law School.
2284. HAZARD STEVENS ESKRIDGE, born at Yuma Depot, Arizona, Feb. 20, 1874; he died at Fort Russell, Wyoming, Oct. 12, 1874.
2285. VIRGINIA ESKRIDGE, born at Fort D. A. Russell, Wyoming, March 2, 1875.
2286. OLIVER STEVENS ESKRIDGE, born at Roxbury, Mass., Oct. 12, 1876.
2287. MARY PEYTON ESKRIDGE, born at Fort Leavenworth, Kan., March 28, 1878.

§ 1357. HARRIET THERESA HAZARD, 8 (Bowdoin, 7; Jonathan, 6; Thomas, 5; Jonathan, 4; Thomas, 3; Robert, 2; Thomas, 1), was born January 15, 1820; she married, March 12, 1843, John Gould Perry; he was born in South Kingstown, Rhode Island, June 2, 1817. For a number of years he was Town Clerk.

CHILDREN

2288. HARRIET ELIZABETH PERRY, born in South Kingstown, Jan. 18, 1844; she married, June 16, 1869, *Clarence Eugene Thomas*.
2289. OLIVER HAZARD PERRY, born June 1, 1845.
2290. JOHN EDWARD PERRY, born May 28, 1847; married, May 1, 1878, *Elenora Crawford*.
2291. SARAH EMILY PERRY, born April 17, 1849; married, Oct. 10, 1877, *Herbert Johnson Wells*.
2292. MILLARD FILLMORE PERRY, born Aug. 27, 1856; married, Nov. 9, 1892, *Edna Aldrich*.
2293. HOWARD BOWDOIN PERRY, born Sept. 20, 1859.

§ 1358. WILLIAM RHODES HAZARD, 8 (Bowdoin, 7; Jonathan, 6; Thomas, 5; Jonathan, 4; Thomas, 3; Robert, 2; Thomas, 1), was born April 1, 1821. He married, first, September 8, 1847, Mary E. Lyon; she died October 30, 1849. He married, second, December 31, 1851, Sarah, daughter of George C. and Mary Niles (Potter) Robinson. She died May 27, 1860, aged thirty-eight. He married, third, August 1, 1865, Adeline A. Wetherell. He died December 29, 1877.

CHILD BY FIRST MARRIAGE

2294. MARY EUDORA HAZARD, born April 1, 1849; died June 15, 1856.

CHILDREN BY SECOND MARRIAGE

2295. EDWARD LYON HAZARD, born Nov. 22, 1852.
2296. WILLIAM A. HAZARD, born Jan. 11, 1854; married, Jan. 13, 1885, *Laura Abell Pelton*.
2297. MARY ELIZABETH HAZARD, born Dec. 8, 1855; died June 28, 1858.
2298. SARAH ROBINSON HAZARD, born July 11, 1858; married *Henry Dunn*.

§ 1359. MARIETTA HAZARD, 8 (Bowdoin, 7; Jonathan, 6; Thomas, 5; Jonathan, 4; Thomas, 3; Robert, 2; Thomas, 1), was born February 18, 1823; she married, January 11, 1849, Joseph Nichols.

CHILDREN

2299. ANNIE E. NICHOLS, born July 23, 1850; married, May 26, 1869, *Charles A. Porter*.
2300. JOSEPH B. NICHOLS, born Oct. 27, 1855; married, 1st, April 10, 1881, *May L. Greene;* married, 2d, March 28, 1886, *Fannie E. James*.
2301. MARY S. NICHOLS, born Feb. 1, 1857; married, June 9, 1875, *Frank Warner Robinson*.
2302. ABBIE A. NICHOLS, born May 11, 1861; married, Sept. 19, 1882, *J. H. Crandall*.

§ 1389.

§ 1389. ELISHA WATSON, 8 (Ann Cole, 7; Mary Hazard, 6; Thomas, 5; Jonathan, 4; Thomas, 3; Robert, 2; Thomas, 1), was born October 8, 1808; he died May 31, 1877. He was born and lived all his life in South Kingstown, Rhode Island. His education was the best that could be obtained in a country town in those days. His father was a large landholder and merchant, the largest in the town at the time of his death, owning thirteen large farms. At an early age his son was often sent to New York, Philadelphia and Baltimore with cargoes of wool, butter and cheese, returning with dry goods and groceries. He was subjected to the caprice of wind and waves in sailing crafts, often meeting with delays that were dangerous and trying, but sometimes amusing. At the age of twenty-one, he married and settled on a farm in the village of Wakefield. This farm had a frontage of nearly two miles on the post-road, and two-thirds of the large and now flourishing village of Wakefield has grown up on this land.

Mr. Watson was ever ready with his influence and money to promote improvements in his native town. He was interested in education, and gave land for school-houses in Wakefield and the adjoining villages, as well as land for churches of different denominations. He was chosen by the Whig and afterwards by the Republican parties to represent them in the Legislature, both as senator and representative. He purchased several large farms besides those given to him by his father. He owned a farm at Narragansett Pier; and foreseeing the future of the village as a watering-place, he divided it into streets, planted trees, and thus gave to this well-known watering-place its first start. He was interested in the Narragansett Pier Railroad, working with zeal for its completion.

Mr. Watson married, first, December 20, 1829, Susan, daughter of John and Mary Watson; she died May 7, 1834, in her twenty-eighth year. He married, second, December 20, 1834, Hannah, daughter of Benjamin and Elizabeth (Brown) Robinson; she died November 18, 1838, aged thirty-six. He married, third, November 18, 1840, Hannah R., daughter of George W. and Mary L. Hazard; she died August 21, 1871, aged fifty-two. He married, fourth, Rebecca, widow of Daniel Gorham. By his last wife he had no children.

CHILDREN BY FIRST MARRIAGE

2303. HENRY CLAY WATSON, born Oct. 16, 1832; died, unmarried, 1863.
2304. RICHARD G. WATSON, born April 22, 1834; died at Fort Scott, Kan., June, 1891; married, and left children.

CHILDREN BY SECOND MARRIAGE

2305. BENJAMIN ROBINSON WATSON, born Dec. 30, 1835; died at Como, Ill., March, 1883; married, and left children.
2306. HANNAH SUSAN WATSON, born Sept. 19, 1837; married, 1st, April 9, 1861, *Altmore Wright;* married, 2d, Dec. 13, 1865, *Charles Hazard.*

CHILDREN BY THIRD MARRIAGE

2307. GEORGE HAZARD WATSON, born May 31, 1842. He enlisted as a volunteer in the War of the Rebellion, and was killed at the battle of Malvern Hill, July 1, 1862.
2308. MARY ANN WATSON, born Jan. 9, 1844.

§ 1390.

§ 1390. MARY ANN WATSON, 8 (Ann Cole, 7; Mary Hazard, 6; Thomas, 5; Jonathan, 4; Thomas, 3; Robert, 2; Thomas, 1), was born May 15, 1810; she died August 3, 1883; she married, November, 1829, John H. Cross, son of Judge Amos and Elizabeth (Barns) Cross, of Westerly, Rhode Island. He was born January 17, 1811; he died November 10, 1874.

CHILDREN

2309. AMOS CROSS, born April 5, 1831; died Dec. 25, 1836.
2310. AMOS CROSS, born Aug. 27, 1841; unmarried.
2311. ELISHA WATSON CROSS, born Sept. 22, 1844; married, Nov. 1, 1872, *Frances Cooper Wright.*

§ 1391. WILLIAM WATSON, 8 (Ann Cole, 7; Mary Hazard, 6; Thomas, 5; Jonathan, 4; Thomas, 3; Robert, 2; Thomas, 1), was born November 6, 1811; he died June 29, 1874; he married Ann Arnold; she was born in 1818.

CHILDREN

2312. CAROLINE S. WATSON, born 1838; died Jan. 25, 1843.
2313. CHRISTOPHER WATSON, born 1840; died Oct., 1842.
2314. ELISHA WATSON, born Aug., 1847; died 1850.
2315. EDWARD WATSON, born 1842; died July 19, 1844.
2316. A DAUGHTER, born and died 1845.
2317. CHRISTOPHER A. WATSON, born 1845; died 1878; married *Sarah Dean.*
2318. ADA WATSON, born 1849; married *Marshal Gilbert.*
2319. FRANK S. WATSON, born 1852; died Dec., 1852.
2320. WILLIAM WATSON, born 1857; married *Abby Holland.*
2321. ANN ELIZABETH WATSON, born 1859; married *Theodore Lawton.*

§ 1395. LAURA WATSON, 8 (Ann Cole, 7; Mary Hazard, 6; Thomas, 5; Jonathan, 4; Thomas, 3; Robert, 2; Thomas, 1). She married, May 20, 1848, Robert Dunbar Watson.

CHILDREN

2322. IRVING WATSON, born June 28, 1849, in New York; married, in Detroit, Mich., Sept. 8, 1875, *Lizzie Campau.*
2323. FRANK WATSON; married *Abby Caswell.*

§ 1396. THOMAS JEFFERSON WATSON, 8 (Ann Cole, 7; Mary Hazard, 6; Thomas, 5; Jonathan, 4; Thomas, 3; Robert, 2; Thomas, 1), married, first, Mary, daughter of Willard Hazard; she died February 26, 1853, aged twenty-one years, eight months. He married, second, Abby Cole.

CHILD BY FIRST MARRIAGE

2324. ANNIE WATSON.

CHILDREN BY SECOND MARRIAGE

2325. THOMAS WATSON.
2326. ELISHA WATSON.
2327. IDA WATSON.

§ 1409. GEORGE THOMAS HASZARD, 8 (James Douglas, 7; Thomas Rhodes, 6; Thomas, 5; Jonathan, 4; Thomas, 3; Robert, 2; Thomas, 1), was
born

born February 1, 1826. In early life Mr. Haszard attended the University of Edinburgh as a medical student for some time, but finding the studies not agreeable to him, he returned to his home in Charlottetown, Prince Edward Island, and succeeded to his father's printing and bookselling business. With enterprise unusual in those days, he imported from New York a cylinder printing-press, from which he issued "Haszard's Gazette," and other publications. This was the first printing-press driven by steam-power used in the Island. About 1855, his brother-in-law, George W. Owen, entered into partnership with him, under the name of Haszard & Owen. This connection continued until Mr. Owen's departure for New Zealand, in 1858. Mr. Haszard retired from the printing and book business about 1863. He married, May 14, 1850, Margaret, daughter of Thomas Owen, Esquire, Postmaster-General of the Colony.

CHILDREN

2328.   GEORGE HERBERT OWEN HASZARD, born June 1, 1851; married, Aug. 13, 1889, *Edith S. Moore.*
2329.   THOMAS WALTER DOUGLASS HASZARD, born Jan. 27, 1854; married, Sept. 13, 1882, *Annie Wilson Campbell.*
2330.   ANNIE SOPHIA CAMPBELL HASZARD, born March 24, 1856.
2331.   HENRY WILLIAM HASZARD, born May 3, 1858; he lives (1894) at Malden, Mass.
2332.   GEORGE ASHLEY HASZARD, born May 15, 1860; married *Sarah Bears,* lives at Melrose, Mass.
2333.   LOUIS ALBERT HASZARD, born Jan. 19, 1863.

§ 1412. CHARLES ALBERT HASZARD, 8 (James Douglas, 7; Thomas Rhodes, 6; Thomas, 5; Jonathan, 4; Thomas, 3; Robert, 2; Thomas, 1), was born February 8, 1838; he married Amelia J. Haszard, daughter of William Jones Haszard; she was his second cousin. He died June 10, 1886.

CHILDREN

2334.   CLARA NELMES HASZARD, married —— *Barnet.*
2335.   INA JANE HASZARD.
2336.   CHARLES EDWARD ADOLPHUS HASZARD.
2337.   EDNA WINIFRED HASZARD.
2338.   MONA VERA HASZARD.
        The three last were killed, with their father, in the volcanic eruption in New Zealand, June 10, 1886.

§ 1413. JANE LIGHTBOURN HASZARD, 8 (James Douglas, 7; Thomas Rhodes, 6; Thomas, 5; Jonathan, 4; Thomas, 3; Robert, 2; Thomas, 1), was born February 10, 1841; she married, first, April 12, 1860, Captain Adolphus Daniel Smith; she married, second, September 4, 1877, Charles H. Robinson, merchant, of Hamilton, Bermuda.

CHILDREN BY FIRST MARRIAGE

2339.   CHARLES SMITH, died in infancy.
2340.   JAMES SMITH, died in infancy.

§ 1422. JESSIE HENRIETTA HASZARD, 8 (James Douglas, 7; Thomas, 6; Thomas, 5; Jonathan, 4; Thomas, 3; Robert, 2; Thomas, 1), was born October 9, 1856; she married, June 19, 1879, Thomas James Harris.

CHILDREN

CHILDREN

2341. ROBERT CLARE HARRIS, born May 5, 1880; died Jan. 18, 1892.
2342. CHARLES ROBINSON HARRIS, born July 29, 1882.
2343. JAMES EDWARD HARRIS, born July 2, 1886.
2344. DORA RUTCLIFFE HARRIS, born March 21, 1892.

§ 1432. CHARLES COLSON GARDINER, 8 (John Rhodes Gardiner, 7; Eunice Hazard, 6; Thomas, 5; Jonathan, 4; Thomas, 3; Robert, 2; Thomas, 1), was born at Centreville, Prince Edward Island, September 10, 1835; he married, first, September 22, 1868, Martha, daughter of J. B. Cox, Esqʳ. She died June 29, 1869. He married second, at Pictou, Nova Scotia, November 25, 1873, Lucy Narraway.

Mr. Gardiner received his preliminary education at Centreville, and afterward spent two years at Mount Alison Academy, Sackville, New Brunswick. In 1854 he entered a mercantile house in Charlottetown, where he remained till the summer of 1856. In that year he went to California, and engaged in gold-mining until the spring of 1858. At that time great excitement sprang up about the new Eldorado in the country then owned and controlled exclusively by the Hudson Bay Company. Mr. Gardiner determined to try his fortune at the new mines, and accordingly proceeded to San Francisco, and took passage up the coast to Portland, Oregon, went thence across the country to Whatcome on Bellingham Bay, and, with a company of five others, started in a canoe for Fraser River, where the mines were said to be richest. On arriving at their destination, Mr. Gardiner and his friends, by prospecting, found gold in many places; but the appliances at their disposal were so ineffectual that all hope of getting the precious metal in paying quantities was abandoned. Accordingly they determined to return to California, which, after experiencing much toil and incurring many dangers, they succeeded in doing.

In 1860, Mr. Gardiner returned to his home and went into business at Centreville. In 1870 he bought a farm near Charlottetown, where he built a comfortable residence and other buildings, and remained there till 1877, when he sold his property, and since has lived as a gentleman of leisure, occasionally visiting California and Europe. When in Rome, Mr. Gardiner and his wife had the honor of being presented to His Holiness, Leo XIII.

Mr. Gardiner has for many years taken an active interest in all matters pertaining to the welfare of the agriculturists of the country, particularly in the department of live stock. In this connection, his name is known far beyond the Maritime Provinces, and he has been appointed, and has acted for many years, as an expert judge of live stock at the New England, Bangor and Lewiston fairs in Maine.

§ 1461. FRANCIS LONGWORTH HASZARD, 8 (Charles, 7; William, 6; Thomas, 5; Jonathan, 4; Thomas, 3; Robert, 2; Thomas, 1), was born at Bellevue, November 20, 1849; he married, October 12, 1876, Elizabeth, daughter of

L.

L. P. W. DesBrisay, Esquire. Mr. Haszard was educated at the Provincial Normal School and the Prince of Wales College. In February, 1867, he entered the office of his uncle, the Honorable John Longworth, as a law-student. On February 28, 1872, he was admitted as attorney of the Supreme Court of the Province, and in March, 1873, he was called to the bar of the same court. In the same year he entered into partnership with his uncle, under the name of Longworth and Haszard, and continued until his uncle's retirement in 1883. From that time until 1887, he conducted business in his own name, when he admitted Oliver Rattenbury as a partner, continuing it thereafter under the name of Haszard and Rattenbury, until November 1, 1890. He then entered into partnership with Honorable L. H. Davies, Q. C., M. P., under the name of Davies and Haszard, now one of the leading law-firms of the Province. On the resignation of R. R. Fitzgerald, Esq'., in December, 1893, Mr. Haszard was appointed Stipendiary Magistrate for the City of Charlottetown, and City Recorder.

CHILDREN

2345. CHARLES FREDERICK LESTOCK HASZARD, born July 28, 1877.
2346. LOUIS GEORGE HASZARD, born Dec. 22, 1878.
2347. MARY ELIZABETH HASZARD, born Sept. 2, 1880.
2348. HILDA MARGARET HASZARD, born May 29, 1882.
2349. HELEN LOUISE HASZARD, born March 7, 1884.
2350. EVELYN BEATRICE HASZARD, born Sept. 24, 1886.
2351. ETHEL CHRISTINE HASZARD, born Dec. 12, 1888.
2352. JOHN FRANCIS HASZARD, born June 18, 1892.

§ 1464. HENRY FENWICK HASZARD, 8 (Henry Bowdoin, 7; William, 6; Thomas, 5; Jonathan, 4; Thomas, 3; Robert, 2; Thomas, 1), was born July 29, 1848, at Charlottetown, Prince Edward Island. He entered the Royal Navy in 1862, and continued in active service until the autumn of 1893, when he retired with the rank of commander. During that period, he served on board many of Her Majesty's ships, in most parts of the world. When on the voyage from England to New Zealand, in the troop-ship *Niagara*, he was shipwrecked on S. Paul's Island. For upwards of three years he commanded the *Cherub*, in the North Sea, protecting the fisheries off the British coast. While in command of the *Cherub*, at the Isle of Wight, he received a visit on board from the Prince of Wales, and shortly afterwards had the honor of dining aboard the Prince's yacht. In September, 1889, he was appointed to the command of the Coast-Guard Service at the Mumbles, near Swansea, in which he continued until his retirement in 1893.

He married, January 24, 1891, Grace C. Webber, daughter of Felix Webber, Esq'., of Glym-dderwin, South Wales.

CHILD

2353. GLADYS GRACE HASZARD, born Feb. 19, 1892.

§ 1468. DAVID FITZGERALD HASZARD, 8 (Henry Bowdoin, 7; William 6; Thomas, 5; Jonathan, 4; Thomas, 3; Robert, 2; Thomas, 1), was born
August

August 31, 1855. He emigrated to New Zealand in 1879, and married, in Auckland, Kate, daughter of H. D. Morpeth, Esq²., where he now (1894) lives.

CHILDREN

2354. MARY CAMERON HASZARD, died when fourteen months of age.
2355. ELSIE HASZARD.
2356. HENRY HORACE HASZARD.
2357. KEITH FITZGERALD HASZARD.

§ 1479. GRIFFEN BARNEY HAZARD, 8 (Jonathan J., 7; Griffen B., 6; Jonathan, 5; Jonathan, 4; Thomas, 3; Robert, 2; Thomas, 1), married, first, Adelaide Hart, daughter of Henry Hart; he married, second, Mary Ann, daughter of Thomas H. Norris.

CHILDREN OF FIRST MARRIAGE

2358. CATHARINE A. HAZARD.
2359. MARY JANE HAZARD.
2360. JONATHAN H. HAZARD.

§ 1504. ANDREW WASHINGTON HAZARD, 8 (Thomas Jefferson, 7; Griffen B., 6; Jonathan, 5; Jonathan, 4; Thomas, 3; Robert, 2; Thomas, 1), was born May 27, 1849; he married Emma Coffin Tucker.

CHILDREN

2361. ALBERTUS WINFIELD HAZARD, born March 27, 1874.
2362. ANDREW GARDINER HAZARD, born Nov. 13, 1875.

§ 1508. MARY JANE HAZARD, 8 (Daniel Williams Hazard, 7; Joseph H., 6; Jonathan, 5; Jonathan, 4; Thomas, 3; Robert, 2; Thomas, 1), was born about 1840; she married, December 6, 1864, Albert D. Brown.

CHILDREN

2363. HAZARD L. BROWN, born June 23, 1871.
2364. ANNIE ELECTA BROWN, born Dec. 1, 1879; died Dec. 3, 1879.

§ 1519. PELEG GARDINER, 8 (Mary Niles, 7; Esther Hazard, 6; Doctor Robert, 5; Caleb, 4; Colonel George, 3; Robert, 2; Thomas, 1), was born November 27, 1808; he died January 15, 1880; he married Mary Harris, of Brenton, New Jersey.

CHILDREN

2365. MARY GARDINER, born Aug. 11, 1840.
2366. KATHARINE GARDINER, born Nov. 17, 1846.
2367. HIRAM GARDINER, born Dec. 24, 1848.
2368. JOHN R. GARDINER, born Dec. 28, 1851.

§ 1521. ELIZABETH NILES GARDINER, 8 (Mary Niles, 7; Esther Hazard, 6; Doctor Robert, 5; Caleb, 4; Colonel George, 3; Robert, 2; Thomas, 1), married John Underwood, of Yatesville, New York; she died July 22, 1857.

CHILDREN

2369. ISABELLA WATSON UNDERWOOD, born Aug. 19, 1842; died April 3, 1863.
2370. HENRY CLAY UNDERWOOD, born Dec. 11, 1844.

§ 1522.

§ **1522.** MARY NILES GARDINER, 8 (Mary Niles, 7; Esther Hazard, 6; Doctor Robert, 5; Caleb, 4; Colonel George, 3; Robert, 2; Thomas, 1), married, after her sister's death, John Underwood.

CHILDREN

2371.  MARY ELIZABETH UNDERWOOD, born Jan. 3, 1860; married *Frank A. Watres.*
2372.  JOHN UNDERWOOD, born Aug. 15, 1863; married *Sarah,* daughter of *John Walin.*

§ **1549.** CHARLOTTE MORGAN HAZARD, 8 (George S., 7; Francis, 6; Doctor Robert, 5; Caleb, 4; Colonel George, 3; Robert, 2; Thomas, 1), was born March 4, 1834; she married, in 1856, Frank W. Fiske.

CHILDREN

2373.  SUSAN REED FISKE, born April, 1857; married Oct., 1889, *Dexter Rumsey.*
2374.  EVELYN FISKE, born Nov. 11, 1863.
2375.  FRANK W. FISKE, born Feb. 28, 1866; married, Dec., 1891, *Margaret Skortiss,* of Albany.
2376.  CHARLOTTE HAZARD FISKE, born July 1, 1868.
2377.  MANSON L. FISKE, born April 15, 1876.

§ **1550.** JOHN ROBERTSON HAZARD, 8 (George S., 7; Francis, 6; Doctor Robert, 5; Caleb, 4; Colonel George, 3; Robert, 2; Thomas, 1), was born February, 1838; he married, 1862, Jane Howel, of Canandaigua, New York.

CHILDREN

2378.  LOUISE HOWEL HAZARD, born Jan. 17, 1863.
2379.  SARAH MERCER HAZARD, born Oct. 26, 1864.

§ **1578.** GEORGE BROWN ROBINSON, 8 (Benjamin Robinson, 7; Sarah Peckham, 6; Mary Hazard, 5; Governor George, 4; Colonel George, 3; Robert, 2; Thomas, 1), was born in South Kingstown, Rhode Island, September 27, 1796; he died May 8, 1872; he married, first, May 17, 1832, Mary, daughter of T. R. Wells; she died March 4, 1838. He married, second, March 14, 1839, Juliana Wells, of Hopkinton, Rhode Island; she died January 15, 1884.

CHILDREN OF FIRST MARRIAGE

2380.  MARIA POTTER ROBINSON, born June 16, 1833; died Sept. 13, 1848.
2381.  ELIZABETH BROWN ROBINSON, born Sept. 30, 1836.
2382.  JOHN WANTON ROBINSON, born Sept. 30, 1837; died Nov. 9, 1837.
2383.  MARY WELLS ROBINSON, born Feb. 27, 1838; died June 18, 1838.

CHILDREN OF SECOND MARRIAGE

2384.  HANNAH WATSON ROBINSON, born June 1, 1840.
2385.  GEORGE BROWN ROBINSON, born March 16, 1842; married Jan. 28, 1869, *Lilla Bryan,* of New York.
2386.  THOMAS WELLS ROBINSON, born Oct. 10, 1843; died Dec. 19, 1893; married Oct. 15, 1878, *Annie J. Livermore,* daughter of *George W. Livermore,* of Nyack on the Hudson.

§ **1581.** SYLVESTER ROBINSON, 8 (Benjamin Robinson, 7; Sarah Peckham, 6; Mary Hazard, 5; Governor George, 4; Colonel George, 3; Robert, 2; Thomas, 1), was born July 16, 1798; he died in January, 1867. From a boy, he seized every opportunity for improvement. He read much, and thus became well informed

informed upon the topics of the day, and in advancing years was the trusted advisor and friend of many of his townspeople.

In 1841–2, he became interested in the temperance movement known as the "Washingtonian," first started in Baltimore, Maryland. In this he worked with the zeal and ardor that characterized any enterprise in which he took part. This work was so thoroughly done that soon there was a marked change in the town. For a number of years it was impossible for a man to obtain intoxicating liquor nearer than Charlestown.

In 1841, he was chosen president of the Wakefield Bank. He held this position until his death, in 1867. He united with the Baptist Church in December, 1838. No one loved the old church better than he, and he was always trying to do something for its prosperity. He filled a large place in the growth and advancement of his town. He married, October 9, 1822, Eliza, daughter of Joseph Noyes, and grand-daughter of Colonel Joseph Noyes, who was an officer in the army, and who served through the war of 1776.

CHILDREN

2387. BENJAMIN F. ROBINSON, born Jun. 9, 1824; married *Caroline E. Redman.* For children see *No. 1958.*

2388. ELIZA ANNE ROBINSON, born Aug. 22, 1826; married *William N. Austin;* died March 19, 1857.

2389. HANNAH BABCOCK ROBINSON, born July 13, 1833; died Oct. 22, 1851.

§ 1582. WILLIAM BROWN ROBINSON, 8 (Benjamin Robinson, 7; Sarah Peckham, 6; Mary Hazard, 5; Governor George, 4; Colonel George, 3; Robert, 2; Thomas, 1), was born in 1800; he died in 1875; he was a merchant in Wakefield, Rhode Island. He was a man respected for his probity of character and his kindly nature, which never allowed him to speak unkindly of any of God's creatures. He married, first, Harriet, daughter of Christopher Robinson, his second cousin; he married, second, October 27, 1831, Eliza Robinson, sister to his first wife.

CHILD OF FIRST MARRIAGE

2390. CAROLINE H. ROBINSON, born Sept. 13, 1828; died May, 1829.

CHILD OF SECOND MARRIAGE

2391. CAROLINE E. ROBINSON, born Sept. 13, 1842; married March 4, 1873, *Benjamin W. Sherman.*

§ 1706. WILLIAM CARDER HAZARD SHERMAN, 8 (Julia Hazard, 7; Carder, 6; Mayor George, 5; Governor George, 4; Colonel George, 3; Robert, 2; Thomas, 1), was born at Norwich, Connecticut, June 28, 1829; he died at Norwich, July 20, 1882; he married, in Providence, Rhode Island, November 20, 1855, Amelia Kimball Taft. She was born September 9, 1831, and died January 25, 1889.

CHILDREN

2392. ORRAY T. SHERMAN, born Aug. 5, 1856.

2393. DANIEL DENNIS SHERMAN, born Dec. 20, 1857; married *Cornelia A. Deyo.*

2394.

2394. WILLIAM HAZARD SHERMAN, born July 14, 1859.
2395. GEORGE K. SHERMAN, born Nov. 10, 1860; died July 12, 1861.
2396. DEBORAH K. SHERMAN, born Jan. 24, 1863.
2397. A DAUGHTER, born and died Jan. 12, 1864.
2398. EDWARD TAFT SHERMAN, born Nov. 28, 1865.
2399. JULIA HAZARD SHERMAN, born Oct. 16, 8167.

§ 1707. JOSEPHINE HAZARD SHERMAN, 8 (Julia Hazard, 7; Carder, 6; Mayor George, 5; Governor George, 4; Colonel George, 3; Robert, 2; Thomas, 1), was born at Norwich, Connecticut, October 9, 1830; she married, August 16, 1855, Daniel Thomas.

CHILDREN
2400. JULIA HAZARD THOMAS, born at Norwich, June 14, 1856.
2401. WILLIAM HENRY THOMAS, born at Norwich, May 18, 1857; died April 26, 1858.

§ 1725. ANN ELIZA HAZARD, 8 (Carder, 7; Doctor George, 6; Judge Carder, 5; Governor George, 4; Colonel George, 3; Robert, 2; Thomas, 1), was born June 6, 1837; she married, June 6, 1860, Jedediah Huntington, of Norwich, Connecticut.

CHILDREN
2402. ANNIE HUNTINGTON, born Jan., 1862; married *Frederick Davis*.
2403. LILLIAN HUNTINGTON, born Sept., 1870; married *Henry Mayhew Hills*.

§ 1726. JULIA HAZARD, 8 (Carder, 7; Doctor George, 6; Judge Carder, 5; Governor George, 4; Colonel George, 3; Robert, 2; Thomas, 1), was born in 1844; she married, April 18, 1866, George Durfee.

CHILDREN
2404. GEORGE NIGHTINGALE DURFEE, born Nov. 12, 1867.
2405. CHARLES HAZARD DURFEE, born Oct. 12, 1870.
2406. NATHANIEL BRIGGS DURFEE, born April 5, 1874.
2407. JULIAN HUNTINGTON DURFEE, born Aug. 16, 1878.
2408. EDGAR GREENE DURFEE, born April 1, 1884.

§ 1727. ELIZA STOCKFORD HAZARD, 8 (George, 7; Doctor George, 6; Judge Carder, 5; Governor George, 4; Colonel George, 3; Robert, 2; Thomas, 1). She married Josiah Crooker.

CHILDREN
2409. GEORGE HAZARD CROOKER.
2410. FOSTER CROOKER.

§ 1735. JAMES ATTMORE ROBINSON, 8 (Laura Hazard, 7; Doctor George, 6; Judge Carder, 5; Governor George, 4; Colonel George, 3; Robert, 2; Thomas, 1), was born January 13, 1842; he married, first, Lizzie Alger; he married, second, Mary Ring.

CHILDREN OF SECOND MARRIAGE
2411. LORENZO CLARKE ROBINSON.

2412.

2412. ETHEL ROBINSON.
2413. GLADYS ROBINSON.

§ **1738.** GEORGE HAZARD ROBINSON, 8 (Laura Hazard, 7; Doctor George, 6; Judge Carder, 5; Governor George, 4; Colonel George, 3; Robert, 2; Thomas, 1), was born March 16, 1847; he married Sarah Delamater.

CHILDREN
2414. RUTH ROBINSON.
2415. EDITH ROBINSON.
2416. LAURA ROBINSON.
2417. ATTMORE ROBINSON.

§ **1745.** JOSEPH EDWARD HAZARD, 8 (Joseph, 7; Richard, 6; Judge Carder, 5; Governor George, 4; Colonel George, 3; Robert, 2; Thomas, 1), was born September 10, 1855. Mr. Hazard worked on a farm until the age of sixteen, when he commenced teaching school, by which he was enabled to pay for his instruction at Chamberlain Institute, in Napoli, New York. He graduated from this Institute with "honors" in 1876, and is now president of the Alumni Association of that institution. In 1876 he began to read law, and in 1880 was admitted to practice in the courts of the State, and in 1885 was admitted to practice in the Supreme Court of the United States. He is an indefatigable worker, and has held a number of positions of trust, which he has filled with credit. In 1880, owing to the illness of the Indian Agent of the State, in whose office he was at that time clerk, he was appointed Acting Agent, and held the position until another agent was appointed by the President. For a number of years he has been Superintendent of the Indian Schools on the Alleghany and Catteraugus Reservation. He married, October 1, 1877, Ada B., daughter of Orrey Snow.

CHILDREN
2418. MARY ELIZABETH HAZARD, born July 13, 1878.
2419. MARGUERITE MINNIE HAZARD, born Oct. 1, 1891.

§ **1746.** DANIEL ARTHUR HAZARD, 8 (Joseph, 7; Richard, 6; Judge Carder, 5; Governor George, 4; Colonel George, 3; Robert, 2; Thomas, 1), was born November 15, 1858. He is a farmer, the only member of the family who represents the time-honored occupation of his Rhode Island ancestors. He lives on a farm in Napoli, New York. He married, October 8, 1879, Ida E., daughter of Eben Sibley.

CHILDREN
2420. LELAND ARTHUR HAZARD, born May 20, 1881.
2421. GEORGE THEODORE HAZARD, born Jan. 5, 1883.
2422. MARY IDA HAZARD, born May 15, 1889.

§ **1747.** THEODORE LINCOLN HAZARD, 8 (Joseph, 7; Richard, 6; Judge Carder, 5; Governor George, 4; Colonel George, 3; Robert, 2; Thomas, 1), was born September 9, 1860. He is a physician. He is a graduate of Chamberlain Institute, and also of the medical department of Ann Arbor, where he graduated
with

with honor in 1883. For eight years he practiced at Anamosa, Iowa. He now lives at Iowa City. He is ex-Secretary and ex-President of the Central Homeopathic Medical Association of Iowa. He has held many minor offices, as alderman, president of eight or ten different organizations, and is now connected with the University of Iowa, as lecturer on pharmacology and allied subjects.

Doctor Hazard married, January 3, 1883, Clara C., daughter of Archibald Merrill.

CHILDREN

2423. CHARLES MERRILL HAZARD, born Dec. 21, 1883.
2424. ARCHIBALD MERRILL HAZARD, born Nov. 10, 1887.
2425. PHILIP LEE HAZARD, born Dec. 16, 1890.

§ 1771. RUTH HAYWARD ROGERS, 8 (Mercy Champlin, 7; Elizabeth Perry, 6; Mercy Hazard, 5; Oliver, 4; Colonel George, 3; Robert, 2; Thomas, 1), was born May 13, 1809, in Hornellsville, New York. She married, April 27, 1836, Elisha Harmon; she died March 6, 1887.

CHILDREN

2426. FRANCES HARMON; married *George Welch*.
2427. WILFORD HARMON, born Aug. 10, 1838; unmarried.
2428. EMMA HARMON, born Nov. 12, 1840; married, Sept. 2, 1863, *Oscar Folsam*.
2429. CARLTON ROGERS HARMON, born March 30, 1842; died April 9, 1862.
2430. HELEN HARMON, born Aug. 11, 1844; married, Aug. 17, 1870, *T. R. Huddleston*.
2431. HOMER HARMON, born Jan. 1, 1847; married, July 9, 1887, *Jessamine Lorgy*; died Feb. 3, 1888.

§ 1772. JOSHUA PERRY ROGERS, 8 (Mercy Champlin, 7; Elizabeth Perry 6; Mercy Hazard 5; Oliver, 4; Colonel George, 3; Robert, 2; Thomas, 1); he married Electa Baldwin.

CHILDREN

2432. JAMES ROGERS, born Aug. 5, 1833; married —— *Jones*.
2433. SUSAN ROGERS, born April 15, 1836; married *John Anderson*.
2434. ELIZABETH ROGERS, born July 11, 1840; married *E. P. Wilson*.
2435. ARTHUR ROGERS, born April 21, 1842; married *Dora Rogers*.

§ 1773. CAROLINE HAYWARD ROGERS, 8 (Mercy Champlin, 7; Elizabeth Perry, 6; Mercy Hazard, 5; Oliver, 4; Colonel George, 3; Robert, 2; Thomas, 1), was born December 18, 1814; she married, September 13, 1836, Reverend Anson Tucker; she died January 17, 1853.

CHILDREN

2436. SARAH TUCKER, born Oct. 16, 1840; married, April 13, 1860, —— *Phelps*.
2437. CAROLINE TUCKER, born May 18, 1843; married, Sept. 20, 1867, *Guy Staffe*.
2438. ERENAH TUCKER, born April 9, 1846.
2439. EMMA TUCKER, born July 31, 1850.
2440. FANNIE TUCKER, born Jan. 20, 1856.

§ 1774. ELIZABETH ROGERS, 8 (Mercy Champlin, 7; Elizabeth Perry, 6; Mercy Hazard, 5; Oliver, 4; Colonel George, 3; Robert, 2; Thomas, 1), was born January 16, 1813; she married Robert Pomeroy.

CHILDREN

CHILDREN
2441. LYDIA POMEROY.
2442. JENNIE POMEROY, married —— *Jarvis.*
2443. ALICE POMEROY, married *George Remington.*
2444. JULIA POMEROY, married *Charles Ayres.*
2445. RALPH POMEROY.
2446. MARY POMEROY.

§ 1775. EVENAH A. ROGERS, 8 (Mercy Champlin, 7; Elizabeth Perry, 6; Mercy Hazard, 5; Oliver, 4; Colonel George, 3; Robert, 2; Thomas, 1), was born December 12, 1816; she married September 28, 1846, John Keeney.
CHILDREN
2447. WILLIAM KEENEY, born Oct. 14, 1847.
2448. EMMA L. KEENEY, born April 4, 1854.
2449. MINNIE KEENEY, born Feb. 13, 1856; married, Aug. 20, 1888, G. O. *Perry.*

§ 1776. RYLAND ROGERS, 8 (Mercy Champlin, 7; Elizabeth Perry, 6; Mercy Hazard, 5; Oliver, 4; Colonel George, 3; Robert, 2; Thomas, 1), married first, Eliza Pomeroy; he married secondly, Eunice Goddard.
CHILDREN
2450. GEORGE P. ROGERS, married *Minnie Huddlestone.*
2451. ELIZABETH ROGERS.
2452. MARY ROGERS, married *A. T. Cuddleback.*

§ 1785. OLIVER HAZARD PERRY CHAMPLIN, 8 (Stephen, 7; Elizabeth Perry, 6; Mercy Hazard, 5; Oliver, 4; Colonel George, 3; Robert, 2; Thomas, 1), was born at Lebanon, Connecticut, November 25, 1818; he married, October 1, 1856, Amelia Tilley, of Newport, Rhode Island.
CHILDREN
2453. HENRY CHAMPLIN.
2454. PERRY CHAMPLIN.
2455. CAROLINE CHAMPLIN.

§ 1787. STEPHEN RAYMOND CHAMPLIN, 8 (Stephen, 7; Elizabeth, Perry, 6; Mercy Hazard, 5; Oliver, 4; Colonel George, 3; Robert, 2; Thomas, 1), was born in Lebanon, Connecticut, April 14, 1823; he died at St. Paul, Minnesota. He married Sophia Borup.
CHILDREN
2456. LIZZIE CHAMPLIN; married Major *Durbam.*
2457. JENNIE CHAMPLIN; married Lieutenant *Badger.*

§ 1788. LYDIA MINERVA CHAMPLIN, 8 (Stephen, 7; Elizabeth Perry, 6; Mercy Hazard, 5; Oliver, 4; Colonel George, 3; Robert, 2; Thomas, 1), was born in Lebanon, Connecticut, in August, 1825; she married, August 14, 1843, Charles L. Emerson, of Buffalo, New York.
CHILDREN

CHILDREN
2458. CHARLES EMERSON.
2459. JENNIE EMERSON.

§ 1789. ELIZA ELLEN CHAMPLIN, 8 (Stephen, 7 ; Elizabeth Perry, 6 ; Mercy Hazard, 5 ; Oliver, 4 ; Colonel George, 3 ; Robert, 2 ; Thomas, 1), was born in Lebanon, Connecticut, Sept. 11, 1827 ; she married, August 30, 1852, John B. Cook, of Erie, Pennsylvania.

CHILD
2460. STEPHEN CHAMPLIN COOK.

§ 1793. SAMUEL G. BAILEY, 8 (Mary Perry Champlin, 7 ; Elizabeth Perry, 6 ; Mercy Hazard, 5 ; Oliver, 4 ; Colonel George, 3 ; Robert, 2 ; Thomas, 1), was born August 1, 1821 ; he married Isabella Sinclair, of Milwaukee, Wisconsin.

CHILDREN
2461. EDWARD S. BAILEY; married *Cora Ormsbee.*
2462. SAMUEL G. BAILEY; married *Kittie Reed*, of Champagne, Ill.
2463. BESSIE BAILEY; married *C. E. Ranney.*

§ 1794. ELIZABETH PERRY BAILEY, 8 (Mary Perry Champlin, 7; Elizabeth Perry, 6 ; Mercy Hazard, 5 ; Oliver, 4 ; Colonel George, 3; Robert, 2 ; Thomas, 1), was born August 9, 1823 ; she married Joseph Eckley.

CHILD
2464. WILLIAM ECKLEY.

§ 1796. MARY JEANNETTE BAILEY, 8 (Mary Perry Champlin, 7; Elizabeth Perry, 6 ; Mercy Hazard, 5 ; Oliver, 4 ; Colonel George, 3 ; Robert, 2 ; Thomas, 1), was born May 13, 1828 ; she married T. C. Rayburn.

CHILDREN
2465. MARY BAILEY RAYBURN.
2466. ARABELLA SINCLAIR RAYBURN; married *Charles Lowell Whiting.*
2467. PERRY CHAMPLIN RAYBURN.

§ 1797. JOHN C. BAILEY, 8 (Mary Perry Champlin, 7 ; Elizabeth Perry, 6 ; Mercy Hazard, 5 ; Oliver, 4 ; George, 3 ; Robert, 2 ; Thomas, 1), was born April 13, 1830 ; he married Anna Grant.

CHILDREN
2468. GORDON BAILEY.
2469. HARRY BAILEY.

§ 1799. LUCIAN C. BAILEY, 8 (Mary Perry Champlin, 7 ; Elizabeth Perry, 6 ; Mercy Hazard, 5 ; Oliver, 4 ; Colonel George, 3 ; Robert, 2 ; Thomas, 1), was born November 30, 1836 ; he married Helen Hayden, of Haydenville, Massachusetts. He, with all his family, is now living in London.

CHILDREN
2470. LILLIAN JUNE BAILEY; married *George Henschel.*
2471. HAYDEN BAILEY.

§ 1801.

§ 1801. ELISHA F. WATSON, 8 (Phebe, 7; Job, 6; Sarah Hazard, 5; Robert, 4; Thomas, 3; Robert, 2; Thomas, 1), was born March 28, 1814, at Boston Neck, in the house owned and built by his ancestor, Robert (4) Hazard. His early education was received from William H. Ghanor, a teacher of repute in the early part of the century. In 1837, he entered Brown University, Providence, and graduated from that institution in 1840. He then began the study of theology at the General Theological Seminary of the Protestant Episcopal Church, concluding the course under Reverend Doctor Francis Vinton, of Newport. He was ordained to the ministry in August, 1843, and for the succeeding three years was rector of S. Paul's Church, Tower Hill, and S. Matthew's Church in Jamestown. Mr. Watson was then called to Christ Church, Lonsdale, in the same State, and for more than three years had charge of the parish.

In 1851 he returned to South Kingstown, and lived on the farm inherited by his wife from her father. In 1861, on the outbreak of the Civil War, he joined the Army of the Potomac, as Chaplain of the Eleventh Massachusetts Volunteers, serving in that capacity for more than three years, with an absence of but two weeks during the entire period. He later acted as volunteer chaplain of the Seventh Rhode Island Volunteers, returning to his home in the autumn of 1864. Mr. Watson's reading of Clarkson's *Abolition of the British Slave Trade* strongly impressed upon his mind the evils of the slave system, and made him an abolitionist. Hence his labors during the late war were not more directed to the preservation of the Union than the abolition of slavery.[1]

He married, June 6, 1843, Mary, daughter of John and Mercy (Peckham) Dockray, of Wakefield. She was born October 23, 1819. They were married by the Reverend James Eames.

CHILD
2472. ARTHUR H. WATSON; married *Annie P. Sprague.*

§ 1802. FREEMAN PERRY WATSON, 8 (Phebe, 7; Job, 6; Sarah Hazard, 5; Robert, 4; Thomas, 3; Robert, 2; Thomas, 1). He married, first, January 24, 1848, Mary Congdon, daughter of Daniel Watson, and Mary, his wife, of Jamestown. He married, second, Abby, daughter of Benjamin Hull, of Tower Hill.

CHILDREN OF FIRST MARRIAGE
2473. LINCOLN P. WATSON.
2474. MARY CONGDON WATSON.

§ 1824. HERBERT HAZARD, 8 (Jonathan, 7; Jonathan, 6; Stephen, 5; Stephen, 4; Stephen, 3; Robert, 2; Thomas, 1), was born in 1848; he married, first, Jennie Hunter; he married, second, Fannie Ross.

CHILDREN OF SECOND MARRIAGE
2475. FANNIE ROSS HAZARD.
2476. JOHN ROSS HAZARD.

§ **1825.** JONATHAN HAZARD, 8 (Sylvester, 7; Jonathan, 6; Stephen, 5; Stephen, 4; Stephen, 3; Robert, 2; Thomas, 1), was born June 19, 1823; he married Elizabeth Pierce; she was born May 3, 1814, and died November 14, 1888; he died September 12, 1877.

CHILDREN
2477. CHARLES HAZARD.
2478. DARIUS HAZARD.
2479. GEORGE HAZARD; married *Sarah*, daughter of *Edward* und *Louisa (Fisk) Hazard.*
2480. ELIZABETH HAZARD; died aged three years.

§ **1827.** EDWARD WEEDEN HAZARD, 8 (Sylvester, 7; Jonathan, 6; Stephen, 5; Stephen, 4; Stephen, 3; Robert, 2; Thomas, 1), was born October 5, 1824; he died June 28, 1889; he married Louisa, daughter of Stephen and Sarah (Dyre) Fisk. She died April 5, 1872, aged thirty years and eight months.

CHILDREN
2481. ALICE HAZARD, born Aug. 23, 1859; died Aug. 24, 1859.
2482. EDWARD HAZARD; married *Mary* ——.
2483. STEPHEN HAZARD, born Dec., 1864; died May 8, 1886; unmarried.
2484. SARAH HAZARD; married *George Hazard.*
2485. SYLVESTER HAZARD, born Sept., 1866; died Feb., 1867.

§ **1828.** GEORGE HAZARD, 8 (Sylvester, 7; Jonathan, 6; Stephen, 5; Stephen, 4; Stephen, 3; Robert, 2; Thomas, 1), was born in 1829; he married Laura Davis, of Orange County, New York.

CHILDREN
2486. GEORGE HAZARD.
2487. ANNA HAZARD.

§ **1832.** HARRIET HAZARD, 8 (Stanton, 7; Joshua, 6; Judge Joseph, 5; Governor Robert, 4; Stephen, 3; Robert, 2; Thomas, 1), was born November 25, 1839; she married, June 17, 1864, Charles H. Rhodes; he was born in 1835, and died April 17, 1878.

CHILDREN
2488. WILLIAM MOSS RHODES, born April 18, 1868.
2489. MATILDA ABORN RHODES, born April 21, 1871.

§ **1833.** CELESTE HAZARD, 8 (Evan Malbone Hazard, 7; Joshua, 6; Judge Joseph, 5; Governor Robert, 4; Stephen, 3; Robert, 2; Thomas, 1), was born July 23, 1837; she married, April 28, 1859, Arius Newton Kingsbury, a lawyer in Hillsborough, Illinois. He was born in February, 1830, and died December 12, 1889.

CHILDREN
2490. MARY EVELYN KINGSBURY, born Feb. 9, 1860.
2491. JESSIE CORINNE KINGSBURY, born April 11, 1862.

2492.

2492. VIRGIL WILLIS KINGSBURY, born Dec. 12, 1864. He is a physician, now in the government service as surgeon in the Alaska Expedition, to establish monuments on the line between the United States and British possessions (1890).

2493. ARIUS ROSS KINGSBURY, born July 31, 1868.

§ 1834. MARY EVELYN HAZARD, 8 (Evan M., 7; Joshua, 6; Judge Joseph, 5; Governor Robert, 4; Stephen, 3; Robert, 2; Thomas, 1), was born February 1, 1840; she married, December 1, 1864, Darius Kingsbury, brother to her sister's husband; he is a lawyer in Carlyle, Illinois.

CHILDREN

2494. IRA DALE KINGSBURY, born Nov. 12, 1866.
2495. HAZARD HUME KINGSBURY, born Sept. 19, 1869.

§ 1835. LAURA JANE HAZARD, 8 (Evan M., 7; Joshua, 6; Judge Joseph, 5; Governor Robert, 4; Stephen, 3; Robert, 2; Thomas, 1), was born March 17, 1842; she married, December 24, 1861, Charles Winston Holliday. He was killed on the railway, March 17, 1879, on the anniversary of his wife's birthday.

CHILDREN

2496. JENNIE WINSTON HOLLIDAY, born March 25, 1864; married Oct. 7, 1886, *Joseph Stanton Wall.*
2497. CHARLES LAMB HOLLIDAY, born Jan. 29, 1870.

§ 1836. WILLIAM PRIME HAZARD, 8 (Evan M., 7; Joshua, 6; Judge Joseph, 5; Governor Robert, 4; Stephen, 3; Robert, 2; Thomas, 1), was born January 3, 1845; he married, February 9, 1875, Celeste, daughter of John Loraine, of Galena, Illinois.

CHILDREN

2498. LORAINE HAZARD, born Nov. 6, 1876; died April 4, 1877.
2499. WILLIAM EVAN HAZARD, born April 19, 1878.
2500. VIRGINIA LAURA HAZARD, born Oct. 24, 1880.
2501. STANTON JAMES HAZARD, born June 13, 1884.

§ 1843. MARY LUNDY DENNISON, 8 (Mary Niles Hazard, 7; Joshua 6; Judge Joseph, 5; Governor Robert, 4; Stephen, 3; Robert, 2; Thomas, 1), was born February 28, 1843; she married Alexis Chappie, of Jersey County, Illinois.

CHILDREN

2502. URANIA CATHARINE CHAPPIE, born Aug. 22, 1872.
2503. DENNISON HAZARD CHAPPIE, born March 21, 1874.
2504. GEORGE F. CHAPPIE, born Aug. 6, 1876.
2505. ALEXIS FRANCIS CHAPPIE, born March 12, 1878.
2506. LOUIS CHAPPIE, born Oct. 31, 1880.
2507. ESTHER CLIFT CHAPPIE, born June 24, 1882.

§ 1844. ROBERT HAZARD CLIFT, 8 (Esther Hazard, 7; Joshua, 6; Judge Joseph, 5; Governor Robert, 4; Stephen, 3; Robert, 2; Thomas, 1), was born
April

April 18, 1838 ; he died September 1, 1868, from exposure in the Civil War. He married, February 14, 1864, Emeline Walton.

CHILD

2508. WATERMAN CLIFT, born Dec. 4, 1866.

§ **1845.** **CHARLES W. CLIFT,** 8 (Esther Hazard, 7 ; Joshua, 6 ; Judge Joseph, 5 ; Governor Robert, 4 ; Stephen, 3 ; Robert, 2 ; Thomas, 1), was born April 21, 1840 ; he married November 3, 1862, Jane Forsith, of Mystic, Connecticut.

CHILDREN

2509. ESTHER HAZARD CLIFT, born Nov. 30, 1869.
2510. ELLEN ELIZABETH CLIFT, born May 15, 1872.
2511. WILLIAM FORSITH CLIFT, born Feb. 27, 1874.

§ **1846.** **JOHN GARDINER CLIFT,** 8 (Esther Hazard, 7 ; Joshua, 6 ; Judge Joseph, 5 ; Governor Robert, 4 ; Stephen, 3 ; Robert, 2 ; Thomas, 1), was born March 25, 1846 ; he married, July 27, 1871, Mary C. Packer

CHILDREN

2512. EDITH ADELL CLIFT, born Dec. 20, 1876.
2513. ROBERT MANTON CLIFT, born Nov. 9, 1878; died Nov., 1879.
2514. JENNIE MORTON CLIFT, born Dec. 1. 1880.
2515. MATTIE MORTON CLIFT, born July 1, 1882.

§ **1864.** **ROBERT FULTON BABCOCK,** 8 (Jared Starr Babcock, 7; Robert, 6 ; Esther Hazard, 5 ; Governor Robert, 4 ; Stephen, 3 ; Robert, 2 ; Thomas, 1). He married, January 15, 1849, Mary S. Gilman.

CHILDREN

2516. GEORGE DOUGLAS BABCOCK; married, Nov. 4, 1875, *Emily Ferguson ;* she died Feb. 29, 1876.
2517. ELLA JANE BABCOCK; married, Jan. 12, 1876, *Charles N. Seward ;* she died Dec. 20, 1881.
2518. EDITH LOIS BABCOCK; died March 4, 1855.
2519. FLORA GRACE BABCOCK; died March 4, 1878.
2520. ÉMILIE CLEMENA BABCOCK; died Dec. 6, 1878.
2521. ROBERT GILMAN BABCOCK; married, Jan. 3, 1883, *Mary Hanly*, of Fales Centre, Kan.
2522. MARY DIADEMA BABCOCK; married ——— *Sawyer*, Feb. 14, 1881, in Kansas.
2523. CLARA FRANCES BABCOCK.
2524. DANIEL JARED BABCOCK.

§ **1865.** **LOIS DOUGLAS BABCOCK,** 8 (Jared Starr, 7 ; Robert, 6 ; Esther Hazard, 5 ; Governor Robert, 4 ; Stephen, 3 ; Robert, 2 ; Thomas, 1). She married, October 20, 1848, Jahiel M. Parkes, of Pittsfield, Illinois.

CHILDREN

2525. THERESA ELIZA PARKES; died June 10, 1857, in Chicago.
2526. MARY ROBERTS PARKES; died July 27, 1855, in Illinois.
2527. ROBERT JAHIEL PARKES; died June 16, 1887, in Chicago.
2528. ANNE DIADEMA PARKES; died June 2, 1887, in Chicago.

§ **1894.** **ELVIRA HAZARD,** 8 (Augustus G., 7 ; Thomas S., 6 ; Stephen, 5 ; Thomas, 4; Stephen, 3 ; Robert, 2 ; Thomas, 1), was born May 15, 1824; she died
March

March 9, 1894. To have known her father and mother was to know the daughter. Generous, sympathetic and kind, her hand never wearied in well doing, scattering its bounties into the homes of the poor, and uplifting the fallen. For the last few years of her life she was an invalid, and was obliged to retire from society, but she never allowed her suffering to interfere with her charities. Her love and affection for her children and grandchildren seemed to increase as she neared the close of her life, and was never greater than when " her life, so true, devoted, patient and loving, closed in peace."

She married, August 29, 1844, Alexander Hamilton Bullock. " He was born in Royalston, Worcester County, Massachusetts, March 2, 1816. He was fitted for college in his native town, and at Leicester Academy. He entered Amherst College in 1832, and graduated in 1836, the second scholar in his class, delivering the salutatory oration at Commencement. After graduating, Mr. Bullock taught school at Royalston, and at Kingston, Rhode Island. He then studied law at Harvard Law School, under Story and Greenleaf. Leaving the law school in 1840, he spent a year in the office of Emory Washburn, at Worcester, and was admitted to the bar in 1841. He soon established a large business as agent of important insurance companies, and withdrew himself altogether from the practice of law. . . March 1, 1842, Mr. Bullock became editor of the *National Ægis*, a weekly Whig newspaper, published in Worcester. He retained this connection several years. Mr. Bullock represented Worcester in the Massachusetts House of Representatives in 1845, 1847, and 1848, and in the Senate in 1849. He spoke infrequently, and only on important questions, and with careful preparation. His eulogy on John Quincy Adams, in 1848, was especially impressive. . . . He was Mayor of Worcester in 1859. His term of office was rendered memorable in the history of the City Library, of whose board of trustees he was the first president. . . . He was appointed Commissioner of Insolvency for the County of Worcester by Governor Clifford in 1853. The jurisdiction of these officers was transferred to the Court of Insolvency by statute of 1856. Mr. Bullock was appointed Judge of that court, for the County of Worcester, in June, 1856, and held the office until 1858. . . . Mr. Bullock was re-elected to the House of Representatives in the fall of 1861. When the Legislature organized in January, 1862, he was elected Speaker, receiving every vote cast. . . . He was elected Speaker again in January, 1863, receiving every vote cast except three for Caleb Cushing."

In 1865 Mr. Bullock was elected Governor of the State of Massachusetts, and from that time until his death, on the seventeenth day of January, 1882, he was more or less actively engaged in public service. Hon. George F. Hoar, in closing the account of Mr. Bullock's life, adds : " Mr. Bullock's refined and delicate nature found, as his life advanced, its most congenial atmosphere within the walls of his home, and led him to shrink more and more from the rough strifes of politics. He delighted in days spent in literary pursuits in his library, and in evenings of hospitable welcome to neighbors, friends and strangers. His strong domestic affections found most abundant satisfaction in his own family circle, where

where, says a near neighbor and intimate friend, ' his home life diffused all around it an influence and charm, and, by its high example, elevated the standard of the domestic and moral life of a whole community.'
" He was stainless, wise, patriotic, fit to be trusted with the administration of great interests, public or private. He was a lover of scholarship. He had the ear of the people during a time of great peril and trial. He never gave it dishonorable counsel, or uttered a word which would debase or degrade it." '

CHILDREN

2529. AUGUSTUS G. BULLOCK; married *Mary Chandler*, of Worcester, Mass.
2530. ISABEL HAZARD BULLOCK; married *Nelson S. Bartlett*, of Boston, Mass.
2531. FANNY BULLOCK; married *William H. Workman*, of Worcester, Mass.

§ 1895. GEORGIANA HAZARD, 8 (Augustus G., 7; Thomas S., 6; Stephen, 5; Thomas, 3; Stephen, 3; Robert, 2; Thomas, 1), was born July 29, 1827; she died September 20, 1882; she married October 22, 1850, Joseph Sexton, of New York.

CHILD

2532. EDWARD BAILEY SEXTON, born Jan. 24, 1852; married Dec. 20, 1883, *Ella Marian Smith*, of New York.

§ 1896. FANNY HAZARD, 8 (Augustus G., 7; Thomas, 6; Stephen, 5; Thomas, 4; Stephen, 3; Robert, 2; Thomas, 1), was born October 1, 1830. She married, November 3, 1869, Ephraim Ward Bond, of Springfield, Massachusetts; they had no children; but previous to her marriage, she adopted the four orphan children of her sister, Mrs. Dakin. The children were taken not only to her home, but to her heart.

Ephraim Ward Bond was born in West Brookfield in 1821. Five years later his father moved to Springfield, and his whole life was practically identified with that place. He entered Amherst College, and graduated at the age of twenty with honours. After leaving Amherst he took a year's course at Yale, and then entered the Harvard Law School, from which he graduated in 1844. In 1845, he began the practice of law in Springfield. Six years later he formed a partnership with the late E. D. Beach, which continued up to 1864, and the firm of Beach and Bond was well known not only in Springfield but throughout the State. Mr. Bond at his death was president of the Springfield Five Cents Savings Bank and the Springfield City Library, and a director of the Pynchon National Bank. He had served as selectman, before Springfield became a city; was largely instrumental in securing a city charter; was subsequently councilman and alderman, and for one term was a member of the Massachusetts House of Representatives.

This in brief, is the record of Mr. Bond's life, but his character and ability have extended in influence for good beyond this bare recitation of facts. He had con-

¹ Bullock's Addresses, by Hon. George F. Hoar.

tributed

tributed generously to the charitable and benevolent institutions of the city. Mr. Bond was greatly interested in the Springfield Library, being one of its incorporators and a director from its organization in 1864; also vice-president until 1880, when he was elected president. He gave largely to it. He died Saturday, December 5, 1891.

§ 1898. EMILY HAZARD, 8 (Augustus G., 7; Thomas, 6; Stephen, 5; Thomas, 4; Stephen, 3; Robert, 2; Thomas, 1), was born June 24, 1834; she died September 18, 1866; she married, September 20, 1859, Francis Elihu Dakin, of Freeport, Illinois. He died December 25, 1867.

CHILDREN
2533. ANNA MUMFORD DAKIN, born Aug. 28, 1860; married *George Bond.*
2534. ARTHUR HAZARD DAKIN, born April 27, 1862. He is a lawyer in Boston, Mass.
2535. ELLIE BULLOCK DAKIN, born Jan. 27, 1864.
2536. EMILY HAZARD DAKIN, born Sept. 17, 1866; married *Joseph H. Spofford.*

§ 1905. ROWLAND HAZARD CARPENTER, 8 (Hannah Oatley, 7; Mary Hazard, 6; Stephen, 5; Thomas, 4; Stephen, 3; Robert, 2; Thomas, 1), was born in 1809; he died in 1869; he married Thankful Rose.

CHILDREN
2537. JOSEPH CARPENTER, born 1833; married *Martha Brown.*
2538. ROWLAND CARPENTER, born 1835; married *Lucy Arnold.*
2539. SARAH HAZARD CARPENTER, born May 19, 1840; married *Robert Gamble.*
2540. EDWARD CARPENTER, born 1844; died 1860.

§ 1906. ROUSE CARPENTER, 8 (Hannah Oatley, 7; Mary Hazard, 6; Stephen, 5; Thomas, 4; Stephen, 3; Robert, 2; Thomas, 1), was born in 1811; he died in 1875; he married Ruth Larkin.

CHILDREN
2541. LAVINIA CARPENTER, born 1833; married, July 28, 1850, *Henry Spear.*
2542. ANNE CARPENTER, born 1835; married *Benjamin Franklin Carpenter.*
2543. NAPOLEON CARPENTER, born 1837; married *Mary Clifton.*
2544. SUSAN CARPENTER, born 1840; married *Adolphus M. Open.*
2545. JOSEPHINE CARPENTER, born 1842; married *Charles Watson.*
2546. HANNAH CARPENTER, born 1844; married Dr. *George Sweet,* "a natural bone-setter.'
2547. RODMAN CARPENTER, born 1846; married *Lucy Case.*
2548. RUTH CARPENTER, born 1848; married *Thomas Rodman;* she died 1883.
2549. ROUSE CARPENTER, born 1851; married *Mary J. Crumb.*
2550. CAROLINE CARPENTER, born 1853; married *Edward Sweet.*
2551. JOSEPH CARPENTER, born 1855; married *Jane Carlisle.*
2552. JOHN CARPENTER, born 1858; died young.

§ 1907. MARY CARPENTER, 8 (Hannah Oatley, 7; Mary Hazard, 6; Stephen, 5; Thomas, 4; Stephen, 3; Robert, 2; Thomas, 1), was born in 1813; she married, first, John Whitford; second, Robinson Perry.

CHILDREN

CHILDREN OF FIRST MARRIAGE

2553. JOHN WHITFORD, born 1834; married *Hannah Church.*
2554. JAMES WHITFORD, born 1836; married *Della Church.*

CHILDREN OF SECOND MARRIAGE

2555. PHEBE PERRY, born 1845; married *Daniel R. Northup.*
2556. OSEANNA PERRY, born 1847; married *Isaac Coe.*
2557. HANNAH PERRY, born 1849; married, May 25, 1868, *Edward Redman.*
2558. CLARA PERRY, born 1852; married *Thomas Gough.*
2559. SARAH PERRY, born 1855; married *Frank Coe.*

§ 1908. HANNAH CARPENTER, 8 (Hannah Oatley, 7; Mary Hazard, 6; Stephen, 5; Thomas, 4; Stephen, 3; Robert, 2; Thomas, 1), was born in 1816; she married Nathaniel Armstrong.

CHILDREN

2560. OLIVE ARMSTRONG, born 1833; died young.
2561. LUCY ARMSTRONG, born 1835; married *Elnathan Albro.*
2562. HANNAH ARMSTRONG, born 1838; died 1864.
2563. ABBY ARMSTRONG, born 1848; died 1850.

§ 1909. ELIZABETH CARPENTER, 8 (Hannah Oatley, 7; Mary Hazard, 6; Stephen, 5; Thomas, 4; Stephen, 3; Robert, 2; Thomas, 1), was born in 1819; she married Robert Armstrong; she died in 1867.

CHILDREN

2564. MARY C. ARMSTRONG, born 1840.
2565. JULIA C. ARMSTRONG, born 1851; married *Frank Holland.*
2566. ABBY C. ARMSTRONG, born 1853; married *George Gardiner.*
2567. NATHANIEL C. ARMSTRONG, born 1855.

§ 1910. ISAAC HAZARD CARPENTER, 8 (Hannah Oatley, 7; Mary Hazard, 6; Stephen, 5; Thomas, 4; Stephen, 3; Robert, 2; Thomas, 1), was born in 1821; he married Abby Perry.

CHILDREN

2568. JAMES R. CARPENTER, born 1843; married *Mary Hill.*
2569. MELISSA CARPENTER, born 1847; married *Elisha Holland.*

§ 1911. JOSEPH CARPENTER, 8 (Betsey Oatley, 7; Mary Hazard, 6; Stephen, 5; Thomas, 4; Stephen, 3; Robert, 2; Thomas, 1), was born April 4, 1804; he married Eliza Quirrer. He died in Cincinnati in 1832.

CHILDREN

2570. WILLIAM CARPENTER, born July 12, 1828.
2571. MARGARET CARPENTER, born March, 1830; died April, 1892.

§ 1913. HARRIET CARPENTER, 8 (Betsey Oatley, 7; Mary Hazard, 6; Stephen, 5; Thomas, 4; Stephen, 3; Robert, 2; Thomas, 1), was born February 3, 1808; she married Eli Knox.

CHILDREN

2572. JOSEPH KNOX.

2573.

2573. KILBORN KNOX; died 1849.
2574. GEORGE KNOX.
2575. NANCY KNOX.
2576. JULIA KNOX.
2577. STEPHEN KNOX; died 1887.

§ 1914. BETSEY CARPENTER, 8 (Nancy Oatley, 7; Mary Hazard, 6; Stephen, 5; Thomas, 4; Stephen, 3; Robert, 2; Thomas, 1), was born September 16, 1813; she married, in 1841, Walter North.
CHILDREN
2578. LOUISA J. NORTH, born Sept. 3, 1843; died July 6, 1886.
2579. ARTHUR J. NORTH, born Dec. 10, 1844.
2580. HELEN E. NORTH, born Feb. 28, 1847.

§ 1915. ALBERT C. CARPENTER, 8 (Nancy Oatley, 7; Mary Hazard, 6; Stephen, 5; Thomas, 4; Stephen, 3; Robert, 2; Thomas, 1), was born March 5, 1815; he died April 8, 1850; he married Electa Lyon.
CHILDREN
2581. ALBERT G. CARPENTER, born April 17, 1841; died June 25, 1876.
2582. EDWARD D. CARPENTER, born Nov. 17, 1844; he was killed at the capture of Fort Harrison, Sept. 29, 1864.
2583. EMMA J. CARPENTER, born Jan. 11, 1846; died Dec. 17, 1883.

§ 1916. GEORGE HAZARD CARPENTER, 8 (Nancy Oatley, 7; Mary Hazard, 6; Stephen, 5; Thomas, 4; Stephen, 3; Robert, 2; Thomas, 1), was born December 21, 1816. He married, first, in 1841, Lydia Cowen; he married, second, in 1854, Caroline Nutting.
CHILD OF FIRST MARRIAGE
2584. HARRIET E. CARPENTER, born Oct. 16, 1843.
CHILD OF SECOND MARRIAGE
2585. GEORGE HAZARD CARPENTER, born May 29, 1856; died May 28, 1882.

§ 1917. JONATHAN CARPENTER, 8 (Nancy Oatley, 7; Mary Hazard, 6; Stephen, 5; Thomas, 4; Stephen, 3; Robert, 2; Thomas, 1), was born November 15, 1818; he died February 9, 1865; he married, in 1842, Eliza Paterson.
CHILD
2586. FRANCIS PATERSON, born Jan. 21, 1843.

§ 1918. JULIA A. CARPENTER, 8 (Nancy Oatley, 7; Mary Hazard, 6; Stephen, 5; Thomas, 4; Stephen, 3; Robert, 2; Thomas, 1), was born March 28, 1820; she died February 12, 1889; she married Henry Ferra.
CHILD
2587. HENRIETTA FERRA, born May 18, 1844.

§ 1919. STEPHEN HAZARD CARPENTER, 8 (Nancy Oatley, 7; Mary Hazard, 6; Stephen, 5; Thomas, 4; Stephen, 3; Robert, 2; Thomas, 1), was born January 13, 1822; he died September 26, 1883; he married Martha Nettleton.
CHILDREN

CHILDREN

2588. ELIZABETH CARPENTER, born Jan. 3, 1850; died 1870.
2589. LUCRETIA CARPENTER, born 1852.
2590. EMMA CARPENTER, born 1854.
2591. MARTHA CARPENTER, born March 9, 1856; died Aug. 30, 1885.
2592. SUSAN A. CARPENTER, born March 8, 1858.
2593. EDWARD CARPENTER, born 1861; died Feb. 17, 1891.
2594. ALVIRA CARPENTER, born 1864.

§ 1920. BENEDICT O. CARPENTER, 8 (Nancy Oatley, 7; Mary Hazard, 6; Stephen, 5; Thomas, 4; Stephen, 3; Robert, 2; Thomas, 1), was born January 1, 1824; he died April 1, 1882; he married Frances Way.

CHILDREN

2595. ANNIE L. CARPENTER, born March 4, 1858.
2596. MARY F. CARPENTER, born Jan. 31, 1866; died May 9, 1892.

§ 1921. SARAH A. CARPENTER, 8 (Nancy Oatley, 7; Mary Hazard, 6; Stephen, 5; Thomas, 4; Stephen, 3; Robert, 2; Thomas, 1), was born October 20, 1825; she married, in 1848, Frederick S. Smith; he was a lawyer in Cleveland, Ohio.

CHILDREN

2597. FREDERICK SMITH, born March, 1849; died 1849.
2598. FLORENCE E. SMITH, born March 25, 1855.

§ 1923. SUSAN EMMA CARPENTER, 8 (Nancy Oatley, 7; Mary Hazard, 6; Stephen, 5; Thomas, 4; Stephen, 3; Robert, 2; Thomas, 1), was born June 4, 1829; she married, May 18, 1849, Richard N. Allen. Mr. Allen was born in 1827, and began his search for fortune when about eighteen, in a subordinate position on a railroad. After several smaller inventions, one of which was a car-wheel oil-box, now in practical use, he, after many years of study and experiments, perfected the paper car-wheel, with a steel tire. When he made his first set of wheels, in 1869, it was with difficulty that he got the use of a wood-car for six months to test his invention. The Pullman Palace Car Company gave him his first order, in 1871, and a few months later the Allen Car Wheel Company made seventeen thousand such wheels in one year. Almost the last act of Mr. Allen's life was to sign the papers applying for a patent for a noiseless wheel on electric motors, which is the last in a series of notable inventions which have made the railroads and traveling public indebted to him for safety and comfort. He was the first to invent the steel tire for the car-wheel, and spent several years in Krupp's works in Germany perfecting the model. He had recently devoted himself to improving paper wheels for street-car service, and had a patent on a model, recently introduced, in use, beside the invention completed before his death. In personal appearance Mr. Allen was singularly like James A. Garfield, late President of the United States. He died suddenly, in Cleveland, Ohio, October 7th, 1892.

CHILDREN

1952

Isaac Peace Rodman.

CHILDREN

2599. SUSAN ELIZABETH ALLEN, born Sept. 29, 1850; died 1856.
2600. GEORGIANA ALLEN, born Nov. 8, 1851; died Aug. 18, 1852.
2601. ALICE GERTRUDE ALLEN, born Aug. 2, 1858; died Jan. 19, 1862.
2602. RICHARD HAZELL ALLEN, born Dec. 22, 1861; died March 23, 1870.
2603. GRACE LOUISE ALLEN, born Aug. 15, 1864; died April 3, 1870.

§ 1952. ISAAC PEACE RODMAN, 8 (Samuel Rodman, 7; Elizabeth Hazard, 6; Stephen, 5; Thomas, 4; Stephen, 3; Robert, 2; Thomas, 1), was born in South Kingstown, Rhode Island, August 18, 1822. He was educated in the public schools of his native town, but early entered the manufacturing business with his father. He had a passionate love for books, combined with a remarkable memory. His leisure hours were for years devoted to study, and thus he was enabled to take his place amongst men of a more liberal education on an equal footing.

After a few years of initiatory labor in his father's mills, he, together with his brother, Rowland G. Rodman, entered into partnership with their father, under the name of S. Rodman and Sons.

He was for several years President of the Town Council of South Kingstown, and was a Representative for several terms in the General Assembly of Rhode Island, and also in the Senate of the State.

When President Lincoln called for seventy-five thousand men, at the commencement of the Civil War, he was among the first to respond to the call. He raised a military company composed of his fellow-townsmen for the Second Rhode Island Regiment of Volunteers, and was appointed by Governor Sprague its captain. For his gallant conduct at the battle of Bull Run, Governor Sprague, when the Fourth Rhode Island Regiment was mustered into service, appointed him lieutenant-colonel, and soon after colonel. He distinguished himself by his gallant conduct in the battle of Roanoke, February 8, 1862, and at Newbern, March 15th, 1862. Abbott, in his *History of the Civil War*, said, in speaking of this battle: "The charge by Colonel Rodman, leading the Fourth Rhode Island Regiment, was one of the most heroic deeds of the day." This gallant charge won a brigadier-general's commission for Colonel Rodman. Yet he always insisted that his regiment deserved more credit for their conduct at the battle of Roanoke Island, in which they took a conspicuous part, than at the battle of Newbern. It was about this time that Mr. Robert Hale Ives, of Providence, asked Governor Sprague to give his son Robert a place on General Rodman's staff. "Do you know what you are asking for?" said the governor; "he is your only son, and to give him this position means certain death, for General Rodman is the bravest man I ever knew, and will lead your son into the very midst of danger. Let me place him on General Burnside's staff, where he will be in comparative safety." Mr. Ives said that his son would take no other position than on General Rodman's staff; and so the brave young man met death, with his brave leader, on the field of Antietam.

After

After the capture of Fort Macon, April 17, 1862, General Rodman contracted typhoid fever, and was obliged to return home, " broken in health, but crowned with the honors he had won."

He remained at home but a few weeks; before his furlough was ended or his health re-established, General Burnside wrote to him, saying that the army was on the eve of a great battle, urging him to return if possible, as there was great need for commanding officers; and, against the remonstrance of his physician, he hastened back.

At the battle of Antietam, September 17, 1862, he commanded the Third Division of the Ninth Army Corps, and fell, mortally wounded, while leading his division to the charge. " Though feeble in health, and exhausted from five days and nights of arduous service, he kept in the saddle from early dawn till sunset, when he fell, pierced with a minie ball through his left breast. Surgical aid and efforts of friends were unavailing to save his life; his system was exhausted. His patience in suffering was equal to his courage on the battle-field. He died as he lived, a Christian soldier. His physician, who had witnessed many death-bed scenes, said that for calm, conscious, peaceful resignation, he never witnessed its equal. From the time he left home in the spring of 1861 to the hour of his fall, his Bible was his daily companion, and was daily read by him. It was found in his bosom, clotted with his blood." [1]

Abbott, in closing a notice of General Rodman, says: " At Antietam, while at the head of his division, and performing the part of major-general, a bullet pierced his breast, and he was carried to a house in the rear. There, after a lapse of thirteen days, he died. His remains were buried at his native place, South Kingstown, with the highest honors. He was mourned as one of the purest and best of men." [2]

The State of Rhode Island brought back his remains amid demonstrations of mourning, and laid them in state in the Hall of Representatives. His funeral was conducted by the State. The State has also placed his portrait in the Memorial Hall of Brown University, at Providence.

Senator Henry B. Anthony, in a funeral oration, said of him: " Here lies the true type of the patriot soldier. Born and educated to peaceful pursuits, with no thirst for military distinction, with little taste or predilection for military life, he answered the earliest call of his country, and drew his sword in her defense. Entering the service in a subordinate capacity, he rose by merit alone to the high rank in which he fell; and when the fatal shot struck him, the captain of one year ago was in command of a division. His rapid promotion was influenced by no solicitations of his own. He never joined the crowd that thronged the avenues of preferment. Patient, laborious, courageous, wholly devoted to his duties, he filled each place so well that his advancement to the next was a matter of course, and the promotion, which he did not seek, sought him.

" He was of the best type of the American citizen; of thorough business train-

<hr>

[1] Bartlett's Rhode Island Officers, p. 357.          [2] Abbott's History of the Civil War, vol. 2, p. 157.

ing,

ing, of high integrity, with an abiding sense of the justice due to all, and influenced by deep religious convictions. In his native village he was by common
consent the arbiter of differences, the counsellor and friend of all." [1]
He was buried in the family burying-ground, at South Kingstown, on the fifth
of October, 1862.
He married, June 17, 1847, Sally, daughter of Governor Lemuel Hastings and
Sally (Lyman) Arnold.

CHILDREN

2604. ISAAC PEACE RODMAN, born April 25, 1848; married *Harriet E. Robinson.*
2605. SALLY LYMAN RODMAN, born Feb. 10, 1850; married *Robert Thompson.*
2606. MARY PECKHAM RODMAN, born March 23, 1852; unmarried.
2607. SAMUEL RODMAN, born Feb., 1854; died Feb., 1856.
2608. THOMAS RODMAN, born March 23, 1856.
2609. SAMUEL RODMAN, born April 23, 1858; married *Cynthia Sheldon;* his name was changed to
       *Samuel Arnold Rodman.*
2610. ELIZABETH ARNOLD RODMAN, born July, 1860; died 1864.

§ 1954. LOUISA HAZARD RODMAN, 8 (Samuel Rodman, 7; Elizabeth
Hazard, 6; Stephen, 5; Thomas, 4; Stephen, 3; Robert, 2; Thomas, 1), was born
March 26, 1826; she died May 2, 1854. Louisa Rodman was born in the first
quarter of the century. Then a village school was as much a place of amusement
as study, so that her opportunities for an education were limited; but so great
was her love for study and books that she rose above her environment. There
were no public libraries in the town until long after her day, but there was hardly
a house in the neighborhood which contained a book that she had not read. She
was wonderfully well informed upon many subjects; the classics were especially
familiar to her.
She was a woman of fascinating personality. Her wit was so pungent and spark-
ling that it was contagious, and brought out the best there was in her friends;
and one left her presence feeling that he himself had been particularly clever.
Her quickness at repartee was unsurpassed, and woe to the poor wight who at-
tempted to crush her with sarcasm. He was annihilated in the answering flood
with which he was assailed, although most kind and gentle in general, especially
to an inferior. This wit was an inheritance from her Rodman ancestors. It was
said that old John Rodman, of Barbadoes, before he left his native Ireland, in
1655, had kissed the " Blarney stone," and the wit for which he asked had flowed
down the advancing years, to break out here and there in some favored descendants, especially the women. A lady once returned a book that her daughter had
borrowed, with the remark, " My daughter is a regular book-worm." Louisa,
looking at the soiled, dilapidated book with a regretful glance, said, " That accounts for the condition in which the books I lend to her are returned; she
leaves her trace on every page."
She was so bright and full of life, and seemed to love life so dearly, that one was

---

[1] This sketch is condensed from one in the History of Washington County.

surprised

surprised at her remark, often repeated, that she wished to die young. When asked what she called young, the answer came, " Twenty-eight,"and she added, " then every one will regret me." Her wish was granted, for she was twenty-eight in March, 1854, and died in May, 1854. She married, October 4, 1849, Colonel Daniel Chase Hiscox.

CHILDREN

2611. SUSAN WOOD HISCOX, born Dec. 13, 1850; married, Oct. 6, 1870, *Eugene F. Beecher*, son of Rev. *Edward* and *Isabella (Jones) Beecher.*

2612. DANIEL CHASE HISCOX, born May 2, 1854; died Aug. 9, 1854.

§ 1955. ROWLAND GIBSON RODMAN, 8 (Samuel Rodman, 7; Elizabeth Hazard, 6 ; Stephen, 5; Thomas, 4; Stephen, 3; Robert, 2 ; Thomas, 1), was born January 10, 1828. At the beginning of the war he was engaged in the manufacturing business, in company with his father and brother, under the name of " S. Rodman and Sons." When the President made his second call for volunteers during the Civil War, Mr. Rodman, following the example of his elder brother, raised a company of men, mostly from his native town. He was appointed by the governor, captain of the company. His first battle was one of the most fearful of the war, and it was his last. Abbott, in writing of this battle of Fredericksburg, says, " Eleven hundred and twenty-eight brave men were dead ; nine thousand and five writhing under tortures of wounds ; and two thousand and seventy-eight men missing, of whom probably many should have been reported dead." Captain Rodman received a fearful wound in the breast. He was carried to Baltimore, and taken to the house of his sister, where he was carefully nursed back to life. But he never entirely recovered from the effects of his wound. Few men made greater sacrifice in fighting for his country than Captain Rodman. From his youth he was not strong, and could never see fresh blood without fainting. After the bloody carnage that he witnessed at Fredericksburg this weakness was taken from him.

Captain Rodman married, September 24, 1856, Maria Macy, daughter of the Hon. Nathaniel Briggs Durfee, and Harriot Greene, his wife. He now lives in Ashland, Wisconsin.

CHILDREN

2614. HARRIOT GREENE RODMAN, born Feb. 19, 1859.

2615. ROWLAND GIBSON RODMAN, born Aug. 22, 1861.

2616. MACY DURFEE RODMAN, born Oct. 7, 1866.

2617. NATHANIEL GREENE RODMAN, born July 27, 1869.

2618. EDGAR GREENE RODMAN, born April 4, 1872; died March 17, 1877.

§ 1957. JULIA MARIA RODMAN, 8 (Samuel Rodman, 7; Elizabeth, 6 ; Stephen, 5; Thomas, 4; Stephen, 3; Robert, 2 ; Thomas, 1), was born September 7, 1831; she died September 27, 1891; she married, June 7, 1852, John Thompson, of San Francisco. A short time before his marriage, Mr. Thompson bought of Attmore Robinson a farm at Narragansett Pier, then known as " Sea View," now

*1961*
MARY PECKHAM RODMAN.
*Mrs. William H. Baldwin.*

now called Canonchet. Here they lived until 1864, when they removed to Brook-lyn, New York. In 1883 they removed to Waco, Texas, where their two sons were established in business. Mr. Thompson died in Waco in 1888 or 1889. Mrs. Thompson, broken in health, but with a yearning desire to see once more her old home within sound of the sea, returned to South Kingstown in July, 1891, and died at the home of her brother-in-law, B. F. Robinson, in Wakefield, September 27, 1891.

CHILDREN

2618. JOHN THOMPSON, born April 28, 1853; died March 24, 1864.
2619. MARY LOUISA THOMPSON, born Oct. 5, 1854; died Sept. 21, 1870.
2620. EDWARD WASHINGTON THOMPSON, born June 26, 1856; married, in Waco, Texas, *Ida Thompson.*
2621. SAMUEL RODMAN THOMPSON, born March 6, 1859; married *Lilian Williams.*
2622. SARAH CAROLINE THOMPSON, born Jan. 11, 1862; died 1883.
2623. JULIA RODMAN THOMPSON, born March 31, 1864; married, Oct. 26, 1892, *E. R. Bryan.*

§ 1958. CAROLINE ELIZABETH RODMAN, 8 (Samuel Rodman, 7; Eliz-abeth Hazard, 6; Stephen, 5; Thomas, 4; Stephen, 3; Robert, 2; Thomas, 1), was born July 4, 1833; she married, November 20, 1854, Benjamin F. Robinson. She was born in the village of Peacedale, in a house that stood almost on the exact site where now stands the "Hazard Memorial Hall," and has always lived within a mile of her birthplace. Mr. Robinson was born within a few rods of the house where he has lived since he was ten years old, in the village of Wakefield.

CHILDREN

2624. ELIZA NOYES ROBINSON, born Dec. 23, 1855; died June 21, 1863.
2625. BENJAMIN FRANKLIN ROBINSON, Jr., born Feb. 22, 1858.
2626. SAMUEL RODMAN ROBINSON, born April 17, 1859.
2627. ROWLAND RODMAN ROBINSON, born Aug. 23, 1862. He is a physician in Wakefield, R. I.
2628. ELIZA NOYES ROBINSON, born Nov. 8, 1863; died Dec. 17, 1863.
2629. CAROLINE ELIZA ROBINSON, born Feb. 18, 1871; died Aug. 15, 1871.

§ 1961. MARY PECKHAM RODMAN, 8 (Samuel Rodman, 7; Elizabeth, 6; Stephen, 5; Thomas, 4; Stephen, 3; Robert, 2; Thomas, 1), was born in South Kingstown, Rhode Island, November 12, 1838; she married, November 10, 1859, William Henry Baldwin, of Baltimore, Maryland, son of William Henry and Maria (Woodward) Baldwin. He is a commission merchant and a large man-ufacturer of textiles.

CHILDREN

2630. WILLIAM HENRY BALDWIN, 3d, born Aug., 1860; died Feb., 1889.
2631. SAMUEL RODMAN BALDWIN; died March, 1882.
2632. MARY LOUISE BALDWIN; died Aug., 1877.
2633. CHARLES BALDWIN.
2634. GORDON BALDWIN.
2635. MARIA WOODWARD BALDWIN.
2636. FRANK BALDWIN.

2637.

2637. CARROLL BALDWIN.
2638. SALLY RODMAN BALDWIN.

§ 1962. SARAH ABIGAIL RODMAN, 8 (Samuel Rodman, 7; Elizabeth Hazard, 6; Stephen, 5; Thomas, 4; Stephen, 3; Robert, 2; Thomas, 1), was born September 15, 1840; she married, September 27, 1865, William Woodward, of Baltimore, Maryland, son of Henry and Mary (Webb) Woodward. He was born in Anne Arundel County, Maryland, on the last day of the year 1836. After his tenth year, the family removed to Baltimore. At the age of twenty-one, he became a partner in the firm of Cary, Bangs and Woodward. In 1864 he removed to New York, and entered the cotton business. In 1869 he was offered a partnership in the firm of Smith and Dunning, general commission merchants, and the firm became Smith, Dunning and Woodward; later, Smith, Woodward and Stillman; and finally, Woodward and Stillman, under which style the firm has been in business nearly twenty years.

By his death, New York lost a strong, vital and commanding personality in its business circles, and withal a spirit genial, friendly, helpful and kind. During the last twenty years his career as a merchant illustrates the value of concentrated energy, strict personal attention to affairs, and absolute integrity in the rise and growth of a business which, at the time of his death, was the largest of its kind in the country. Mr. Woodward was a man of sanguine spirit, tempered with a keen power of discrimination and an almost unerring judgment, and through the ups and downs of general business for twenty years, the firm of Woodward and Stillman has been synonymous with good management and success. Mr. Woodward took an active part in the organization and advancement of the New York Cotton Association. He was a member of the original committee appointed to draft its by-laws. Later, he served very effectively as member of its building committee, and, upon the completion of the magnificent Cotton Exchange Building, as chairman of the committee of arrangements, he began the ceremonies of its formal dedication "according to the usages of a God-fearing people," by introducing the Right Reverend H. C. Potter, who offered a prayer of blessing.

He was a valued member of the Union, Manhattan, Tuxedo, South Side, New York Yacht Clubs, and of Holland Lodge. He was a man of sturdy physique, the apparent embodiment of health, success and happiness, — cheerful, hopeful, confident, and with a delightful dry humor of his own. He enjoyed the respect and confidence of all who knew him, and stood among those honored and distinguished merchants of New York, who, through their own efforts and natural force of character, attained success. His charities were unostentatious, but many and great. He helped many business men in days of trouble, and gave many young men a start in life. His kindness extended to the humblest of his employees, and his benevolence was not bounded by creeds, conditions or circumstances. To the hearts of all who knew him, the news of his death came with a painful shock. He died suddenly in March, 1889.

CHILDREN

CHILDREN
2639. MARY WOODWARD, born Oct., 1868; died Oct., 1868.
2640. JULIA WOODWARD, born Feb. 28, 1871; died March 2, 1871.
2641. EDITH WOODWARD, born Dec. 29, 1873.
2642. WILLIAM WOODWARD, born April 7, 1876.

§ 1963. SAMUEL RODMAN, 8 (Samuel Rodman, 7; Elizabeth Hazard, 6; Stephen, 5; Thomas, 4; Stephen, 3; Robert, 2; Thomas, 1), was born November 4, 1842, in Rocky Brook, Rhode Island; he died in January, 1890; he married, May 1, 1881, Mary McDaniel, daughter of John and Emma McDaniel.
CHILDREN
2643. MARY P. RODMAN, born Feb. 21, 1882.
2644. SALLY WOODWARD RODMAN, born July 17, 1884.
2645. ETHEL RODMAN.

§ 1965. EDWARD RODMAN, 8 (Samuel Rodman, 7; Elizabeth Hazard, 6; Stephen, 5; Thomas, 4; Stephen, 3; Robert, 2; Thomas, 1), was born December 14, 1845; he married, May 25, 1868, Hannah, daughter of Robinson and Mary (Carpenter) Perry.
CHILD
2646. WILLIAM WOODWARD RODMAN, born 1870.

§ 1975. ELIZA CHASE HISCOX, 8 (Abby Rodman, 7; Elizabeth Hazard, 6; Stephen, 5; Thomas, 4; Stephen, 3; Robert, 2; Thomas, 1), was born September 18, 1826; she died in 1861; she married, December 25, 1848, Daniel Wall, of Wickford, Rhode Island.
CHILDREN
2647. SUSAN FRANCES WALL, born Oct. 5, 1849; married *Edward C. Gardiner.*
2648. JOHN GARDINER WALL, born April 27, 1852; died Feb. 21, 1878, at Rio Janeiro, Brazil.
2649. ELIZA CHASE WALL, born Feb. 10, 1859.

§ 1981. ALFRED KNOWLES, 8 (Sarah Rodman, 7; Elizabeth Hazard, 6; Stephen, 5; Thomas, 4; Stephen, 3; Robert, 2; Thomas, 1), was born November 2, 1838; he married, April 7, 1868, Ellen, daughter of Thomas and Eliza Howard, of Newport, Rhode Island.
CHILDREN
2650. THOMAS KNOWLES, born 1869; died 1875.
2651. JOHN KNOWLES, born 1870.
2652. ELIZABETH KNOWLES, born 1872; died 1888.
2653. MARTHA KNOWLES, born 1874.
2654. DANIEL KNOWLES, born 1876; died 1877.
2655. CAROLINE KNOWLES, born 1879.
2656. ELIZABETH KNOWLES, born 1881.
2657. GEORGE KNOWLES, born 1882; died 1883.

§ 1982. WARREN KNOWLES, 8 (Sarah Rodman, 7; Elizabeth Hazard, 6; Stephen, 5; Thomas, 4; Stephen, 3; Robert, 2; Thomas, 1), was born November 2,

2, 1838; he married, November 8, 1866, Susan, daughter of Thomas Harvey, and Susan Brown, his wife, of North Kingstown, Rhode Island.

CHILDREN
2658. LOUISA KNOWLES, born 1867.
2659. FRANK KNOWLES, born 1868.
2660. GILBERT KNOWLES, born 1872.

§ 1991. MARY ELIZABETH GOULD, 8 (Penelope Rodman, 7; Elizabeth Hazard, 6; Stephen, 5; Thomas, 4; Stephen, 3; Robert, 2; Thomas, 1), was born at South Kingstown, September, 1842; she married, first, July 2, 1860, Doctor Jonathan Sweet. She married, second, 1882, Ezekiel H. Browning.

CHILDREN OF FIRST MARRIAGE
2661. MARY PENELOPE SWEET.
2662. LOUISA SWEET; married —— *Potter.*
2663. JOB SWEET.

CHILD OF SECOND MARRIAGE
2664. ROWLAND S. BROWNING.

§ 1992. JULIA GOULD, 8 (Penelope Rodman, 7; Elizabeth Hazard, 6; Stephen, 5; Thomas, 4; Stephen, 3; Robert, 2; Thomas, 1), was born January 19, 1844; she married, July 7, 1862, Peleg Brown; died 1894.

CHILDREN
2665. JULIA BROWN, born Dec. 3, 1866.
2666. ALICE BROWN, born Feb. 11, 1868.
2667. ELIZABETH BROWN, born Sept. 25, 1870.
2668. PELEG BROWN, born Jan. 18, 1872.
2669. MARY BROWN, born Sept., 1877.

§ 1993. SARAH R. GOULD, 8 (Penelope Rodman, 7; Elizabeth Hazard, 6; Stephen, 5; Thomas, 4; Stephen, 3; Robert, 2; Thomas, 1), was born September 11, 1847; she died September 29, 1877; she married, 1871, Lorenzo Chase.

CHILD
2670. GEORGE CHASE, born 1872; died 1873.

§ 1994. LYDIA ANN GOULD, 8 (Penelope Rodman, 7; Elizabeth Hazard, 6; Stephen, 5; Thomas, 4; Stephen, 3; Robert, 2; Thomas, 1), was born April 27, 1849; she died December 3, 1880; she married, December 25, 1870, George Fitzgerald.

CHILD
2671-3. IONA FITZGERALD, born Feb. 18, 1877.

§ 1996. HARRIET NEWEL RODMAN, 8 (Benjamin Rodman, 7; Elizabeth Hazard, 6; Stephen, 5; Thomas, 4; Stephen, 3; Robert, 2; Thomas, 1), was born in South Kingstown, July 31, 1837; she married, November 23, 1863, Peleg F. Pierce, of North Kingstown, son of William and Abby (Sandford) Pierce. He
was

was born in 1835. Early in life he was engaged in teaching, and later in business; but about 1870 he retired to his farm in North Kingstown, and has since that time been engaged in farming. He is interested in antiquarian research, and has done excellent work for many historical publications. His paper on *Land Titles* is not only extremely interesting, but valuable for its accuracy, showing much patient study and research. He is almost the only man besides the town clerk who is allowed to handle the tattered, burnt records of North Kingstown, preserved at Wickford, Rhode Island. From his study of these records, many discoveries have been made most valuable to historians and genealogists.

CHILDREN

2674. FRANK HOWARD PIERCE, born in North Kingstown, Oct. 15, 1866; died Feb. 25, 1871.
2675. HANNAH MARY PIERCE, born Aug. 26, 1874; died Sept. 5, 1874.
2676. WALTER RODMAN PIERCE, born Aug. 24, 1876.
2677. HARRIET SANDFORD PIERCE, born March 2, 1878.

§ 1997. JOHN BROWN RODMAN, 8 (Benjamin Rodman, 7; Elizabeth Hazard, 6; Stephen, 5; Thomas, 4; Stephen, 3; Robert, 2; Thomas, 1), was born February 15, 1839; he married, November 18, 1874, Sarah Elizabeth Babcock, daughter of Edward and Martha Babcock.

CHILDREN

2678. MARY HANNAH RODMAN, born Aug. 30, 1875.
2679. BERTHA E. RODMAN, born June 3, 1878.

§ 1999. ROWENA HAZARD CAMPBELL, 8 (Hannah Rodman, 7; Elizabeth Hazard, 6; Stephen, 5; Thomas, 4; Stephen, 3; Robert, 2; Thomas, 1), was born September 29, 1834; she married, October 10, 1854, Stephen H. Crary.

CHILDREN

2680. BLANCHE ELLA CRARY, born Aug. 26, 1855; married, Aug. 1, 1875, *Andrew Jackson*.
2681. GRACE CRARY, born March 1, 1859; married, Oct. 19, 1880, *William D. Daggett*.
2682. ROWENA CAMPBELL CRARY, born Jan. 31, 1868; married, Dec. 1, 1884, *Nelson E. Longe*.
2683–6. STEPHEN RODMAN CRARY, born Jan. 17, 1873.

§ 2023. JOB WATSON HAZARD, 8 (Arnold Hazard, 7; Thomas, 6; Jeremiah, 5; Jeffrey, 4; Robert, 3; Robert, 2; Thomas, 1), was born in 1816; he married, first, Ann Eliza, daughter of John and Ann Weeden; he married, second, Sarah Ann ——. He had by his second wife three children, all of whom died in infancy. He died August 4, 1884. His first wife died March 7, 1841, aged twenty-nine years.

CHILD OF FIRST MARRIAGE

2687. LUCY ANN HAZARD, born Nov. 28, 1837; married, Feb. 3, 1859, *Eben N. Tefft*.

§ 2030. JOHN HAZARD, 8 (Jeremiah, 7; Robert, 6; Robert, 5; Jeffrey, 4; Robert, 3; Robert, 2; Thomas, 1), was born November 26, 1848; he married Mary Whaley.

CHILDREN

CHILDREN
2688. WILLIAM HOXSIE HAZARD, born Aug. 2, 1870.
2689. LILLA HALE HAZARD, born Aug. 13, 1879.
2690. SUSAN WHALEY HAZARD, born June 22, 1884.

§ 2034. JASON P. HAZARD, 8 (Thomas T., 7; John, 6; Robert, 5; Robert, 4; Robert, 3; Robert, 2; Thomas, 1), was born in West Greenwich, Rhode Island, February 21, 1823; he married, March 15, 1847, Betsey Lewis, of Exeter, Rhode Island.

CHILDREN
2691. THOMAS T. HAZARD, born May 12, 1848; died Aug. 19, 1871.
2692. DUTY J. HAZARD, born June 23, 1850; died Aug. 6, 1857.
2693. STEPHEN A. HAZARD, born Oct. 20, 1852; married *Bertha Sprague*.
2694. ALICE HAZARD, born Sept. 29, 1854; died Nov. 7, 1878.
2695. CHARLES HAZARD, born Jan. 12, 1860.
2696. GEORGE B. HAZARD, born Oct. 14, 1861.

§ 2036. ALEXANDER S. HAZARD, 8 (Thomas T., 7; John, 6; Robert, 5; Robert, 4; Robert, 3; Robert, 2; Thomas, 1), was born January 25, 1836; he married, September 5, 1875, Elizabeth York. She was born August 15, 1859. They live at San Luis Obispo County, California.

CHILDREN
2697. FREDERICK ALEXANDER HAZARD, born May 17, 1876.
2698. MABEL ESTELLA HAZARD, born Jan. 18, 1878.
2699. LELAND STEWART HAZARD, born Dec. 6, 1879; he was drowned Jan. 1, 1884.
2700. MERLIN CARTER HAZARD, born Sept. 21, 1883.
2701. MARGIE LOUISE HAZARD, born April 20, 1888; died May 15, 1888.
2702. NELLIE ELIZABETH HAZARD, born Aug. 8, 1892.

§ 2041. JOHN G. HAZARD, 8 (John, 7; Governor Jeffrey, 6; Jeremiah, 5; Robert, 4; Robert, 3; Robert, 2; Thomas, 1), was born in Exeter, Rhode Island, April 15, 1832. Previous to the Civil War, General Hazard was engaged in business, but he was one of the first to offer his services to his country. He was commissioned first lieutenant, First Rhode Island Light Artillery, August 8, 1861, and has a long and honorable war record. At Fredericksburg, his battery was ordered into a position of extreme danger. General D. N. Crouch, the major-general commanding, made the following report: —

"Never men fought more gallantly. Never before, I believe, has artillery so far advanced in plain sight, without cover, against an intrenched enemy. The object of the daring enterprise was accomplished. The guns were ultimately withdrawn without the loss of a single piece; and Battery B, First Regiment Rhode Island Artillery, Captain John G. Hazard commanding, was placed upon record." [1]

He adds (December 13, 1862): "While Humphreys was at work, Getty's division of Wilcox's corps was ordered, about three o'clock, to charge on our left, by the unfinished railroad. I could see the men were being dreadfully cut up, al-

---

[1] History of Battery B, p. 142.

though

281

John G. Hazard.

though they had not advanced as far as my men. I determined to send a battery upon the plain to shell the line that was doing them so much harm, so I ordered an aide to tell Captain Morgan to send a battery across the canal, and plant it near the Brick House. Morgan came to me and said: 'My God, general, you will lose your guns; a battery cannot live there.' My reply was: 'Then it can die there! I would rather lose my guns than so many of my men; put them in.' Hazard's Battery B, First Regiment Rhode Island Light Artillery was the one to be sacrificed."

"Without a murmur, Captain Hazard dashed, with his six twelve-pounders, into the street, over the bridge, and getting into action on the left of the road, opened fire with a rapidity which well served my purpose to hearten our men lying down in front, and create in the mind of the enemy the expectation of a new assault, which would draw their fire, and relieve the pressure on the Ninth Corps." [1]

§ 2042. JEFFREY HAZARD, 8 (John, 7; Governor Jeffrey, 6; Jeremiah, 5; Robert, 4; Robert, 3; Robert, 2; Thomas, 1), was born in Exeter, Rhode Island, September 23, 1835. "He received his education in the Providence High School, and, previous to the breaking out of the Civil War, was engaged in the Manufacturers' Bank, as teller. He was commissioned second lieutenant of Battery A, in the First Regiment of Rhode Island Light Artillery, on the 5th of October, 1861, and appointed adjutant. While connected with this battery, he distinguished himself by his bravery in the many battles in which it took part. Among these were Ball's Bluff, Yorktown, Fair Oaks, Malvern Hill, and Antietam. At the latter engagement, the only officers present with Captain Tompkins were Captain Hazard (then first lieutenant), and first lieutenant Charles F. Mason. The battery gained for itself great credit at this battle, holding as it did an advanced and important position under a heavy artillery and infantry fire. On the 1st of October, 1862, he was promoted to the captaincy of Battery H." [2]

Captain Hazard married, October 20, 1865, Anne Hartwell.

CHILDREN

2703. LAURISTON HARTWELL HAZARD, born Nov. 22, 1866.
2704. JEFFREY HAZARD, born Dec. 28, 1867.
2705. JOHN HARTWELL HAZARD, born May 20, 1870.
2706. MARGARET CRANDALL HAZARD, born April 10, 1872.
2707. MARION HAZARD, born Aug. 3, 1874.
2708. HARRIET HALL HAZARD, born Aug. 11, 1877.
2709. ANNA ROSALINE HAZARD, born Oct. 8, 1882.

§ 2046. GEORGE POTTER HAZARD, 8 (John Boss, 7; John, 6; Jeremiah, 5; Robert, 4; Jeremiah, 3; Robert, 2; Thomas, 1), was born October 19, 1809; he died September 18, 1887; he married, about 1834, Rachel, daughter of Samuel and Freelove Joy.

CHILDREN

2710. INFANT DAUGHTER, born and died June 21, 1835.

---

[1] Contributed by Caroline Hazard.    [2] Memoirs of Rhode Island Officers, by John R. Bartlett.

2711. GEORGE JOY HAZARD, born Nov. 7, 1836 ; married, March 3, 1860, *Elvira*, daughter of *Henry A.* and *Margaret (Spencer) Abbot ;* she was born July 27, 1842 ; died Oct. 3, 1870 ; s. p. he married, 2d, May 8, 1872, *Helen F.*, daughter of *Cortez* and *Prussia Darling.*
2712. SAMUEL ANTHONY HAZARD, born Dec. 24, 1839; unmarried.
2713. MARY HAZARD, born March 19, 1843; unmarried.

§ 2048.  JOHN HAZARD, 8 (John Boss, 7; John, 6; Jeremiah, 5; Robert, 4; Jeremiah, 3 ; Robert, 2 ; Thomas, 1), was born May 22, 1812 ; he died July 2, 1845 ; he married Isabella, daughter of Arthur and Zilpha Potter, of Cranston, Rhode Island.

CHILDREN
2714. JOSEPHINE HAZARD, born Jan. 18, 1838; married *Amos A. White.* s. p.
2715. ARTHUR POTTER HAZARD, born June, 1841 ; married *Mary*, daughter of *Lorenzo* and *Harriet K. Hervey ;* she was born 1844.
2716. ALMIRA HAZARD, born April 17, 1843; died Nov. 28, 1844.

§ 2051.  HARRIET MOORE HAZARD, 8 (Jeremiah, 7; John, 6; Jeremiah, 5; Robert, 4; Jeremiah, 3 ; Robert, 2 ; Thomas, 1), was born July 17, 1817 ; she married, January 23, 1842, George Hunt Wilson, of Newport, Rhode Island.

CHILDREN
2717. JAMES HAZARD WILSON, born Feb. 24, 1843 ; married, April 23, 1874, *Louisa Coggeshall*, daughter of *James Monroe Coggeshall* and *Mary Isabella Van Vechten*, of New York.
2718. CLARA HUNT WILSON, born Nov. 10, 1847; died Jan. 5, 1872; unmarried.

§ 2055.  JOHN ATWOOD HAZARD, 8 (Benjamin S., 7; Wilbor, 6; Jeremiah' 5; Robert, 4; Jeremiah, 3 ; Robert, 2 ; Thomas, 1), was born June 2, 1854; he married, December 1, 1886, Fannie E. Tiffany.

CHILDREN
2719. AMEY STANTON HAZARD, born Dec. 26, 1890.
2720. WILLIAM STANTON HAZARD, born Oct. 14, 1892.

§ 2060.  JULIA TALMAN HAZARD, 8 (Daniel, 7; Wilbor, 6; Jeremiah, 5; Robert, 4; Jeremiah, 3 ; Robert, 2 ; Thomas, 1), was born in Providence, Rhode Island, February 7, 1863 ; she married, October 7, 1884, Charles Frederick Cooper.

CHILDREN
2721. ETHEL HAZARD COOPER, born Sept. 5, 1885.
2722. CHARLES FREDERICK COOPER, born Sept. 9, 1887.

§ 2061.  BENJAMIN HAZARD, 8 (Robertson, 7; Freeborn, 6; Gideon, 5; Robert, 4; Jeremiah, 3 ; Robert, 2 ; Thomas, 1), was born September 29, 1819; he married, first, Jane Knox, September 16, 1841 ; he married, second, Alexandrina Farrier.

CHILDREN
2723. LIZZIE M. HAZARD.
2724. FRANK A. HAZARD.

§ 2062.

§ 2062. LOUIS HAZARD, 8 (Robertson, 7; Freeborn, 6; Gideon, 5; Robert, 4; Jeremiah, 3; Robert, 2; Thomas, 1), was born October 27, 1820; he married, March 27, 1842, Harriet G. Harwood, daughter of Samuel Harwood, of Connecticut. She was born June 16, 1823, and died May 17, 1883. Mr. Hazard died April 16, 1892.

CHILDREN

2725. GEORGE R. HAZARD, born April 1, 1847; died April 11, 1847.
2726. WALTER R. HAZARD, born April 15, 1854; married *Cora E. Burton*.
2727. CHARLES C. HAZARD, born Dec. 17, 1855; died Nov. 17, 1859.
2728. MARION A. HAZARD, born July 1, 1860; married *William A. Pierce*.
2729. HENRY T. HAZARD, born Sept. 26, 1861 ; married, Nov. 30, 1887, *Nellie Shields*, of St. James, L. I. He lives at Stamford, Conn.

§ 2063. MARY ELIZABETH HAZARD, 8 (Robertson, 7; Freeborn, 6; Gideon, 5; Robert, 4; Jeremiah, 3; Robert, 2; Thomas, 1), was born June 17, 1829; she married, November 3, 1851, John Q. A. Gardiner, son of Herrington and Susan Gardiner, of North Kingstown. He lives at Barrington Centre, and was representative to the General Assembly from that town in 1887.

CHILDREN

2730. ALONZO COTTRELL GARDINER, born Sept. 29, 1853; married, June 1, 1876, *Abby N. Brown*, daughter of *William* and *Eliza Brown*.
2731. HERBERT MARSHALL GARDINER, born Feb. 6, 1855.
2732. SARAH KNIGHT GARDINER, born June 12, 1858; married, Sept. 16, 1885, *Mervin H. Pierce*, son of *Albert* and *Caroline Pierce*.
2733. ARTHUR ROBERTSON GARDINER, born Sept. 5, 1859; married, Oct. 6, 1891, *Helen Robbins*.
2734. JOHN LINCOLN GARDINER, born Oct. 28, 1865; married, June 31, 1891, a daughter of *Charles Jones*.
2735. NELLIE ELIZABETH GARDINER, born April 1, 1863.
2736. EVERETTE IRVING GARDINER, born May 4, 1869.

§ 2071. SARAH ROUNDS HAZARD, 8 (Robertson, 7; Freeborn, 6; Gideon, 5; Robert, 4; Jeremiah, 3; Robert, 2; Thomas, 1), was born January 17, 1839; she married, November 21, 1859, George Briggs Willis, of Providence, Rhode Island, son of William and Eliza Willis. He was born in Pawtucket, Rhode Island, November 16, 1837.

CHILDREN

2737. GEORGE SUMNER WILLIS, born Oct. 6, 1861; died June 5, 1870.
2738. CLARA LOUISE WILLIS, born Dec. 22, 1870.

§ 2074. HANNAH HAZARD, 8 (Susan, 7; Freeborn, 6; Gideon, 5; Robert, 4; Jeremiah, 3; Robert, 2; Thomas, 1). She married, January 9, 1843, Samuel R. Phillips, son of Nicholas H. Phillips; she died in May, 1881.

CHILDREN

2739. ANDREW P. PHILLIPS, born Oct. 16, 1843.
2740. ABNER L. PHILLIPS, born June 12, 1845.
2741. CANDACE V. PHILLIPS, born Jan. 16, 1848.

2742.

2742. JOSEPHINE H. PHILLIPS, born May 15, 1849.
2743. PAREDES E. PHILLIPS, born Nov. 6, 1851; died June 24, 1853.
2744. HIRAM M. PHILLIPS, born Oct. 8, 1853; died Feb. 13, 1854.
2745. MARY E. PHILLIPS, born March 17, 1856.
2746. JESSE FREMONT PHILLIPS, born May 21, 1857; died Oct. 14, 1857.
2747. SUSAN E. PHILLIPS, born April 5, 1858.
2748. MARTHA L. PHILLIPS, born March 4, 1859.
2749. EUGENIA C. PHILLIPS, born June 11, 1860.
2750. LAURA E. PHILLIPS, born July 27, 1861.
2751. LILIAN V. PHILLIPS, born June 18, 1863; died April 4, 1864.

**End of the Eighth Generation.**

THE

# THE HAZARD FAMILY

## 𝔑𝔦𝔫𝔱𝔥 𝔊𝔢𝔫𝔢𝔯𝔞𝔱𝔦𝔬𝔫

SARAH CATHARINE HOWLAND, 9 (William Hazard Howland, 8; Sarah Hazard, 7; Thomas, 6; Thomas, 5; Robert, 4; Thomas, 3; Robert, 2; Thomas, 1), was born in New York, May 5, 1846; she married, June 10, 1869, Millen Ford.

CHILDREN

2752. ANNIE HOWLAND FORD, born at Morristown, N. J., July 8, 1870.
2753. WILLIAM HOWLAND FORD, born at Morristown, N. J., Feb. 8, 1872.

§ 2104. JOHN HOWLAND PELL, 9 (Mary R. Howland, 8; Sarah Hazard, 7; Thomas, 6; Thomas, 5; Robert, 4; Thomas, 3; Robert, 2; Thomas, 1), was born in New York, December 23, 1830; he died at Yonkers, New York, October 6, 1882, and was buried at New Rochelle. At the beginning of the Civil War, he enlisted in Duryea's Zouaves, and was stationed at Fort Schuyler, New York. He was commissioned ensign in the Fourth Regiment, New York State Volunteers, July 6, 1861. When a lieutenant, he was honorably mentioned for gallant conduct at the battle of Antietam. His commission as Captain, Company K, Fourth Regiment New York State Volunteers, was dated October 14, 1862. He was then compelled to resign on account of physical disability brought on by the hardships of the campaigns in which he participated. His company attained great perfection in skirmish drill.

John H. Pell married, first, Cornelia Corse, of Flushing, Long Island; she died May 13, 1864; he married, second, April 20, 1870, Caroline E., daughter of Stephen Hyatt.

CHILDREN OF FIRST MARRIAGE

2754. RODMAN CORSE PELL, born at Flushing, L. I., March 31, 1861; married, 1887, *Antoinette G. Pell*. He enlisted in Company I, Seventh Regiment N. G. S., New York, 1883. He is in business in San Francisco, Cal.
2755. FLORENCE CORNELIA PELL, born at Flushing, L. I., Jan. 17, 1864.

CHILDREN OF SECOND MARRIAGE

2756. CLARENCE PELL, born in New York, Jan. 10, 1871; died July 20, 1874.
2757. JOHN H. PELL, born in New York, May 30, 1872. His name changed to *Howland Pell Haggerty*.
2758. STEPHEN HYATT PELL, born at Flushing, L. I., Feb. 3, 1874.
2759. SAMUEL OSGOOD PELL, born at Montclair, N. J., July 3, 1875.
2760. MARY HOWLAND PELL, born at Yonkers, N. Y., Dec. 12, 1876.

2761.

2761. THEODORE ROOSEVELT PELL, born at Yonkers, May 12, 1878.
2762. HORACE PORTER PELL, born at Yonkers, Aug. 30, 1879.

§ 2105. WILLIAM HOWLAND PELL, 9 (Mary R. Howland, 8; Sarah Hazard, 7; Thomas, 6; Thomas, 5; Robert, 4; Thomas, 3; Robert, 2; Thomas, 1), was born at Bloomingdale, September 3, 1833; he married, September 30, 1852, Adelaide, daughter of Benjamin Ferris and Anna Maria Schieffelin.

CHILD
2763. HOWLAND PELL, born March 19, 1856; married, April 12, 1887, *Almy Goelet Gallatin.*

§ 2140. ROWLAND GIBSON HAZARD, 9 (Rowland, 8; Rowland Gibson, 7; Rowland, 6; Thomas, 5; Robert, 4; Thomas, 3; Robert, 2; Thomas, 1), was born January 22, 1855; he married, November 16, 1880, Mary Pierpont, daughter of Reverend George Bushnell, of Beloit, Wisconsin. He was graduated from Brown University in 1876, and immediately entered the Peacedale Manufacturing Company, of which he is treasurer. He is active in all town improvements; was elected a trustee of Brown University in 1893, and is also vice-president of the Solvay Process Company, of Syracuse, New York.[1]

CHILDREN
2764. ROWLAND HAZARD, born Oct. 29, 1881.
2765. ELIZABETH HAZARD, born April 27, 1883.
2766. MARGARET HAZARD, born Jan. 25, 1886.
2767. MARY HAZARD, born April 11, 1890.
2768. THOMAS PIERPONT HAZARD, born Oct. 27, 1892.

§ 2142. FREDERICK ROWLAND HAZARD, 9 (Rowland, 8; Rowland G., 7; Rowland, 6; Thomas, 5; Robert, 4; Thomas, 3; Robert, 2; Thomas, 1), was born June 14, 1858; he married, May 29, 1886, Dora G. Sedgwick, daughter of Charles B. Sedgwick, of Syracuse, New York. He graduated from Brown University in 1881, and after a year spent in the Peacedale Mills, went abroad to study the manufacture of soda-ash. On his return he entered the Solvay Process Company, of which he is treasurer. He lives at Upland Farm, near Syracuse, New York.[2]

CHILDREN
2769. DOROTHY HAZARD, born May 21, 1887.
2770. SARAH SEDGWICK HAZARD, born Aug. 2, 1889.
2771. KATHARINE HAZARD, born Nov. 7, 1890.
2772. FREDERICK ROWLAND HAZARD, born Dec. 6, 1891.

§ 2143. HELEN HAZARD, 9 (Rowland, 8; Rowland Gibson, 7; Rowland, 6; Thomas, 5; Robert, 4; Thomas, 3; Robert, 2; Thomas, 1), was born January 15, 1861; she married, October 6, 1885, Nathaniel Terry Bacon, a grandson of Dr. Leonard Bacon, of New Haven.

---

[1] Contributed by Miss Caroline Hazard.          [2] By the same.

CHILDREN

CHILDREN
2773. LEONARD BACON, born May 26, 1887.
2774. SUSAN BACON, born Nov. 12, 1889.

§ **2144.** MARGARET HAZARD, 9 (Rowland, 8 ; Rowland G., 7; Rowland, 6;
Thomas, 5; Robert, 4; Thomas, 3 ; Robert, 2; Thomas, 1), was born in Peacedale,
Rhode Island, May 31, 1867 ; she married, June 24, 1893, Doctor Irving Fisher.
Doctor Fisher graduated from Yale as the valedictorian of his class in 1888. In
1891 he took the degree of Doctor of Philosophy, presenting as his thesis a paper entitled *Mathematical Investigations in the Theory of Value and Prices,* which
attracted much attention. In 1893–4 he studied at the universities of Berlin and
Paris, and delivered an address before the economic section of the British Association at its Oxford session, August, 1894. He is a professor in the mathematical department of Yale University.'

CHILD
2775. MARGARET FISHER, born in Paris, France, April 30, 1894.

§ **2230.** CLARA GARDINER HAZARD, 9 (Christopher Grant Hazard, 8 ;
Sylvester, 7; Thomas A., 6; George, 5; George, 4; Thomas, 3; Robert, 2; Thom-
as, 1), was born April 11, 1841 ; she married Reverend Charles Wiltshire Wood.
She is an active worker in the cause of temperance.

CHILDREN
2776. GERTRUDE H. WOOD, born Sept. 4, 1869.
2777. CHARLES E. WOOD, born Feb. 21, 1871.
2778. EFFIE WILCOX WOOD, born and died Feb. 21, 1871.
2779. GRACE S. WOOD, born Oct. 23, 1873.
2780. FREDERICK M. WOOD, born Feb. 18, 1886.

§ **2231.** CHRISTOPHER GRANT HAZARD, 9 (Christopher Grant, 8; Sylvester, 7; Thomas A., 6; George, 5; George, 4; Thomas, 3; Robert, 2; Thomas,
1), was born May 9, 1852. He is a clergyman in the Presbyterian Church. Mr.
Hazard married Fannie Seward Post.

CHILDREN
2781. FLOYD SEWARD HAZARD.
2782. GRACE WOLCOTT HAZARD.
2783. MARY ELIZA HAZARD.

§ **2232.** FREDERICK SYLVESTER HAZARD, 9 (Christopher G., 8 ; Sylvester, 7; Thomas A., 6; George, 5; George, 4; Thomas, 3; Robert, 2; Thomas,
1), was born March 26, 1856; he married, December 24, 1880, Emilie Cook.
They live in Denver, Colorado.

CHILDREN
2784. GRANT HOWARD HAZARD, born Oct. 28, 1883; died Sept. 10, 1884.
2785. FREDERICK EMANUEL HAZARD, born Nov. 1, 1885.

Contributed by Miss Caroline Hazard.

2786.

2786. EMILIE LOUISA HAZARD, born Oct. 23, 1887.
2787. GEORGE SEWARD HAZARD, born Dec. 13, 1888; died Dec. 31, 1888.


§ 2238. ADA HAZARD, 9 (Louis L., 8; George, 7; Thomas A., 6; George, 5; George, 4; Thomas, 3; Robert, 2; Thomas, 1), was born about 1857; she married, in Newport, Rhode Island, Thomas G. Brown.

CHILDREN
2788. HELEN H. BROWN.
2789. MARY BROWN.
2790. THOMAS G. BROWN.


§ 2239. HELEN MAUD HAZARD, 9 (Louis, 8; George, 7; Thomas A., 6; George, 5; George, 4; Thomas, 3; Robert, 2; Thomas, 1), was born in 1859; she married, in Newport, Rhode Island, Lieutenant I. Goodwin Hobbs, U. S. N.

CHILDREN
2791. J. GOODWIN HOBBS.
2792. MAJORIE GOODWIN HOBBS.


§ 2245. JEREMIAH POTTER ROBINSON, 9 (Jeremiah, 8; Mary Niles Potter, 7; Sarah Hazard, 6; Enoch, 5; George, 4; Thomas, 3; Robert, 2; Thomas, 1), was born in Brooklyn, New York, March 13, 1846; he married, November 12, 1867, Margaret Downing Lanman, daughter of David Trumbull Lanman. She is a descendant, through the Trumbulls, of the Reverend John Robinson, who blessed the first pilgrims as they left for their journey across the Atlantic.

CHILDREN
2793. DAVID TRUMBULL LANMAN ROBINSON, born Nov. 14, 1868, in Brooklyn, N. Y.
2794. ELIZABETH DeWITT ROBINSON, born April 28, 1870, in Brooklyn.
2795. MARY HELEN ROBINSON, born Oct. 15, 1871, in Brooklyn.
2796. MARGARET FAITH ROBINSON, born April 22, 1883, in New York.


§ 2246. ELIZABETH DeWITT ROBINSON, 9 (Jeremiah, 8; Mary N. Potter, 7; Sarah Hazard, 6; Enoch, 5; George, 4; Thomas, 3; Robert, 2; Thomas, 1), was born August 12, 1851; she married, Jan. 10, 1870, Lewis Herman Leonard, son of William B. Leonard. He was born August 13, 1850.

CHILDREN
2797. ESTHER HENRIETTA LEONARD; married, June 1, 1892, *John Griffen Underbill.*
2798. JOSEPHINE BUCKLEY LEONARD.
2799. WILLIAM BOARDMAN LEONARD, born Aug. 14, 1873.
2800. MABEL ROBINSON LEONARD, born May 1, 1876, in Brooklyn, N. Y.


§ 2247. HARRIET WOODRUFF ROBINSON, 9 (Jeremiah, 8; Mary N. Potter, 7; Sarah Hazard, 6; Enoch, 5; George, 4; Thomas, 3; Robert, 2; Thomas, 1), was born March 11, 1853, in Brooklyn, New York. She married, June 21, 1883, John E. Leech, of Brooklyn.

CHILDREN

CHILDREN

2801. ROBINSON LEECH, born May 4, 1884, in Brooklyn, N. Y.

2802. CHARLOTTE LEECH, born July 30, 1886, in Brooklyn, N. Y.


§ 2248. ISAAC RICH ROBINSON, 9 (Jeremiah, 8; Mary N. Potter, 7; Sarah Hazard, 6; Enoch, 5; George, 4; Thomas, 3; Robert, 2; Thomas, 1), was born in Brooklyn, New York, July 8, 1856; he married, November 21, 1877, in Brooklyn, New York, Ellen Louise Pate, daughter of William and Harriet (Wastelle) Pate. She was born July 21, 1856.

CHILDREN

2803. RUTH ROBINSON, born Dec. 7, 1879, in Brooklyn, N. Y.

2804. ELSIE POTTER ROBINSON, born at Edgewood Farm, Wakefield, R. I., Nov. 23, 1884.


§ 2250. LOUISA LYMAN ROBINSON, 9 (George Champlin Robinson, 8; Mary N. Potter, 7; Sarah Hazard, 6; Enoch, 5; George, 4; Thomas, 3; Robert, 2; Thomas, 1), was born in Brooklyn, New York, May 24, 1856; she married, October 27, 1880, George F. Weeden, of Brooklyn, New York.

CHILDREN

2805. MARIE LOUISE WEEDEN, born Sept. 1, 1881, in Brooklyn, N. Y.

2806. ELIZABETH SPENCE WEEDEN, born April 30, 1885, in New York.

2807. MARGARET WEEDEN, born Sept. 23, 1889, in Wakefield, R. I.


§ 2257. GEORGE ROBINSON PEARSE, 9 (Mary Robinson, 8; Mary N. Potter, 7; Sarah Hazard, 6; Enoch, 5; George, 4; Thomas, 3; Robert, 2; Thomas, 1), was born July 7, 1852; he married, October 14, 1880, Nellie Morse, in Wakefield, Rhode Island.

CHILDREN

2808. LE BARON PEARSE, born May 14, 1881; died Aug. 17, 1881.

2809. GEORGE M. PEARSE, born May 17, 1882.

2810. MARY F. PEARSE, born Feb. 1, 1884.

2811. RUTH L. B. PEARSE, born March 5, 1886.

2812. MARGUERITE PEARSE, born Dec. 6, 1887.


§ 2288. HARRIET ELIZABETH PERRY, 9 (Harriet Theresa Hazard, 8; Bowdoin, 7; Jonathan, 6; Thomas, 5; Jonathan, 4; Thomas, 3; Robert, 2; Thomas, 1), was born in South Kingstown, Rhode Island, January 18, 1844; she married, June 16, 1869, Clarence Eugene Thomas, of Wickford, Rhode Island.

CHILD

2813. HARRIET EUGENIE THOMAS, born April 11, 1870.


§ 2290. JOHN EDWARD PERRY, 9 (Harriet T. Hazard, 8; Bowdoin, 7; Jonathan, 6; Thomas, 5; Jonathan, 4; Thomas, 3; Robert, 2; Thomas, 1), was born May 28, 1847. He is a physician, and settled in Wakefield, Rhode Island. He married, May 1, 1878, Elnora Crawford.

CHILD

CHILD
2814. HARRIET ELNORA PERRY, born in Wakefield, R. I., Oct. 27, 1881.

§ 2291. SARAH EMILY PERRY, 9 (Harriet T. Hazard, 8; Bowdoin, 7; Jonathan, 6; Thomas, 5; Jonathan, 4; Thomas, 3; Robert, 2; Thomas, 1), was born in Wakefield, Rhode Island, April 17, 1849; she married, October 10, 1877, Herbert J. Wells. They live on Kingston Hill (formerly called Little Rest). He is son of Thomas P. and Julia Johnson Wells.

CHILDREN
2815. GRACE PERRY WELLS, born in Providence, R. I., Feb. 15, 1879.
2816. HERBERT COMSTOCK WELLS, born in Providence, Nov. 21, 1880.
2817. EMILY POTTER WELLS, born in Kingston (South Kingstown), R. I., Sept. 8, 1882.
2818. THOMAS PERRY WELLS, born in Kingston, April 5, 1884.
2819. JOHN HAZARD WELLS, born in Kingston, Dec. 29, 1885.
2820. ELIZABETH JOHNSON WELLS, born in Kingston, April 20, 1890.

§ 2296. WILLIAM A. HAZARD, 9 (William R., 8; Bowdoin, 7; Jonathan, 6; Thomas, 5; Jonathan, 4; Thomas, 3; Robert, 2; Thomas, 1), was born in South Kingstown, Rhode Island, January 11, 1854; he married, in New York, January 13, 1885, Laura Abell Pelton, daughter of William and Catharine (Abell) Pelton.

CHILDREN
2821. FRANCIS MOULTON HAZARD, born Oct. 24, 1885; died Jan. 2, 1890.
2822. MARY PELTON HAZARD, born May 18, 1887.
2823. JESSIE ASHLEY HAZARD, born Sept. 4, 1890.

§ 2299. ANNIE E. NICHOLS, 9 (Marietta Hazard, 8; Bowdoin, 7; Jonathan, 6; Thomas, 5; Jonathan, 4; Thomas, 3; Robert, 2; Thomas, 1), was born in South Kingstown, Rhode Island, July 23, 1850; she married, May 26, 1869, Charles A. Porter.

CHILDREN
2824. JAMES EDWARD PORTER, born March 29, 1870.
2825. HATTIE NICHOLS PORTER, born June 9, 1872.
2826. MARIETTA PORTER, born Oct. 22, 1874.

§ 2301. MARY S. NICHOLS, 9 (Marietta Hazard, 8; Bowdoin, 7; Jonathan, 6; Thomas, 5; Jonathan, 4; Thomas, 3; Robert, 2; Thomas, 1), was born February 1, 1857; she married, June 9, 1875, Frank Warner Robinson, son of Elisha and Mary (Hull) Robinson.

CHILDREN
2827. ANNA ROBINSON, born Feb. 24, 1881.
2828. ELIZA HAZARD ROBINSON, born Aug. 5, 1882.
2829. FANNY ROBINSON, born Jan. 7, 1885.
2830. FRANK A. ROBINSON, born Aug. 11, 1887.
2831. ELISHA N. ROBINSON, born Jan. 25, 1892.
2832. THURSTON ROBINSON, born Aug. 9, 1893.

§ 2302.

§ 2302. ABBIE A. NICHOLS, 9 (Marietta Hazard, 8; Bowdoin, 7; Jonathan, 6; Thomas, 5; Jonathan, 4; Thomas, 3; Robert, 2; Thomas, 1), was born May 11, 1861; she married, September 19, 1882, John H. Crandall.

CHILDREN

2833. CHESTER HAZARD CRANDALL, born Sept. 11, 1883.
2834. LEROY PRINCE CRANDALL, born Nov. 24, 1886.
2835. JOSEPH NICHOLS CRANDALL, born Aug. 1, 1889.

§ 2306. HANNAH SUSAN WATSON, 9 (Elisha, 8; Ann Cole, 7; Mary Hazard, 6; Thomas, 5; Jonathan, 4; Thomas, 3; Robert, 2; Thomas, 1), was born September 19, 1837; she married, April 9, 1861, Attmore Wright, son of Stephen and Susan (Allen) Wright. He died in less than a year after their marriage, a few weeks before the birth of their child. She married, second, December 13, 1865, Charles Henry Hazard, her first cousin.

CHILD OF FIRST MARRIAGE

2836. GEORGIANA ATTMORE WRIGHT, born Jan. 14, 1862; married *Joseph Milne*, of Fall River, Mass.

CHILDREN OF SECOND MARRIAGE

2837. CARDER HAZARD, born March 12, 1867.
2838. CHARLES H. HAZARD, born Feb. 22, 1868; died Aug. 3, 1868.
2839. ELISHA WATSON HAZARD, born Oct. 18, 1870; died Sept. 4, 1871.
2840. JANE HULL HAZARD, born July 22, 1874.
2841. ANNIE HUNTINGTON HAZARD, born May 27, 1876.

§ 2311. ELISHA WATSON CROSS, 9 (Mary Watson, 8; Ann Cole, 7; Mary Hazard, 6; Thomas, 5; Jonathan, 4; Thomas, 3; Robert, 2; Thomas, 1), was born September 22, 1844; he married, November 1, 1872, Frances Cooper Wright, daughter of Stephen and Susan (Allen) Wright. She was born June 17, 1843.

CHILDREN

2842. HENRY PARSONS CROSS, born Sept. 29, 1873.
2843. SUSAN WRIGHT CROSS, born Nov. 14, 1875.
2844. MORTON ROBINSON CROSS, born Jan. 29, 1878.

§ 2317. CHRISTOPHER WATSON, 9 (William, 8; Ann Cole, 7; Mary Hazard, 6; Thomas, 5; Jonathan, 4; Thomas, 3; Robert, 2; Thomas, 1), was born in 1845; he died in 1878; he married Sarah Dean.

CHILD

2845. ADELAIDE WATSON.

§ 2318. SUSAN ADA WATSON, 9 (William, 8; Ann Cole, 7; Mary Hazard, 6; Thomas, 5; Jonathan, 4; Thomas, 3; Robert, 2; Thomas, 1), was born in 1849; she married Marshal Gilbert.

CHILD

2846. MARSHAL C. GILBERT.

§ 2320.

§ 2320. WILLIAM WATSON, 9 (William, 8; Ann Cole, 7; Mary Hazard, 6; Thomas, 5; Jonathan, 4; Thomas, 3; Robert, 2; Thomas, 1), was born in 1857. He married Abby Holland.

CHILDREN
2847. MARGARET E. WATSON.
2848. ADELAIDE G. WATSON.

§ 2321. ANN E. WATSON, 9 (William, 8; Ann Cole, 7; Mary Hazard, 6; Thomas, 5; Jonathan, 4; Thomas, 3; Robert, 2; Thomas, 1), was born in 1859. She married Theodora Lawton.

CHILDREN
2849. BYRON LAWTON; died in infancy.
2850. WILLIAM LAWTON.

§ 2322. IRVING WATSON, 9 (Laura, 8; Ann Cole, 7; Mary Hazard, 6; Thomas, 5; Jonathan 4; Thomas, 3; Robert, 2; Thomas, 1), was born June 28, 1849, in New York City. He married, September 8, 1875, Elizabeth C. Campau, of Detroit, Michigan.

CHILDREN
2851. HENRY VON RENSSELAER WATSON, born in Wakefield, June 9, 1876; died Feb. 21, 1879.
2852. HELEN CAMPAU WATSON, born in Wakefield, Aug. 14, 1878.
2853. ANN HARRIET WATSON, born in Wakefield, Aug. 6, 1881.
2854. WALTER IRVING WATSON, born in Wakefield, Sept. 8, 1883.

§ 2328. GEORGE HERBERT OWEN HASZARD, 9 (George Thomas, 8; James D., 7; Thomas R., 6; Thomas, 5; Jonathan, 4; Thomas, 3; Robert, 2; Thomas, 1), was born June 1, 1851. He is a printer and bookseller, of the firm of Haszard & Moore, Charlottetown, Prince Edward Island. He married, August 13, 1889, Edith, daughter of Reverend F. W. Moore.

CHILDREN
2855. HELEN MARGUERITE HASZARD, born May 19, 1890.
2856. EDITH FREDERICA ELAINE HASZARD, born May 22, 1894.

§ 2329. THOMAS WALTER DOUGLAS HASZARD, 9 (George Thomas, 8; James D., 7; Thomas R., 6; Thomas, 5; Jonathan, 4; Thomas, 3; Robert, 2; Thomas, 1), was born January 27, 1854. He married, September 13, 1882, Annie Wilson Campbell.

CHILDREN
2857. ALLAN CAMPBELL HASZARD, born July 5, 1883.
2858. JEAN DOUGLAS HASZARD, born Jan. 2, 1885.
2859. ARTHUR ALEXANDER HASZARD, born Nov. 1, 1886.
2860. MARGUERITE MARCELLA HASZARD, born Sept. 3, 1891.
2861. WILLISTON HASZARD, born Dec. 6, 1893.
2862. JESSIE E. HASZARD, born Oct. 29, 1895.

§ 2332.

§ 2332. GEORGE ASHLEY HASZARD, 9 (George Thomas, 8; James D., 7; Thomas R., 6; Thomas, 5; Jonathan, 4; Thomas, 3; Robert, 2; Thomas, 1), was born May 15, 1860, at Charlottetown, Prince Edward Island. He married, Feb. 6, 1880, Sarah Bears of Murray River. He removed from Charlottetown to the United States, in July, 1880, and lives in Melrose, Massachusetts.

CHILDREN
2863. MINNIE ADELE ASHLEY HASZARD, born Jan. 11, 1881.
2864. EDITH OWEN HASZARD, born June 6, 1883; died July 18, 1884.
2865. MARGARET VICTORIA HASZARD, born Feb. 8, 1885.
2866. OLIVE GRAY HASZARD, born Nov. 1, 1886.
2867. HARRY ASHLEY HASZARD, born Sept. 4, 1888.
2868. GRACE FAIRCHILD HASZARD, born April 15, 1890; died Sept. 29, 1890.
2869. MAY KATHLEEN HASZARD, born May 2, 1891.
2870. FRANK KELLOG HASZARD, born Aug. 3, 1893.
2871. JAMES DOUGLAS HASZARD, born Sept. 13, 1895.

§ 2373. SUSAN REED FISKE, 9 (Charlotte M. Hazard, 8; George S., 7; Francis, 6; Doctor Robert, 5; Caleb, 4; Colonel George, 3; Robert, 2; Thomas, 1), was born April, 1857. She married, October, 1889, Dexter Rumsey, of Buffalo, N. Y.

CHILD
2872. RUTH RUMSEY, born May, 1891.

§ 2385. GEORGE BROWN ROBINSON, 9 (George B., 8; Benjamin, 7; Sarah Peckham, 6; Mary Hazard, 5; Governor George, 4; Colonel George, 3; Robert, 2; Thomas, 1), was born March 16, 1842; he married, January 28, 1869, Lilla Bryan, of New York. He is a merchant in New York.

CHILD
2873. KATE BRYAN ROBINSON, born July 16, 1870.
2874. GEORGE BROWN ROBINSON, born Aug. 13, 1872.
2875. JOHN BRYAN ROBINSON, born Oct. 5, 1874.
2876. LILLA BRYON ROBINSON, born June 30, 1879.
2877. FREDERICK RUSSELL WELLS ROBINSON, born Sept. 22, 1880; died Sept. 11, 1881.
2878. JULIA MARGUERITE ROBINSON, born Jan. 11, 1882.
2879. THOMAS WELLS ROBINSON, born Aug. 1, 1884.
2880. BENJAMIN ROWLAND ROBINSON, born May 28, 1887.

§ 2402. ANNIE HUNTINGTON, 9 (Ann Eliza Hazard, 8; Carder, 7; Doctor George, 6; Judge Carder, 5; Governor George, 4; Colonel George, 3; Robert, 2; Thomas, 1), was born January 3, 1863; she married January 20, 1886, William F. Davis, of Boston, Massachusetts.

CHILD
2881. MARION HUNTINGTON DAVIS, born July 3, 1889.

§ 2403. LILLIAN HUNTINGTON, 9 (Ann Eliza Hazard, 8; Carder, 7; Doctor George, 6; Judge Carder, 5; Governor George, 4; Colonel George, 3; Robert,

Robert, 2 ; Thomas, 1), was born September 28, 1867 ; she married, April 27, 1891, Henry M. Hills, of New York.

CHILD
2882. JEDEDIAH HUNTINGTON HILLS, born July 23, 1892.

§ 2428. EMMA HARMON, 9 (Ruth Hayward Rogers, 8 ; Mercy Champlin, 7 ; Elizabeth Perry, 6 ; Mercy Hazard, 5 ; Oliver ; 4 ; Colonel George, 3 ; Robert, 2 ; Thomas, 1), was born November 12, 1840 ; she married, first, September 2, 1863, Oscar Folsom. She married a second time.

CHILD OF FIRST MARRIAGE
2883. FRANCES FOLSOM, born 1865 ; married *Stephen Grover Cleveland*, President of the United States. They have three children, *Ruth, Esther*, and *Marion*.

§ 2604. ISAAC PEACE RODMAN, 9 (Isaac Peace Rodman, 8 ; Samuel, 7 ; Elizabeth Hazard, 6 ; Stephen, 5 ; Thomas, 4 ; Stephen, 3 ; Robert, 2 ; Thomas, 1), was born in South Kingstown, Rhode Island, April 25, 1848 ; he married, April 28, 1880, Harriet E. Robinson, daughter of Doctor Morton and Anna (Collins) Robinson.

CHILDREN
2884. HELEN SMITH RODMAN, born Sept. 9, 1883.
2885. ISAAC PEACE RODMAN.

§ 2605. SALLY LYMAN RODMAN, 9 (Isaac P., 8 ; Samuel, 7 ; Elizabeth Hazard, 6 ; Stephen, 5 ; Thomas, 4 ; Stephen, 3 ; Robert, 2 ; Thomas, 1), was born February 10, 1850 ; she married, June 15, 1875, Robert Thompson, attorney-at-law, son of Robert and Nancy (Gilmore) Thompson.

CHILDREN
2886. LOUISA HAZARD THOMPSON, born July 25, 1876 ; died Sept. 5, 1876.
2887. SALLY RODMAN THOMPSON, born Feb. 12, 1879.
2888. NANCY GILMORE THOMPSON, born May 19, 1881 ; died Oct. 15, 1881.
2889. EDWARD HAZARD THOMPSON, born Feb. 14, 1884.

§ 2611. SUSAN WOOD HISCOX, 9 (Louisa Hazard Rodman, 8 ; Samuel, 7 ; Elizabeth Hazard, 6 ; Stephen, 5 ; Thomas, 4 ; Stephen, 3 ; Robert, 2 ; Thomas, 1), was born December 13, 1850 ; she married, October 6, 1870, Eugene F. Beecher, son of Reverend Edward and Isabella (Jones) Beecher.

CHILDREN
2890. LOUISA ISABELLA BEECHER, born Sept. 27, 1871 ; married, 1892, *William Chancelor*, of Worcester, Mass.
2891. CLARE RODMAN BEECHER, born Jan. 9, 1873.

§ 2620. EDWARD WASHINGTON THOMPSON, 9 (Julia Rodman, 8 ; Samuel, 7 ; Elizabeth Hazard, 6 ; Stephen, 5 ; Thomas, 4 ; Stephen, 3 ; Robert, 2 ; Thomas, 1), was born in Point Judith, at what is now known as "Canonchet" farm, April 28, 1856. He is now settled at Waco, Texas. He married at Waco, October

October 6, 1881, Carrie Ida Thompson, daughter of Hugh Montgomery and Carrie Virginia (Wolfe) Thompson, of Mississippi.

CHILDREN

2892. EDITH RODMAN THOMPSON, born Aug. 25, 1882.
2893. MARY LOUISA THOMPSON, born March 18, 1886.
2894. IDA BLAND THOMPSON, born April 24, 1888.
2895. EDWARD THOMPSON, born Dec. 30, 1891.

§ 2621. SAMUEL RODMAN THOMPSON, 9 (Julia Rodman, 8 ; Samuel, 7 ; Elizabeth Hazard, 6 ; Stephen, 5 ; Thomas, 4 ; Stephen, 3 ; Robert, 2 ; Thomas, 1), was born in Point Judith, South Kingstown, March 6, 1859 ; he married, in Brooklyn, New York, June 29, 1887, Lillian Williams. He lives in Waco, Texas.

CHILDREN

2896. SAMUEL RODMAN THOMPSON, born June 13, 1888.
2897. WILLIAM BUCKLAND THOMPSON, born July 13, 1892.

§ 2687. LUCY ANN HAZARD, 9 (Job W., 8 ; Arnold, 7 ; Thomas, 6 ; Jeremiah, 5 ; Jeffrey, 4 ; Robert, 3 ; Robert, 2 ; Thomas, 1), was born November 28, 1837 ; she married, February 3, 1859, Eben M. Tefft. They live at Jamestown, Rhode Island.

CHILDREN

2898. THOMAS ARNOLD HAZARD TEFFT, born March 22, 1861.
2899. JEREMIAH HAZARD TEFFT, born May 21, 1865.
2900. HANNAH WATSON TEFFT, born Feb. 11, 1870.
2901. JOB WATSON TEFFT, born April 24, 1872.
2902. JESSE COTRELL TEFFT, born Aug. 3, 1873.

§ 2693. STEPHEN ALLEN HAZARD, 9 (Jason P., 8 ; Thomas T., 7 ; John, 6 ; Robert, 5 ; Robert, 4 ; Robert, 3 ; Robert, 2 ; Thomas, 1), was born October 20, 1852 ; he married, December 11, 1879, Bertha Sprague.

CHILDREN

2903. ALICE M. HAZARD, born Feb. 20, 1881.
2904. GEORGE J. HAZARD, born July 2, 1882.
2905. MARY L. HAZARD, born Feb. 11, 1884.
2906. JOHN C. HAZARD, born Nov. 8, 1885; died July 8, 1886.

§ 2695. CHARLES S. HAZARD, 9 (Jason P., 8 ; Thomas T., 7 ; John, 6 ; Robert, 5 ; Robert, 4 ; Robert, 3 ; Robert, 2 ; Thomas, 1), was born January 12, 1860 ; he married, at Voluntown, New London County, Connecticut, September 14, 1886, Lucy R. Main. They live at Bayonne, New Jersey.

CHILDREN

2907. BYRON E. HAZARD, born July 24, 1888.
2908. BESSIE M. HAZARD, born Oct. 10, 1889.
2909. LOIS E. HAZARD, born Nov. 8, 1891; she died April 4, 1892.
2910. GERTRUDE HAZARD, born Oct. 17, 1882.

§ 2711.

§ **2711. GEORGE JOY HAZARD,** 9 (George Potter Hazard, 8 ; John Boss, 7 ; John, 6 ; Jeremiah, 5 ; Robert, 4 ; Jeremiah, 3 ; Robert, 2 ; Thomas, 1), was born November 7, 1836 ; he married, first, March 3, 1860, Elvira, daughter of Henry A. and Margaret (Spencer) Abbott ; she was born July 27, 1842, and died October 3, 1870 ; no children. He married, second, May 8, 1872, Helen F., daughter of Cortez and Prussia Darling.

CHILDREN
2911. SAMUEL JOY HAZARD, born July 14, 1873; died Jan. 4, 1878.
2912. GRACE DARLING HAZARD, born Dec, 21, 1874.
2913. HELEN RACHEL HAZARD, born July 26, 1877.
2914. GEORGE CORTEZ HAZARD, born July 19, 1880.

§ **2717. JAMES HAZARD WILSON,** 9 (Harriet M. Hazard, 8 ; Jeremiah, 7 ; John, 6 ; Jeremiah, 5 ; Robert, 4 ; Jeremiah, 3 ; Robert, 2 ; Thomas, 1), was born in Newport, Rhode Island, February 24, 1843 ; he was educated in the fine public schools of his native town, and began his career as a teacher of vocal music at the age of eighteen. Since then he has studied abroad at the Leipzig Conservatory, in Dresden, and in Florence. On his return, he was engaged by Ole Bull, the famous violinist, for a series of concerts in New York and Boston. At the conclusion of these engagements, he settled in New York, where, from 1869 until the present time, he has been actively engaged, except in summer, when he lives in Newport. Professor Wilson married, April 23, 1874, Louisa Coggeshall, daughter of James Monroe and Mary Isabella (Van Vechten) Coggeshall, of New York.

CHILDREN
2915. GEORGE COGGESHALL WILSON, born March 3, 1875; died April 16, 1875.
2916. LANTON HAZARD WILSON, born Dec. 18, 1876.
2917. JAMES COGGESHALL WILSON, born Feb. 18, 1878.

§ **2726. WALTER R. HAZARD,** 9 (Louis, 8 ; Robertson, 7 ; Freeborn, 6 ; Gideon, 5 ; Robert, 4 ; Jeremiah, 3 ; Robert, 2 ; Thomas, 1), was born April 15, 1854 ; he married Cora E., daughter of Doctor George S. and Abbie E. Burton, of Warwick, Rhode Island. She was born July 30, 1860. Mr. Hazard is captain of the steamer New Hampshire, of the Stonington line.

CHILDREN
2918. HATTIE HAZARD, born July 1, 1879; died same year.
2919. ELIWORTH JOSEPH HAZARD, born April 29, 1880.
2920. WILSON REYNOLDS HAZARD, born March 19, 1887.

**End of the Ninth Generation**

THE

# THE HAZARD FAMILY

## Tenth Generation

FLORENCE CORNELIA PELL, 10 (John H. Pell, 9; Mary R. Howland, 8; Sarah Hazard, 7; Thomas, 6; Thomas, 5; Robert, 4; Thomas, 3; Robert, 2; Thomas, 1), was born at Flushing, Long Island, January 17, 1864; she married, at Paris, June 25, 1887, Nathan Clifford Brown, of Portland, Maine.

CHILD

2921. CORNELIA CLIFFORD BROWN, born at Portland, Me., July 12, 1888.

§ 2763. HOWLAND PELL, 10 (William H. Pell, 9; Mary R. Howland, 8; Sarah Hazard, 7; Thomas, 6; Thomas, 5; Robert, 4; Thomas, 3; Robert, 2; Thomas, 1), was born at Flushing, Long Island, in his father's house on Main Street, March 19, 1856. He entered the School of Mines, Columbia College, Class of 1876, but left in 1874 to enter business. He enlisted in Company I, Seventh Regiment N. G. S., New York, June 7, 1875; honorably discharged September 7, 1881; second-lieutenant Company E, Twelfth Regiment N. G. S., New York, February 8, 1884; first-lieutenant Company G, June 3, 1884; Company A, August 25, 1885. He married, April 12, 1887, Almy Goelet Gallatin, daughter of Frederic Gallatin and his wife, Almy Goelet Gerry.

CHILDREN

2922. GLADYS ALMY PELL, born in New York City, March 14, 1888.
2923. HOWLAND GALLATIN PELL, born at East Hampton, L. I., August 17, 1889.

FOLD-OUT HERE

FOLD-OUT HERE

# THE INDEX

# THE END.

*Printed under the supervision of*
D. B. Updike, 7 *Tremont Place,*
*Boston, Massachusetts.*

www.ingramcontent.com/pod-product-compliance
Lightning Source LLC
Chambersburg PA
CBHW020942030726
47496CB00005B/1318